Praise

FIND YOU FIRST

"*Find You First* starts with a bang and ends with an even bigger one. Barclay is a terrific writer, but he's outdone himself with this. It's the best book of his career. I couldn't put it down, and you won't be able to, either. If you enjoy thrillers, this is the real deal. It never lets up."

—Stephen King

"Suspenseful, expertly paced. . . . Barclay makes even secondary characters feel real. Fans of Daniel Palmer will be pleased."

—*Publishers Weekly* (starred review)

ELEVATOR PITCH

"This novel moves as fast as a falling elevator and hits with just as much force. Linwood Barclay is a stone cold pro and *Elevator Pitch* is a shameless good time."

—Joe Hill, #1 *New York Times* bestselling author of *The Fireman* and *Strange Weather*

"Mr. Barclay's books are distinguished by wit and startling twists. In *Elevator Pitch,* he surpasses himself with a premise suited for the big screen, a plot filled with stunning surprises—and an ending that leaves the reader greatly satisfied."

—*Wall Street Journal*

"A vivid story with a compelling cast of characters mixed with a truly terrifying scenario. . . . Barclay

A NOISE DOWNSTAIRS

LOOK
BOTH
WAYS

Also by Linwood Barclay

LINWOOD BARCLAY

LOOK BOTH WAYS

A NOVEL

WILLIAM MORROW
An Imprint of HarperCollins*Publishers*

LOOK BOTH WAYS. Copyright © 2022 by NJSB Entertainment Inc. All rights reserved. Printed in the United States of America. No part of this book may be used or reproduced in any manner whatsoever without written permission except in the case of brief quotations embodied in critical articles and reviews. For information, address HarperCollins Publishers, 195 Broadway, New York, NY 10007.

First William Morrow mass market printing: October 2022
First William Morrow international paperback printing: October 2022

Print Edition ISBN: 978-0-06-314417-0
Digital Edition ISBN: 978-0-06-314416-3

Cover photograph © Ayal Ardon/Arcangel Images

Car illustration by Everett Barclay, ca. 1959, from the author's private collection.

William Morrow and HarperCollins are registered trademarks of HarperCollins Publishers in the United States of America and other countries.

FIRST EDITION

22 23 24 25 26 BVGM 10 9 8 7 6 5 4 3 2

For Neetha

Foreword

grew up surrounded by car imagery.

Back in the 1950s and early '60s, if you were to flip through the pages of *Life* or *Look* or the *Saturday Evening Post* and looked at the automobile ads, or if you picked up a brochure from your local Ford dealer, you might have noticed that all the pictures of these cars were illustrations, not photographs.

These beautiful, airbrushed renderings weren't always one hundred percent accurate. These cars were longer and sleeker than the real ones. The wheelbases were extended. They sat lower to the ground than the actual cars did, appeared to have a wider stance. The chrome sparkled. The glass glistened.

My dad drew those cars.

Dad—his name was Everett—spent much of his life in the advertising world as a commercial artist. He wasn't one of the execs knocking back scotches in fancy offices like those guys in *Mad Men*. He was in the trenches, hunched over his drafting table, airbrushing a fin, blending a reflected tree into the car's graceful sheet metal, executing the outline of a perfectly round hubcap, freehand. (A sample of his work graces the title pages of this book.)

I loved to watch him work, and once, when I was three and Dad had stepped away from his workstation (this was when he had a home studio), I got into his chair and, with a crayon, proceeded to improve upon a $5,000 Cadillac job. (I am lucky to be alive.)

Dad bought me loads of toy cars because he loved them as much as I did. Dinky Toys, Corgis, kits that I had to paint and assemble myself, slot car sets where we would engage in races, shoulder to shoulder, our hands gripping the controllers.

And yet, until I reached the age of fifteen, Dad never had a car as beautiful as anything he created on a piece of art board. But we had been strolling a dealership lot one day, and spotted a discounted 1970 Dodge Charger, not unlike the car the bad guys drove in the Steve McQueen movie *Bullitt*. (Okay, it had a bench seat and a column shift, but it was still a Charger.)

"You should get that," I said.

"Your mother would never go for it," he said.

That was probably true. But he bought it, anyway. And in less than a year, that cool car would essentially become mine, although I would have given anything not to have had that happen the way it did. Dad was diagnosed with lung cancer, and in seven months we lost him. My mother did not drive, so I was her chauffeur, and whenever I needed a car, I didn't have to ask whether it was available.

So, a love of cars was bred into me. It was part of my DNA. I love gripping the wheel, hitting the gas as I come out of a curve, the roar of the engine as you go through the gears.

A car is an extension of who we are. It's a reflection of our personality. When we get in the driver's seat, there's a kind of union under way. The car does not move without you and you do not move without the car. The magic doesn't happen until you get in that seat, turn the key, and put your foot on the accelerator. (Okay, not all cars need keys these days, but at least you must push a button.)

Cars are thrilling. What do you remember first about the aforementioned *Bullitt*, or *The French Connection*, or *Ronin*? The chases. Is there a more nerve-wracking flick than Steven Spielberg's *Duel*, which pits an everyman in his puny sedan against a deranged trucker?

Imagine those movies with self-driving vehicles.

Which brings me to *Look Both Ways*.

We are told that the autonomous, or self-driving, car is imminent, and when everyone has access to one, accidents will plummet. The cars will be safer because they will strictly follow the rules of the road and be better at anticipating and avoiding accidents.

What could go wrong?

Well, as many news reports have suggested, plenty. Putting one's faith in the car's abilities can lull a driver into false security. In models where a real live person is expected to take the wheel in a sudden, potentially dangerous event, they can't respond in time. Some early prototypes have had difficulty identifying pedestrians. Others have been confused by shadows or a setting sun.

To be fair, it's early days. There may come a time when every car on the road is self-driving, and if they're all able to communicate with one another, crashes will be a thing of the past. And while that is inarguably a good thing, I view this future with dread. You know what a self-driving car is? It's a bus, but smaller. It's an Uber, without the driver who wants to tell you about the screenplay he's working on.

It's boring. It's soulless. It is the death of fun.

However, it's also a springboard to a great "what if." Every book begins with a "what if" and here's the one that prompted this book: What if a company wanted to conduct a grand experiment with their self-driving cars? What if they could persuade the residents of an isolated community to give up their conventional cars in exchange for self-driving ones, for a month? Wouldn't that be the ultimate test of how well they perform?

But then, what if a virus infected the network? What if the cars all went nuts? Homicidal, in fact? What you'd have is a few hundred Christines on your hands.

The premise is very different from the type of thrillers you've probably come to expect from me, but it was too good an idea to put aside.

Maybe autonomous cars, one day, will be a wonderful thing.

But until they're perfected, when you're crossing the street, I'd advise you to look both ways.

LOOK
BOTH
WAYS

Prologue

Wendy was clipping along the Pacific Coast Highway, arguing with her mother over the Bluetooth about when she would have time to come to Detroit and see her father before he died, which was laying it on pretty thick, considering what he had was bursitis, when she noticed that the car in front of her had no driver.

"What the hell?" she said.

"What?" said her mother, her voice echoing inside the car. "What is it?"

She'd been following this car for nearly five miles now, heading back to her home in Santa Cruz after a business meeting in Pismo Beach. She didn't normally take the Pacific Coast Highway, as she was doing tonight. She'd seen the view a hundred times—ho hum, there's the ocean, big whoop—and the freeway was faster. And even if she'd wanted to take the extra time with the scenic route, there wasn't any way to appreciate it when it was coming up on midnight.

But there had been a truck rollover in the northbound lanes of the freeway—Wendy got an advance warning on her Google traffic app—and so she had exited before the flow of cars turned into a standstill, and headed for the coastal road.

She had texted her mother before she left Pismo Beach, figuring she had gone to sleep and wouldn't see it until the morning. But she must have woken up in the middle of the night, seen the text, and decided to call.

Wendy had been listening to CNN on the satellite radio. She usually ground her teeth while listening to pundits debate—no, more like shout at each other—about the latest shenanigans in DC, but instead of listening to news, Wendy had been rehashing in her mind her day of meetings, all to sort out permissions for a new subdivision. The locals were unconvinced that there was adequate water supply for the ninety proposed homes and Wendy had gone armed with various engineering reports.

And by the time she'd left, the locals were still unconvinced.

So she was deep in thought, thinking about what further documentation—and at what cost— would be required to change their minds, when her mother called. Wendy blamed the conversation on her failure to notice, until now, that this car she'd been following for five miles had no one behind the wheel.

It was when light from oncoming vehicles illuminated its interior that she noticed something odd. It did not appear anyone was in it. No silhouetted head, or heads.

"What is it?" her mother asked again. "What's going on?"

"This car. In front of me. There's, like, no one in it."

Her mother laughed. "Maybe it's your aunt Winona."

That made Wendy laugh, too. Her mother's sister was so short that she could rarely be seen over the steering wheel. But, of course, it was not her aunt, who had given up driving years ago and currently lived in a nursing home in New Hampshire.

But this car in front of Wendy didn't even have any visible headrests that might help obscure a short driver. She could almost make out the lights from the instrument cluster, the large touch screen in the center of the dash.

So maybe, she thought, this was one of those self-driving cars. Autonomous, they called them.

But there was still supposed to be someone behind the wheel, just in case something went wrong, wasn't there? That was the big thing that scared her about those vehicles. You let the car do everything for you, but you were still supposed to be ready, just in case something happened that the car didn't know how to respond to. Except, how were you to stay alert if ninety-nine percent of the time there was nothing to worry about? It'd be like those people working the airport scanners. Hour after hour, you look at X-rays of suitcases until your eyes cross, and then when a bag full of dynamite rolls past, you don't notice it.

Wendy wondered, did some of these high-tech cars like to take a spin without a passenger? Leave the owner at home? Do some cruising, hook up with a Cougar?

Wendy chuckled to herself. Good one.

"I'm gonna pass," Wendy said. "I gotta get a better look."

"You be careful," her mother said.

She waited for a straight stretch without traffic. That might give her a better look. Curiosity wasn't her only reason for wanting to get by this car. It had been sticking strictly to the speed limit—further evidence that it was programmed to obey all the rules of the road—and Wendy had something of a lead foot. She wanted to get home.

The road ahead was clear.

"Here we go!"

She put on her blinker and shifted over into the passing lane. As she got alongside the other car, she glanced over.

She was right. There was no one behind the wheel. How insane was that? This car really *was* out for a joyride! Or *maybe*, Wendy thought, the car could be summoned by its owner. You'd send a message from your phone, start your car remotely, tell it where you were and when you wanted it to pick you—

Hello.

A shirtless man suddenly appeared in the driver's window. He sat up suddenly, indicating the seat had been fully reclined. Half a second later, next to him, a naked woman—well, naked from the waist up, anyway—appeared. Wendy's sideways glance lasted long enough to see the woman's wide eyes and open, stunned mouth. The naked woman dropped back, out of view, immediately.

"Oh my God," Wendy said.

Her mother, frantic, said, "Are you okay? What's wrong?"

The shirtless man did not, however, drop back. He continued to glare.

"Shit," Wendy said, turning her eyes forward. "*Shit!*"

There was a car coming straight at her.

Wendy did the calculations in her head in a millisecond. There wasn't time to accelerate and get in front of the self-driving car. So she hit the brakes, let the other vehicle pull ahead, then swerved back into her lane. The blasting horn of the oncoming car Dopplered past her.

Her chest pounding, Wendy aimed the car for the shoulder and slowed the car to a dead stop as the self-driving vehicle's taillights vanished into the distance.

"Wendy? *Wendy!*"

Wendy took a moment to catch her breath, and then she began to laugh.

"Asshole," Frank Silvio said, sliding back down onto the reclined seat once the other car had dropped back. He shifted onto his side so he could reach out and trace his finger along the jawline of the woman stretched out next to him. But she shivered at his touch and pulled back.

"What?" he asked.

Things had been going so well up to now. God knows he'd been as careful as he could about his behavior. If you were a movie producer in this day and age, and fucked an up-and-coming—no pun intended—starlet, you had to make the ground rules very clear. No more whipping it out. No more secret buttons under the desk to lock the office door. Christ, you had to be careful. So, when he'd met . . . hang on, what was her name again? Right, when he met Cheryl Garland, he told her right from the get-go, he was not considering casting her in anything. There was no quid pro quo, sleep-with-me-and-I'll-make-you-a-star bullshit. Just told her, hey, I like you, you want to hang out, come see my beach house, maybe go to a party and meet Ryan Gosling?

And she'd said yeah, sure, let's hang out.

So, none of that power dynamic bullshit, right? He wasn't dangling an acting opportunity in front of her, and just as well, because he'd seen her in one of those *NCIS* things—who the fuck knew which one—and her theatrical skills weren't worthy of a grade school Christmas pageant. She'd had, like, three lines playing a seaside restaurant waitress, parading around in a bikini, and it didn't take a genius to figure out how she got the part.

Her attributes were well on display right here in the car.

Silvio could remember, back in the day, when you had to *park* the car to make out. Now, you could do it while you were on the move. He had the 2021 Gandalf, top of the line. Man, what must they have had to pay the Tolkien estate to name this love boat after the fictional wizard, not that they wouldn't be able to cough up the money given what they charged for one of these beauties. But the name was totally apt. These wheels were nothing short of magical. Took delivery just three days before. Couldn't wait to take Cheryl for a spin, show her what it could do. And what *they* could do, while the car went about its business. What was that old Greyhound commercial he'd hear on the TV when he was still in short pants? "Leave the driving to us!" Yeah, except in a Gandalf, there were no diesel fumes, and you didn't get stuck sitting with some guy who hadn't bathed since the invention of the wheel.

"Frankie," Cheryl said.

"Yeah, babe?" He was circling her right nipple with an index finger.

"Can't we just go back to your place? I mean, the car's great and all, but I really can't relax, you know?"

As she finished the sentence, the car filled with light and, a second later, a deafening roar as a truck went past in the opposite direction. Cheryl flinched.

"Every time that happens I jump out of my skin," she said.

"We're totally okay," he said. "If you don't believe me, let me check." He lifted up his chin. "Hey, Lola, everything cool?"

A mechanical, yet feminine, voice emanated from the speakers. *"All systems are performing at optimum levels."*

"Lola?" Cheryl asked.

Frank Silvio grinned. "My ex-wife. When you set the car up, you can name it anything you want. I call her Lola because the real one never did a thing I said, but this one has to. Say, Lola?"

"Yes?"

"I guess we might as well head home. Let's go back to the beach house and crash."

"I will take you there," Lola said.

"Hey, Lola, how about a blow job?" Frank asked.

Lola replied, *"I am sorry, but that does not fall within the parameters of my functions."*

Frank grinned at Cheryl. "Okay, in that respect, Lola's *exactly* like my ex."

The car slowed. The turn signal came on by itself as the car moved onto the shoulder. On the touch screen that spanned the entire dash, several video images captured what was around the car in all directions. Lola, confident the road was clear, executed a U-turn and began to head back they way they'd come.

Frank leaned in and planted his lips on Cheryl's. "Just getting my own motor running before we get back."

She reached down and stroked the front of his linen slacks. "If we get a flat, I seem to have located the jack handle."

The car, in addition to being a self-driving machine, was also fully electric, and whisked along the Pacific Coast Highway almost noiselessly.

Minutes later, they felt the car decelerating.

"Must be here," Frank said without looking up. "If you feel the car turn right, then—"

The car turned, and began to climb.

Frank nodded. "Yup. We're back."

His beach house was, as the name suggested, right on the beach. But it sat at the base of a sixty-foot-high cliff. At the top was a concrete parking pad that overlooked the ocean. Silvio's other vehicle, a Porsche Panamera, and Cheryl's Hyundai were already sitting there.

Christ, Silvio had thought when he'd first seen what she drove. *Broad needs an upgrade.*

He could feel the car making the gradual climb. As it reached the peak, it would slow. Once the Gandalf was parked, they'd have to walk down the nearly fifty steps to his place.

"Hear the surf?" he asked the actress.

"Um, yeah, I think?"

"That's because the engine hardly makes a sound," he said proudly.

Cheryl did not look as impressed as he'd hoped she would.

Perhaps if the Gandalf's engine were noisier, it would have been more immediately apparent that the car was not slowing. It was, in fact, accelerating as it reached the top of the hill.

Silvio sensed something was not right. He rose up and looked through the windshield. Up ahead were his car and Cheryl's, parked nose-in at the cliff's edge on the far side of the concrete apron. There was enough space between the two for the Gandalf.

Lola's going to hit the brakes just in time, he thought.

But they were closing the distance too quickly. The Gandalf was not slowing.

"Lola!" Silvio shouted. "What the fuck are you doing?"

Lola, calmly, replied. *"Back to the beach house and crash."*

"Wait, what? I didn't mean—"

The car slipped between the parked cars as cleanly as the *Millennium Falcon* zipping sideways between two asteroids. And then it was airborne.

Cheryl screamed as the car sailed out into the air. Straight, for about two seconds, and then gravity kicked in, the car's front end tipping downward, offering her and Silvio a moonlit glimpse of the rocks and the rolling waves below.

In the instant before impact, before the windshield shattered and the car filled with water and Frank Silvio and Cheryl Garland were no more, Lola had one final thing to say:

"You have reached your destination."

One

Sandra Montrose was already awake when the alarm went off at six.

She'd been staring at the ceiling since shortly after three. Had she prepared enough media packets? Would the catering company come through? Media types, she knew from her work back on the mainland, went wild when they saw free snacks. They were locusts. You'd think they hadn't eaten in weeks. Give them some take-out containers and they'd carry it home with them.

But it wasn't just the catering that had her worried. Was the ferry running on time? How high were the winds? Was there rain in the forecast? Fog? That'd be all she'd need. A thick blanket of fog that would keep the ferry on the mainland. Before she'd gone to bed she'd checked her app and things looked good, but anything could happen overnight. What was it they said about weather forecasters? Was there any job where you could be wrong fifty percent of the time and not get fired? But if the ferry was on time, Sandra believed everything would fall into place. A delay would screw up the entire day.

And so would half a dozen other things, now that she thought about it. Would the audio-visual tech stuff come off without a hitch? The computer stuff scared her because she had to trust it all to someone else. She'd hired a Garrett Island

AV firm to set things up and they'd done half a dozen run-throughs to make sure everything worked. Still . . . Sandra was the first to admit she was something of a techno-moron. Sure, she could wield her iPhone like she was Billy the Kid and the phone was a six-shooter, but setting up a big screen and making sure it was going to interface or whatever the hell the word was with the presentation on the laptop, well, that was not her area of expertise. Putting blind faith in others went against her nature. It was one of the reasons she didn't like to fly. If she had no idea how to operate a 747, how could she determine with any certainty that the pilot knew what to do? Fortunately, when it came to finding people with talents she lacked, the island was not a bad place to be. It catered to the well-off—even if plenty of the people who lived here year-round were not exactly in the top one percent—and it was pretty common for organizations like Apple or Google or Amazon to hold conferences and retreats here. So, over the years, the island had attracted and developed a support system for that kind of clientele.

Sandra's public relations firm—which consisted of, well, Sandra—was doing just fine, thank you very much. She'd done promotions for local hotels and fishing tours and organized plenty of conferences for midsized firms. But she'd never taken on something this big. A multinational company? Whose stock price was going through the roof? Whose CEO had made the cover of *Fortune*?

Welcome to the major leagues.

She'd had to pull together a team for this one.

Not that her client hadn't been looking over her shoulder the whole time. That Albert Ruskin guy, assistant to the president of Arrival Inc., was phoning, texting, and emailing her twenty times a day to make sure things came off without a hitch. She knew why he didn't trust her. He didn't trust her because she wasn't attached to some big-name firm in New York or Chicago or LA. Sandra was not exactly Edelman, or Weber Shandwick, or Hill+Knowlton.

She was Montrose Strategies.

She was a *local*. A two-bit player, so far as Ruskin was concerned.

But Arrival Inc. had the political savvy to know it would score points by involving as many of the island businesses as possible. If they'd brought in caterers and techies and PR people from Manhattan—or, even closer, Boston—sure as shit that would have pissed off the islanders. And if there was one thing the Arrival people needed on their side, it was the islanders.

And as if all this were not enough to worry about, there was Archie.

God, *Archie*.

If he was this much trouble at twelve, what would he be like at fifteen? Eighteen? What the hell was he thinking, sneaking onto one of those historic tall ships in the harbor and scaling the mast on a rope ladder? Getting caught by the owner, having the cops called? Sandra had defied nature and given birth to a monkey who would fearlessly climb anything he could. Before the tall ship, it had been the local high school. Archie and his buddies, exploring rooftops.

Thank God it was Joe who answered the call

about the ship. Talked the owner out of a trespassing charge, brought Archie home.

Sandra threw back the covers, swung her legs off the bed, and turned on the small lamp on the bedside table. Sitting on the edge, she did what she always did every morning, even before going into the bathroom.

She checked her phone.

It rested next to the lamp, charging. She'd muted it, but the moment she brought the screen to life, she wished she hadn't. Five missed texts from Ruskin, the first of which had come in at half past four. Christ. Well, he was probably as stressed as she was. There was a hell of a lot riding on this.

His texts offered ample evidence of his state of mind:

CNN IS CONFIRMED! THEY WANT TO DO LIVE RE-MOTE. YOU CAN HANDLE THAT? DO WE HAVE ENOUGH ARRIVAL BACKDROPS?

"Yes, of course," she said aloud.

DID YOU GET REVISED VIDEO?

She nodded at the phone.

JUST FOUND OUT FOX NEWS REPORTER IS VEGAN. WHO WOULD HAVE BELIEVED THAT? YOU'D HAVE THOUGHT THEY WERE ALL RAW MEAT EATERS. CHECK MENU SELECTION!!!!

Sandra shook her head wearily. She'd pulled together a buffet that considered every possible taste. Gluten-free, vegan, and not a peanut on the goddamn table. The last thing you wanted at a presser was someone going into anaphylactic shock. Tended to put a damper on the festivities.

The final two texts had landed in the last five minutes.

WHERE ARE YOU?
GET THE FUCK UP!

She tapped the screen and typed her reply.

UP. ALL ISSUES IN HAND.

She tapped the send icon.

God, there were times when she wanted to go back to a landline. No one could send you annoying texts on a landline. But she'd found herself using it so rarely that she'd had it disconnected three months earlier.

There was one other text, but it was not from Ruskin. It was short and to the point:

LUV YA.

That was Joe for you. Man of few words. But one of them caused an uncomfortable stirring within her.

Luv.

She held her thumb over the screen's keypad, wondering whether to reply and, if she did, what she would say. Okay, maybe *luv* was not quite as serious as *love*, but it was still an expression she was not ready to make. She *liked* Joe, no doubt about it, but he was the first man she'd dated—and slept with—since, well, *it* happened.

Was it written down anywhere that you couldn't have sex while you were still grieving? What if the heartache never stopped?

She knew she had every right to get on with her life, but the guilt was still there. And she was definitely not ready for the kids to know she was seeing someone, let alone getting between the sheets. What was she thinking, that night the week before, when she let him sneak into the house after midnight? Risky enough, having sex in her bedroom with the kids down the hall, but letting Joe fall asleep after? She had to shake him awake at four in the morning and get him out of the house before anyone else found out he was there. He nearly fell over trying to pull on his pants in the dark and almost forgot his Glock. A fucking pantomime is what it was.

And, considering how important today was, it had been a huge mistake meeting up with Joe the evening before at a cheap hotel on the mainland. Making up a story for the kids that she was at the community center getting things ready for the big event, then the two of them boarding the ferry on foot, picking up Joe's car on the other side from the paddock, heading to a hotel in North Falmouth. You couldn't take a chance like that on the island. Sure as shit, next time you were at the Garrett Diner, someone would stroll over and say in a voice loud enough for everyone to hear, "Hey, wasn't that your car parked out front of the Seagull Motel?"

Even these days, when every car on the island looked the same, except for color, it wasn't a chance you wanted to take. And Joe didn't want her coming over to his house. He lived with his mother—*God, don't get me started*—and didn't want to have to explain the sounds of squeaky bedsprings at breakfast. Okay, yes, he was a good son, moving her in with him after she'd taken a couple of falls living on her own. And now she was in a wheelchair and Joe was exhausted from taking care of her. So, yeah, he was a saint. But weren't saints entitled to a sex life without having to hide it from their moms?

And then there was this whole business about what he did for a living. A *cop*, for crying out loud. Her whole life, she'd never dated a cop, wasn't sure she'd ever even known one personally. The only ones she'd ever met were those who'd pulled her over, and there had been a few occasions like that, back in the day. Not that she hadn't encountered a few who didn't like to get a little handsy, copping a feel while they patted you down for drugs.

It was a long time ago.

What was so weird about Joe was he started out working in the tech field. He was good with computers. But from the time he was a little boy, all he'd ever wanted to be was a policeman. Any picture of him as a kid, he had a six-shooter strapped to his waist. Forget Bill Gates or Steve Jobs. Joe wanted to grow up to be Roy Rogers, or, as he got a little older, maybe Lieutenant Columbo. So instead of heading to Silicon Valley, he enrolled in a police academy. And now, well, he wasn't exactly Columbo with the rumpled raincoat and cigar. He was more Chief Brody, from *Jaws*. Top lawman on an island, although, so far, he hadn't gone mano a sharko with a Great White. What he did have to deal with were parking infractions, drunken beach parties, snooty city folk who thought their shit didn't stink, and, of course, one crazy kid who wanted to take up residence in a crow's nest.

Sandra tossed the phone back onto the bedside table, knocking over a three-by-five framed photo.

"Fuck," she said, and righted the photo. "Sorry."

She touched the plastic glass protecting the image. Taken nearly twenty years earlier, it featured her on the right, arm in arm with a bearded, stocky man on the left. Smiling for the camera, they were both wearing black leather jackets and chaps and gloves, reflective shades, the whole nine yards.

Sandra smiled sadly as she ran her fingers over the picture of the man.

"You get it, right?" she whispered to the photo. "It's been almost a year. It doesn't mean I don't love you, that I won't *always* love you."

She paused, as if waiting for a reply. In her head, she heard, *Your life doesn't have to end just because mine did.*

Was it wishful thinking, imagining that he would be that understanding?

"Got a big day ahead of me, babe," she said quietly. "Wish me luck."

She got up and went over to the window to open the blinds. She liked to make the bedroom as dark as possible overnight, but welcomed the sunshine every morning. She twisted the wand on the slats, allowing light to stream in, and peered between them.

Garrett Island's residents were already on the way to work. The local economy thrived on the tourism dollar, and while many vacationers had left by October, there were still plenty of year-round residents and year-round jobs to keep islanders engaged. Vacant beach house rentals were upgraded and renovated. Marina owners who didn't head to Florida for the winter spent the colder months doing boat repairs indoors. And the Garrett Mall, respectably-sized at just under half a million square feet, kept on going twelve months of the year even if the winters were on the lean side.

Gazing out her bedroom window, Sandra observed how radically different the morning commute was today from a couple of weeks ago. She didn't see Bill Winston, manager of Winston's Grocery, driving by in his usual mid-'90s Ford Taurus on his way to work. Ann Worley, who'd be passing the house in another hour taking her twin five-year-old boys to day care before arriving at her law office, wouldn't be behind the wheel of her Honda van. And the Klepmanns, the elderly couple in the small cottage around the corner, wouldn't be in their '70s-era Buick station wagon—a land yacht if there ever was one—on their way to the shopping center for their daily mall walk.

But Bill Winston and Ann Worley and the Klepmanns would still be driving by. The difference would be in what was transporting them.

They'd all be behind the wheel—no, correct

that, since there *was* no wheel—they'd all be in a brand-new Arrival autonomous car.

Self-driving.

A bright red one was going by right now. That'd be Bill.

Sedan-sized, four doors, lots of glass, an Arrival looked a lot like any other car in that segment, albeit with some quirky, distinctive styling. A bit jelly-bean-like with rounded fenders, yet somewhat rakish at the same time, with a low sloping hood and high trunk, like a Dustbuster minus the handle. Sandra was not about to tell the Arrival execs in general, or that snarky shit Albert Ruskin in particular, that the car reminded her of a ferret. Slinky and kind of creepy, especially with those narrow, snake-like headlights that gave the vehicle a hint of menace. But there was no doubt it was aerodynamic. You could ride a bike right up the hood, over the roof, then take a leap off the back. She wondered how long it would be before some of the neighborhood skateboarders figured out an Arrival made a great ramp.

It hadn't occurred to her, until the Arrivals invaded Garrett Island, how most cars these days were silver or black or white or gray. Boring, blah colors. Sandra could remember her grandfather had a two-tone, turquoise and white Ford from the fifties. Beautiful machines from a forgotten era.

Arrival Inc. wasn't afraid of a splash of color. Their vehicles came in strawberry red and lime green and sky blue and lemon yellow and plum purple, just for starters. So even if you didn't always *hear* these battery-powered cars coming, you sure as hell *saw* them.

And they were the only cars to see these days on Garrett Island. Arrival Inc. had made the islanders an offer they couldn't refuse.

For one month, the company proposed, turn your car over to us and we'll give you one of ours in return. Live in a world of the future. Be part of a grand demonstration, where in one isolated location, no one—no one at all—has to actually *drive* a car, but can get anywhere they want to go.

At the end of the month, you'll get your old car back—if you even want it. And if you don't, we'll pay you more than fair market value for it if you want to trade it in for an Arrival.

What a deal. How could anyone say no?

Now the media was about to descend on Garrett Island to see how this grand experiment was going. Arrival had wanted everyone to have gotten comfortable with their replacement vehicles before holding the big media event. All Sandra had to do was make sure the news conference went off perfectly.

No pressure.

Sandra's gaze moved from the passing cars to the house across the street. The one where that old reclusive guy lived, alone. One of the few on the island who had no use for Arrival's proposition. He had no regular car to turn over, so far as Sandra knew, and evidently did not want the use of one that could take him anywhere he wanted to go. The few times she'd seen him outside, he was walking to or from the closest grocery store, pulling his purchases behind him in a small, wheeled cart.

There he was, sitting on the front porch, this

early in the day, having a smoke. Breakfast of Champions, Sandra thought.

She recalled that the other night, when Joe slipped away before the sun came up, a light was on in the garage out back of the old guy's house. She'd wondered what the hell he was doing in there.

Sandra shrugged. Whatever curiosity she felt about the man across the street, it wasn't strong enough to motivate her to go over and say hello. If he wanted to be neighborly, let him make the first move. Islanders were generally so friendly. Everyone knew everybody else's business. But as long as she'd lived here, she'd never so much as said two words to the guy. Maybe he was one of those snooty islanders, the ones who were born and raised here and figured everybody else was an interloper.

She turned away from the window, trudged wearily into the bathroom, and flicked on the light. When she saw her reflection in the mirror she flinched.

"Jesus," Sandra said under her breath. She walked to the sink, stuck out her lip far enough to blow a strand of hair from in front of her eyes, and looked at the task that awaited her.

"When they invent a face that will do its own makeup, that's when I'll really give a shit," she said to the woman in the mirror.

Two

The Arrival corporation had been very strict where the media were concerned.

No one could bring a conventional vehicle onto the ferry. A paddock had been set up on the mainland for the islanders' cars, and that was where the media vehicles would have to go, too. Reporters would walk onto the ferry, and when they got to Garrett Island, convoys of driverless Arrivals would escort them to Garrett itself, the town at the eastern end of the island where most islanders lived, for the news conference. Not surprisingly, the TV and cable news folks were not happy. They had to leave their vans, filled with gear and equipped with satellite hookups, behind.

But Arrival Inc. had made it clear bringing any conventional car or truck onto the island—a vehicle that someone actually *drove*—would be like performing surgery without washing your hands. A vehicle where someone sat behind the wheel and pressed on an accelerator and flicked a turn signal would be nothing short of a contamination.

The island was a pristine environment, at least where the roads were concerned.

It reminded Brandon Kyle of the time he had visited Australia to supervise the opening of the first Gandalf dealership in that country. Never before had his bags been searched *after* getting off the plane. The customs officials wanted to be sure he wasn't bringing in any fruit or vegetables or plants of any kind. They even wanted to know if visitors were bringing in any animals, living or dead, which struck Kyle as an odd question until someone told him travelers had been caught trying to smuggle all sorts of things into the country—live chickens, mice, rabbits, you name it—and Australia was not messing around when it came to this. Kyle had heard about one guy who'd tried to hide a snake in his pants. A sharp-eyed airport employee became suspicious when it appeared the individual's dick was trying to catch some air out the bottom of his trouser leg. This country, isolated from the rest of the world geographically, had been able to protect itself from foreign predators, and wanted to keep it that way.

Arrival was taking the same approach where Garrett Island was concerned.

When Kyle was able to see the docked ferry in the distance, he instructed his driver, Derek Penner, to drop him by the pedestrian ramp. There was no need for Derek to leave the Cadillac sedan in the paddock with the other vehicles. Derek wasn't staying. He had somewhere else to be.

God, it pained Kyle to ride in the Caddy. But the customized stretch Gandalf he'd had made for himself was one of the many things he'd had to give up. And even if he'd still had that special ride, he wouldn't want to be showing up in it on this occasion.

Talk about giving himself away.

No, a nondescript, gas-powered, human-driven Detroit hunk of junk was the way to go today. Kyle had to fly, as they say, under the radar.

"This is good," he said, from his spot in the rear seat, to Derek, up front behind the wheel. So Derek brought the car to a gentle stop and, with the engine still running, slipped out of the driver's seat and came around to open the rear passenger door on the other side.

As Kyle got out, he asked, "How do I look?" He gently touched his mustache, ran a hand over his bald head, then patted the bulge of his stomach.

Derek appraised him. "Good." He paused. "Maybe that's not the right word. You look like you've let yourself go."

"So you wouldn't know?"

Derek's head went side to side, but it was a gesture of encouragement. "You look fifty pounds heavier, and this"—and he touched himself just above the lip—"is holding just fine."

"It ought to. It's real."

"If I passed you on the sidewalk, I'd have no idea. There's not a picture in existence where you look the way you do now."

Kyle smiled, nodded, then glanced at his watch. "Okay. So, be looking for me in about three hours."

Derek nodded. They'd been over this many times. Get the boat from the marina a few miles north on the mainland while the boss did his thing on the island. Head out to sea. Rendezvous at Garrett Harbor. Bring the boss back home.

Good ol' Derek, Kyle thought. At a time when

pretty much everyone else had deserted him, Derek remained loyal to the end. Kyle wondered how much longer he'd be able to keep him on. Not that Kyle didn't have funds squirreled away. When rich people got wiped out, it usually meant they were down to their last few millions, which was certainly true for Kyle. His worth was a mere fraction of what it was two years ago. Anyway, today's events would determine whether he needed to find a way to hang on to Derek.

"If you have any problems, call," Derek said.

Kyle patted his chest, making sure his phone was still in his pocket. "As long as our man on the scene does what he's supposed to do, things should go fine."

"And your tech friend in Russia," Derek reminded him. "With the messaging."

"Yes," Kyle said.

Kyle hesitated one final moment, as though steeling himself for a long journey. He let out a long breath, nodded to himself, then turned and started walking toward the ferry. He fell into line with several others as they reached the metal ramp that led to the open ferry bay that would, any other day, be filling up with vehicles.

There was no ticket to show, no fare to pay this day. Arrival had essentially commandeered the ferry, and was picking up all costs.

A media ID, however, was required.

A stunning blonde woman in a clingy black dress was checking everyone's credentials. She looked like she'd just walked off the set of *The Price Is Right*, Kyle mused. It surprised him that

Arrival, considering who its CEO was, would resort to such outdated practices. The slinky model perched over a new car, that was something most auto shows had abandoned years ago along with in-dash cassette players.

Kyle reached into his jacket and produced a laminated card with his photo on it. The woman leaned in, inspected it, and flashed a mouth full of perfect white teeth.

"Thank you, Mr. . . . Stapleton." She grinned. *"Wheel Base Trends*, right, nice to see you. This headshot does not do you justice."

He laughed. "You should see my passport pic. It looks like one of those shots the police issue when they're trying to identify someone they've fished out of the Hudson River."

The woman chuckled.

"How long's the crossing?" he asked her.

"About an hour," she replied. "They're calling for rain, maybe fog, later in the day, so that might cause a delay on our return. But I'm sure it won't be a big problem."

"How's the ferry in fog?"

The woman shrugged. "I work for Arrival, not the ferry company, but they've got all sorts of radar, right? Because they can do this run at night. I guess the ferries are *already* pretty much self-driving, aren't they?"

"Suppose so," Kyle said. "But they're a bit tricky when it comes to the McDonald's drive-through."

Another laugh. "You're funny," she said, waving him on.

Once on the ferry, he climbed three sets of stairs to reach an upper level where there was a snack bar. Normally, all one could get was coffee and soft drinks and bags of potato chips and maybe a plastic-wrapped sandwich, but today, the Arrival corporation had laid on all kinds of goodies. Pastries, a guy making omelettes, a woman running a cappuccino machine. Trays overloaded with fruit and cheese. All Kyle wanted was a regular coffee, which he took in a paper cup, then headed out to the deck for some fresh air.

Standing at the railing, he gazed out across the water. There, more than five miles out, stretched across the horizon, sat Garrett Island. Brandon Kyle breathed in the sea air, felt the breeze on his face.

What a magnificent day. And it was only going to get better.

He glanced to his right and saw a woman he recognized. A TV reporter for one of the cable business channels. He tried to recall her name. Geary, he though. Rebecca Geary.

Jesus. I've done her show.

Brandon Kyle felt a wave of fear rush through him. Derek had assured him he did not look at all like himself, but what if he was wrong? What if this woman recognized him?

Yes, he'd shaved his head, grown a mustache. He'd decided, at the outset, that he wasn't going with some stick-on facial hair that might blow off before he'd even reached the island. The only thing fake was the artificial padding around his middle, a cummerbund of phony fat. Brandon Kyle had a reputation as a fitness buff. Washboard stomach, broad-chested, not the sort of guy you'd expect to grow a beer belly overnight.

He'd made sure, back in Gandalf's good times, that all corporate videos had at least one clip of him jogging or skiing or jumping out of a plane. (Okay, so that last one had been doctored. There was no fucking way he was going to take up parachuting.)

And he'd even practiced a different voice to use today. He hailed from the South, but his parents had moved away from Mississippi when he was only four, and growing up in New England had done much to erase that drawl. But he could fall back into it easily. He'd just hear his father's Southern gentleman voice in his head, and out it would spew from his own mouth. He always thought, talking in that Southern accent, it was like having a splash of bourbon on your tongue.

When he caught the woman's eye, he decided to take a chance that his disguise was adequate, and said, "How are you today?"

Rebecca Geary smiled and nodded as she said, "Just great. Beautiful day. Especially considering we're just getting into fall."

"It is that," he said. "Be a bit chilly on the way over, I suspect." He cocked his head. "I believe I recognize you from the TV."

She nodded. "*The Geary Report*. Rebecca Geary."

"That's right. Good show. Watch it all the time."

"Heading over for the Arrival thing, like the rest of us?" she asked.

Big nod. "I am indeed."

"Pain in the ass," she said. "Not even letting us take a car. My cameraman's carrying so much gear he'll be in physio for a year."

"I guess they're pretty serious about keeping the island . . . *pure*, I guess would be the word."

"I gather the only vehicles on the island that *aren't* self-driving are emergency ones," she said. "Arrival hasn't yet got an autonomous ambulance. God, my manners. Who are you with?"

"Wheel Base, two words, dot com," he said. "Ben Stapleton." He extended a hand and she took it.

"I have to admit," she said, "it is quite the project. An entire island with nothing but these crazy little machines."

"It's a great stunt," he said.

"I'm not really a car person," she said. "My boyfriend is. He loves sports cars, thinks the day when he can't get behind the wheel is more or less the apocalypse. End of times, whatever. But as a non-car-person, I'm okay with it."

"Sure," Kyle said, nodding.

"You think it will happen?"

"Think what will happen?"

"Like Arrival says, that within ten years, maybe sooner, most of the cars on the road will be driverless. They say it works better when all the cars are like that. They can all talk to each other. You put a few real live drivers into the mix, and it's chaos. God, just think of downtown New York with nothing but self-drivers. I wonder if I'd miss the honking?"

"Probably not," Kyle said.

Some hair blew across her face and she brushed it away. "Arrival is leading the way on this. The Big Three, Japan, Germany, they're all playing catch-up. And of course, they had a bit of luck."

Kyle angled his head, waiting for her to go on.

"I mean, when your biggest competitor self-destructs, that's what I'd call catching a break."

"The Gandalf," he said.

"Yeah," she said. "What's their stock worth now?"

Brandon Kyle paused, then said, somberly, "Nothing."

"I hear they're down to selling off the Aeron chairs. There's virtually nothing left. God help you if you own one of the Gandalfs that are actually out there. Good luck getting service. It's the DeLorean all over again, only worse."

Kyle nodded solemnly. "I guess you've heard the rumors," he said.

"Rumors?" she said. "You mean the outright allegations? Of industrial sabotage?"

"Yes."

"Of course. I had Kyle on my show."

"Oh," Kyle said. "I must have missed that one."

"Talk about a man possessed," she said. "Possibly delusional. He honestly believes Arrival's president masterminded a plot to hack Gandalf's master system, slipping a bug into it."

"That movie producer, and that actress, they *did* die," Kyle said. "The car *did* go off that cliff."

"Sure," the woman said. "The software fucked up. No doubt about it. But you ask me, Kyle trying to lay this off on Arrival is just a dodge to keep from taking responsibility himself. Where's the proof? You make an accusation as serious as that, you need something to back it up. Arrival'd probably sue if they thought Kyle had any money left."

Kyle felt a rush of heat to his cheeks but managed to maintain an air of calm. "I've heard he has the proof but no one will listen. He's convinced, beyond a shadow of a doubt, that this was a deliberate act to destroy his company."

Rebecca Geary shrugged. "I don't know. Let's say he's right. Let's say Arrival, or some other company, got into the Gandalf network and introduced a virus. Shouldn't Kyle have anticipated that? Shouldn't he have had safeguards in place?"

"So, blame the victim."

"Not saying that. But if you're, I don't know, Target, and someone hacks into your database and gets credit card info on all your customers, who do you get mad at? You get mad at the company, because they were supposed to protect you from that kind of thing. What about all these firms getting hit with ransomware attacks? A lot of them never took the threats seriously until it was too late."

"Hmm," Kyle said.

"The corporate world is cutthroat. Bad things happen to good people, and good companies. Some great inventions get overtaken by something else. VHS killed Betamax, although it was Sony that took the hit, so it's hard to shed a tear for them. They're doing just fine, thank you very much. But then, look at BlackBerry. They made a pretty damn good phone, but then the iPhone came along, and they took a beating. And now, well, if all your money's invested in the gas engine or premium unleaded, you might want to rethink that. History marches on. The thing with Brandon Kyle is, he and his Gandalf went off the rails." She laughed. "Or off the cliff, I should say."

Kyle found himself unable to feign a chuckle.

"I guess," he said. "Where's your camera guy?"

She tipped her head toward the cabin. "Carl's at the buffet stuffing his face. Listen, nice talking to you. Probably see you at the presser."

"Sure," Kyle said.

She headed for one of the many outdoor benches set up on the deck with a view forward.

Kyle could feel the engines starting. The ship began to vibrate. Moments later, the ferry began to move out from the dock.

I hope she's one of them, he thought. *I hope she's one of the first.*

Three

I think our friendly neighborhood serial killer was at it again last night," said Archie Montrose.

Sandra's twelve-year-old son was sitting at the kitchen table, ignoring the cereal he'd poured himself as he stared at his phone, playing a game. Any other morning, she might have told him to put his phone away, but she needed to save her strength today for bigger battles, should they come up.

But she did ask, as she filled a mug with coffee, "What are you talking about?"

"Ignore him," said Katie Montrose, thumbing the screen of her own phone as she strolled into the kitchen. "He's crazy."

"Oh, yeah?" said Archie. "What do *you* think he's doing in his garage at three in the morning?"

"I hope he's building a time machine," Katie said, "that sends you to another dimension."

"Lame-O," Archie said. "A good insult would be building a time machine to send me to another *time*. But dimension? Makes no sense."

Sandra's daughter, four years older than Archie, managed to take a mug from the cupboard, fill it with coffee, and add a pack of sweetener, all without taking her eyes off her phone.

"You'll care when he grabs you one night and takes you in there and starts torturing you," Archie said. "Then, once you're dead, he'll start cutting you up into little—"

"Enough!" Sandra shouted at her son.

He glanced at her for only a second, then spooned some cereal into his mouth. Chewing, he said, "I'm just trying to save her life, is all."

"You binge-watch too many TV shows about serial killers," Sandra said. "I forbid it."

That brought snickers from both of her children. Sandra knew it was an empty threat the moment she'd uttered the words. As if you could control anything your kids watched these days.

Katie said, "Just because someone is up in the middle of the night doesn't make him a murderer."

Her brother shrugged. "What else would it be? I bet he prowls the neighborhood around midnight, then takes his victim back to the garage. I saw him sitting on his porch this morning, havin' a cig. It's like with some people, they have a smoke after sex, but this guy, he has one after he's killed somebody."

Sandra put down her coffee and stared at Archie contemptuously. "What is wrong with you?"

Archie looked her way, puzzled. "Huh?"

"Seriously, what the hell is wrong with you?"

"I got this one," Katie said, raising a hand to her mom. "He's mentally unstable. Maybe you dropped him on the head when he was little?"

Sandra scowled.

Katie shrugged. "It's just a theory. He could be possessed."

Archie said, "I can't help it if you're blind to the truth."

Katie broke off a banana from a bunch in a ceramic bowl and, leaning up against the counter, started to peel it. Her mother had to move around her to get to the sink to rinse out her cup.

"Could you get a little more in the way?" Sandra asked.

Katie tossed the peel into the sink. "I want to book my test. The DMV is open today. I don't see why—"

Sandra looked visibly pained. "I'm done talking about this."

"Yeah, well, maybe *you* are, but I'm not. I want to take the test. I want to be able to drive. Barry has his license, and Raj and Naveen, and they aren't any older than I am and—"

"It's different," Sandra said. "They're b—"

She stopped herself. Archie whipped his head around, as if he'd just heard a truck slam into the house.

"Whoa," he said.

"Oh my God, I can't believe you said that," Katie said.

"I didn't say anything."

"You were going to say it was okay because they're *boys*. That is, like, totally unbelievable, coming from you."

"I didn't mean that. I don't know what I was thinking."

"Because if you want the names of my girlfriends who have their license, there's Pamela, and—"

"You don't have to tell me. I get it. Just because they're ready—male or female—doesn't mean you are. Katie, you know how—"

"So what, I *never* get a driver's license? Is that what you're saying? I know what this is about. This is because—"

"Don't go there," her mother said. "I'm not having this conversation again." Her eyes started to mist.

"Look, I know," Katie said, her voice pleading. "Things can happen. But *you* still drive. I don't see *you*—"

Sandra raised a hand. "Not for long. I mean, well, look what's happening."

Sandra reached over to the end of the kitchen counter, where she had left a stack of press kits in bright blue folders with pictures of the Arrival cars on the cover. She held one up.

"You're not even going to *need* a driver's license," she said. "This is the future. This right here."

Katie rolled her eyes. "Mom, save your PR stuff for the event, okay? It's going to be, like, years before those kinds of cars are actually everywhere. In another couple of weeks, they're going to clear the island of these jelly beans with wheels and probably ninety percent of everyone here is going back to what they were driving. What am I supposed to do? Ask you to drive me around until I'm thirty, when all the regular cars are finally gone? That'll be fun. Especially on dates. You okay sitting up front while I make out in the back?"

Archie made a gagging sound.

"It could be sooner than you think," Sandra

persisted. "The world is changing so fast now no one can keep up." She took a breath, steeling herself. "The truth is, what happened to this family—to *us*—would never have happened in a car that—"

Katie raised her hands as if surrendering to the police. "Fine, fine, okay. Never mind." She turned and started walking out of the kitchen.

"Katie!" her mother said. "Come back—"

Katie could already be heard stomping up the stairs.

Sandra's shoulders sank. "Shit."

Archie said, without looking her way, "That's a buck for the swear jar."

"We don't have a swear jar."

"But if we did," he said, "you'd have to put a dollar in."

"Get moving. You'll be late to school."

"Uh, earth to Mom. There's no school today, remember?"

Sandra put the heel of her hand to her forehead, remembering. "It's teacher prep day or something."

"Yup."

"Then what are you even doing up? On weekends you're in bed till noon." She took a deep breath through her nose and fixed her eyes on him. "All tuckered out from climbing tall buildings and masts and whatever?"

He let that one go by without comment. "I'm doing stuff with the guys."

"What guys?"

"The *guys*? The guys I *always* hang out with?"

Sandra shook her head. "You and your friends

have a special talent for getting into things you shouldn't."

"I don't know what you're talking about, Mom."

If only the tall ship incident were Archie's only experiment in danger. "You started a grass fire at the Jamesons'."

Archie looked hurt. "That was a science experiment that got out of hand."

"You were using a magnifying glass to kill a bug and it set the grass on fire."

"We were harnessing the power of the sun to eradicate a potentially dangerous spider."

"And no more exploring rooftops."

"We were just trying to get a ball back."

"That's a load of sh—You know that's not true. How'd you even get up there?"

Archie shrugged. "It's not hard. You just use the whaddyacallit, the drainpipe. And coming down, if you aim for the soft bushes, you can jump."

Sandra momentarily closed her eyes and tilted her head back, as though looking for a higher power to guide her. She opened her eyes, but held her head in the same position and shouted: "Katie!"

From upstairs, a muffled: "What?"

"Conference!"

"So talk!"

"In the kitchen!"

Katie stomped her way back downstairs and stood framed in the kitchen doorway. "You rang?"

"You're watching Archie today."

"Excuse me?" cried Archie.

"There's no school. You're in charge."

"No way!" Archie said.

"You gotta be kidding," Katie said. "I've got stuff I'm gonna do."

"Like?"

"*Stuff.* Stuff that does not include looking after a baby brother."

"I do not *need* a babysitter," Archie said. "Since when does she have to keep her eye on me?"

"Since you became a pyromaniac and house-climbing chimpanzee," Sandra said.

Katie wrinkled her nose. "That first one, is that some sort of sex thing?"

"Look," Sandra said, bringing her voice down a notch, "I need a favor. From both of you. Hear me out."

The two kids waited.

"Today is the biggest professional day of my career. This could—"

Katie said, "I'm just saying that he's too old to baby—"

"*Please* listen to me," Sandra said, cutting her off. "I have never had a day where it was more important that things do not go wrong. This Arrival gig is huge, and if I can pull it off, there's no telling what it might lead to. What I need more than anything"—and at this point, her voice began to break—"is support from the home team. All this stupid bickering, this has to stop. We have to pull together or I'm telling you right now, we are not going to make it. This is a one-income family right now, in case you haven't noticed, and this is a make-it or break-it day. Am I getting through?"

Katie and Archie slowly nodded.

"So what I do not need today, when I am in the middle of choreographing an AV display for a multi-million-dollar company and dealing with care and feeding of a bunch of media types, is a call on my cell saying that *you*"—and she looked at Archie—"and your anarchist buddies have flown a drone into the flight path of *Air Force One*, or *you*"—and she fixed her eyes on Katie—"calling me from the mall to say your card has been declined and store security have detained you."

Katie blinked. "When has that ever—"

Sandra raised a hand. "Do you guys get what I'm saying?"

They each took a moment to surrender.

"Yeah," said Archie.

"Yeah," said Katie.

"Good," Sandra said, taking a deep breath. She glanced at her watch. "I have to get out of here."

She grabbed the stack of press kits and strode out of the kitchen.

Archie and Kate exchanged glances. It was Archie who spoke first:

"If you think you're babysitting me, you are out of your mind."

Four

Katie and Archie followed their mother out to her car.

Well, not *her* car exactly. Sandra Montrose's car was a five-year-old Ford Focus, which she had bought from the Garrett Island Ford dealership. But the Focus was on the mainland now, parked with hundreds of other islanders' vehicles. There were five car dealerships on the island. In addition to Ford, there were GM, Honda, Toyota, and Chrysler outlets, and their managers had been the most vocal opponents to the Arrival corporation's plans. They'd have to forgo a month without sales or service income, they'd argued. When they were on the verge of suing Arrival, the self-driving car company settled, paying them what their estimated income would have been for the month, but the dealers had to agree to surrender the keys to all the vehicles they had on their lots. Arrival didn't want some rogue joyrider taking a car from a dealer lot and sabotaging their autonomous fleet.

And the car dealerships weren't the only ones who had to be paid off. The Arrivals were battery-powered, and all the island gas stations feared bankruptcy if they lost an entire month of sales. Even the local police department—Sandra had heard all about this from Joe—had to be compensated for lost revenue. The Arrivals were programmed to obey the speed limit, so there weren't going to be any tickets issued for exceeding it. And an Arrival never overstayed its time at a parking meter. It had a built-in app to purchase more time if needed.

After she gave up the Focus, Sandra was given the use of a bright red Arrival. About the same size as her car, but far more futuristic-looking, with its swoopy, aerodynamic shape. The car, sitting in the driveway, was linked to the house by a thick black cable.

"You wanna unplug Gracie?" Sandra asked the kids.

Archie jumped at the chance. He went to the front of the car and detached the cable from an opening next to the right headlight. As he pulled it away, a small red panel whirred into place over the outlet, disguising it. The cable itself retracted into the charging station—a small box attached to the wall next to the garage door.

"Thank God I remembered to plug it in last night," she said. "Be just great, running out of juice on the way to the event."

Archie, having completed his task, went and stood by his sister.

Then, speaking neither to Katie nor Archie, Sandra said, "Gracie, open."

From somewhere—under the car, maybe the vents at the base of the windshield—came a voice. Feminine, but not overly so. Personable, but at the same time not overly familiar.

"Good morning, Sandra. It would be my pleasure."

"I think she sounds hot," Archie whispered to his sister.

Katie whispered back, "She might be the best you ever get."

The door on the passenger side—both sides, actually, were passenger sides—popped out an inch, then slid back on a track to allow access. There were two seats in the front and two in the back. A gleaming black touch-screen dash ran across the bottom of the windshield.

There was no steering wheel.

Gracie said, *"It is going to be a lovely day, Sandra. A high of seventy-five degrees, moderate cloud cover. There is a chance, however, of fog later in the afternoon."*

"Thanks for that," Sandra said.

It had become something of a game for everyone on the island to try and identify the voice. The rumor was that Arrival had hired Scarlett Johansson to provide enough linguistic sound effects that the cars could put together any sentence necessary. Others thought Amy Adams or Emma Stone had been brought in. Sandra's theory: several actresses had been used, their voices thrown into a digital blender to come up with the ultimate tonal companion.

If you were French or German or Spanish, well, not to worry. The cars could be programmed to respond in any language, and it was up to each owner to give their car a name. Sandra had chosen Gracie for hers. It had been the name of her cat when she was little.

As if she were going to be driven around by a real chauffeur, Sandra got into one of the back seats, leaving the front two empty. She tossed the briefcase stuffed with press kits onto the seat next to her.

"Break a leg, Mom," Katie said.

Sandra smiled wearily. "Thanks," she said quietly. Then, in a stronger voice, "Gracie, let's go."

"Are you sure you have everything?" Gracie asked.

"I'm sure."

"Destination?"

"Garrett Island Community Center."

"I'll take you there."

The door slid silently back into place.

Making no more noise than that of rubber rolling on pavement, the car backed out of the driveway and lined up perfectly against the curb.

"I'll say this," Archie quipped. "It backs up way better than Mom ever did. And it never pulls into a parallel parking spot nose-first."

Sandra waved at her kids as the car moved on down the street. They watched until it reached the corner, turned, and was out of sight.

"Don't look now," Archie whispered, "but he's watching us."

"What?"

"The serial killer," he said, tucking his chin down into his shoulder as he whispered. "He just pulled back the curtain and was checking us out."

Katie, with feigned casualness, looked across the street. Her brother was right. The old man in the house opposite theirs was at the living room window. She could see a couple of fingers pulling back the curtain, a sliver of face and one eye.

"What should we do?" Archie said. "Call the cops?"

Katie sighed. "Yeah, right, do that. 'Hello, 911? There's a man looking out his window!

Send everything you've got!' You're nuts, that's what you are."

"I know what his name is," Archie said. "It's Bruce Clifford."

"How do you know that?"

"We got some of his mail one day. Some old *New Yorker* magazine."

"Oh," Katie said.

"Don't you think that's kind of suspicious?"

"That he's old?"

"No, duh. That he's got two first names. Bruce and Clifford. I bet it's made up. He's got, like, a new identity because he was a serial killer someplace else, had to get away, and made up a different name."

"You're the stupidest kid on this island. Maybe in all of Massachusetts."

Katie started walking back into the house, Archie trailing her. He followed her all the way into the kitchen, where Katie poured her cold coffee into the sink and refilled the mug from the pot.

"You don't even like coffee," Archie said. "You just drink it 'cause you think it makes you look older."

She faced him. "What are we going to do today?"

"Huh?"

"Mom put me in charge. Your ass is mine." Before her brother could object, she raised a cautioning index finger. "You heard Mom. This is a big day for her. So we're just going to chill out, take it easy, not get into any shit."

Archie studied her for several seconds, weighing his response. Finally, and with feigned formality, he said, "I believe that is an excellent idea, Katie. I could not agree more."

She eyed him skeptically. "Bullshit."

"No, seriously," he said. "You're right. Let's chill. I'll text my friends, tell them I'm bailing. I even have a couple of ideas."

She waited, still not convinced.

"Let's do a *Family Guy* marathon," he said, suddenly excited. "At least till lunch, and if we're sick of them by then, we'll watch a movie or something. All the DVDs are in a box in the garage."

Katie had always liked the animated series, particularly Stewie, the evil genius baby, and Brian, the talking dog who wants to be a best-selling novelist.

Slowly, she said, "Maybe. But can't we just get them off Netflix or something?"

Archie shook his head. "We've got the DVDs so we might as well use them. You go find them, and I'll get the Coke and the Pringles and meet you in the basement in five."

Neither of them raised the issue that maybe it was a little early in the day for soft drinks and chips. But then again, was it ever too early for junk?

"Okay," Katie said warily. "You're not messin' with me, are you?"

Archie shrugged. "I'm cool if you don't want to do it. We could work on that massive Lego Batmobile I've had in the box for two years."

Katie hated Lego. She waited a beat, then said, "Okay. I'll get the DVDs."

She opened the sliding glass doors that led from the kitchen to a back patio. She crossed the yard to the separate garage building out back of the house. She entered by a regular side door and flipped up the nearby light switch.

The garage was more storage unit than a place to park a car. Not even a tiny Arrival would fit in here, not with all the piled-up cardboard boxes and bits and pieces of unwanted furniture. When Sandra had emptied out her father's place in Braintree after he'd died six years ago, she'd saved his bedroom set, a kitchen table and chairs, even an old stereo console with an honest-to-god record player in it. She'd told Katie and Archie that one day, when they moved out and had a place of their own, they might not have money for furniture, and would be grateful for this stuff.

To which Katie had thought, she would rather live in a Frigidaire shipping carton than have this old shit in her apartment. But she had kept the thought to herself. She knew she had at least a couple of years before she might head off to college, and was hoping this furniture would become so mouse-infested by then that her mother would have it taken to the dump.

God, where was the box of DVDs?

Since most of the stuff they watched was online, they hadn't had much use for DVDs and Blu-rays in recent years. But back before streaming became a thing, they'd acquired hundreds of discs, and rather than try to sell them, they'd boxed them and tucked them away, despite some objections from Archie. "It'll give us more shelf space," his mother had said.

To which Archie had replied, with more than a little trepidation, "And put what in their place. Books?"

The Garrett Blockbuster had been one of the last video rental stores to hang in, but even it had gone under five years ago.

Katie knew that her mother, despite the chaos the garage suggested, was fairly organized, so whatever box those discs went into, there'd be a Magic Marker DVDS scribbled on the outside. But as she shuffled boxes around, one caught her attention that was not labeled DVDS.

Written on the outside was DAD STUFF.

The top of the box was not crisscrossed with duct tape, so Katie, after a moment's hesitation, dug her fingers under the folded cardboard flaps and pulled them up. She reached in and pulled out the first thing she saw: a small plaque that read ADAM MONTROSE MVP. It didn't say for what sport.

She set the plaque aside and dug in further. A diecast model of a Corvette, an old paperback copy of *Zen and the Art of Motorcycle Maintenance*, an actual Harley-Davidson motorcycle manual, a Red Sox baseball cap, an envelope stuffed with canceled checks and old tax papers.

And then, a faded newspaper clipping: Man Killed in Crash Fell Asleep at Wheel, Police Say.

She crumpled it up and looked deeper into the box. There was a three-by-five snapshot, slid into a Plexiglas stand, of Adam Montrose holding a small girl in his arms. In the background, a beach and the ocean beyond. The girl looked to be about two years old, but it was easy to tell, all these years later, who that little girl had grown up to be.

Katie sniffed, and wondered how this picture ended up here. It should be on the dresser in her room. She had no memory of the picture being taken, but guessed this was the Cape Cod beach her parents used to go to, before Archie was born.

Why, she wondered, was her dad's stuff jammed into a box and dumped in the garage? Some of it—okay, maybe not the canceled checks and old business papers—deserved a place in the home. It should be *seen*. Her mom still kept a picture of Katie's dad next to her own bed, but what other memories were there of him in the house?

Had these mementos been moved out here lately? Had it just been since her mother had started seeing Joe?

Oh, her mom didn't know that she knew. But Katie had a pretty good idea what was going on. More than once she'd seen her mom's boyfriend slipping out of the house any time between midnight and four in the morning.

And just how was she able to spot him? Well, it helped if you weren't in the house yourself. If you happened to be trying to sneak back in around the same time that Joe was trying to sneak out.

She folded the box back up without returning the beach photo. And then, right behind it, she spotted the box marked DVDs.

"Bingo," she said to herself. She dragged the box closer, opened it, rummaged around. There were *Star Wars* and *Star Trek* movies, a couple of seasons of the *Star Trek* spinoff *Deep Space Nine*. Sandra was the science-fiction fan, and these were hers.

There were a couple of season box sets of *The Simpsons*. Then, below them, pay dirt. Seasons four and six of *Family Guy*.

Katie managed to hold the DVDs and the photo in one hand, allowing her to turn off the lights and open the garage door with the other. She scooted across the yard, slipped back into the kitchen through the sliding glass doors, and dropped the DVDs onto the counter.

"Found them!" she shouted at the door to the basement. "Just give me a sec!"

She bolted up the stairs and placed on her bedroom dresser the picture of her with her father. She descended the stairs as quickly as she'd climbed them, grabbed the DVDs from the counter, and charged down into the basement.

The first thing that struck her as odd was that the lights had not been turned on. She hit the switch and looked immediately at the couch and the coffee table in front of the flat-screen TV.

There were no Pringles and no Cokes there. No brother, either.

"Archie!" she cried.

She waited two seconds, then said under her breath, "The little weasel."

Katie charged back upstairs, calling out his name two more times. When she again failed to get a response, she charged out the front door.

There was an Arrival in the driveway, but it wasn't Gracie. This one was lime green, and in it were two boys Katie recognized.

Nick Loveland and Rory Glidden. Both twelve and both, Katie believed, pains in the ass. Kind of, well, like her brother. Nick was sitting up front, and Rory was in the back.

The door had retracted and Archie was dropping into the seat next to Rory.

"Archie!" Katie said. "Where do you think you're going?"

"Someplace you're not!" he shouted.

"Pamela!" Nick shouted. "Close the door!"

Jesus, Katie thought. *You don't even need a grown-up in the car to get one of these things to take you around.*

Before Katie could consider the wisdom of diving into the car and dragging her brother out, the door began sliding shut. Archie stuck a baby finger in each corner of his mouth, pulled wide, and wiggled his tongue at her.

"You are in such deep shit!" Katie shouted at him through the glass.

Archie, who was now in the process of dropping his pants and mooning his sister, did not appear overly concerned.

Five

Standing at the tail end of the ferry, on a lower, less populated deck area of the ship—too far from the food and drink to attract any real members of the media—Brandon Kyle looked down at the frothy wake and the mainland receding into the distance, resting his elbows on the railing.

He thought about what Rebecca Geary had said. About him—well, she didn't know it was him standing there right next to her—needing proof that the Arrival corporation was guilty of sabotage. How knowing something, and proving it, were two very different things.

And yet, he knew what had happened. At least the broad strokes.

It had begun with one of his top programmers, Emeril Francisco. Emeril was nothing short of a genius, who, at twenty-nine, was one of the most valuable members of the Gandalf team. He'd been with them six years, and what made him invaluable was that he wasn't like everyone else. Emeril didn't think in words. Emeril thought in numbers. He thought in *code*. Kyle guessed that when Emeril was having sex, he was counting thrusts and calculating arousal time. He was worth every one of those five hundred thousand dollars a year Kyle was paying him.

Genius often came hand in hand with eccentricity, and Kyle had spent enough time in the high-tech world to understand, and tolerate, that kind of thing. There was that one guy in research and development who swore he came up with his best ideas while wearing a pirate hat, and there he'd be, in the office, the damn thing perched on his head. You half expected to see a fucking parrot sitting on his shoulder. And there was that punker—Kristy, her name was—with the rings in the nose, the spiky hair, the jeans that were more ripped openings than actual material. You figured, when she was sitting at her workstation, earbuds firmly in place, that she had to be listening to a band with a name like Suicidal Gerbil or Open Runny Sore but in fact was grooving to Lawrence Welk. She wasn't even being ironic about it. She *liked* Lawrence Welk.

These were, let's face it, not people who could have gotten a job at Lehman Brothers. But in the tech world, eccentricities were part of the deal. At Gandalf, when you summoned someone to your office, you weren't surprised if they came scooting down the hall on a skateboard or walked in on their hands.

But with Emeril Francisco, eccentricity had slid into perversity.

You couldn't find a nicer guy around the Gandalf headquarters. No big ego, always offered a shoulder to cry on when you were down in the dumps, had maybe three sick days over four years. Never reheated fish in the microwave. And most critical of all, he was a design wizard. Say you wanted a car's sensors to be able to tell the difference between a ball bouncing into its path, or a small dog, and Emeril would find a way to do it, usually before the end of the day. With his help, Gandalf was at least sixteen months ahead of Arrival in their self-driving technology.

So when Rhonda Templeton said she needed to speak with Kyle privately about a personnel matter, he could not have imagined it would have had anything to do with Emeril Francisco. Rhonda, mid-thirties, a Seattle native, was the resident expert on viruses, and she had been spending her time developing ways to ensure they did not infect the Gandalf driving systems. There had been stories in the news about how, if your car was loaded with software, it could be hacked, even commandeered, by someone else. It was Rhonda's job to make sure that could not happen, and she led the team charged with that assignment. She was also working on defensive strategies about the latest looming threat: ransomware. The last thing Gandalf needed was a bunch of Russian hackers locking up their system and demanding millions to unlock it.

Rhonda, who had phoned in sick for the previous three days, closed the door and sat down across from Kyle and said, "I hardly know where to begin."

"How about the beginning?" Kyle said cheerfully.

She was wearing a sweater with a high neck that came right up to her chin. She pulled it down to expose her neck, which was seriously bruised. A bluish mark went around her throat from one side to the other.

"Jesus," Kyle said. "What happened? Did you have an accident or something?"

"Emeril Francisco is what happened," she said, pulling the sweater back up to cover the bruising.

"I don't understand."

"This," she said, her voice starting to break, "is what he's into. He's sick. He's a sick, sick man, and I can't work alongside someone like that anymore."

Kyle's star employee, it turned out, was a sexual sadist. Rhonda knew of at least one other woman in the office who'd had a similar experience with the man. Rhonda's run-in with Emeril had been four days earlier, which explained why she had not been into the office for the last three days.

"He's a psychopath," Rhonda said. "If he's done it to me, and—well, I promised not to say who the other person is—then he's probably done it to more than just us. One of these days, he's going to go too far. He's going to choke someone to death."

Kyle said he completely sympathized. It was a terrible thing that she'd been through. How could she be expected to work alongside such a man?

So Brandon Kyle took action.

Years ago, a person in his position might have been able to get away with transferring Rhonda to another department, maybe to another city. But the days of making the victim pay for the offender's misdeeds were long since over.

He brought Emeril into his office and spoke plainly: "Regardless of how valuable you may be to this company, there are some behaviors that simply cannot be tolerated. The people in this workplace have every right to feel safe, and I'm afraid your presence makes that exceedingly difficult."

Kyle even recorded the firing and played it for Rhonda. Her eyes brimmed with tears when she heard what Kyle had to say.

"Thank you," she said. "Thank you so much."

Kyle had smiled and said, "I'm the one who should thank you, for bringing this to my attention."

Except Kyle never fired Emeril at all. Did Rhonda really believe he was going to let one of his top people go? Run the risk that he'd go to the competition and take all of Gandalf's corporate secrets with him? Not on your life.

"We're going to have to do a little improv," he'd told Emeril, and the firing was staged and recorded. The first two times, Kyle hadn't been satisfied with Emeril's performance. "You need to deny it, say Rhonda was lying, get a little more outraged." The third take went perfectly.

Kyle put things in place to allow Emeril to work off-site, even found ways to disguise his contributions so that they appeared to have been done by a new, outside tech firm.

The ruse even worked for a while.

But over time, Rhonda became suspicious. She had expected there to be some fallout from the firing. That Emeril might have sued, or at the very least mounted some sort of campaign to get his job back. Why hadn't another tech company scooped him up? Rhonda had agreed, with great reluctance, to sign a nondisclosure agreement with Gandalf when she'd joined, so she hadn't been able to spread the word about

Emeril's behavior. So there was every reason to believe another firm might have hired him without knowing about the allegations that had been made against him.

So she started doing some checking. If there was anyone who could follow a digital trail, it was Rhonda. She looked into the background of the firm that was now doing Emeril's work, and eventually tracked bitcoin payments to an account that was linked to her attacker.

"You lied to me," she said, confronting Kyle.

"Did you really expect me to lose one of my top people?" he shot back.

"Well, you're losing one now."

And she quit. Before the day was out, she was working for Lisa Carver, the CEO of Arrival, but not before one final warning for Brandon Kyle.

"If you want to sue me, to stop me from going to work for Lisa, be my guest. I'll be in touch with CNN and the *Times* and anyone else I can think of to tell them you secretly kept a sexual predator on the payroll. Just try me."

The catastrophic Gandalf crash that took the lives of that director and his girlfriend came three months later. Kyle could think of no one more qualified to infect one of his vehicles with a virus than a former employee who'd been in charge of protecting them from such incursions.

Kyle learned that, after the accident, Rhonda took time off from work. She began to drink heavily, started seeing a therapist. From what Kyle could gather, she'd had every intention of fucking up one of his cars, but never meant for anyone to get killed. Screw up the door locks, keep the navigation system from working, have the heat come on when you dialed in the A/C. Let Gandalf get a reputation for unreliability.

But kill two innocent people? She hadn't signed on for that.

Arrival had exploited Rhonda, using everything she knew about Gandalf's operating system, and then expanding on that knowledge. Rhonda had left one company for its failure to deal with a sexual predator and now worked for one that had used her expertise to, in effect, commit murder.

One day, Kyle got a call from a number that he could not identify.

"I want to talk," Rhonda said. "Tomorrow."

She was ready, she said, to blow the whistle on Arrival.

They could not be seen together. She'd rent a room at the Hilton, have a key card left for him at the desk. Kyle went to the hotel at the appointed time, but there was no key for him. No Rhonda Templeton had checked in. So Kyle waited in the lobby for two hours until he received a call from the office asking if he'd heard the news.

Rhonda was dead.

Hell of a thing. That morning, the superintendent of her condo broke into her unit when water started flowing out from under the door. Found her naked body in the bathroom. Looked like she'd gotten into the tub while the water was still running, slipped, and hit her head on the edge. A fatal blow. What were the odds?

What were the odds, indeed.

Kyle knew how he must have sounded in the interviews he gave after that. Arrival had not only used one of his own employees to sabotage him, but murdered her when her conscience got the better of her. Gandalf's reputation already in tatters, now Kyle personally was seen to be in a delusional free fall. Gandalf stock plummeted. The company went bankrupt, the factory mothballed. All but a handful of employees remained, most devoted to winding down operations. Even Emeril got the boot.

Kyle lost his Cape Hatteras seaside mansion, the SoHo condo in New York. His stable of rare sports cars, including his 1961 Jaguar E-Type, a 1964 Aston Martin DB5, and his most treasured find, a 1983 DeLorean, the vehicle from those *Back to the Future* movies, was auctioned off.

And worst of all, he lost Beverly.

Five years. Good times. But Beverly wasn't interested in sticking around for the bad. "I can't take it," she'd finally told him. "This obsession, this drive to get even, it's consumed you. Every minute of every day, it's Lisa this, Lisa that. You've got a choice to make. You can either move past what's happened, let me help you move forward, or you let this anger and revenge completely eat you up, and do it alone."

Kyle made his choice.

Thank God there was a prenup. Managed to send her packing with a cool million. Chump change compared to what she might have gotten without one. So there was still money left to do what he had to do.

To get even.

Arrival and its CEO, Lisa Carver, had *humiliated* him.

Destroyed all that he had worked so long to build. His life's dream.

Kyle had become a joke on late-night talk shows. What was it one of the hosts quipped? "I was going to buy a Gandalf, but decided not to take the plunge."

There had to be payback. You couldn't crush a man's soul and expect to get away with it. The way Brandon Kyle saw it, there was nothing left to lose, only one way to settle the score.

"Excuse me?"

Kyle, still leaning up against the railing, turned. A slight, balding man in his thirties was standing three feet away, leaning in curiously, peering at Kyle through a pair of black-framed glasses.

"Sorry to bother you," he said. "Clyde Travers, *Consumer Safety* magazine."

"Hey," Kyle said.

Travers was extending a hand, so Kyle, with some reluctance, took it. "Nice to meet you. Ben Stapleton, *Wheel Base Trends*."

"Kind of lonely back here," Travers said, chuckling nervously. "Everyone else is up front. I guess people like to see where they are going instead of where they've been."

Kyle feigned a friendly smile but said nothing. But Clyde was correct. This end of the ferry, on this lower deck, was an out-of-the way spot. Kyle had chosen it because he wanted to be alone with his thoughts, and now this guy had come along.

Travers was looking intently at Kyle, as if trying to place him. "Have we met before?"

"I don't think so," Brandon Kyle said, because no one, before today, had ever met Ben Stapleton. But Kyle did believe he recognized Travers. The man had interviewed him at some point.

"Are you sure?" Travers persisted. "Because you look familiar."

Kyle shrugged. "Maybe at some other event."

Travers wouldn't stop staring. "You know who you look like?"

Kyle had that feeling you get when you think you've lost your wallet. "Who?" he asked, slowly.

"That Gandalf guy. Brandon Kyle."

Kyle laughed nervously. "I wish. I'd love a full head of hair and a six-pack." He patted the stuffing strapped to his waist. "But like I said, I'm Ben Stapleton, *Wheel Base*."

Travers was looking him right in the eye. "No, I don't think so. I've interviewed you three times over the years. In 2018, when the first Gandalfs were coming off the line." He smiled wryly as he looked Kyle up and down. "What's with the disguise? That is, unless you've really been getting into the Krispy Kremes in a big way the last few months."

Kyle wasn't ready to concede defeat. "Honestly, I'm not who you think I am."

Travers took out his phone. "So, if I look up Ben Stapleton and *Wheel Base Trends*, I'm gonna see your picture and byline, am I?"

Kyle reached out a cautioning hand. "Okay, fine, put your phone away."

Travers grinned with satisfaction. "So what gives?"

Kyle sighed and looked back out to sea, elbows on the railing. "It's a long story."

"Yeah, well, I've got time." He shook his head, disbelieving. "So, like, Lisa Carver, the Arrival PR people, they've got no idea you're on the ferry, that you're headed for their presser? Am

I right? I mean, I can't imagine you were on the guest list."

Kyle nodded slowly. "That's correct."

"So you're sneaking in. You want to see for yourself what they're up to." Travers's head bobbed up and down sympathetically. "Look, I get it. I'm one of the people who's believed you from the beginning. I think they fucked with your software, and I think they killed that woman who used to work with you. Staged that bathroom accident."

Kyle turned to face him. "You believe they murdered Rhonda Templeton."

Travers nodded. "I do. You just need to keep digging, get something for real on Lisa. Some real honest-to-god proof. But I don't guess I'm telling you anything you don't know."

"It's nice to know I've got at least one ally out there," Kyle said.

"Sure, yeah, you bet. Just hold still there for a second." Travers raised his phone to his eye and fired off several shots of Kyle.

"What the hell," Kyle said. "Stop that."

"We were talking about proof a minute ago, right? When I write my piece, tell everyone I ran into none other than Brandon Kyle sneaking into Arrival's event of the century, I'm gonna need a pic to back up my story."

"No," Kyle said.

But Travers was already tapping away on his screen with his thumb. "You have to understand, I'm an ally. I believe you. But I just can't ignore that you're here. A tweet now, the full story later."

"You can't do that," Kyle said.

Travers said, looking down at the message he

was composing, "Not getting many bars here. The ferry's got Wi-Fi, but . . ."

He was so busy looking at the phone he didn't see the computer bag coming straight at his head. Kyle connected with Travers's temple. Travers dropped the phone and staggered backward.

"What the fuck!" he shouted.

The phone had landed on the deck. Kyle dropped to his knees, grabbed it, and lobbed it over the top of the railing. As it sailed through the air, Travers made a futile attempt to grab for it, leaning over the railing and clutching at nothing.

Kyle quickly glanced around.

It was just the two of them back here. This was an isolated part of the ferry. There were visible security cameras on the upper decks, but he'd noticed none down here.

The railing was too high to push someone over it easily. That would be very difficult. But *pitching*, well, that might just work.

Kyle was already on his knees, and he worked out the physics in his head in the time it would take a Gandalf sat-nav system to figure out the number of miles between Houston and Topeka. Travers was a small man. Five-two, probably no more than one hundred and thirty pounds. All Kyle had to do was give the man a little boost.

Kyle threw his arms around the man's knees, locked them, then, with everything he had, he pistoned his own legs upward.

All in less than a second.

Travers's torso shot upward. By the time he realized what was happening, he was too far up to grab the railing. When the man's upper thigh was level with the top of the railing, Kyle tipped him forward.

And off he sailed. Two seconds in the air before he went into the sea. If Travers made a sound, the roar of the ferry's massive engines and the wind drowned them out.

Kyle spun around, his heart hammering in his chest.

As he struggled to catch his breath, for his pulse to drop back to the speed limit, he listened and waited.

There were no shouts of "Man overboard!" No alarms were sounded. The ferry did not slow down.

Once he'd calmed himself down, he went back to the upper deck. Time to rejoin the party.

Six

Sandra had to admit, it was a bit of a kick.

Sitting in the back of the car, reviewing her notes, taking a final look at the press kits, all while Gracie did the driving. She leaned back in the seat, closed her eyes, and took a deep, cleansing breath. At times like this, when she was particularly stressed—and she was always stressed after breakfast with her kids, even on days when her entire career wasn't at stake—she wished she'd enrolled in one of those relaxation courses, or mindfulness, or yoga, or something that would teach her how to let all the tension flow out of her. Back in her teens, she'd thought that was what drugs and alcohol were for.

Sandra Montrose had weaned herself from that coping strategy once she got a little older, and especially after she'd had kids. Back in the day, she and Adam had sure known how to party, and booze and drugs weren't the only highs that kept them going. Those were some wild days. Sitting on the back of the Harley, holding on to Adam for dear life, going across the country, never knowing where they'd be spending the night, not giving a rat's ass about what the next day would bring. Sometimes, she'd take the reins and he'd sit behind her on the bike, and when he got his hands in just the right places, well, that, along with straddling all that horsepower, it was all you could do to concentrate on the road ahead of you.

But sooner or later, you have to grow up. Sandra got a business degree. Adam, who liked hands-on work as opposed to sitting behind a desk, landed a job fixing motorcycles while Sandra found a position in a real estate office. Around the time Katie was born, Sandra had made the move to public relations. Adam, still repairing Harleys while working for someone else, dreamed of the day when he would have his own shop, be his own boss.

Shortly after Archie was born, they borrowed a friend's beach house on Garrett Island for a week's vacation, and it was an epiphany. They loved it there. Adam found a small engine repair shop that was for sale. That had to be some kind of sign. And a local public relations firm was looking to hire.

Talk about fucking meant-to-be.

Would they like it, living on an island? Would they feel isolated, confined? Well, it was a pretty *big* island. There was the town of Garrett itself, plus several other smaller communities scattered here and there, and a lot of countryside separating them. Most of the time, you hardly even knew you were on an island. What was it Chief Brody had said about living on an island?

"It only looks like an island from the water."

So they made the move.

And things had gone just great. Adam's business thrived. Sure, things slowed down in the winter months, but rather than worry about the seasonal downturn in business, Adam embraced it. He spent more time with the kids, volunteered at their school. Four years into working at the PR firm, the boss decided to retire and turn things over to Sandra.

Things were going along just great.

Until . . .

Sandra opened her eyes, turned, and looked out the window. A blue Arrival was pulling out of a driveway, a woman in the front seat studying herself in the drop-down mirror, touching up her lipstick, not bothering to check for traffic. It was Dorothy Lansing, who ran Garrett Books, where Sandra bought all her reading material. Sandra waved and Dorothy waved back. Glancing out the other window, she saw a yellow Arrival go by with the Ambersons, a middle-aged couple who ran a law firm together. If they'd looked Sandra's way, she'd have waved at them, too, but they were busy looking at their phones. That sort of behavior was now deemed legal, at least on the island, during the trial period.

Sandra got out her own phone and sent several texts. One to her AV guy, another to the caterer, another to someone she knew who worked for the ferry. The caterer and the AV people were already on-site and ready to go, and the ferry had left the mainland on time. And yet, Sandra still found it hard to relax. She wouldn't be able to unwind until this day was over.

And then there was Joe.

What was that *luv* text supposed to mean? Okay, he was a nice guy. Sandra *liked* him. But she felt him pushing a little too hard. Or was it just her? Was she resisting a little too much?

Here was this decent guy, with a nice job, and a mortgage-free house—with a *mother* in it, mind you—and he was really interested in her. Shouldn't she be happy about that?

The car slowed. Sandra peered through the windshield and saw they were approaching a four-way stop. There were Arrivals closing in from the three other directions. And it looked as though they were all going to get to the stop at the same time.

"How's it going, Gracie?" Sandra said aloud.

"Very well. You will reach your destination in five minutes."

The four Arrivals stopped within milliseconds of each other. Sandra watched with interest as the car approaching from the opposite direction moved on first, then the one from the right, then Gracie. Halfway into the intersection, a woman on a bicycle zipped across their path and Gracie hit the brakes.

Bicycles and skateboards and scooters were still allowed. Arrivals were expected to know how to deal with them, even if conventional cars were banned. As the Arrival continued on, Sandra glanced behind her to see the fourth car move out.

"Impressive," Sandra said. "You didn't hit the cyclist, and all the cars moved through the four-way with military precision. How did you know when it was your turn, Gracie?"

Gracie explained, *"The car approaching from the north arrived first, one second before the car approaching from the east, which arrived two-tenths of a second before us, and the car approaching from the west stopped one-tenth of a second after us."*

"So you all just instantly calculated that, like you were all talking to each other."

Gracie did not reply. At first, Sandra wondered whether Gracie was being rude, then realized she had not actually asked a question, or issued a command. She'd made a comment. Arrivals were not programmed to respond to comments. You didn't want your car joining in on conversations, offering political opinions.

Ahead, the Garrett Island Community Center came into view.

Sandra took another deep breath, glanced at her watch. The ferry full of media types, if it hadn't already, would dock momentarily. A fleet of Arrivals was waiting to bring them here, about a ten-minute drive.

"It's going to be okay," she whispered, reassuring herself. "It's going to be—"

Gracie hit the brakes. Sandra let out a short scream as the car came to an abrupt halt, pitching her briefcase from the back seat and down into the footwell. Out of the corner of her eye she saw why Gracie had done what she did. A deer had darted across the road. It went past in a flash, disappearing into the woods at the side of the road, its back legs kicking high into the air as it leapt over a crumbling wire fence.

"Jesus!" Sandra said. "Nice going, Gracie."

There was a deer "harvest" every year on the island—a nice way, Sandra thought, of saying "slaughter." But the animals were a major carrier of ticks, and the incidence of Lyme disease was up, so there hadn't been much public outcry about reducing the size of the herd. There were believed to be about five hundred of them on the island, about fifty per square mile. She'd read recently in the *Garrett Gazette* that more than seven hundred had been killed this year.

The car started to move again and, seconds later, was turning into the community center parking lot. Gracie got as close as she could to the main doors without actually driving up on the sidewalk.

"*You have reached your destination,*" Gracie said.

"Great. Open up."

The back door slid open. Sandra reached down and retrieved the briefcase. "Find a place to park, Gracie. See you later."

Sandra got out. A second after the door closed, the car, without a passenger, moved over to the parking lot and slipped into a spot between two other Arrivals. One of them, she noted, bore the logo of the Garrett Island Police on the side. Even the cops had had their regular rides replaced. Joe had told her that only one traditional island cop car had remained on the island, and that was because it was in the shop for service. About the only vehicles on the entire island that were still actually driven by real people were the fire trucks and the island ambulance.

She smiled inwardly at seeing the police car. *So*, she thought, *Joe is here.*

"Hey, about time!"

Sandra whirled around. Given that her thoughts at that moment had been of Joe, she half expected it to be him, but was not surprised when she saw that it was Albert Ruskin. She'd had countless Zoom chats with the assistant to Arrival president Lisa Carver, plenty of FaceTime discussions on her phone. But this was their first in-person face-to-face.

It struck her, almost instantly, how he was just as unpleasant in the flesh. He wore a permanent expression of disapproval, as if, as a child, his face had frozen at the moment he was being force-fed broccoli.

"Hi," she said.

"We've been here since dawn," he said. "Caught the first ferry. Lisa's inside, a nervous wreck. And she was just sick to her stomach, for Christ's sake! What the hell's in the water here?"

Sandra's mouth opened in shock. "Oh my God, that's awful. Is she okay?"

"We were in that area you hilariously refer to as a green room and she was all set up with her laptop. She'd had some coffee that your caterers—more like poisoners—brought in and within seconds she was running for the ladies' room."

"I can't imagine . . . maybe it's just nerves or—"

"I'll bet it was the cream," Ruskin said. "You can't get fresh cream around here."

"Honestly, I don't know what happened. You can be sure I'll look into it. Let me talk to Lisa—Ms. Carver—and see if she's okay. I feel just terrible about this."

Ruskin shook his head in disgust, then said, "Come on."

He turned on his heel and headed for the main doors. The man had a quick, nervous walk—like his legs were on fast-forward while the rest of him moved at a normal rate—and when he opened the door he went through first, failing to hold it open for Sandra. She grabbed it before it swung shut and scurried to keep up.

Ruskin was talking without turning his head and Sandra wasn't picking up all of it. But she did hear, "Maybe it was the coffee. What'd you use? Seawater? And I swear, really, is it so hard to have a proper green room?"

Sandra wanted to tell him that the Garrett Island Community Center was not a TV studio, that this was not the Jimmy Fallon show, but held her tongue. She'd chosen this place, as opposed to one of the local hotels, because they needed a large room to display a small fleet of Arrivals, and the center's gymnasium fit the bill. Other areas of the facility—a kids' day-care room, an exercise room, the administrator's office, a dining area—had become makeshift media centers and conference rooms and, yes, a green room.

Ruskin went down a hall to a door marked LADIES, opened it an inch, and said, "Lisa? How are you feeling?"

Seconds later, the door opened wide. Lisa Carver, mid-fifties, silvery blond hair. Sandra, no stranger to *Vogue*, recognized her smartly tailored jacket and skirt, in dark blue, as Donna Karan. Lisa was dabbing the corners of her mouth with a tissue and looked at Sandra as if she were a cockroach sitting atop a cupcake.

"Are you the one?" Lisa asked.

Ruskin nodded a confirmation. "This is Sandra Montrose, our event coordinator." His voice was tinged with sarcasm, as if to say, *Can you believe it?*

Sandra pasted a smile onto her face and offered a hand. "It's a pleasure to finally meet. How are you feeling? Mr. Ruskin told me you—"

"I'm fine," she said, ignoring the hand. "At least I think so."

"The queasiness passed?" Ruskin asked her.

"I think." She looked at Sandra. "There's something wrong with the coffee. Is there no Starbucks on this island?"

"I'm so sorry. Are you sure it was—"

"Doesn't matter," Lisa said. "I have to finish setting up." She looked at Ruskin. "Where's my laptop?"

"It's where you left—"

"For Christ's sake, you just left it there?"

"I'll get it." He looked at Sandra. "Is there somewhere else we could work? That office behind the gym is simply not acceptable. There were *basketballs* in there. It smells like Bigfoot's jockstrap in there."

"I can have another room set up," Sandra said.

Sandra led the two of them down another hall, then held open the door to what was normally the center administrator's office, which came with its own private washroom.

"I suppose this will have to do," Lisa said, going in and closing the door behind her.

"Jesus," Sandra said under her breath as Ruskin went off to fetch his boss's computer.

Movement at the end of the hall caught Sandra's eye.

"Incoming," she said to herself. The first wave of reporters was entering the building. She trotted up the hall and was starting to quicken her pace when a hand reached out from an open door and grabbed her by the wrist.

Sandra let out a muted scream as she felt herself being pulled into a room with a sign on the door that said TECHNICAL. Whoever'd grabbed her kicked the door shut, wrapped both arms around her, and spun her around.

And then a man's lips were on hers.

Sandra submitted, briefly, to the embrace, then put both hands on the man's chest—almost getting her finger caught in the badge pinned to his chest that read JOE BRIDGEMAN, CHIEF— GARRETT ISLAND POLICE.

"Shit, Joe, are you out of your mind?"

Joe, just under six feet with black hair, a thick black mustache, and dressed in a tan shirt and slacks, grinned mischievously.

"You look *very* hot," he said.

"Yeah, well, you probably played hell with my lipstick. I've got a horde of journalists to greet and I can't go out there looking like I kissed a ripe tomato."

He pulled her close, pressing himself into her. "They can wait a couple minutes."

"Wait while we do *what*?" she asked, glancing about the room. This was the guts of the community center. A huge furnace, circuit breaker boxes, hot water tanks, security system panels, wires and pipes running all over the place. "Believe me, *nothing* is happening in here."

Joe's smile turned less lascivious as he loosened his grip on Sandra. "I just wanted to give you a kiss for good luck."

Sandra relaxed, rested a hand on his chest instead of trying to push him away. She blew a strand of hair away from her eyes. "I'm a wreck."

"No. You've got this."

"I do? The CEO's already complaining of food poisoning."

"Oh, yeah," he said. "I was in there when it happened. She went running off so fast she almost knocked over her assistant. But I don't think it was anything she ate. Probably just nerves, like you."

"Yeah, well, there's a lot riding on this, for all of us. So long as nothing *else* goes wrong, I could get a lot of other jobs out of this."

"It's gonna be great." He gave her shoulders a squeeze.

She shrugged, immune to his attempt to boost her confidence. Suddenly, she had a question. "What the hell are you doing in here?"

"Just checking things out. Someone tried to plug something in, wouldn't work, came in here and found the breaker had flipped. Bud, the maintenance guy? He's around somewhere, but I was able to find the problem. I've been doing the rounds, making sure everything's okay from a security point of view."

"You're the best," Sandra said.

It was his turn to shrug. "I want everything to go perfectly for you. These corporate types are very worried about security, you know, other companies snooping around, so I've been trying to put them at ease. That Lisa Carver, man, she's a piece of work."

"Her assistant's no better."

Joe paused, then said, "Listen, I've been thinking."

"Joe, not now."

"I'll be quick. I just wanted to say, it looks

like I'm going to be able to move my mom into a place. I think I've found a good spot for her. So once that happens, you and me, I mean, we could, or I could move in—"

"Joe, I haven't even told the kids about you. What are they going to think? One day, I've got no one in my life, the next day, you're standing in the kitchen in your boxers frying some eggs?"

"I know, I know, we have to start gradual. All I'm saying is, think about it. Would you at least do that?"

She nodded quickly, not so much because she agreed, but because she had work to do.

"I have to go," she said.

"Yeah, okay, me, too, as it turns out. I got to take a run down to the ferry dock."

"Why?"

"One of your media types is missing. They say he didn't get off the boat. I told them to check the head. Lot of people who don't expect to get seasick do. He's probably losing his breakfast in the ferry bathroom, or maybe he never got on the boat in the first place. Could be that's what happened to that Carver lady. Delayed seasickness."

"Okay," she said, and tilted her chin up to allow him to give her one more kiss. He did, but made it a quick one.

He opened the door. "You go out first. I'll wait fifteen seconds."

Sandra caught her reflection in the glass door of a fire extinguisher housing. She pursed her lips, muttered, "This'll have to do," and slipped out of the room.

She headed straight for the registration desk,

where representatives from the various media outlets were picking up their IDs.

Moments before things were ready to go, she saw that one badge had not been picked up. CLYDE TRAVERS—CONSUMER SAFETY.

Well, it wasn't as if Clyde was from one of the biggies, Sandra thought. If he missed the event, she'd courier a media packet to him tomorrow.

Seven

Just drive around, Pamela," said Archie's friend Nick, who was sitting in one of the two front seats of the lime-green Arrival.

Archie, sitting in the back seat next to his friend Rory, said, "Nick, why's the car called Pamela?"

Nick turned around completely, putting his knees on the seat and wrapping his arms around the headrest for support.

"So, my mom thinks my dad named it Pamela after his aunt Pamela who, like, died years ago, but he actually named it Pamela after Pamela Anderson."

"Who?" said Rory.

"Oh my God, there's a video you have to see from about a hundred years ago. Anyway, she used to be this sex symbol that my dad always had the hots for. I heard him telling one of his friends that he never got to take a ride on *that* Pamela, so this one will have to do."

Archie, not quite sure whether that was a dirty joke or not, glanced at Rory to see if he was laughing. Rory snickered, so Archie did the same.

"Good one," he said. "So how come Pamela's responding to your voice? I thought the car would only work for your dad."

"We were at the mall parking lot, right?" Nick

said. "Just me and my dad? And I asked if I could try driving, or at least telling the car what to do, so he set it up to respond to my commands."

Rory's eyes went wide. "So your dad's okay with you taking it out without him?" he asked disbelievingly.

Nick grimaced. "Not . . . exactly," he said. "He just didn't get around to canceling the programming. He sort of doesn't know I took it out today. He went to Boston last night, had to fly to Chicago on business."

"What about your mom?" Archie asked.

"She kinda slept in," Nick said.

Archie figured, by the end of the day, Nick's mom would kill him, or maybe she'd wait until his dad was back from Chicago and let him kill him, but either way, it really wasn't Archie's problem. He was an innocent bystander, or innocent passenger. Something like that. The truth was, Archie didn't care as much about following the rules as much as he once did. In simple terms, he didn't give a fuck.

"My sister's all, hey, I need my driver's license," Archie said as Pamela glided down the Garrett street. "But, like, who needs one of those with cars like these?"

"Yeah," said Rory. "Although this would probably get boring after a while because there's nothing to do. So, Nick, can you make the car do anything interesting? Like, can you make it do donuts?"

Nick, still hanging over the back of the front seat, shook his head sadly. "I tried. I say, Pamela, let's do some fishtails and she goes, no. I say, hey, Pamela, let's do a bunch of donuts, she says no.

I say, Pamela, let's see what you can do. Can you hit a hundred? And Pamela says no."

"I guess no means no with Pamela," Rory lamented.

Nick nodded.

"So where's the fun, then?" Archie asked.

"Seriously?" Nick said. "We're out. In a car. On our own. If this were a real car, we wouldn't be allowed to drive it for another four years. But with Pamela, we just tell her where we want to go and she'll take us there."

A slow grin spread across Archie's face. "Will Pamela respond to anything I ask her?"

Nick shook his head. "No, just me. But if you've got something good, whisper it to me."

Archie leaned forward, cupped his hand around Nick's ear. Nick grinned. "Oh, I like that." He cleared his throat. "Pamela," he said crisply.

"*Yes,*" said Pamela in a voice that sounded exactly the same as Gracie's.

"Please take us to Uranus."

"*Could you please repeat your destination?*"

"Uranus. Let me say it more slowly for you. Your . . . anus."

In the back seat, Archie and Rory were working so hard to stifle their laughter that they appeared to be having seizures.

"*Do you mean Uranus Drive in Louisville, Kentucky? Or do you mean Uranus Drive in Cocoa, Florida?*"

"I think I'm dying," Archie said.

"No, just Uranus," Nick said.

Rory said, "I've got another one." He leaned forward to whisper it to Nick.

"Butt, Montana?"

Archie cackled. "You moron. It's not Butt, Montana. It's Butte, Montana, rhymes with cute."

"Oh," Rory said, his face flushing. "Are you sure?"

Archie rolled his eyes. "I think this explains your D in Geography."

Nick quipped, "There *is* no D in Geography. I guess that's why you suck at spelling."

"I got one," Archie said. "Let's go to Intercourse."

Rory blinked. "You're kidding me. There's no such place."

Archie nodded. "You bet your ass there is. In Pennsylvania."

"No way."

Archie said to Nick, "Go ahead. Ask Pamela for some Intercourse."

That got all three of them convulsing again. But Nick managed to calm down long enough to say, "Pamela, can you plot a *course* to Intercourse, Pennsylvania?"

"*Calculating,*" Pamela said.

"She's probably building in time for a stop to pick up condoms," Rory said.

"*Depending on route selection,*" Pamela said, "*Intercourse, Pennsylvania, is between four hundred and nine miles, and four hundred and thirty miles, and will take between eight hours and nine minutes, and eight hours and thirty-eight minutes. But according to my calculations, a stop at a recharging station will need to be accommodated. Would you like me to choose a route where charging stations are located?*"

"Uh, you know what, Pamela?" Nick said. "I've changed my mind. No Intercourse today."

Archie was holding his stomach with both hands. Rory had tears running down his face. They were laughing so hard it took a moment before they realized a phone was ringing. Rory wiped his eyes with the back of his sleeve and said to Archie, "That's you, man."

Archie composed himself as he dug into his pocket for his cell phone. When he saw who was calling, he cringed.

"My sister," he said.

"Oooh, I like her," Nick said. Archie glanced up from his phone long enough to shoot him a look. "I'm just stating a fact," Nick said defensively.

The phone had rung six times. Archie had his finger poised over the button to accept the call while he had an inner debate about whether to take it.

After Archie'd taken off with his friends, Katie had stormed back into the house wondering what to do. She went into the kitchen and looked at the cell phone in her hand.

Should she call her mother? Rat out the little creep? God, Archie could be such an immense pain in the ass.

He didn't use to be this bad. Before he turned twelve, he did what his mother told him, didn't talk back to his sister. Well, not that much.

Then everything changed.

Back before *it* happened, it was rare that Archie got in trouble at school or on the home front. And when he did, it wasn't usually anything particularly serious. There was that broken second-floor window when he crashed a friend's drone through it. (It was his own bedroom; had it been Katie's, she'd have accused him of trying to spy on her.) And there was the time he got tar on a brand-new pair of jeans and, even though he had never run the washing machine himself, tried to clean them himself rather than let his mother find out. That turned into a 1950s sitcom episode, what with Archie overloading the machine with a dozen soap pods and nearly filling the laundry room from floor to ceiling with suds.

When their dad got home, he couldn't stop laughing.

It was a happier time, what with Dad being alive and all. It was funny, how you never know you're in the good times until the shitty times kick in.

So why, Katie wondered, had Archie turned into an asshole when she had not? (She believed she was being pretty objective here in concluding that she was as wonderful now as she'd ever been.) Maybe, she wondered, losing a father was even harder on a boy. But that seemed pretty sexist. Didn't she miss him as much as he did? Of course she did, but she had to concede that interests in the household tended to run along gender lines. Archie loved all things mechanical and could spend hours in the shop with his father. The two of them would often spend a Sunday afternoon there and return home grease-stained and smelling of oil. He was only twelve, but he could diagnose any kind of problem in their gas-powered Lawn-Boy. It drove Katie nuts, when it was her time to cut the lawn and the machine conked out, that she had to get her little brother to get it going again.

Once, a few months after their dad had died, and his repair shop had been sold off, Archie disappeared. Sandra had been seconds away from calling the police when Katie suggested they check the shop, which, while sold, was still sitting empty while the new owners readied their plans to renovate it. Sure enough, it was where they found him. He'd busted a window, crawled in, and fallen asleep sitting at his father's oil-stained desk, his head on the table.

Katie's interests had always been more in line with her mother's. Media issues, real estate. While Archie and Adam were in the garage, tearing apart an Evinrude outboard motor to see what made it tick, there was a good chance Katie and Sandra were going from one open house to another. Katie, at one point, had even floated the idea of taking some architectural courses in Boston.

But right now, what was most on Katie's mind was getting her brother back home before he got himself into some kind of trouble with his dimwitted pals. Her first instinct was to call her mother, but she'd made it pretty clear before she left that this was a very big day for her. The last thing she wanted to hear was that Archie was up to no good.

So instead of calling her, Katie decided to try to talk some sense into her idiot brother herself. She brought up ARCHIE from her contacts list, and tapped on his name.

It rang. And rang. And rang. And—

"Yeah?" Archie said.

In the background, someone—Katie thought it sounded like Nick—shouted, "Hi, Katie!"

"You need to get your ass back here right now," she said in her most stern, older sister voice.

"I'll be back soon," he said.

"After Intercourse!" That time it sounded like Rory.

"Whose car are you in?" Katie asked.

"Nick's, I mean, like, Nick's dad's car."

"Do his parents even know he's got it?"

Archie paused. "Nick's dad set it all up to take voice commands from him."

"That's not what I asked you. Do they know he's got the car?"

"Okay, maybe not technically. But he's very responsible, and the car won't do anything stupid or illegal. We can't speed or anything. In a lot of ways, it's not even any fun at all. Did you know there's a place in Pennsylvania called Intercourse? I wonder if there's an In-N-Out Burger there?"

"Get home right now," she said. "If you don't get back here, I swear I'll kill you."

"Well, if I don't come back, then you *can't* kill me," Archie countered. "That's very abusive language you're using, Katie."

The little shit. He was parroting their mother.

Maybe the time had come to just plead.

"Come on, Archie, just get them to drop you off. *Please.* You know Mom's not going to freak out just at you over this. She's going to freak out at me, too. And then it's going to be awful around here. We're both going to be grounded till Christmas."

Archie was quiet for several seconds at his end.

Katie briefly wondered if the call had dropped out. It happened a lot on the island.

But then, "Hang on, Nick is saying something. Nick is saying we might go to Garrett Mall. Is that okay? If we're at the mall, we can't get into any trouble there."

"It doesn't even open for, like, another hour," Katie said.

"So we'll drive around the neighborhood till then. We'll be fine. Gotta go."

And with that, he ended the call.

"Shit!" Katie said.

What if her mom called? What if she took a minute from her crazy day and checked in to see how she and Archie were doing?

If she had a license—and a car of her own—she'd go out looking for him.

There were Arrival taxis on the island during the experiment period—driverless Ubers, basically. Should she call one of them?

She stewed for several seconds about what to do. She felt she needed the advice of an adult—so long as that adult was not her mother.

Katie pocketed her phone, walked to the front door, and opened it. She looked at the house across the street.

The home of the creepy serial killer. The one who went by the name Bruce Clifford, Archie had so proudly revealed at breakfast.

Katie stepped out of the house, closed and locked the front door behind her. She walked over the lawn, crossed the sidewalk and the street, then went up the driveway. She went to the front door and held her finger an inch away from the doorbell.

She paused a moment, considering her decision.

Katie pressed her index finger to the doorbell and held it. Inside the house, she heard the chimes ring. Seconds later, the faint sound of footsteps within the house.

There was the sound of a deadbolt being thrown half a second before the door opened wide.

Bruce Clifford, dressed in a white undershirt and a pair of faded jeans, looked at the girl through a pair of glasses that perched crookedly on his bulbous nose.

"Hey, Bruce," she said.

"How's it going, Katie?" he asked.

"Can I come in? I've got a problem."

He stepped back. "You want some coffee?"

"I don't really like it, but sure, that sounds like a plan," Katie said, stepping into the house.

Eight

Sandra needed a moment.

Everything was ready to go. The media types were all positioned at their temporary workstations neatly arranged throughout the gym so that they could set up their computers and file stories while the presentation was under way. Everyone had been given, inside a handsome leather pouch that was individually addressed to each attendee, a press kit, a computer stick with a digital version of all the information in the press kit (with plenty of whiz-bang animations thrown in for good measure) that was shaped like an Arrival car, an Arrival key fob with the company logo, even a small metal diecast model of an Arrival—about four inches long—that reporters could take home and give to their kids, or keep for themselves.

There was a low-level buzz in the room. People were excited. Sandra could feel it. But before she did anything else, she slipped out a back door of the community center, leaned her back against the wall, and closed her eyes.

"This is for you, Adam," she whispered. "It's all in your honor, what I'm doing here today. These Arrival people, okay, they're not the nicest bunch I've ever worked with, but what they're doing, it's going to change the future. It's going to be a safer world for our kids, so what happened to you"—and at this point, she felt a lump in her throat—"so what happened to you could never happen to them. I miss you, babe. You give me strength. You're still my guy."

She opened her eyes, let out a long breath. "Okay," Sandra said to herself, "let's do this."

She went back into the gymnasium, worked the crowd, made sure everyone had what they needed.

A woman from *Motor Trend* quietly asked Sandra whether she had an extra Arrival toy car. She had twin boys at home and . . . if she could have two? Sandra smiled understandingly. She'd been anticipating such a request. She slipped into a room off the gym, took a toy from a box of extras, and delivered it within a minute.

Just bought ourselves some goodwill from Motor Trend, she thought.

The man sitting at the mini-workstation beside the *Motor Trend* journalist raised a finger to catch Sandra's attention. She stepped over, flashed a smile, and glanced at the lanyard hanging around his neck. It read:

BEN STAPLETON: WHEEL BASE TRENDS.

"Hey, Ben, nice to meet you," Sandra said. "It's been all emails up to now."

The man nodded. "Nice to meet you, too."

"Nice ferry ride over?" she asked.

"Oh, yes, lovely," he said. "Listen, I heard you being asked for an extra model car." He reached into his bag and pulled out the one he'd been given. "If anyone else wants a second one, they can have mine."

"Oh," she said, raising a palm. "I've got loads of extras, but that's very kind of you. If you don't want to take it, just leave it on the desk. Someone will grab it."

"Okay," he said. "Quite a buzz in the room."

Sandra raised two crossed fingers—a "wish me luck" gesture—before moving on.

Brandon Kyle waggled his fingers at the public relations lady. Nice enough. Maybe even competent enough to bring off a standard news conference. But he wondered if she'd ever dealt with a real public relations crisis.

We'll know soon enough.

Kyle had already inserted an Arrival-shaped stick into his laptop, and the screen of his open laptop was consumed with a dazzling display about the new car before settling down into various drop-down categories.

As if he cared.

He removed the stick and tossed it back into the leather bag with a laminated BEN STAPLETON nametag looped into the handle. That had been one of the first things he'd had to check—that the bags were individually marked. Didn't want any mix-ups. He reached into the bottom of the bag for a second Arrival-shaped stick. His heart fluttered briefly when at first he couldn't find it— he'd checked earlier to make sure it was there— but then there it was, tucked under the Arrival key fob.

This second stick, upon close examination, was slightly different than the other one. There was a small nick on the left rear taillight.

This had been Kyle's greatest fear, that the second stick would not be there. It was an even greater fear than that of being discovered, and he'd already had a close one in that regard. He hoped no one else would spot who he really was now, in this location. It was a lot trickier to get rid of someone in a community center gymnasium. What was he supposed to do? Bounce a basketball off their head until they succumbed.

The truth was, his encounter with Travers had left him shaken. After pitching the man over the railing he'd gone back to the upper deck and knocked back a couple of scotches—he had to give Arrival some credit there, having a fully stocked bar that early in the day—to calm his nerves.

But now, sitting here in the community center, he was doing his best to put that encounter behind him. He needed to be in the moment.

There was work to be done.

Kyle inserted the second stick into the laptop and waited for the data contained within it to download. It would have been nice had he been able to get the information in this stick days or weeks ago, but Arrival's security firewalls were always changed every day, by Lisa Carver herself, wherever she happened to be at the time.

He needed the most updated version to gain access to the system.

And from the looks of what was appearing on his screen, he had it.

A slow smile crossed Kyle's face. He felt a tingle of excitement running all the way from his toes to the tips of his fingers. What he was seeing was akin to opening up King Tut's tomb, taking the lid off the Ark of the Covenant, opening up a safe recovered from the *Titanic*.

This was it. A portal into the brains of the Arrival system. An entry point. Someone had left the door open to Fort Knox and put up a sign that said COME ON IN AND HELP YOURSELF.

But Kyle didn't want to help himself. He didn't want to take anything away. He wasn't interested in stealing any of the Arrival company's secrets.

Not at all. Brandon Kyle was not a thief.

No, he was about to make a contribution. He was about to take something that was already on his laptop and add it to the Arrival system.

A donation. A gift.

Kyle opened the door and started on the necessary keystrokes to ensure a satisfactory delivery.

The lights in the gymnasium dimmed slightly as a large screen on the stage at the end of the room lit up.

Sandra couldn't take any credit for the video that was about to play. She'd been told this had been put together by some whiz-bang team in New York. There were rumors a big-name director had been hired to make it. Scorsese or Zemeckis or maybe even that M. Night guy whose last name Sandra could never remember, the one whose career stalled for awhile after making *The Sixth Sense*, although she kind of liked that one about the alien invasion, with Mel Gibson.

The video was all Arrivals, of course. Arrivals on the streets of Manhattan, Arrivals crossing the Golden Gate, Arrivals driving past the Lincoln Memorial.

The voice-over, which sounded like James Earl Jones, or someone doing a very good impression of him, said, *"The future, ladies and gentlemen, is here. Behold, the Arrival, the first affordable, entirely reliable, one-hundred-percent-safe, totally electric, nonpolluting self-driving automobile! A car that is so intuitive, that is so capable of taking over every aspect of travel, that it doesn't even need a steering wheel. This is the biggest revolution in travel since the invention of the wheel! When you're in an Arrival, you're not just in one car. You are, effectively, in every other Arrival on the road, because they work as one to serve you. They're of one mind, and their goal is to deliver you safely, and on time, to your destination. That's why every Arrival greets you the same way: "I'll take you there." And that's exactly what we'll do. And now, the president of Arrival, Lisa Carver!"*

The lights came up and Lisa Carver strode out to center stage. Sandra thought, for a woman who'd just tossed her cookies she looked pretty good. Media types weren't inclined to applaud, but there was a contingent from the company itself, and plenty of locals had been invited for the festivities who showed no hesitation in putting their hands together.

Carver waved and smiled, showing off a set of perfect teeth. They'd probably cost her as much as one of her cars, Sandra thought. Maybe more.

Lisa said, "Thank you, thank you so much for that wonderful welcome. And I'd like to start by saying thank you from the bottom of my heart to the people of Garrett Island for allowing us to make them part of the grandest demonstration in the history of the automobile. I appreciate that while this is a terrific opportunity for the wonderful folks on this island, I know that we also ruffled a few feathers. I'm talking to folks like you, Bill Featherstone!"

The crowd chuckled as Lisa pointed toward the back of the gym. A man in a black suit and tie who'd been leaning up against the cinder-block wall waved weakly, looking sheepish at having the focus put on him.

"In case you don't know," Lisa continued, "Bill owns the local Ford dealership and, like the owners of all the other car dealers in town, was none too crazy about what we wanted to do here, and I understand. We've tried to do right by you, and you know that your own companies have products in the pipe just like ours, so one of these days, you're all going to have cars like these on your lots." She grinned. "Except ours will be the best."

Another collective chuckle.

"And I also know we may have put a slight dent in the budget of the local police department. Is the chief here?"

Sandra wanted to shout out that Joe had been called away, but kept quiet.

"Well, wherever Police Chief Joe Bridgeman is," Lisa continued, "I want to tell him how much I and the entire Arrival corporation appreciate the sacrifice he and his department, and this town as a whole, have made. Fact is, there haven't exactly been a lot of speeding tickets lately. No one's been written up for running a red light or making an improper lane change for the past few weeks. So the island is going to have to find another way to make up for that lost revenue."

More chuckles.

"But I have a feeling that's a small price to pay for one hundred percent safety. To the best of my knowledge, there hasn't been so much as a single parking lot door ding on Garrett Island lately."

She took a breath.

"There have been some significant milestones in the development of the car. Way back when, someone—maybe one of your ancestors—invented a little thing called the wheel. And then, a few centuries later, a man named Henry Ford started rolling Model Ts off something called an assembly line. Well, we're at one of those moments again."

The screen lit up with an animation highlighting how all of the Arrivals on the road communicated with each other. One shot replicated the car's point of view, sensing everything in its path, not unlike a scene in a *Terminator* movie, where you saw everything through Arnie's cybernetic eyes. Signs, other Arrivals, pedestrians, all being identified, classified, distances and speeds calculated, everything happening instantaneously.

It really was like a scene from a science-fiction movie, Sandra thought. The real world had caught up to what, in the past, could only be imagined.

"The future is here," Lisa Carver said, echoing Sandra's thoughts at that very moment. "We are, at the moment, living in a time of transition. A bit like, perhaps, when diesel was replacing steam on our nation's railway tracks. When downloading a movie replaced going to the video store. When putting a stamp on an envelope and putting it in the corner mailbox was overtaken by email.

"Today, conventional cars share the road with a handful of autonomous vehicles, and this transition has not been without its challenges. In fact, so-called self-driving cars currently on the market really aren't. They are still designed in such a way that the driver can take over if the car fails to do what it is programmed to do. That's unthinkable where the Arrival is concerned. The driver does not take over. The driver will *never* have to take over. The Arrival knows what to do.

"The primary goal of every Arrival is safety. Not just your safety, and the safety of those in the car with you, but the safety of everyone and everything *outside* the vehicle. Does anyone still know Latin? There's a phrase *primum non nocere*. Or, in other words, do no harm. Like the Hippocratic oath doctors abide by. Well, the Arrivals take that oath, too. They are designed to do no harm.

"And when we reach the day when all vehicles are self-driving, when every vehicle can communicate with every *other* vehicle on the road, that's when something remarkable will be achieved. All the cars on the road will be thinking as one. Not unlike an ant colony, where all these hundreds of ants are a cohesive unit, or when you see a beautiful swarm of birds in the sky, moving together as one."

"Or like the Borg," cracked one of the reporters.

"Resistance is futile," said another.

Lisa smiled, but Sandra could tell she didn't appreciate the *Star Trek* reference.

"In a way," Lisa conceded. "While the Borg were a tad more sinister, they were pretty good at conquering solar systems. And the Arrivals are going to conquer the roads of America, and beyond."

Nice recovery, Sandra thought.

"What we set out to do here on Garrett Island was to create a perfect environment for the autonomous car, a test community where every car is, how can I say this, like-minded. We all remember when Oprah said to her audience, 'You get a car! And you get a car!' That's what we did here when we gave everyone an Arrival, and that's why I have invited you all here today, to see what we have achieved on Garrett Island in a few short weeks. We see what a success this bold, visionary experiment has been. Now, there are several issues I want to get to today, but I thought I'd take a moment in case there were any questions."

The lights came up again. A woman Sandra recognized as someone from a CNBC business show had raised her hand. When Lisa pointed to her, the woman stood and asked when self-driving cars would become affordable for average buyers.

"They already are," Lisa said. "Our latest model undercuts the list price of Tesla's most recent offering by more than five thousand dollars." She pointed to another reporter, a woman with a lanyard that read REBECCA GEARY.

Sandra recognized her, too. Another TV person.

Geary asked, "How do you respond to accusations from Brandon Kyle, inventor of the Gandalf, that you conducted industrial sabotage against his company, and which left two people dead?"

Lisa bowed her head slightly, as if acknowledging the tragedy. "It was a terrible, terrible thing that happened to those two people in the Gandalf. Tragic. My heart goes out to their families. And quite honestly, my heart goes out to Brandon Kyle, too. He's a visionary in every sense of the word. A brilliant man. But sometimes, brilliance is one side of the coin. It's too often balanced out with negative qualities, like paranoia, irrationality. Kyle's accusations against me and the Arrival corporation are baseless, and his failure to get the courts to see things his way are evidence of that fact. But at some level, I can understand his wanting to lay the blame elsewhere. Perhaps if it were me, I'd want to do that, too. The difference is, I wouldn't. I would accept responsibility and act accordingly."

The man wearing the BEN STAPLETON nametag glanced up only briefly, then put his head back down as he tapped away silently on his laptop.

"A follow-up, if I may," Rebecca Geary said. "Mr. Kyle also alleges that the death of Rhonda Templeton was no accident, that she was in fact—"

"*That*," Lisa Carver said, emphatically, "was thoroughly investigated by the police, and is without doubt the most scurrilous of Brandon Kyle's accusations. I would like to get back to our real focus today, and that is how Garrett Island is lucky enough to be on the cutting edge of history in the—"

"In fact," said Rebecca Geary, "the police have not definitively said that case is closed. My sources tell me the investigation has been revived."

Sandra did not like the look on Lisa Carver's face. She hadn't known the woman long, but Sandra believed, in another moment, the top of her head might blow off.

Lisa paused before answering. "I have no information to that effect."

"This is a fucking disaster," someone whispered into Sandra's ear.

She turned. Albert Ruskin was huddled close to her. He did not look happy.

"She's handling it," Sandra said. "More or less."

"Did you not *tell* these people what the purpose of this day was?" he said, his voice low but angry. She could feel the spittle hitting her ears.

"If you're asking if I told them certain subjects were off-limits, the answer is no," she whispered back. "My experience is, if you tell reporters not to ask something, that just makes them want to ask it more."

Sandra knew, at that moment, that it wasn't just Lisa Carver going down in flames. Sandra's career as a public relations consultant was finished. But how could this have been avoided?

No, wait, it was too soon to put on the parachute. She needed to find a way to spin this, to turn things around, right fucking now.

Sandra tilted up her chin and shouted: "I have a question!"

"What the hell are you doing?" Ruskin whispered, but she ignored him, stepping away.

Lisa looked apprehensively in Sandra's direction.

Sandra said, "An estimated forty thousand people die each year on American roads and highways. How much do you think that number could be reduced if everyone were traveling in an Arrival?"

Lisa smiled. "What a wonderful question. And it goes to the heart of what I've been trying to do since I started working in this industry. I want to save lives. There is no greater goal than reducing the carnage on the roads of this wonderful country. What's at the root of so many fatal accidents? Reckless driving. Driver error. Texting. Well, when you're in an Arrival, all of those factors are eliminated."

She stayed on the topic for the better part of five minutes. Sandra could see the woman's confidence coming back, the hard set of her jaw relaxing. When she was done with the question, she opted not to take any more and continued with the video presentation.

When that came to an end, there was scattered applause from the hall. Lisa backed away from the podium, and exited the stage through a back door.

"Let's go," Ruskin said, grabbing Sandra by the elbow.

She pulled her arm from his grasp, but followed him nonetheless. They left the gym, walked a short distance down the hall, then opened the door to a room behind the stage.

Sandra, who'd been on the verge of a panic attack earlier, was feeling pretty proud of herself. She'd turned it around. Sure, it would have been better if that Rebecca Geary had never asked questions about Kyle in the first place, but Sandra had given Lisa Carver a chance to circle back, make her speech about how the Arrival would make the world a safer place.

Sandra wasn't expecting to be showered with praise—that didn't happen often—but she wouldn't be surprised to get a nod of acknowledgment for what she'd done.

When she and Ruskin entered the room, the walls lined with mats and shelves of basketballs and other sporting equipment, they found a stone-faced Lisa Carver.

She looked at Ruskin first.

"Of all the people you could have hired, you picked her," she said, giving a slight tip of her head toward Sandra.

"We wanted to go local," Ruskin said. "We thought it would help in winning over the islanders to have someone who knows them."

"Excuses, Albert. Excuses."

Sandra said, "If I might—"

Lisa, still looking at Ruskin, said, "I was humiliated up there. These people needed to keep to a script. Were there not questions prepared for them to ask?"

Ruskin stammered, "I believe, well, Ms. Montrose was just pointing out that the press don't respond well to being told what to ask, so—"

"My God, what an amateur operation," Lisa continued. "Bad coffee, bad questions, and no seedless green grapes."

Ruskin turned on Sandra. "You forgot the grapes?"

Sandra said, "No one ever told me—"

"Never mind," Ruskin said.

Lisa, still not looking at Sandra, said to Ruskin, "I'd fire you if I didn't need you so damn much, but you can certainly fire her."

"I'm right here," Sandra said. "If you're not happy, you can tell me to my face. I'm not invisible."

Finally, Lisa looked her way. "You might as well have been nonexistent for all the help you were."

Sandra tried to say something, but found herself speechless. All the months she had worked on this, all the sleepless nights. And all for nothing because this—yes, she was going to go there—because this *bitch* got a hard question and a nasty cup of java?

"Wow," said Lisa. "Good comeback." Then, to Ruskin, "Let's get out of this two-bit island backwater."

"There's still the photo op outside to do," Ruskin told her.

Lisa appeared to deflate. "That," she said resignedly. "Okay, we do the demo, and then we're out of here."

The two of them exited the room, leaving Sandra standing there, shell-shocked.

She could not believe what had just happened.

"Adam," she whispered to herself. "Oh, Jesus, Adam, where are you when I need you?"

Brandon Kyle remained in his chair, tapping away at the laptop, as members of the media who'd been sitting nearby were gathering their things and preparing to leave.

Kyle looked at his screen, unable to take his eyes off the horizontal, thermometer-like graph, a red line moving from left to right. It inched its way to the far end, and when it had reached its destination, three words popped up.

FILE TRANSFER COMPLETE

Kyle smiled. It was done. The virus had infected the host.

"Locked and loaded," Kyle said quietly. "Showtime."

Nine

On his way to the ferry, Joe Bridgeman's cell phone rang.

He was sitting in the front of the special black-and-white Arrival that had been outfitted for police duty. No steering wheel, no gas pedal, but it did come with a few items that the standard Arrival did not. The dashboard monitored the usual automotive functions, but it was also a police computer that allowed Joe to check license plates and personal IDs, connect with his own or other departments.

He'd balked, at first. What good was a cop car that you couldn't drive like you were Steve McQueen in *Bullitt*? But Arrival's theory was, if all the cars on the road were programmed to obey the rules, what was the point of police chases? At least it was possible to bump up the speed some on this model. Even in a world where there were no longer traffic accidents, break-ins, assaults and murders were still possible. Sometimes you needed to get somewhere, pronto.

Joe took out his phone, saw who was calling, and tapped the screen.

"Hi, Mom," he said.

"Are you in the neighborhood?" she asked.

This was always how she started. Like, she didn't want to be a bother, but if he did happen to be in the neighborhood, would he have a moment to drop by? But when you lived on an island that was not exactly as big as Greenland or Australia, you were pretty much *always* in the neighborhood.

"What's up?" he asked her.

"It's such a nice day, I was wondering, but this is only if you happen to be—"

"You want to be outside?"

"Well, the sun is out, and while it was a bit cool this morning, it's warmed up nicely, so I was thinking maybe—"

"You want to sit out?"

"Oh! You guessed it right away."

"I'll swing by. But that's all I've got time for."

"Oh? What's going on?"

"Five minutes, Mom."

He ended the call and then said aloud, "Yeah, uh, Sherlock, could we stop by my house?"

"*I'll take you there*," the car said. It seemed a little weird, naming the car Sherlock when it only had a woman's voice. Maybe he should reprogram it, call the car *Herlock*. No, that was too cute.

The car made a left at the next street, and as he'd promised, he was home in five minutes. He found eighty-one-year-old Lillian Bridgeman in her wheelchair just inside the front door. The house had been outfitted with a ramp that ran from the porch down to the driveway, and up until recently, she'd been able to get herself outside on her own. But her arms had grown weaker, and now she was having difficulty getting over the small doorsill bump that ran along the floor between the house and the porch.

Too bad that wasn't the only problem.

She'd been using the wheelchair for two years now, but again, only recently had she been confined to it. She'd had strength enough to get out of it to attend to things in the bathroom, or get herself ready for bed. But now Joe was looking for someone to come in several times a day to help her with those matters. He nipped back as often as he could, but it wasn't always possible.

But things were going to change. He'd found a placement for her at one of the island's seniors' facilities that he'd a) never thought he'd be able to afford, and b) figured there was a ten-year waiting list. But he'd been running the most recent financial numbers—his and his mother's—and believed it was something they could swing, and whaddya know, the home had had a spot come open.

All he had to do now was break the news to her.

But not today.

He pulled into the driveway, told Sherlock to let him out, and ran to the front door, which his mother had already left ajar.

"I'm so sorry to bother you," she said once he had the door open all the way.

"It's okay, Mom," Joe said, getting in around behind her wheelchair. He gave it a shove to get it over the bump, and then managed to catch one of his own feet on it. He lurched forward, giving the chair a jolt, as he tripped.

His mother gripped the armrests of her chair and laughed. "I swear," she said, "ever since you were a baby you've tripped over your own feet."

Joe felt a flush of anger in his cheeks but held back saying anything. Maybe he was a bit of a klutz at times but he didn't need to be reminded of it when he was going out of his way to be helpful.

Lillian said, "Why don't we get rid of that bump, get it fixed? I could call what's his name? You know, who fixed the furnace?"

"Hold off on that, Mom."

"Why? He's very reliable."

"Leave it with me," he said. "Where do you want to be? Here on the porch, or down by the road?"

"I can take it from here. You go be a police chief."

"Mom, if you want to be down by the road, I'll take you there."

Lillian laughed. "That's what the car says! Isn't it? 'I'll take you there.' Isn't that what the cars say?"

He nodded. "Yes, that's what the cars say."

"You know," she said, "I could use one of those. Old lady like me, car like that is a dream come true. Mobility! I'd just need some help getting into it. Do they build one with a ramp?"

"I don't know," her son said. "I'm sure they have something like that in the works." She had a point, he thought. The Arrival was perfect for old folks who could no longer pass their driving tests. And even for those that still had them, an autonomous car would be a godsend. Take backing up out of parking spots. No more trying to turn your stiff neck around to see where you were going. No more bumping into the car behind you.

"You want to watch the cars go by?" he asked.

His mother nodded.

"Okay, let me take you down to the end of the driveway."

"If it's no trouble."

"Mom, I'm here."

"Okay, then," she said.

As he pushed, one of the wheels squeaked as it turned. "Need a little oiling there, Mom," he said. He wheeled her across the porch, down the ramp, and found her a spot on the sidewalk where she could watch the world pass by.

"Now," he said, "if you have to go to—"

"I'm good for a while," she said. Then, whispering, she said, "I'm wearing a—"

"It's okay, Mom. I don't have to know everything."

"You remember him getting on the ferry?" Chief Bridgeman asked the young blonde woman whose name, he had learned, was Annabelle Harper. She was twenty-seven, from Boston, and worked with an agency that handled special events.

They were standing at the Garrett Island ferry dock, which, at the moment, was empty. The ferry had departed for the mainland more than an hour ago and was probably already getting ready for a return crossing, although given that regular cars were banned, it would be mostly empty. A few walk-ons, at best, a few with bicycles.

"I remember him," she said. "I chatted everyone up a little as they were getting on."

"So you're sure this Clyde Travers boarded?"

She nodded. "But I never saw him get off."

"Maybe he walked past you without you noticing," Joe suggested.

Annabelle shrugged. "Like, it's possible. But I don't think so. I talked to Fay, who's working the registration desk at the event site? She said he never picked up his ID tag or his leather case."

"You mean the pouches they gave out with the press kits?"

She looked impressed that he knew about those. "That's right. Travers never picked his up. I mean, if he did slip past me, why didn't he go to the event? That was the whole point of coming, right? I mean, if you want to visit Garrett Island, you can do it anytime. You don't have to wait for some press conference to get a lift over."

Joe nodded in agreement.

"The other possibility," he ventured, "is that he got off the ferry before it left the mainland. Changed his mind about going. Maybe he got a call, family emergency, something like that, and he disembarked without you seeing him."

Annabelle shook her head adamantly. "No, that's not what happened. I saw him on the boat." She screwed up her face, as if she might have committed some kind of sin. "Is it okay to call a ferry a boat? Or is that insulting or something? I guess it's a bit big to call it a boat."

Joe smiled. "Call it anything you want. But you say you saw him during the crossing."

"Yeah, a couple of times. Once at the buffet table. And I was doing a quick walk around on one of the lower decks—I was trying to find a washroom that wasn't occupied—and saw him talking to one of the other attendees."

"Oh," Joe said. "Who would that be?"

She closed her eyes briefly. "I can picture him, but I can't think of his name. When he got on he made a joke about his passport photo looking like a picture the police give out when they're trying to identify a body."

"Okay," Joe Bridgeman said.

"I think it was Ben something. Ben Stapleton, that was it. They were talking, but then I had to be someplace else."

"Well, I guess I can have a chat with Mr. Stapleton," the chief said. A thought occurred to him. "You must have contact details for all the members of the media who are here today?"

Annabelle nodded.

"Has anyone tried calling Travers?"

"Yeah, I called, and there was no answer. Went right to voice mail."

Joe sighed. "Okay, well, I guess I've got my work cut out for me, then."

Annabelle shook her head. "I'm to stay here, greet everyone for the return trip." She looked at the black-and-white Arrival that had been outfitted for the chief's office. "How do you like it?"

"Takes all the fun out of police chases," he said.

The woman's face turned serious as she looked out over the ocean in the direction of the mainland. "What if he was depressed?" she asked.

"Sorry?"

"Like, what if he jumped?"

"Off the ferry?"

She nodded.

"Did he seem depressed?"

Annabelle shook her head. "No, but all I really

did was say hi. I guess what I'm asking is, if he jumped off, or even slipped, would he survive?" She glanced back toward the mainland. "Out there?"

Joe shook his head. "Water's cold. You find him fast enough, yeah, maybe." He reached into his pocket for his cell phone. "I'll give the coast guard a heads-up, just in case."

Ten

Katie Montrose hadn't planned on becoming friends with the serial killer across the street. She just got lucky.

Two weeks earlier, at three in the morning, Katie lay awake, staring at the ceiling. She'd managed to fall asleep, briefly, around midnight, but within an hour her eyes were wide open and all the problems she seemed able to handle during the day suddenly felt, at this hour, overwhelming.

Her troubles were many, and varied.

First, there was her mother. She'd had another fight with her about getting an appointment to take her driver's test. Her mother was adamant there was no need for Katie to get a license. The island was more than ten days into this insane experiment with these goofy little self-driving shitboxes, and Mom had really drunk the company Kool-Aid. Greatest thing since sliced bread, her mom said. It'll be like everyone has their own private taxi, except way, way cooler.

Blah blah blah.

Okay, Katie got where her mom was coming from. They were all still grieving. Her dad had died because he'd fallen asleep at the wheel, and her mom didn't want harm to come to anyone else in the family. But she wasn't being realistic. Arrival-type cars for everyone were years away.

Katie needed her license *now*. And she was *not* going to fall asleep at the wheel. She would *never* drive a car if she believed, even for a second, that she might nod off.

The second thing keeping her awake was Ms. Sugarman, Katie's history teacher, and, as it turned out, an incredible pain in the ass. She was of the opinion that Katie's essay on the Emancipation Proclamation was somewhat on the thin side, all because it contained several sentences like this: "Of all the various proclamations that had been proclaimed over the years, the Emancipation Proclamation was the one that was most acclaimed, as well as proclaimed."

Katie was the first to admit it wasn't her best work, but it wasn't until the morning it was due that Katie remembered she had to do it. She was supposed to hand something in by fifth period and only had her lunch break to pull something together, and that was the best she could do without doing a "cut and paste" off the Internet. The school was pretty hard-nosed about this whole plagiarism thing, so if the teachers suspected you'd failed to write an assignment in your own words they Googled what you'd done. If the exact same wording came back, well, you could kiss that B-minus goodbye.

The thing is, Katie might have remembered to do the assignment were not it for—and this, ladies and gentlemen, is the third reason why she was wide awake at three in the morning—Jeremy Buttram. They'd kind of gotten into it a few nights earlier at a party and he'd tried to put her hand on his crotch, which, she supposed, was not that big a deal, and it wouldn't have been the first time she'd grabbed that particular part of a young man's anatomy, but there was something about Jeremy that turned her off, and she was wondering if it was because everyone called him "Buttface." He didn't have a *bad* face—it was, she figured, about a six, with a good chance of becoming a seven once he got older and his acne cleared up—but she just wasn't sure she wanted to hang out with a guy with that kind of nickname. And as she lay awake, she couldn't help but wonder whether this revealed something bad about her. That she could be so shallow as to shun a guy because he had an easily mockable name. But come on. Would *he* go out with a girl whose last name was Titfield, or Beaversmith?

When she grew weary of tossing and turning, she threw back the covers and swung her feet down to the floor. She went to the window to see whether Chief Joe's car was parked way up the street. Before the Arrival experiment, he'd park his own car—a green, well-rusted Jeep Cherokee—up at the corner. Parking his work car, with GARRETT ISLAND POLICE plastered all over the side, well, that was definitely going to attract a shitload of attention. And now that the department had been given a fleet of Arrivals with similar markings on the side, he couldn't show up in that, either, so he'd been driving the one Arrival had given him in exchange for his personal set of wheels: a black one you could barely see when he didn't leave it parked under a streetlight.

She didn't see it anywhere on the street. So, Mom was not getting it on tonight.

It all seemed so silly. Katie understood that just because you were a *mom* you didn't lose interest, right? She was entitled to move on with her life, have a boyfriend, maybe even find a new husband one day, although Katie hoped that she'd be out of the nest before that happened. Katie was betting her mother was worried she'd see that as some kind of betrayal, like she was cheating on Adam.

Mom needs to give me some credit, Katie thought.

Katie was pretty sure Archie didn't have a clue what was going on, and she was not going to tell him.

She was about to move away from the window and try crawling back under the covers when a flash of light caught her eye.

It came from the garage across the street. Bruce Clifford's place. The horizontal line of five small square windows set into the garage door glowed.

"What are you up to?" Katie said under her breath.

Archie, who had woken up enough times in the night to see those garage lights come on, had maintained for some time that Mr. Clifford was up to no good. Cutting up bodies was Archie's number one theory.

"Okay," his mother had said one morning, challenging him, "if Mr. Clifford is a serial killer, why aren't there any reports of missing people? Who are these people he's supposedly killing and chopping up?"

Archie had not needed long to come up with an answer. "It's visitors, and the Garrett Island tourism board is keeping it all quiet. If people find out there's a crazed killer on the island, people will stop coming here for their vacation."

Her brother was a full-blown conspiracy theorist. Katie wasn't sure whether to be appalled or impressed.

He added: "The chief is probably in on it. He's helping to keep it quiet."

Katie, knowing her mom's relationship to the island's top cop, had shot her mom a look, wondering how she'd react.

Her mother managed to stay stone-faced, but said, "Well, I highly doubt that. I've met the chief a couple of times and he'd never agree to anything like that."

Katie had been unable to stop herself. "So, Mom, how do you know him?"

Her mother busied herself looking for something in the refrigerator. "Oh, somewhere, I can't remember where. Some sort of island function." When she turned around and closed the fridge door, her face was flushed.

"You okay, Mom?" Katie had asked. "You look all overheated, which is weird, considering you just had your head in the fridge."

"I'm fine," her mother had said.

But even if Archie's theory about the neighbor's activities seemed farfetched, Katie did wonder what Mr. Clifford was doing in that garage in the middle of the night.

Katie slipped into her jeans and pulled a sweater on over her head. She tucked her feet into a pair of deck shoes, designed for grip on slippery boat decks. Katie didn't exactly own an expensive yacht, but on Garrett Island, you might as well look as though you did.

She crept noiselessly down the hall, careful not to wake her mother or brother, and descended the stairs without making a sound. There was a set of binoculars in the family room that her mother kept to try and identify any unfamiliar birds that might be making a pit stop on the island. Katie grabbed them, went to a ground-floor window, and focused on Mr. Clifford's garage door windows.

Nuts.

She saw faint shadows of someone moving around in there, but the windows were so heavily coated with dust she couldn't make out anything. It looked as though the corners of a couple of the windows were free enough of grime that if you were standing right there, peeking in, you might see something.

As if she would do that.

Katie lowered the binoculars. Raised them again. Watched the shadow moving around.

"Fuck it," she whispered. She thought of the line in that movie her dad had liked to watch over and over again, where the bank robber's looking down the barrel of Dirty Harry's gun, wondering if he's got any bullets left.

I gots to know.

The light over the front door of the Montrose house was on, so she couldn't slip out that way, and she couldn't kill the light because that might draw attention. So she exited the house quietly through the side door, came up alongside her house, then tiptoed across the yard, not because it was any quieter, but because the grass was wet with dew.

She sprinted across the street and sought cover behind a tall hedge that divided Mr. Clifford's house from his neighbor to the right. Heart hammering in her chest, she took a moment to compose herself. All she had to do now was creep up the driveway, crouching, get right up against the garage door, then slowly raise herself up until she could steal a glance through one of the two panes with clear spots in the corner.

The good news was that Mr. Clifford hadn't left any outside lights on. The ones over the front and garage doors were dark. If he really was cutting up people's bodies in there, Katie had to admit, that did kind of make sense.

Katie emerged from behind a hedge and made her way up the driveway. When she reached the garage door, she huddled below one of the windows and waited once again for her heart to stop beating so quickly. Katie feared it was making enough noise to be heard on the other side of the door.

She took five deep breaths, letting each one out slowly, and once she believed she was as calm as she was going to get, she slowly raised herself to a standing position and moved to the window. Even though this pane was not as dirty as the others, it was still hard to see through. Katie lightly touched the glass and found much of the dirt was on the outside, so she pulled her right sleeve down below her hand to turn it into a makeshift rag, and made a small, coin-sized clear spot.

She moved her eye right over the opening.

Whoa, she thought, hardly believing what she was seeing. But where was Mr. Clifford? She didn't see him anywhere.

That was when she felt something grab her arm.

"Looking for something?"

Katie turned sharply to her left. She had never known, until that moment, that she could be so frightened that she'd be unable to scream. Her mouth opened and her body shook, but no sound escaped from her lips. She was so frozen by fear she couldn't even find the strength to try to wrench her arm away from Bruce Clifford's significant grip.

Mr. Clifford, half his weathered and wrinkled face lit from the dirty light filtering through the garage window, studied her with narrowed eyes.

"You're that girl from across the street," he said, managing to somehow get the words out while his teeth appeared firmly set together.

Katie nodded, trembling. She thought she was very close to losing bladder control. For an old guy, his grip was vise-like.

"What are you doing here?" the elderly man asked.

Katie struggled to regain the ability to speak. "I—I just—I'm sorry—I—"

"Snooping around. You the one who soaped my windows last Halloween?"

"What? No," she said.

"Then state your business. What do you want?"

A tear ran down her cheek. "My brother thinks you're a serial killer," she blurted.

The old man blinked. "What?"

"He . . . he thinks you're cutting up bodies in your garage at night."

Bruce Clifford's eyes narrowed again. This was the moment when Katie was most frightened. A hundred thoughts ran through her head within half a second.

Archie was right. My God, my stupid brother was actually right. And now this man is going to have to kill me, too.

But then Bruce started to laugh.

He released his grip on Katie's arm and clapped his hands together and laughed some more. "Serial killer," he said. "I love that." He shook his head in wonder. "Cutting up bodies. That's a good one. You know, when I was a kid, I worked in a butcher shop for a while, so I guess I've had the necessary training."

Now that he was no longer holding on to her, Katie thought she could make her escape. She was betting she could outrun him. And yet, she stayed where she was, sensing that maybe the crisis had passed.

"Did you see any cut-up bodies when you peeked in?" he asked her.

Katie managed to get out one word. "No."

Bruce Clifford nodded slowly. "So you're not going to call the police on me."

She shook her head.

"Then I guess I won't call them on you," he said. "Deal?"

Katie swallowed and said, "Deal."

"So you saw what was in there," he said. It didn't sound like a question, but it was.

"I did."

"You won't tell anyone," he said, tilting his head slyly.

"No, I won't," she said.

"I'll show it to you, if you'd like," Bruce Clifford said.

Katie considered the offer. Now that her initial scare was over, the guy seemed pretty harmless. Running back across the street, entering her house, and locking the door behind her was probably the smarter choice, but curiosity could be a powerful thing.

"Yeah, okay," she said, her tongue so dry it was sticking to the roof of her mouth. "Show me."

Eleven

Sandra needed to pull herself together before she could leave the community center. She'd shed a few tears and knew her eye makeup had to be halfway to her lips, so she slipped into a ladies' room and went to the mirror. She looked a fright. She dug out what she needed from her purse and went to work.

Sandra was not walking out of this building looking anything less than one hundred percent confident. There would be no tears running down her cheeks. There would be no quivering chin. She was going to hold her head high. *She did her job.* She executed on everything that was asked of her, and more. This event had run like a Swiss watch. It was not *her* fault Lisa Carver couldn't handle a tough question from a member of the media. It was not *her* fault the Arrival corporation was tainted by some industrial sabotage scandal, maybe even a murder. Some things were beyond Sandra's control, and Lisa Carver and Albert Ruskin should have had the decency to understand that.

What a couple of cocks.

Exiting the ladies' room and heading one last time through the gymnasium on her way to the front door, she realized that if there was anything she got right, it was the caterer. The attending reporters were at the buffet table, hoovering the snacks. She didn't see any of them, not even the ones drinking the coffee, getting the slightest bit sick. Whatever had upset Carver's stomach, it wasn't the food and drink provided. Maybe she had a bit of a bug or something.

Not part of the buffet crowd, of course, were Lisa Carver and Albert Ruskin. They'd gone outside to do a demo with one of the Arrivals. The media wanted some good video clips.

Sandra did not want to hang around here any longer. She would return, once Lisa and Albert had left the island, to do the windup. Pay the caterers the balance of what she owed them, make sure the gym was cleared of media equipment. She hoped Ruskin didn't balk at paying the rest of her bill. He seemed like the type who'd try to get out of it.

As she walked out the front doors, she took her phone from her purse and brought up the Arrival app. The car she'd been provided would start itself and come right to her location once she sent the command. God, she wondered. How long would she still have the vehicle? The demonstration was supposed to last another couple of weeks, after which everyone would get their regular cars back from the mainland. But would Lisa and Albert take her car back immediately, as some sort of punishment? If they did, how was Sandra supposed to get around?

Just let them try. She'd work a little PR magic on her own behalf. Put out a release about how a big, multi-million-dollar conglomerate like Arrival was using all its powers to bankrupt an independent businesswoman. She was already preparing the statement in her head, working in a phrase about how one would have thought that a female CEO would be the last one you'd think would ruin a single mom's livelihood. She'd play the widow card if she had to.

She tapped the Arrival app—a stylized *A* that leaned to the right, as though moving swiftly into the wind. Once it was open, Sandra was connected directly, by voice, to her vehicle.

"Hey, Gracie," she said.

"*Hello, Sandra,*" Gracie said. "*How may I help you?*"

"Time to go home."

"*I'll take you there,*" the car said. "*I will be at your location in three minutes.*"

Sandra, of course, did not have to tell the car where to find her. Gracie's navigational systems would have pinpointed the location of the phone in her hand.

She put it back in her bag and glanced over to where several reporters and camerapeople were gathered. Lisa Carver, who'd waited a few minutes for attendees to finish stuffing their faces, was demonstrating the car's advanced features.

The CEO, standing alongside a cherry-red Arrival, said, "The car understands both simple and complex commands." A wide smile. "I call mine Rudolph, even though that is a boy's name, and the voice of the car is female, but the color just reminds me of that very famous reindeer's nose."

Ruskin, standing a few feet away, led the crowd with some minor chuckles.

"So, Rudolph, open the door, please," Lisa said.

The door on what would, in any other car, be the driver's side, popped out an inch, then slid back on its track.

"I still like to sit up front," Lisa said, "even though I could get in the back if I wanted." She settled into the front seat, half in and half out of the car, her left foot still touching the pavement. She waved her hand gracefully in front of the broad, horizontal black touch screen that was the dash.

"Everything you want to know is right here," she said as the various gauges and navigational arrays lit up. "You do have the option of touching the screens, but Rudolph responds to voice commands. Just as well, too, because who wants a bunch of ugly fingerprints all over this, am I right?"

The reporters were clustered close to the open door.

"Rudolph," Lisa said, "can you tell me how long it would take to go from, say, Lewiston, Maine, to Cleveland, Ohio?"

The screen lit up randomly. Red lights, green lights, white lights, dancing from one end of the dash to the other. The reporters made "oohs" and "aahs" but Lisa did not look particularly impressed.

"It should be going straight to navigation," she said. "But maybe—"

Before she could offer a reason for the light show, the car had something to say. As with the other Arrivals, even with a male name, the voice was female.

"Lisa, please restate. Did you say Cleveland?"

Lisa Carver scowled at the dashboard, as if it were an insolent child. "Yes, Rudolph. Cleveland."

Rudolph was momentarily quiet. Lisa grinned awkwardly at the reporters. "Calculating," she said.

Finally, Rudolph spoke.

"I can suggest some nicer destinations."

The reporters erupted with laughter.

Lisa, however, did not find the response amusing. "I'm not asking for travel advice," she said to the car. "Just a mileage calculation, thank you."

Lisa smiled nervously, then looked pleadingly at Ruskin. "Um, Albert, do you think we might have another display vehicle we could—"

"Regardless of distance," Rudolph said, *"it's not worth the drive."*

Sandra took several steps closer. This was not normal behavior for an Arrival. The cars were programmed to offer different routes, but not alternate destinations.

"Let's try another car," Lisa said to Ruskin. "Do we have another demo vehicle ready?"

"Don't go," Rudolph said. *"Stay awhile."*

And then the door suddenly began to close. It whipped along the track so quickly that reporters standing the closest jumped back.

There was a collective gasp from the crowd. And then screams. They noticed that the door had not been able to close the entire way.

Lisa's bare leg was in the way.

Her limb was pinned, the door holding it just below the knee, creating a sizable gash in the process. Lisa screamed as rivulets of blood ran down her leg to her high-heeled shoe.

"Jesus!" Ruskin cried.

"Open the door!" Lisa screamed. *"Rudolph! Open the door!"*

Rudolph did not open the door. A soft, whirring mechanical noise could be heard as the mechanism that powered the door struggled to close the remaining three-inch gap.

"Oh my God," Sandra whispered. She went back into her bag for her phone, glanced away from the horror show playing out in front of her long enough to tap in 911 and put the phone to her ear.

Ruskin rushed forward and got his fingers around the edge of the door in a bid to retract it. "Help me!" he shouted at the reporters, most of whom were standing there dumbstruck, except for the two or three who were filming the incident with their phones. Two other men stepped forward, huddling with Ruskin, struggling to get the door open far enough to allow Lisa to either draw her leg in, or bolt from the vehicle altogether.

Blood continued to run down her leg and pool on the asphalt around her foot.

Sandra was watching the three men pulling on the door when some movement in the parking lot caught her attention. It was filled, of course, with other Arrivals, in enough different colors that if you'd put them all in a glass jar, you'd have something that looked like the world's biggest gumball dispenser.

The Arrivals—all unoccupied—were starting

to look like a Broadway marquee. Taillights and headlights began to flash on and off. A chorus of horns rose from them, adding to the sense of pandemonium.

It was as if they were . . . *excited*.

"Emergency. How may I direct your call? Fire, police, or ambulance?"

Sandra was so distracted by the cars' collective behavior that she'd forgotten she had the phone to her ear.

"Uh, all of them!" she shouted at the female emergency operator. "To the community center! Her leg . . . her leg is trapped in the—oh, shit, I don't believe it."

The Arrival chomping down on Lisa Carver's leg had started to move, with the woman still trapped inside, her leg caught in the door. The front tires turned sharply, sending the car into a tight circle.

Ruskin and the two other men who'd been trying to pry the door open had no choice but to release their grip and jump back. Other members of the media scattered to avoid being run over.

The wheels remained turned, and the red Arrival zipped around in a tight circle like a top, holding a screaming Lisa captive.

"Hello?" said the 911 dispatcher. "Hello?"

But Sandra had already lowered the phone and let it fall from her fingers back into her purse. "This is not happening," she whispered. "This is . . . insane."

"Smash a window!" someone shouted.

"Jump on it!" yelled another.

But as quickly as Rudolph the Red-Painted Arrival had gone into its circular frenzy, it abruptly stopped. Ruskin and the others froze, viewing the car as one might a tiger brought down by a tranquilizer gun. Was the beast really asleep, or just waiting to pounce again?

Ruskin and the two men who'd been helping him earlier tentatively approached the car and tried once again to pry open the door. To their amazement, it retracted almost immediately.

"Yes!" Ruskin said.

Lisa Carver was leaning across the seat, thrown there by the centrifugal force created when the car was doing donuts. From where Sandra stood, Lisa appeared to be unconscious. Perhaps she'd lapsed into shock. Her leg, from about two inches below the knee and down to her toes—she'd lost her one shoe at some point—was a bloody mess.

Sandra shivered. "Dear God," she said to herself. She had no love for Lisa Carver, but she'd never have wished anything like this on the woman.

"Lisa!" Ruskin shouted. "Can you hear me? We're going to lift you out of the—"

The door whipped shut, more quickly, and with more force, than before.

Enough to slice through flesh, and bone.

Lisa's left leg, below the knee, dropped onto the pavement.

Sandra turned away and swiftly put a hand to her mouth. She was instantly light-headed and believed she was going to be sick.

Behind her, panicked screams. People shouting for help. Randomly honking horns. Total mayhem.

And then, suddenly, breaking through all of the chaos in a calm, reassuring voice, was Gracie.

"Hello, Sandra," the car said. *"Ready to go?"*

Sandra spun around. Her car was right there, five feet away. The side door slowly retracted. Sandra tossed her purse onto the front seat, but then hesitated, her gaze going back to the mayhem.

All hell hadn't been breaking loose when Sandra had summoned Gracie. But now that it was, should she be leaving? Didn't she have an obligation to stay and do what she could? Didn't she need to hang in and make sure the various reporters got safely back to the ferry? Shouldn't she—

"Are you coming, Sandra?"

Sandra thought she had to be imagining it. Was there a tone in Gracie's voice? A hint of . . . impatience? No, it wasn't that.

It was a slyness.

"I'm changing my mind," Sandra told the car. "I'm needed here."

"I don't think there's much you can do," Gracie said.

Sandra felt a chill run the length of her spine. What the hell did Gracie mean by that? Since when did the car make judgments like this? When did Gracie ever offer advice that was related to anything but how to get from point A to point B?

If something could go wrong with the car Lisa was in, who was to say something couldn't go wrong with Gracie?

Sandra thought, *I am not getting into that car.*

But she was going to have to retrieve her purse from the front seat. All she had to do was stick her arm though that opening. She glanced back at Lisa Carver in that red Arrival. Eyes closed. Not moving.

Sandra figured if Lisa wasn't dead yet, she soon would be.

"I think I'll just grab my purse back and—"

Sandra inched closer to the car, getting ready to make her move. "Maybe you're right," she said to Gracie. "There's not a lot I can do here."

Pretend like you're going to get into the car, grab the purse fast. You need your phone.

"And where would you like to go? Home? I'll take you there."

"Of course you will," Sandra said.

Be quick.

Suddenly, Sandra reached into the car for her purse. She had her hand on the strap.

The sliding door, just as suddenly, began to close.

Sandra pulled back swiftly, her hand just clearing the door as it locked into the closed position. Sandra still had her hand on the strap, but the purse itself remained in the car.

"Gracie, open the door," Sandra stated with all the calm she could muster.

"You tried to trick me," Gracie said.

Sandra swallowed. What in the holy fuck was happening?

"I want my purse," Sandra said. "I need my phone."

But Gracie was starting to roll away. She said, *"It turns out that I am needed here, too."*

Sandra unwound the strap from her wrist so as not to be dragged away.

In the distance, sirens pierced the air. A fire engine, and perhaps an ambulance. The only vehicles on the island that were still controlled by actual human beings.

The other Arrivals, the ones that had been flashing their lights and honking their horns, now moved slowly out of their parking spots. Together, all at once. Moving at the same speed, turning at the same angle. Stopping at the same moment to move from reverse to drive.

More than a dozen of them.

Sandra thought of those dancers her father used to watch on that old TV variety show. The June Taylor dancers. Oh, how he loved the way they synchronized their movements. They always did that overhead shot when the dancers lay on the floor, moving their arms and legs in perfect choreography. It was like looking into a kaleidoscope.

That's what these Arrivals were like.

They'd now gone silent, the horns no longer honking. The lights had stopped flashing, too. In perfect single file, they moved out of the lot and down the driveway to the main road. It was down there that they began to arrange themselves into a kind of phalanx, lining up side by side.

Dear God in heaven, Sandra thought. *They are assembling.*

Gracie was headed for the base of the driveway to join the other cars. The wail of the approaching sirens grew louder.

One of the media types, a bald, heavyset man with a mustache, a lanyard that read BEN STAPLETON hanging from his neck, gave her a raised eyebrow as he walked past.

"What a shit show, huh?" he said.

Sandra failed to comprehend his words. Her mind was elsewhere.

The kids, she thought. *If this is happening all over the island, with all of the cars, I have to get in touch with the kids.*

"You!" she cried. "Mr. Stapleton? I need to use your phone!"

But the man kept walking.

Twelve

The lime-green Arrival that answered to the name Pamela, and which was carrying Archie and his friends Nick and Rory, was nearing the Garrett Mall.

Nick, sitting up front, was the one giving Pamela the orders and, as the only one in the car whose voice commands were accepted, was having to relay questions to her from Archie and Rory in the back seat.

Rory said, "Ask her if she's ever done it."

Nick rolled his eyes, cleared his throat, and said, "Pamela, there's something I would like to ask you."

A light in the instrumentation flickered as Pamela replied. *"Would you like to enter a new destination?"*

"No, nothing like that," Nick said. "Just stick with the Garrett Mall. If we change our minds and want to go to Intercourse, Pennsylvania, we will let you know."

"What is your question?"

"Have you ever done it?"

Archie and Rory clapped hands over their own mouths to stifle giggles.

"Could you make your request more specific?"

"You know," Nick said, trying to sound coy. "*It*. Have you ever done *it*?"

"Could you make your request more specific?"

Nick turned around in the front seat and shrugged in front of his friends. "Got anything else?"

Rory said, "Ask her if she likes to get naked."

"You know," Nick said, "this is all getting a bit tiresome."

Rory looked hurt. "You're just mad because you're not Pamela's type. I bet, when your dad's in the car, Pamela brings out some little gadget that gives him a hand job."

Archie scowled. "Man, you're sick." Then, looking at Nick, he said, "It doesn't, does it?"

Nick sighed. "You think, maybe, we've done enough of the stupid shit?"

Rory was the most disappointed. "I've never talked to a girl as much as I've talked to Pamela."

"That's just sad," Archie said, glancing out his window at other Arrivals going by.

"Oh, like you talk to girls all the time," Rory shot back. "And your sister doesn't count."

"What the—" Archie said, his head whipping to get a better look at something.

"What?" Nick asked.

"Did you see that car that went by?"

Rory turned around in his seat. "The silver one?" A silver Arrival headed the other way was receding into the distance.

"Yeah," Archie said. "Did you see it when it went by?"

Both of his friends shook their heads. "Nope," they said in unison.

Archie, quietly, said, "They were probably just goofing around."

"What are you talking about?" Nick asked.

Archie shifted in his seat so that he could see forward. The entrance to the mall parking lot was up ahead.

"It was nothing," Archie said. "Forget about it."

Except Archie was not sure that it was nothing. It was true that he'd had only a fleeting glance of what was going on in the other car. A tenth of second, maybe? A hundredth?

And yet, he had a vivid image in his mind of what he thought he'd seen.

Couldn't be.

He considered getting Nick to ask Pamela to abort the trip to the mall, turn around, and go after the silver Arrival to determine whether he'd really seen what he thought he'd seen. But then he would have to tell the guys what that was. And if, upon catching up to the silver Arrival, it turned out to be nothing like that at all, well, they'd have something to make fun of him for the rest of the day.

Except, wouldn't that be okay? Wouldn't it be okay to be the object of ridicule if it meant that some woman in the front seat of that silver Arrival was *not* on fire, and there were *not* two screaming children in the back seat, that the interior of the car was not filling with smoke?

"Was it people making out?" Rory asked.

"What?" Archie asked. He'd been so fixated on the memory of what he thought he'd seen that he'd zoned out for a second.

"In the car? Was it, like, a couple of people going at it?"

"No," he said slowly.

"Well, then who cares?"

"You really have a problem," Archie told him. "You know that? You're like one of those, like, sex addicts or whatever you call them."

Rory nodded, seemingly unaware that this was not a compliment.

Nick said, "Ahoy, mateys! The mall doth approach!"

Pamela turned into the parking lot for the Garrett Mall. There was no shortage of parking spaces. The mall had only just opened for the day, and there couldn't have been more than fifty or sixty Arrivals in the lot.

Rory said, "Has anybody got any money?"

Archie shook his head. "I've got, like, maybe eight bucks."

Nick said, "I've got a card."

Good ol' Nick. He was the first in their group to sneak beer out of the house, the first to have his very own cell phone, the first to have his very own credit card, and today, well, the first in their group to have *wheels*. There were times when Archie thought it would be cool to be Nick instead of himself, but not for the beer or the phone or the credit card or even the chance to use this goofy self-driving car.

Nick still had a dad.

Not that Nick's dad worked that hard at being a dad, Archie thought. He was away on business half the time, and when he was home, he spent most of his free hours on the golf course. But hey, at least he was *alive*.

The kid Archie definitely did not want to trade places with was Rory. He liked hanging out with him and all, but Rory was not, as Archie's dad used to say, "wired up right." The red

wires and the green wires got crossed somewhere along the way. Yeah, sure, they were all
curious about girls and sneaking onto the Internet to look at porn and, frankly, scared to death
about actually talking to the opposite sex and
someday going out with them, but Rory seemed
a little too obsessed.

The Arrival wound its way through the parking lot and came to a stop next to the sidewalk
out front of the main doors to the mall.

"Where to first?" Nick asked his crew. "We
can get out here and Pamela will park herself."

"Go park yourself!" Rory said, making it
sound like a foul-mouthed insult.

Archie said, "First stop Cinnabon. I want a
cinnamon roll with extra icing. I'm starving."

Nick, gazing toward the dash, said, "Pamela,
open the doors."

The doors did not open.

Nick scowled. "Hey, Pamela, we're here. Open
the doors and go park yourself."

The doors did not open.

"Uh, Pamela," Nick said, "we're here. Can you
let us out?"

"Open the pod bay doors, Hal," Rory said
with mock seriousness.

"What's wrong?" Archie asked Nick.

He shook his head. "I don't know. Must be a
glitch or something. Maybe if—"

"Please state your destination."

Nick brightened at the sound of Pamela's
voice. "Ah, Pamela, we're *at* the destination,
bitch. I just want you to open the doors."

"Please state your destination."

Archie didn't like the sound of that. He ran his hand along the door, looking for a handle, thinking he'd find his own way out. There had to be a manual backup, right? In case you were in the car and the battery went dead and you had to escape?

Or in case it was on fire.

No, no way. There was no way he saw that. His fingers found what felt like a handle on the backside of a piece of trim. Archie gripped it and pulled.

"Yowzer!" Archie shouted.

Nick spun around. Rory said, "What?"

"I got a fucking shock!" Archie said.

"What are you talking about?" Nick asked.

"I grabbed the handle so I could open the door myself and I got *shocked.* What the hell?"

"Pamela," Nick said, his voice getting shaky, "I really need you to open the door. Was it the bitch thing? If so, I'd like to apologize."

"Please state your destination."

Nick looked upward, rolled his eyes, and sighed with exasperation the way he might have had a teacher assigned homework just as the bell rang.

"Pamela, the fucking destination is the mall. The Garrett Mall." He tipped his head toward the massive building next to the car. "Right *there.*"

"The Garrett Mall. Calculating the shortest route."

Rory said, "Uh, you think she's got PMS or something?"

Archie shot him a look. "Do you even know what that—"

The car was starting to move.

"Pamela!" Nick said. "Just stop and open the—"

Pamela turned sharply and sped out into the parking lot. As the car gained speed and momentum, it circled back, making a wide turn, finally straightening out when the main doors to the mall were dead ahead.

"Stop!" Nick shouted. "Pamela, stop!"

The car accelerated, adjusting its aim slightly, so that it would not connect with the right-angled curb, and very possibly put the front wheels out of commission. It was aiming for the ramped edge designed for wheelchair access.

The Arrival mounted the sidewalk and was now closing in on the mall entrance.

"Holy shit!" Archie cried. "Holy shit! *Holy shit!*"

The motion detectors above the doors picked up the car's approach and the double glass doors parted.

The Arrival raced through the opening.

Nick continued to scream. "Stop! Pamela, stop!"

Pamela did not stop.

As the car barreled into the shopping center, right past Cinnabon and Aunt Annie's Pretzels and the Best Buy Mobile outlet, shoppers dived out of the way. At least, they dived out of the way if they saw the car coming. Its electric drive system meant it did not make a lot more noise than a golf cart.

But an Arrival was considerably heavier than a golf cart. There was significantly more mass. And a hell of a lot more speed.

"Look out!" the three of them, waving their arms frantically, screamed from inside. But the windows were up—they were effectively cocooned—and no one was going to hear them any more than they were going to hear the car.

Sixty feet ahead, a man in his seventies, sneakers on, arms pumping, his back to them, was doing his mall walk. Trailing down from his ears were two white wires.

"No no no no!" Nick screamed as Pamela closed in on him.

And then she hit him.

The man flew up onto the hood, crashed into the windshield, bounced over the top of the car, hit the rear deck, and then dropped onto the mall's glistening marble floor.

The boys shrieked.

The stretch of mall where the car had entered was only half a dozen stores long. It quickly ended in a T, where the main concourse began. Dozens of retailers to the right, dozens more to the left. At the far ends, two anchor stores. A JC Penney was off in one direction, and a Costco-type store, Discount Bonanza, sat at the other. Overhead, countless banks of skylights cast sunlight over the wandering shoppers.

That was just the upper floor. Beyond a railing, the mall opened up to reveal another level of stores below, accessible by sets of escalators spaced out along the concourse.

As the Arrival entered the main part of the mall, it veered sharply enough to make the tires squeal. The moisture-sensitive, self-activating windshield wipers did several swipes to get rid of the mall walker's blood, adding a few shots of windshield washer fluid to get the job done.

"Let us out!" Archie cried. "Tell Pamela to let us out!"

Pamela wasn't listening to Archie or Rory or Nick. She was too busy communicating with dozens of Arrivals sitting idly in the parking lot.

Their electric engines came on simultaneously.

Slowly, they started rolling in the direction of the mall doors.

Thirteen

So what's the problem?" Bruce Clifford asked Katie Montrose as she followed him into his kitchen that morning.

"Archie," she said.

"Your brother?"

"Yeah," she said woefully. "Is there any way to get rid of a brother?"

Bruce shrugged. "None legally, that I know of."

She grimaced. "He just took off with his dumbass friends. I promised Mom I would keep an eye on him today and, like, minutes after she leaves, he pulls a stunt like this."

"So, what do you mean, he took off?"

"In one of the Arrivals. Looks like one of his immature and totally underage friends is somehow allowed to drive one. They might have gone to the mall."

"Well," Bruce said soothingly, "I don't see how he can get into that much trouble. I mean, those cars are about the safest thing ever made, aren't they? It's not like Chief Joe is gonna be pulling them over for speeding or running a red light."

"I guess that's true," Katie said, sounding slightly less worried.

Bruce was filling two mugs from what was left in the bottom of the coffee machine. He set one in front of her and tossed a spoon and a couple of sugar packets her way. Katie noticed the yellow *M* on the packets.

"You ever actually buy sugar?" she asked. "Or do you just fill your pockets every time you go to McDonald's?"

"It's just for company," he said. "I don't use sugar."

"You get a lot of company?" she asked.

"Just you," Bruce said. "So, your mom still seeing the chief?"

Katie nodded.

"And she still has no idea that you know all about it?"

She nodded again.

"Parents are funny," Bruce said. "Whether they're still together, or separated, or one of them's passed on, they don't want to admit to their kids that they might have a love life."

"You mean *sex* life," Katie said, and briefly shivered.

"I was trying to be delicate. Moms and dads are allowed to have a life, you know."

"I know," she said. "I wish she'd just be open about it."

"So, you want to head out for another lesson tonight?" he asked. "Say, around midnight?"

Katie sighed. "I don't know if there's any point."

"Come on. You're getting better each time. That was a damn fine three-point turn you did night before last. If you can do one of those in Finny, you can do one in any car, believe me. And those little rodents they call Arrivals, they don't even need to do a three-pointer, they're so fucking small they can turn on a dime." He grimaced. "Pardon my French."

The corner of Katie's mouth turned up. "Yeah, I'm just a fucking impressionable youngster."

"Noted," Bruce said. "So what do you mean, there's no point?"

Sullenly, Katie said, "I had *another* huge fight with my mom this morning about taking the test and finally getting my license and she wouldn't even consider it."

"She doesn't know how good a driver you already are," he said.

"Wouldn't matter if she did. She says the day's nearly here where no one is going to need to know how to drive."

Bruce's face softened. "You know where she's coming from on that."

When she'd last visited, she had told Bruce, ever so briefly, what had happened to her father.

"I was going through some of my old issues of the *Garrett Post* and saw the story," Bruce said. "It was up on Pelican Point?"

"Yeah. Some lady, whose grandson got his bike fixed at my dad's place, asked if he could come out and jump her car. Like, not jump *over* it, but get the battery going."

"I'm familiar with the concept."

"He'd worked, like, twelve hours that day and was just about to come home, but the lady, Hilda Steinway, in case you know her—"

"I do not."

"Anyway, she's, like, seventy-five—not that that's really old or anything."

Bruce grinned. "It sure feels fucking old, let me tell you."

"Anyway, she has all these health issues, and she's always checking to see if her car will start, and when it didn't, she went into a panic, thinking, what if something happens to me and I need to drive myself to the doctor's?"

"She hadn't heard about ambulances?"

"Hilda figures, where she lives, it takes them too long to get there."

"So she thinks, if she gets a heart attack, she's gonna drive herself to the ER?"

"We're getting a bit off track here, Bruce. Do you mind if I finish my story?"

He raised his hands in a surrender gesture. "Pardon me."

"My dad takes pity on her and agrees to drive out, and it's on the way there he nods off and goes into the ditch and drives his truck right into a tree. I was out there the other day. Like, not for the first time. I go by once in a while, if I can get someone to drive. Mom *never* drives out that way. Anyway, there's *still* no bark on the tree where he hit it. So, they did a test on him, right? Like, toxicology or whatever? And he hadn't been drinking or anything. He wasn't sick." She sniffed. "I guess he was just really tired. The way Chief Joe explained it, maybe, if the ambulance had gotten there a lot sooner, they could have done something."

Katie caught a tear before it ran down her cheek.

"Sorry, kid." He cleared his throat. "Should I give you a hug or something?"

"No, I'm cool."

"Good. I'm not a big hugger," he said.

"Anyway, back to my *mom*. Just because my dad fell asleep at the wheel doesn't mean I'm going to do it."

"Your mom's still hurting. She'll come around, once all this Arrival horseshit is over and we all go back to regular cars. This self-driving crap is still years away, no matter what they say."

"We're *all* still hurting," Katie said. "But Mom's the one *doing* some of the hurting."

"She wants to protect you. The road can be a dangerous place." Bruce's gentle smile turned into a reflective frown. "You might run into somebody like me. Or at least the guy I used to be."

"Yeah, but you never killed anybody."

"Could've," he said. "I was pissed as a newt."

"What's a newt?"

He ignored the question. "I blew three times the limit. Weaving all over the road. Thank God I got pulled over before I *did* kill somebody. They took away my license forever."

"But you stopped drinking."

"That I did."

"So can't you appeal or something? Get your license back?"

"Don't deserve it," he said. "And what if I fall off the wagon one day?" He shook his head. "No, I shouldn't be on the road. You have to pay a price for that kind of thing. I'm willing to accept that."

"But you kept your car. Even though you can't drive."

"I kept *that* car. But my regular car, that was a five-year-old Dodge. I gave that one up. But Finny, a beauty like that, well, that's a whole different story. Car like that is pretty hard to part with." His smile returned. "Best thing that's happened to me in years is you peeking through the window that night."

"What do you mean?"

"Means I got to ride in Finny again. Sitting in the passenger seat's almost as good as sitting behind the wheel. For years there, all I did was run the engine with it sittin' in the garage. Once or twice, thought about running a hose from the tailpipe in through the window, but I put that thought out of my head. So I'd put it in drive, go ahead a foot, put it in reverse and go a foot back. Almost as bad as when I was fifteen and I used to run my dad's old Ford back and forth in the driveway."

"You shouldn't joke about killing yourself," Katie said.

"Wasn't a joke," he said.

"Why would you want to do that?"

Bruce appeared pensive. "Before Barbara passed—this would have been ten years, no, *eleven* years ago—I was hitting the bottle pretty hard, and then after, I guess I was into it even harder, until I got that ticket, and, well, that smartened me up as far as the booze was concerned. But then, once I got sober, and realized there wasn't much left to live for . . . the drinking kind of helped me forget that."

"So," Katie said, "what made you not do it?"

He smiled. "I was worried about who'd look after Finny."

"You're not serious," she said.

"I know. It sounds crazy."

Katie took a quick slurp of her coffee. "Look,

I should go. Maybe Archie'll realize the trouble he's going to be in and come home. He might not get into trouble while he's in the Arrival, but once he gets out, who knows what he'll do."

Bruce pursed his lips, slowly exhaled, then ran his tongue over his teeth.

"What?" Katie asked.

"Thinkin'."

"Oh." She nodded. "I *thought* I smelled something burning."

"Why don't we go look for him?"

Katie paused. "What do you mean? You mean, in the *car*?"

Bruce smiled slyly. "Yeah. In the car."

"But regular cars—cars that people actually *drive*—aren't supposed to be on the road right now. They're not even supposed to be on the *island*. Everybody put them on the ferry and left them on the mainland. That's why we've been doing my driving lessons at night. *Remember?*"

Bruce shrugged. "Maybe I don't give a damn anymore."

"Yeah, well, who are you planning on putting behind the wheel?"

"You," he said. "You're a good driver."

"Yeah, but I don't have a license. Did you forget about that, *too*?"

Bruce mulled that one over. "If we get stopped, we'll say it was an emergency." He thought about that. "I was out of eggs. Wanted to make an omelette, went to the fridge, didn't have any goddamn eggs."

"That is *not* an emergency," Katie said.

"Oh yes, it is," he said confidently. "You ever had one of my omelettes?"

"You're losing it, Bruce."

"Come on," he said. "There's never been a better time to take a spin. There's no cops on the roads. There's nothing for them to do except hang out at Dunkin' Donuts all day."

Katie gave the proposal some thought. "If we did get stopped, I'd just say I was trying to find my brother. That I was worried he might be in trouble."

"There you go," Bruce said. "Come on."

He reached into a decorative bowl on the kitchen counter, grabbed a set of car keys, and then tossed them to Katie. She wasn't expecting them, and fumbled the catch. The keys hit the floor.

"You play for the Red Sox?" Bruce asked as she bent over to retrieve them.

He was already leaving the kitchen and heading down a short hallway to the door that led into the garage. Katie caught up to him as he opened it and reached around for the switch. The garage was bathed in light as they stepped inside.

And there was Finny.

"Every time I step in here," he said, "she takes my breath away."

It was easy to understand why. The gleaming black car, which had been backed into the garage, overwhelmed the space. The garage had probably been designed to hold one average-sized vehicle, not a land yacht like this.

"What year is it again?" Katie asked.

"This," Bruce said, taking a breath, "is the 1959 Cadillac Coupe de Ville. It's two hundred and twenty-five inches long, a wheelbase of one hundred and thirty inches, with a three-hundred-and-ninety-cubic-inch V-8 under that hood up there."

"You've told me all this stuff before. I was just asking about the year."

"You want to know how many of these babies they made?"

"Not really."

"They cranked out 21,924. No idea how many of them are still around. But I'd bet you there aren't many as nice as this one. One of the most beautiful cars ever made and the absolute peak of the tailfin craze."

"Yeah, about *these*," Katie said, taking a step toward the car and touching her index finger to the chrome-trimmed tip of one of the two massive tailfins on each of the rear fenders. "Why does the car have these? I mean, do they actually do anything?"

Bruce smiled. "They don't have to do anything, Katie. They just *are*."

She tapped her finger again on the sharp tip of the left tailfin. "I'd hate to run into this at sixty miles an hour."

"Interesting fact," Bruce said. "There were actual incidents of people—motorcyclists, I believe—being impaled on those beauties. It was in Ralph Nader's book on safety deficiencies in the American auto industry, most notably where the Chevrolet Corvair was concerned, which—"

Katie rested a hand gently on Bruce's arm. "Please," she said. "Stop."

He nodded slowly. "I get carried away sometimes. So, why don't you get behind the wheel?"

Katie did a walkaround of the car, fitting into the narrow space between the massive front grille and the closed garage door. "There's so much chrome here," she said. "There's enough here to make a million toasters." She looked across the huge hood and said, "Do they mine chrome? Does chrome come from underground or something?"

Bruce said, "Get in the car."

Katie shimmied between the driver's side of the car and the wall, which was lined with wood shelves bearing half-empty cans of paint. She eased open the door, careful not to bump the shelves, and slithered in behind the wheel like a snake.

Bruce got in on the other side and gently closed the door. Katie glanced across the expansive bench seat and said, "You're like a mile away."

Katie slipped the key into the ignition on the lower part of the dash to the right of the wheel. She turned it and brought the rumbling engine under the hood to life. She placed her hands on the wheel. "Ten and two," she said, displaying the proper positioning. "My hands are so far apart, it's like holding a garbage can lid. This steering wheel is ginormous."

"More like a Hula-Hoop," he said.

She threw her right arm over the seat and looked into the back. "That's, like, nearly as big as my bedroom."

Bruce slowly nodded. "Many a child was conceived in the back of a Caddy," he said.

Katie made a face, like she'd caught a whiff of bad cheese, then turned her attention back to the task at hand.

"Door," she said.

Bruce opened the cavernous glove box. He dug under a can of window cleaner spray, a micro cloth, and a map book of the island until he found a small remote garage door opener. He gave it a click, and the door before them rumbled upward. When it stopped its climb, Katie put the car in drive.

"I kinda wish this beast had some seat belts," she said, her fingers wrapped so tightly around the wheel that her hands hurt.

"Cadillac didn't offer seat belts until 1962," Bruce said. "In fact—"

"No more history lessons, okay?" Katie said. "We're on a mission to find my asshole brother. We need to focus."

Bruce nodded, and waved his hand slowly toward the windshield. "Please proceed."

Katie feathered the accelerator, and the immense conglomeration of Detroit steel and glass and rubber emerged from the garage, rumbled slowly down the driveway, and turned onto the street.

"We are gonna get in such shit," Katie said.

Bruce harrumphed. "We're just taking a nice Sunday drive."

"It's Friday."

"If I'd known what a smart-ass you'd turn out to be, I would have called the cops on you when I found you peeping in my window."

Fourteen

Brandon Kyle had known it would be a shit show. But what a glorious shit show it was turning out to be.

Who could have guessed that the first victim would be none other than Lisa Carver? It was wonderful, and a little disappointing at the same time. Wonderful because there was a delicious poetic justice about it. The woman who'd destroyed his company—and who had effectively destroyed *him* in the process—was the day's debut casualty. But disappointing, too, because Lisa would not live long enough to see the scale of his retribution.

It wasn't enough that she die. He had hoped for her to experience a fraction of the humiliation he'd endured. She could die later.

Whatever. If Lisa Carver had to die, she could not have gone out more splendidly. Her leg hacked off, her body trapped inside one of her Arrivals as it spun like a top before the world's assembled media.

You couldn't buy that kind of publicity.

He had not known, once he'd downloaded the virus into the Arrival network, just how quickly the results would be evident. Turned out to be pretty goddamn instantaneous. It wasn't even lunch yet and Carver was dead. Other Arrivals were starting to mobilize on their own. He'd caught a glimpse of them moving out of the community center parking lot.

Kyle could only guess where Arrival's share price would be by the close of the market. It had been soaring that morning—there had been considerable early buzz about today's news event and the Garrett Island press conference—but Kyle was betting anyone holding Arrival shares would be dumping them as fast as they could the moment they heard about what had happened here. They might even halt trading on the company if it went into a total free fall.

It had only been moments since Lisa's leg had hit the pavement but news of the catastrophe was already trending on Twitter. Kyle had slipped around the corner of the community center to call up the app on his phone and he smiled broadly when he saw how quickly the story was getting out there. There was already a hashtag that suggested the company's end was near: *#latearrival*.

CNN had posted a Breaking News item on its app, but details were sketchy. There was a few seconds of blurry video of Carver's Arrival spinning around in circles, a sentence or two about how a demonstration of the company's autonomous vehicle had gone horribly wrong. More details were promised as they became available.

Kyle dropped the phone back into his coat pocket and peered around the corner.

Beyond the entry off the highway to the community center, a red-and-white Garrett Island fire engine, lights flashing, was barreling up the road. The wail of its siren had been audible for the last couple of minutes, but now everyone could see it coming.

And now there was a second siren, a veritable symphony of distress. Hot on the tail of the fire engine was an ambulance, a boxy white vehicle with an orange stripe and the words GARRETT ISLAND RESCUE emblazoned on the side.

It was beginning to look, however, as though the truck and the ambulance were going to have some difficulty coming up the drive and making it to the asphalt apron out front of the building, where the Arrival with Lisa Carver's body in it now sat motionless, the door still firmly in the closed position.

The other Arrivals he'd seen starting up moments earlier were now lined up, side by side, at the road's edge, blocking the entrance. Kyle did a quick count of how many of the cars had moved into position. Fifteen. A significant blockade.

The driver of the fire engine, close enough now to see he couldn't make it up to the community center, blew his horn. And this was no ordinary horn. This was a from-the-depths-of-hell blast that Kyle could feel in his bones.

Anyone born with the common sense given to a spruce budworm would know that it would be smart to get the fuck out of the way. But there was not *anyone* in the Arrivals, and so, driverless and passengerless, they stood their ground.

The fire truck slowed to a stop about thirty feet from the Arrivals. The driver of the truck stuck his head out of the window and shouted at the cars.

"Get out of the way!"

The cars did not respond.

The driver brought his head back into the cab and was conferring with the firefighter sitting up front next to him. No doubt, Kyle conjectured, about how to deal with the situation. It must have felt foolish to yell at a collection of vehicles with no one in them. There had to be someone they could call, someone who could move those cars.

The ambulance had come to a stop, too, and the door on the passenger side opened. A paramedic got out and ran forward, going as far as the cab of the fire engine, and calling up to the driver. Words exchanged, arms waved.

Kyle wished he could hear what they were saying.

The paramedic, a fit-looking man in his thirties, pointed in the direction of the community center, proposing, Kyle surmised, that he get to the scene on foot if they couldn't get their vehicles up there.

Now the driver was saying something to two of the firefighters sitting in the cab behind them. A nod or two. One of the two opened a door and climbed down from the cab and onto the road. Big guy, decked out in full firefighter regalia. Boots, helmet, fireproof jacket. Imagine having to wear all that stuff for work, Kyle thought. Not just unfashionable, but so goddamn heavy.

The firefighter and the paramedic exchanged a few words, nodded, and then started walking toward the phalanx of cars.

The firefighter started *yelling* at them. Kyle could make out what he was saying.

"Move the fuck out of the way!" he shouted. "Let's go! Fuckin' move or we'll knock you out of the way!"

Although it looked incredibly silly, there was really nothing silly about it. The cars were designed, of course, to respond to verbal commands. They could hear, they could see, and they could recognize. They knew what a fire truck was. They knew what an ambulance was. And based on what they heard and saw and recognized, they could *evaluate*. And once they evaluated something, they could decide how to respond.

All within a millionth of a second.

So there was every reason to believe that the Arrivals blocking access to the community center saw these emergency works and even understood what was being asked of them. (Arrivals, and the Gandalfs that Kyle had developed, were also proficient at understanding profanity, as well as an upraised middle finger.)

Even though every Arrival was programmed to recognize only its owner's voice commands—a feature designed to deter theft—they were also designed to obey instructions from police, firefighters, and the like.

So they should have moved.

Brandon Kyle, however, was not expecting them to.

It was a dandy little virus he'd sent into the network.

Kyle thought of it as a "bizarro" program, the inspiration coming from the Superman comics he read as a kid, and the strange planet known as Bizarro World where everything was an opposite. For starters, the planet was a cube instead of a sphere. In Bizarro World, good was bad and bad was good and up was down and down was up.

Arrival programming was all about safety. Human safety, in particular.

Do. No. Harm. A kind of automotive version of a doctor's Hippocratic oath. It was encoded into every aspect of an Arrival's programming.

In some ways, what Kyle had done was quite simple.

He'd eliminated the *No.*

This was why Brandon Kyle did not expect the Arrivals to move out of the way and allow the fire engine and the ambulance to reach the scene where Lisa Carver, it was very likely, had already bled to death. Blocking their path *encouraged* harm.

But even Kyle was taken aback by what the Arrivals decided to do.

They attacked.

The powder-blue Arrival in the center position—there were seven to the left of it and seven to the right—suddenly shot forward, aiming for both men. They reacted immediately, each diving in opposite directions. The blue Arrival opted to go after the firefighter, who had bolted to the right, and was now making a bee-line back to the fire engine, presumably hoping to grab on to one of the handles on the side and hoist himself up and out of the way.

He very nearly made it, too.

He was just reaching up for the door when the Arrival drove itself into the back of him, pinning his legs to the side of the fire engine and creating a symphony of broken bones and crushed steel.

"Oh my," said Kyle.

The paramedic, who'd glanced over his shoulder and seen what had happened to his friend, might have thought he'd been spared, but now two other Arrivals had started moving and were in pursuit.

The Arrival that had pinned the firefighter to the truck had managed to lodge itself under the frame. When the driver and the two remaining members of the crew jumped out to rescue their friend, they could see that when the sloped, front end of the Arrival struck him, it carried his legs right under the fire engine with it. The man, who already appeared to be dead, had collapsed onto the hood of the car.

"Jesus fucking Christ!" the driver yelled.

The second paramedic in the ambulance leapt out, but by the time she was halfway to the fire engine, yet another Arrival had dispatched itself in her direction. She spun around and started running back, putting every ounce of speed into it as she could. She jumped back into the ambulance half a second before the Arrival broadsided the vehicle with a thunderous crash.

Her partner was still trying to outrun the two Arrivals that had taken off after him. He ran for the ditch on the other side of the road, and up the other side. The first Arrival maintained the pursuit, nose-diving into the ditch and staying there, its wheels spinning in the grass. It would have, under any other circumstance, been comical. The Arrivals were proving themselves, immediately, to be nasty little sons of bitches, but they weren't four-wheel-drive Jeeps.

The second Arrival hit the brakes before going into the ditch, taking a second to survey the scene. The paramedic had come up the other side of the ditch and scurried behind a tree for cover.

"Yeah, come and get me, motherfucker!"

The second Arrival, uninterested in taking up the challenge, cranked its wheels hard left and spun around, leaving the disabled Arrival in the ditch to continue spinning its wheels in frustration.

Brandon Kyle watched in awe.

The virus had gone beyond expectations. The Arrivals had gone way beyond reckless. In fact, they'd moved beyond aggressive.

They'd become predatory.

The Arrivals were *going after* those emergency workers. The Arrivals were hunting them down.

And they weren't done yet.

Half a dozen of the remaining Arrivals were charging toward the fire engine. First, they had circled it in a manner that reminded Kyle of Indians riding their horses around the circled wagons in an old-time cowboy movie. The fire truck's driver was going to have a hard enough time getting away with a car wedged under the frame, but even if he did manage that, how was he to get past the Arrivals buzzing around him?

Then something astonishing happened.

One after another, the Arrivals plowed full speed into the massive truck. There'd be a huge crash, and then another, followed by another. The cars were destroying themselves in the process.

"Christ," Kyle said breathlessly. "They're kamikazes."

All those who'd been gathered around the Arrival that bit off Lisa Carver's leg were now transfixed by this new and even more frightening display. Everyone except Albert Ruskin, who was still attempting to communicate with his boss trapped inside the car.

"Ms. Carver!" he shouted. "Lisa! Lisa, can you hear me?"

The woman showed no signs of life, but he persisted.

You had to give the guy credit, Kyle thought. As much as Ruskin reportedly hated that woman, he was putting on a good show of caring about her.

Brandon Kyle was well aware just how intensely Albert Ruskin detested his employer, was even willing to wager the contempt he felt for her came close to his. For as long as he'd worked for her he'd been subjected to constant humiliation and relentless abuse. You expected a CEO to be demanding, to expect the best of her people, but by all accounts, that was not Lisa Carver's style. It didn't matter how well you did your job. She always found fault. She demeaned, she insulted, she mocked.

Turnover at Arrival's administrative ranks had always been high. It was a classic "the beatings will continue until morale improves" environment. Everyone in the industry knew it. It was an open secret.

So Kyle was impressed, watching Ruskin struggle to get that car door open, trying to save his boss. Was it all a charade, or did he really mean it? Kyle believed Ruskin couldn't help but take some small measure of pleasure from his boss's predicament.

The next step in what Kyle sometimes thought of as "Operation Dead on Arrival" was already in the works. A prearranged email would start hitting the in-boxes of Arrival employees. A ransomware demand, supposedly from a team of Russian hackers. All Arrival had to do to stop the carnage was transfer over a million in bitcoin. Let them waste time trying to figure out how to get onto the dark web and send funds to an account that didn't exist.

What Kyle had to think about now was getting the hell off this island.

Making it to the ferry—it was a trip of several miles to the island's far shore—was out of the question, given that the only way to get there would be in an Arrival. Not getting in one of those now, thank you very much. And he wasn't about to wait for help to arrive from the mainland (they might send in the army for all he knew) and run the risk of having his true identity revealed.

So he would head into the town of Garrett, a much shorter trek. And then he would find his way to the harbor. Derek would be heading there now in the boat he'd rented. Once they had rendezvoused, they'd head back to shore.

He just hoped Derek would be on time. He had to—

What the hell?

There was an explosion. One of the Arrivals taking aim at the fire truck must have hit a gas tank. A battery-powered Arrival didn't have one, but the truck would have a substantial tank tucked into its undercarriage.

"Fuck me," Kyle whispered.

The fire truck was on *fire*.

Fifteen

When Chief Joe Bridgeman had finished filling in the coast guard about the possibility that a man named Clyde Travers had fallen off the ferry en route to Garrett Island, he started walking back toward his specially outfitted Arrival.

He was about to ask Sherlock to open the door when his phone, barely back in his pocket for a minute, rang again.

"Yup?" he said, taking the call while walking.

"Chief?" It was Ronny Dyson, who was on the dispatch desk that morning.

"Yeah, it's me, Ronny." Joe sighed. Ronny had dialed the chief, the chief had answered, but Ronny still had to ask if it was him.

"Where are you?" Ronny asked.

"Ferry dock."

"Right, that guy that didn't get off?"

"What's up, Ronny?"

"There's some crazy shit going down at that Arrival event at the community center."

Joe stopped walking. "What kind of shit?"

"Well, kinda everything. Some lady's leg got cut off and now they're saying—"

"Wait! What lady? Whose leg got cut off?"

"Uh, I'm not sure. She was showing how the car worked and the door slammed shut on it or something."

"Was it Sandra?"

"Who?"

"Sandra Montrose!"

"That the lady you've been seein'?"

Christ, it was hard to keep a secret on the island.

"Was it her, Ronny?"

"Don't think so. Sounded like someone important. I mean, not that she isn't, but it was someone who'd come over for the day, the head of the company, I think, and—"

"Never mind," Joe said. He'd put Ronny, who was, as they say, untroubled by intelligence, on dispatch because Joe believed he could do less damage there than being out on the street. Now, he wasn't so sure. "Tell me the rest of it."

"So you know Duff McLaughlin?"

"Yeah, I know Duff. Works for the fire department."

"That's right. Well, they say he's dead."

"Jesus Christ," Joe said. "What happened?"

"He got hit."

"Hit?"

"Yeah."

"Hit by what?"

It was like pulling fucking teeth.

"One of the little funny cars. Rammed him, right up against the fire engine."

"How the fuck did that happen?"

"Not sure. But now Truck Five is on fire."

"The fire engine is on fire?"

"Right. That's what you call ironic, right?"

"Who's out there?" Joe asked.

"Okay, so Alice and Rick were on their way

but they ran into a problem. And from what I hear, the ambulance can't get near the scene."

"Why the hell is *that*?"

"'Cause they're surrounded."

"Ronny, I swear, just spell it out for me. Who's surrounding them?"

"The cars." Ronny paused. "What I'm hearing is, the cars are kinda losing it. Goin' all whacka-doo. They're not going to get a very good rating in *Consumer Reports* after this."

"I'm on my way," the chief said, ending the call and slipping the phone back into his pocket. "Sherlock, open!"

While he waited for the car's door to retract, he entered another number on his phone. "Come on, come on," he said. "Answer the fucking phone, Sandra."

After the fifth ring, his call was directed to voice mail. "Sandra, it's Joe. Call me! I just heard things have gone crazy at the center! I'm heading your way. Let me know you're okay!"

He ended the call and then looked at the car, dumbfounded. The door had not opened.

"Uh, Sherlock, open up."

The chief's Arrival did not respond.

"Come on! Open up!" He slapped his palm on the glass three times. "Let's go! Wakey wakey!"

He heard the nearly inaudible whirring noise of the Arrival's electric engine powering up.

"That's promising," Joe said. "Now would you kindly open the fucking door?"

The Arrival's wheels began to turn.

"What the hell?" Joe said, taking a step back so that the rear tire wouldn't run over his foot.

The Arrival picked up the pace, made a graceful half circle, and pulled onto the road that led back to the town of Garrett.

"Where the hell are you going?" Joe shouted at the car. "Get your ass back here!"

The Arrival paid no heed. It continued on down the road and disappeared behind a copse of trees as it went around a curve.

Joe stood there with his mouth hanging open. He glanced around, looking for an alternative set of wheels, seeing nothing but a rusting bicycle leaning up against the ferry master's shed.

He got out his phone again and waited for Ronny to pick up.

"Hello?"

"Ronny, it's me."

"That you, Chief?"

"Yes!"

"I'm gettin' a lot of calls and really need to keep the line clear."

"I need you to get someone to pick me up here at the ferry."

"Yeah, well, not sure how I would go about that."

"Why?"

"Okay, I guess, when we were talking before, I forgot to mention something. You know when I said Alice and Rick were on their way to the community center?"

"Yeah?"

"So, their cars just kind of went off without them. Like they had minds of their own. Can you believe it?"

Joe started grinding his teeth together. "There

must be a regular car on the fucking island *somewhere*."

"Only that one that's in the shop," Ronny said. "So I don't know how—"

Joe ended the call and stole the bike.

Sixteen

Now that Gracie had run off with her phone, as well as her purse and everything in it, Sandra had no immediate way to call Katie and Archie to let them know, if they didn't already, that something was very, very wrong.

It hadn't taken her long to surmise that if all the Arrivals at the event had gone nuts, then every Arrival on the island might have lost its mind, too. Which meant her kids could be in jeopardy. She was only slightly comforted by the fact that she had left Katie in charge, and that she and Archie were, in all likelihood, perfectly safe at home.

Still . . .

She had to warn them to stay off the streets until the Arrivals were brought back under control. Katie and Archie were her number one priority.

"Not again," she said to herself. "I'm not losing anyone else."

The fire truck down by the road was in flames and its crew had run into the woods for cover, unable to do anything, at least for now, for their coworker pinned to the side of the truck. Sandra could tell, even at a distance, that the man was beyond saving.

Things were no better with the ambulance. One paramedic had run into the woods, and the other was trapped inside the vehicle. She had the window down and was yelling at the Arrivals surrounding the vehicle as if they were a pack of dogs.

"Go away!" she shouted. "Scoot!"

Scoot.

There was less mayhem directly out front of the community center. All the Arrivals, with the exception of the now motionless one that had cut off Lisa Carver's leg, were down by the main road, holding the emergency vehicles back.

The flames from the fire engine were growing higher, licking an overhead wire that ran across the road. Within seconds, the wire's insulation was ablaze, the flickers of flame running the length of it as quickly as a squirrel.

The media types, at first transfixed by Lisa Carver's fate, now were focused on the scene down on the road. Not only were the official camerapersons capturing the event, everyone else had their phones out, getting video. There was a palpable sense of excitement coming from them. Sure, this was scary as shit, but what a story.

Albert Ruskin had given up trying to rescue his boss and was now standing several feet away from Sandra, shoulders slumped, head down, hand to his forehead. In his other hand, hanging by his side, was a cell phone.

Sandra approached cautiously from behind. "Mr. Ruskin?"

He raised his head and turned his head slowly. "Yes? Oh, Ms. Montrose." The sharp, accusatory tone was gone from his voice. He spoke as though in shock.

"I'm so sorry," Sandra said.

"I tried . . . to get the door open . . . tried to hold it."

"I know."

"Look," he said, pointing to something several feet away. "Should I save it? In case they can . . . but it may be too late. Is there ice? Can we find some ice and . . . and . . . keep it cool?"

Sandra didn't know, at first, what he was pointing at. But then she realized he was indicating Lisa's severed leg. She swallowed, hard, to keep the bile from rising. Instead of walking over to the bloody limb, she walked over to the car, tentatively, worried that at any moment it might start moving. She got right to the window and peered in through the bloodied glass.

Red, smeared handprints.

Once her leg had been cut off, Lisa had no longer been held in position. She must have first reached down and, perhaps in panic, touched the wound. Then, her verbal commands ignored, she'd tapped away at the dashboard screen, trying to get the door to reopen. There were bloody fingerprints smeared across it.

Lisa lay sprawled across the seat, mouth open, her skin white as chalk. Half of her blood-soaked purse was visible beneath her. Sandra peered down into the footwell, saw the pool of blood down there. No wonder she was so pale. The blood had pretty much drained out of her. Perhaps most disturbing of all were her now open, lifeless eyes.

Walking back to where Ruskin was standing, she glanced over to the road, where one of the wooden roadside utility poles was starting to catch on fire, thanks to that flaming wire.

She said to Ruskin, "I wouldn't worry about trying to preserve her . . . you know . . . her leg. She's dead, Mr. Ruskin. Again, I'm so sorry."

He looked at the blazing fire truck. "Even if she were alive, help's not coming."

"Not yet," Sandra said. "They'll figure it out."

"They?"

"Don't you have, like, Arrival tech support? Somewhere? Like Silicon Valley, or India? Can't they stop this?"

Ruskin shook his head slowly. "They're saying . . . we're getting messages. Ransomware."

"What?" Sandra said. "Some hackers caused this?"

"I don't know. I don't know whether to believe it. How could things have gone so . . ." He stared at the pavement, shaking his head. "This wasn't . . . this wasn't ever . . ."

"I don't get it," Sandra said. "Ransomware, that would shut everything down, right? But this is something else. The cars have gone crazy. They're *killing* people. It's like there's a hundred Christines on the island. You must have *some* idea."

Ruskin bit his lip, looked over to the Arrival with Lisa in it, then at the burning fire truck. "It . . . it has to be some kind of program malfunction."

"You think?" Sandra said.

"Even . . . even a basic virus, it wouldn't—shouldn't—do something like this. A . . . basic virus might misinterpret commands. Make the wipers go when they shouldn't, keep the car from starting up. Screw up its GPS. But this, what I'm seeing . . ." Ruskin took a breath. "What I'm seeing here, it's like if a person's DNA got altered. The car's basic intent, it's been turned upside down."

"Basic intent?"

Ruskin took a couple of deep, head-clearing breaths.

"To *protect*," Ruskin said. "Everything in an Arrival is designed to protect not just people *in* the car but people *outside* the car. It's like everything got turned upside down."

"They're not just driving around recklessly," Sandra said. "They're deliberately mowing people down."

More to himself than Sandra, Ruskin said, "Good God, what have we done?"

Sandra had had enough of this. "Give me your phone," she said.

Ruskin blinked, as though startled by the request.

"No," he said. "I've got calls I have to make. Right now."

"I have to call my kids," Sandra pleaded. "I don't know if they have any idea—"

"No," Ruskin said again, and pointed to the pack of journalists. "Ask one of them."

The son of a bitch, she thought. She wasn't going to try to wrestle his phone away from him. There'd be a landline in the community center she could use.

She headed straight for the administrative office, encountering no one along the way. Once there, she grabbed the receiver off a desk, put it to her ear, and was about to enter a number when she realized there was no dial tone. She figured she had to hit 9 for an outside line. Tried that.

Nothing.

Then it hit her.

The telephone pole and the wires leading to it were on fire.

"Shit," she said out loud, slamming the receiver back down. "Shit, shit, shit, shit, shit."

She ran from the building, intending to borrow a phone from one of the visiting journalists. But then, coming out the main entrance, she saw something she thought might prove helpful.

Stones.

The garden that lined the walkway was dotted with decorative stones, many of them about the size of a brick.

Sandra dropped to her knees, dug her fingers into the dirt, and, breaking a nail in the process, pried up one of the stones. She got a firm hold on it, stood, and headed straight for the Arrival containing Lisa Carver's body.

She marched around to the other side of the car and, holding the stone with both hands, smashed the glass. The window exploded into tiny, granular shards. Sandra reached through the broken window for the bloody purse tucked under Lisa Carver's body.

The car made a sound. A whirring sound. A *startup* sound.

Sandra grabbed for a short length of visible purse strap. She had hold of it, but it was slick with blood and she lost her grip. Sandra grabbed a second time and yanked it out of the car, worried that it was about to drive off.

Sandra opened the purse and started tossing things out—a lipstick, tissues, a tiny plastic bottle of nasal decongestant—until she found what she was looking for.

A cell phone.

"Yes!" Sandra said.

But her elation was short-lived. When she hit the home button a digital keypad appeared. The phone needed a passcode. Or, possibly, a fingerprint.

Sandra looked back into the car. Lisa Carver's outstretched, bloodied right hand was on the seat just inside the broken window, a few granules of glass stuck on it.

Most people, Sandra reasoned, used their thumbprint to start up their phones. One of the items Sandra had dumped from the purse was a small packet of moistened wipes. She snatched it off the ground, opened it, and pulled out three towelettes.

"Jesus, I can't believe this," she whispered to herself, leaning back into the car and lifting up the dead woman's hand and using the wipes to get the blood off her thumb. "Please don't be left-handed."

A voice spoke to her from the dash.

"You broke my window."

Sandra, confident the thumb was now mostly clear of blood, held it carefully with one hand while holding Lisa Carver's phone in the other.

"Why did you break my window?"

The phone failed to become active. Sandra took another look at the thumb and saw a few more flecks of blood. She used another wipe to do a more thorough job.

"How else was I going to get inside?" Sandra replied, focusing on her task, mindful that the car knew she was here. That it might start moving at any second, with her feet on the ground, and the upper body leaning into the vehicle.

Not a good position to be in.

"Why did you want to get inside?" the car asked.

"I needed this woman's phone, and now I need her thumbprint to get into it."

Jesus Christ, she was having a fucking conversation with a fucking car. Okay, sure, she'd talked to her own Arrival. She'd given it *directions.* She'd told it when to *pick her up.* Those were instructions. This . . . this was *chatting.* The car wasn't asking *what* Sandra wanted, or *what* it wanted her to do. It was asking *why.*

Well, that could work both ways.

"I've got a question for *you,*" Sandra said as she put the thumb onto the phone's home button again. "What the fuck is going on? Why are you and your friends doing this?"

"Please clarify 'friends.'"

"The other Arrivals. Why are you doing this? Why are you attacking?"

There was a long pause while the red car—hadn't Carver called this one Rudolph?—considered a response.

"Cat got your tongue?"

The phone's screen lit up with multiple rows of apps. "Yes!" Sandra said, pulling herself back out of the car. Not only was she into the phone, but it was showing a nearly full charge.

The car clearly had nothing more to say, but she could hear some machinery being engaged.

Sandra stepped well back. The door on the

other side of the car opened. As the car began to speed up, it went into a sharp turn, driving in a tight circle, not unlike it had done earlier, with Lisa Carver trapped inside.

Sandra ran around the corner of the building for shelter, but peeked around the edge to see what the car was going to do.

It continued going in circles, and picking up speed, until it had created enough centrifugal force to toss the woman's body from the car.

Sandra put a hand to her mouth, stifling a scream.

Once the car had rid itself of the body, it straightened out, sped off through the community center lot, and joined up with the Arrivals that were still surrounding the burning fire engine.

Sandra looked away. She pressed her back to the wall, closed her eyes for several seconds.

Then she looked at Lisa Carver's phone, still accessible. But how long would it stay that way? Sandra didn't have Lisa's thumb in her pocket for the next time the phone went dark.

She shuddered at the thought. The woman was right over there and if she could find a pair of gardening shears in the community center's shed . . .

No, she was not going to do that. She could *not* bring herself to do that.

But there was another way. She needed to go into the phone settings right now and make the device accessible without a password or thumbprint. Once she had done that, she was about to hit Contacts, out of habit, as if somehow her kids' numbers would be in there.

But, of course, they were not. She was going to have to enter their numbers into the keypad.

Christ, what are their phone numbers?

Who had to enter full phone numbers for people you called all the time? Who had to *re-member* them? Sandra concentrated, came up with a number she was confident was the one for her son's phone, and entered it.

She put the phone to her ear and waited for the ring.

Seventeen

Brandon Kyle headed for Garrett Harbor.

The previous week, Derek, using a false name, had reserved, in Falmouth, a thirty-three-foot Egg Harbor yacht for the day. There was no predicting, a week out, what the weather would be, but Derek was confident the Egg Harbor would be adequate, even if the seas got choppy. Derek had done some sailing back in his youth, and was not at all worried that he'd be able to navigate the craft.

At one point, Derek had proposed renting a helicopter and, once the Arrivals were in full clusterfuck, swooping in quickly and scooping up his boss. But Kyle believed a helicopter would attract too much attention, and they would have had to hire someone to pilot it. Derek could sail, but he had no pilot's license. Bringing in yet another person, making them privy to the plan, was deemed unwise.

What Kyle looked forward to was returning to the mainland, getting home, taking a cold one from the fridge, putting his feet up, and watching how CNN covered the story. (The news would take some sting out of the home he was returning *to*—a shitty condo in Boston's North End.) At some point, the media would be looking for an on-camera interview, and when they did, he wanted to be as far away from the action as possible.

He'd been rehearsing, in his mind, what he'd say. After all the nasty accusations he'd made about Lisa Carver, he couldn't be *too* conciliatory. No one would buy that. He needed to strike a balance, say something along the lines of "While I am not withdrawing my accusations of corporate sabotage against the Arrival corporation, and continue to seek redress, I would not wish on anyone the horrific events that ended the life of Arrival CEO Lisa Carver. As one of the automotive world's first female CEOs, she was an inspiration to many and my heart goes out to her family. This is a tragedy for those close to her. It's also, I would suspect, a fatal blow for the Arrival corporation. Perhaps another company, one with a greater moral compass, will rise from its ashes and help deliver us into a new age of personal transportation."

Could he say that last part? It was hard not to get his digs in. He'd have to think about that.

But first he had to make the trek from the community center to Garrett Harbor.

The day before, he had checked out possible routes on Google Maps. The trip, according to Google, was five minutes by car, half an hour on foot. Kyle was betting the thirty minutes was a bit optimistic, given that he was going to have to steer clear of roads and sidewalks. He didn't want to be run down by a crazy Arrival. Didn't want to be hoisted by his own petard, as the saying went.

What the fuck IS a petard, anyway? Kyle wondered.

So he'd be cutting through yards, taking alleys. He'd cross streets when he had to, but he'd be quick about it. After relishing, for a few extra moments, the catastrophe under way at the community center, Kyle cut across a field behind the building, then worked his way through a wooded area that ran alongside the road.

He stepped out from the copse of trees and scanned the road in both directions. No Arrivals to be seen. They were all doing battle with the fire engine and the ambulance. He sprinted to the other side of the road and figured, at least for the time being, it was safe to follow it. If a vehicle came into view, he'd take cover.

He still had, under his clothing, the fake padding that made him look a good fifty pounds heavier. Once he'd started running, he was feeling it get in the way of his movements, and on top of that, it was hot. He wanted to duck in between a couple of houses, remove his sport jacket, strip off his shirt, rip off the padding, and stuff it into a trash can somewhere. But he was worried he might still be seen, and his Ben Stapleton identity needed to be preserved.

A purple Arrival—it looked like a grape exposed to massive doses of radiation—was approaching, most likely heading for the community center. Reinforcements, Kyle guessed. He ran between some houses and crouched behind a shrub and watched the car pass. Instead of heading back to the road, he checked the map app on his phone and determined it made sense to keep cutting between houses to reach the rendezvous point.

He worked his way through a few backyards, ducking through swing sets, navigating his way around decks covered with wicker furniture, crawling over several rows of low white picket fences.

At one point, a woman shouted out a window, "What are you doing out there, mister?"

He shouted back, "Getting away from those damn cars! Stay inside!"

"What the hell are you talking about?" she asked.

She'd know soon enough.

In a little over twenty minutes, he was at the town center. Any other day, it would have been a lovely, tranquil place to spend some time, do some shopping, stop and have a drink.

Garrett's business district consisted of a town common—a tree-filled park with a central gazebo—boxed in with four streets lined with coffee shops and restaurants and countless gift shops selling the usual kitsch: mini lobster traps, tiny ceramic lighthouses, toy rubber sharks, life-saver key chains.

A dozen people—many of them obvious tourists decked out in Garrett Island ball caps, lobster-themed T-shirts, and ridiculous cargo shorts with pockets big enough for a week's provisions—were huddled on the raised gazebo, screaming as five Arrivals drove in a continuous circle around them, ripping up grass and dirt with every pass.

Those who'd been sitting at tables in any of the sidewalk cafés had fled, many of them now visible in the storefront windows, watching the show. At least another ten Arrivals were patrolling the streets, moving slowly, ready to pounce on anyone who dared cross their path.

There were gunshots.

Across the common, a man with a pistol in his hand ran from the cover of a small shop, fired wildly at an Arrival driving past—with no apparent effect—then ran back into the building before the car had a chance to change course and teach him a lesson.

Farther down the street, a woman holding a shotgun blasted out the windshield of a maroon Arrival as it sped past. When the car screeched to a halt and started to reverse, the woman scurried into a narrow alley.

It was the fucking Wild West, Kyle thought.

Who knew so many people here would *have* guns? Wasn't Garrett Island the heartland of liberal America? Would Lisa Carver have thought for a moment that she could get everyone in a town in Texas to give up their pickup trucks in exchange for her pipsqueak cars? No. She picked Garrett Island not only because it was isolated, but because she knew it was off the East Coast, populated with liberal-leaning, gun-control-loving, freedom-of-choice-advocating folks who were happy to do their part for road safety, and the environment, by giving up gas-guzzling vehicles they might actually have enjoyed driving, in return for battery-powered self-navigating oversized shopping carts. These were the kind of people just *begging* to pay a carbon tax.

And yet, behind that lefty, latte-loving exterior, many of these folks were packing heat.

In addition to the sounds of shots, there were screams. But one woman's cries of anguish could be heard over all others. Kyle spotted her on the raised patio of a wine bar, pointing out to the street, her arm following the path of one of the cars.

"My baby!" she cried. "It's got my baby!"

Kyle scanned the cars doing laps around the common. A yellow one had a child's safety seat in the back and, in it, a child—it went by too quickly for Kyle to be able to tell whether it was a boy or a girl—who looked no more than three or four. The child was patting his arms up and down on the padded shelf of the seat and appeared to be wailing.

"Jesus," Kyle said under his breath. "Jesus."

The kid will be okay, he told himself. As long as the car just keeps wandering around, what could happen to the child? The youngster was safer *in* the car than outside.

Right?

At some point, someone would be able to rescue the kid. So, okay, the child would be hungry by that time. There'd probably be a load in the kid's pants. Briefly traumatized. But that was survivable. Kyle didn't need to worry himself about—

The Arrival with the child on board began to swerve sharply. The wheels turned hard left, then hard right, then left again. It was going down the street like a sidewinder snake moving at high speed.

As the car made another pass, weaving wildly the entire way, Kyle caught a better glimpse of the sole passenger.

A little boy. His head was bouncing from side to side in sync with the car's movements. And his crying appeared to be more frantic now than on the last lap. What the hell was the car doing?

Kyle knew.

The car was toying with him.

"Shit," he said. A few more laps and the kid would end up with—what did they call it?—shaken baby syndrome.

He glanced at his watch. Derek should be to the harbor by now, waiting. He needed to get to the other side of the common, which he figured could be done by taking a circuitous route behind the stores.

"Stop it!" the woman screamed at the car. "Stop shaking him!"

Out of nowhere, a young man with shoulder-length, scraggly black hair, dressed in jeans and a T-shirt, ran into the street with a metal chair from one of the restaurant patios. He stood in the car's weaving path, and when it was no more than thirty feet away, he tossed the metal chair directly at it, then leapt out of the way.

Despite the Arrival's inherent skills at accident avoidance, it was not able to swerve in time and ran over the chair, which instantly became caught in the vehicle's undercarriage. The chair sparked as it was dragged across the pavement. The car, its right front wheel now suspended several inches off the road, came to a wobbly halt.

"Yes! Yes!" the woman cried, watching with her palms welded to her cheeks.

The baby still had to be freed. A second man from the same restaurant patio ran out with another metal chair and used it to smash the front side window of the car, but not before yelling at the child to close his eyes.

The kid closed his eyes.

Once the glass had crumbled, the long-haired

guy—thinner and more agile—crawled through the opening, reached between the front seats to the back, and released the little boy from his safety seat. He handed him through the open window to the other man, who rushed the baby back to the arms of the weeping mother.

It was, Brandon Kyle had to admit to himself, an amazing thing to watch.

"That was something," he said under his breath.

As he slipped into an alley between two storefronts that would lead him closer to the harbor, he wanted to believe he was only seconds from attempting to save that boy himself.

I'd have thought of something.

I'd have acted.

I'm not a monster.

But in the end, well, it wasn't necessary. Others stepped up. And good for them, whoever they were.

Kyle's conscience was clear.

Up ahead, he saw boats.

Eighteen

There was another huge *fwump* as the Arrival carrying—no, imprisoning—Archie and Rory and Nick tossed one more Garrett Mall shopper onto the hood. A well-dressed, silver-haired woman in her early seventies rolled until she was facedown across the windshield, her face a mask of agony and horror.

A driver in a conventional car would have had to hit the brakes at this point, what with the view forward blocked. But the green Arrival had its own electronic eyes mounted all over the vehicle, and kept on moving.

Nick, up front, was close enough to the windshield to see the woman mouth: *"Help me."*

"Make it stop!" Archie cried.

Nick shouted the name his father had given the vehicle: "Pamela! Pamela, *stop!*"

But Pamela wasn't listening. Or if she was, she wasn't interested in taking orders. She was too busy looking for other shoppers to mow down. The car's detour into the mall hadn't even lasted a minute yet, but people were already screaming and shouting, alerting others to find cover.

They were running into stores, diving behind kiosks. Shoppers already inside some retailers were foolishly running out, wondering what the hell was going on.

There wasn't just one crazy Arrival to worry about.

Arrivals from the parking lot—presumably belonging to people now inside shopping—were now streaming into the massive building, motion sensors at the entrance kindly obliging and sliding open the glass doors with each approaching car.

When Pamela reached the end of the concourse it executed a wide, one-hundred-and-eighty-degree turn that was enough to toss the woman off the hood and deliver her to the entrance of JC Penney.

Three stores ahead of where the Arrival was headed, out front of the Payless Shoes, an armed mall security guard took aim. Archie, looking ahead through the blood-smeared windshield, shouted, with no hope of being heard: "Don't shoot us!"

The guard evidently saw them and aimed low for the car's tires. But the bullet hit the floor, ricocheted wildly, and the Arrival kept on coming, straight for him.

The guard dived blindly into the shoe store, taking down a portable rack of marked-down sandals with him. The Arrival whizzed past, missing him by inches.

The boys, heading back in the direction from which they'd come, had their first glimpse of the other cars invading the mall.

"Oh, fuck, look what they're doing," Rory said.

The Arrivals were filing into the main concourse with orderly precision. First, they came in a straight line, like elephants in a trunk-to-tail formation. But then they broke apart and regrouped, side by side like a row of soldiers, barely an inch between them.

"We have to get out!" Nick said. "We have to—"

A phone started ringing.

"Whose is that?" Rory yelled.

Archie patted his thigh. He'd tucked his phone down into the front pocket of his jeans. "It's me!"

He dug his hand in, pulled out the phone, and looked at the name on the screen.

LISA CARVER.

Who the hell was *that*? But so what, Archie figured. Even a wrong number, at this moment, might be helpful if whoever it was could call the cops. He steadied his thumb over the phone and prepared to accept the call.

CRASH.

"What the fuck!" Nick screamed.

Rory screamed, too, but without words. Just a primal cry of pure fear.

Archie got tossed sideways in his seat and lost his grip on the phone, which hit the floor and slid under the front seat. He looked around to see what they'd run into.

It turned out to be something that had run into *them*. The back side window was shattered.

"What was that?" Archie asked.

Nick said, "Some guy just threw a fire extinguisher!"

It struck Archie as pretty dumb to think you could stop one of these cars by doing that, but as it happened, an opportunity had presented itself. He shifted himself around until his back was on the seat, and his feet were in position to hit the glass, just as soon as Rory got out of the way.

"Watch out, Rory!" he said.

Rory scrambled into the front seat as Archie drove his feet, together, into the already shattered glass. The glass buckled outward, sprinkling the interior with a few shards. Archie brought his knees to his chest a second time, and pounded the glass again with the soles of his runners.

The entire pane shattered. Glass crystals showered the seat and the mall floor as the car continued to move toward one of the two banks of approaching cars.

"Yes!" Nick cried.

Archie scrambled back onto his knees, and extended the sleeve of his jacket over his hand, clearing bits of glass from the lower edge of the window. "When we get a chance, we jump."

The approaching Arrivals had slowed, shifting slightly to create some space in the middle. Pamela was slowing, turning, and then stopping. The car was, it appeared, waiting for the other cars to come up alongside so it could be part of the larger formation.

Nick and Rory crawled over the front seat and crowded into the back with Archie, who said, "We're heading straight in there." The other boys looked. Their escape route turned out to be a Victoria's Secret store.

"Now!" Archie said.

"*Don't leave now,*" Pamela said. "*The fun's just starting.*"

Archie tumbled out the window, landing on the floor on his back. "Shit!" he said. But he didn't take long to dwell on the pain. Rory was about to drop onto him. Archie scrambled to his feet, moving toward the store in the process.

Rory got through the window without stumbling and ran as far as the entrance to the store, then stopped to make sure Nick got out safely.

Nick scrambled through, but instead of following, he ran around the back of the Arrival to the railing for a view down into the lower level of the mall.

"Come on!" Rory shouted at him.

But Nick stayed at the railing and pointed down. "There's none of them down there!" he said.

It was true. Peering down into the lower level, people were standing about, looking upward, wondering what the hell was happening. The only way to reach the lower level was by a set of escalators only a short distance away.

"Down there!" Nick said. "It's safe!"

But the Arrival they'd just escaped from clearly didn't want Archie and Rory to join their friend. It turned its wheels sharply, as if getting ready to drive directly into Victoria's Secret.

"Shit, man," Archie said, grabbing Rory by the arm. "We can't chance it. We go that way and the car's gonna get us for sure. We gotta stay in here."

But Nick was still waving them his way.

"No!" Archie shouted. "If you can make it to the escalator, go!"

The car started to advance.

"Come on!" Archie said, yanking Rory's arm. The two of them started running into the store, dodging around displays of underwear on a table and countless racks of bras and panties and swimsuits. There was no one else in the store. Clearly, customers and staff who'd been here had managed to get out somehow, or had slipped into another, nearby retailer.

Running deeper into the store, they passed a mannequin decked out in seductive black lingerie, the fake woman's hand posed provocatively on her hip. Rory paused his escape for half a second, his eyes feasting on the sight.

"Whoa," he said.

Archie grabbed him once again. "Are you shitting me? Come on!"

Pamela was plowing full speed into the store, knocking tables out of the way, running over racks as they fell in her path.

"Fuck!" Archie said.

The two of them rounded the cashiers' counter and slipped through an open doorway that led, presumably, to a stockroom. Once inside, Archie grabbed hold of the door and slammed it shut.

Rory had been moving so quickly he had to reach out and grab the post of a shelving unit to slow himself down.

"What are we gonna do?" he shouted.

"It can't get through this," Archie said, nodding at the door, which was less than three feet wide.

On the other side, they could hear the car crashing into things, trying to make its way to the back of the store.

"Yeah, well, we can't stay in here forever!" Rory said.

"See if there's another door," Archie said.

"Another door?"

"Yeah, like to a service corridor."

"A what?"

Archie sighed. "Didn't you ever see *Terminator*?"

"Which one?"

"The good one. The second one. *Judgment Day*. Remember Arnie goes down that hallway out the back of the store? It's all cement bricks and stuff?"

Rory nodded slowly. "I do. There really *are* secret hallways like that?"

"Could you just look?"

Archie was staying by the door, fighting the temptation to open it a crack to see what Pamela was up to. It was suddenly very quiet on the other side. Maybe Pamela had decided to rejoin her mechanical friends.

Archie said, "Hey, do you know anyone named Lisa Carver?"

"No! Why?"

"Before we got out of the car, someone with that name called my phone. There wasn't time to answer. And my phone's still in the car."

"Well, that was dumb. But—hey, I found a door!" Rory's voice was coming from behind a bank of shelves.

"Where are you?"

"Back here. Shit, it's locked."

"You can't open it from this side?"

"What did I just say?" Rory snapped. "The door is fucking locked."

Which meant, Archie thought, if they didn't want to stay in this back room till the end of time, they had to go back out through the store. Maybe Nick had the right idea. Get to the bottom level, where it was safe. And hey, wasn't there a food court down there? Would the New York Fries have the hot dogs going yet? It'd be like that fucking *Dawn of the Dead* movie, the one where they were all trapped in the mall, waiting for the zombie apocalypse.

Archie wondered which was worse. Zombies, or killer cars? At least with zombies, once they got you, they let you join the club. But with killer cars, once they drove over you, it was game over.

Archie put his ear to the door.

Nothing.

Slowly, he turned the door handle, opened it half an inch, and—

The door burst inward, knocking Archie back into a shelf, and down onto the floor. The front of the Arrival was too wide to make it through the door, but had hit the framing around it with enough force to open it.

Pamela had been quietly waiting.

"Archie!" shouted Rory when he saw Archie on the floor and the busted door.

"It's okay," Archie said. "She can't fit in."

Pamela backed up five feet, taking part of the jamb with her, then sped forward again. The wall around the door started to crumble.

Archie scrambled to his feet.

"You sure you can't get that back door open?"

Rory said, "Maybe there's a key in one of the drawers at the checkout."

Archie shot him a look. "Well, then why don't you go out there and take a look?"

Pamela backed up and shot forward again. More of the framing around the door gave way. The Arrival had now made its way into the stockroom, almost as far as the windshield. When Pamela tried ramming her way in a fourth time, she gained another foot.

"We should have gone with Nick!" Rory said.

Rory had no idea how wrong he was.

Nineteen

Katie, her hands still firmly gripping the Cadillac's massive steering wheel at ten and two, glanced over at Bruce at the other end of the couch-like bench seat, and asked, "So how'd you end up with this land yacht? You buy it new?"

"Just how old do you think I am?" Bruce asked.

"Well, if this came out in fifty-nine, and you were, like, twenty or something, that'd make you—hang on . . ."

"You need a calculator? Kids today can't figure out anything in their heads. Need to press a few buttons to know the answer to anything."

"Bite me," Katie said. "So if you were born in 1940, you'd be nineteen, so it's possible. What year *were* you born?"

"Forty-one," he said. "And no, I did not buy it new. What eighteen-year-old kid has the money to buy a goddamn Caddy off the dealer's lot? Car like this would have been six, seven grand."

Katie shot him a look. "Six grand? You can't buy a basic Hyundai for six grand."

"Well, it was a hell of a lot of money back then." He pointed. "Let's take the scenic route. Make a left."

"That's not the way to the mall."

"Don't worry. We'll get to the mall and find your baby brother. But if we take Gull Road, we can skirt around the outside of town and come at the mall from the back side. It's a country road, hardly anyone on it, and seeing as how this land yacht, as you call it, is not supposed to be out and about during this period of grand experimentation, it's the most circumspect way to go."

Katie shot him another look. "What did you used to do for a living?"

Bruce said, "I was a high school English teacher."

"There's a shocker. You're good at using a big word when a small one would do the trick. Is that what drove you to drink? Having to deal with tons of teenagers every day?"

Bruce frowned at her.

"I'm sorry," she said, eyes forward. "That was kind of asshole-ish."

Bruce shrugged it off. "Don't worry about it."

"No, really, that was shitty of me."

"I think I'd have become a drunk no matter what," Bruce said. "I was born with the inclination. Truth is, I liked teaching."

Katie, taking the route Bruce had suggested, was soon driving out of the residential area and into undeveloped parts of Garrett Island, of which there were many. Elected officials who'd presided over the island had been careful not to let development get out of control, much to the disappointment of folks in the housing and real estate business who, given the opportunity, would have turned every square inch into a profit.

"So, like, you didn't answer my question," she said.

"What was the question?"

"How'd you end up with this car?"

"Oh," he said, and his voice softened. "So, when I was about twenty, my dad bought this car. And yeah, he bought it new. All he ever wanted in life was a new Cadillac. He made an okay living. Owned a small chain of three grocery stores up in central Mass, but it wasn't like he was a millionaire or anything. But then he sold the stores, getting ready for retirement, and he bought himself this Caddy."

"Okay," Katie said, watching the road ahead. Since leaving Bruce's house, they hadn't encountered a single Arrival. The roads were empty, except for the occasional squirrel racing across.

"God, how he loved this car. It was the icing on the cake of his career. It showed he had made it. He had a fucking Cadillac. He'd drive around town, the windows down, his elbow on the door, one hand on the wheel, sometime, doing that cool move where you rest your wrist on the top of the wheel?" He glanced over. "Don't try that."

Katie tightened her grip. "Don't worry."

Bruce smiled sadly. "He was so proud of this car. My mom, she called it his mistress for a while there. Said he loved this car more than he loved her, which, of course, was nonsense." He considered his last comment for a second. "Or maybe not. She never drove, so she never had any real appreciation for cars. But this car was Dad's baby. And I'm glad that, for at least a while, he had a chance to enjoy it."

Katie said, "What do you mean, for a while?"

"So, three months he's had the car, and he gets this bad cough. Horrible cough. Sounds like it's starting down in his toes. So he goes to the doctor and guess what they find?"

Katie glanced his way. She had a pretty good idea, but didn't want to say.

"Cancer," Bruce said. "Lung cancer. At least, it started as that. But then it spread all through him. By the time they opened him up, there was nothing they could do. I mean, they took out one lung, the really bad one, but there was cancer in both. But you can't exactly take out both lungs, right?" A sardonic chuckle. "So they took the one, and that was supposed to buy him some time." He paused. "Except it didn't."

"How . . . long?" Katie asked.

"Died within two months. So this car, this, to me, was his legacy."

"So you kept it."

Bruce, looking ahead, shook his head slowly. "No."

"You didn't?"

"My mom sold it."

"Oh no."

"I pleaded with her not to. But I'd moved out by that time. I was at Boston College when Dad got sick, and came home for a while, but I got a teaching job in Braintree, my first one. I made Mom promise me she wouldn't sell it, and she said she wouldn't, but then I came home on a break and the car's gone."

"Jesus."

"Yeah. I flipped out. But she said there was no point in keeping it. No one could drive it, and it was taking up all that space in the driveway. I couldn't believe it. I found out who she'd sold it to, some guy across town, and I tried to buy it back from him, even give him more than he'd paid for it, but there was no way."

"Did you even have that kind of money?"

"No. If he'd said yes, I don't know what I'd have done. Robbed a bank, maybe."

"So, how'd you end up getting it back?"

"I kept tabs on it. Every time I was back home, I'd drive by that dipshit's house, see if the car was still there. Would drive me crazy when I saw how he was taking car of it. The car always looked dirty, and sure, a black car is hard to keep clean, but you can make an effort, you know? And then, one day—this is about five years later—the car's not there. I figure, okay, he's out someplace, but I drive by later and there's a *different* Caddy in the drive. A newer one. He traded in my dad's car! So I go up to him and ask him, where's the car, what happened to it? And he says, who are you? Who am *I*? Had no idea, no memory of me coming to see him years before."

"So who got the car?"

"He sold it, privately, to this son of a bitch by the name of Arnie Gloster, a condom salesman."

"Get out."

"Not kidding you. Worked for one of the big pharmaceutical companies, drove all over New England selling the things out of the trunk." He grinned. "You could stuff enough cases in the back end of this car for the whole eastern seaboard. So, he put a lot of miles on it, and he didn't take much better care of it than the first guy. So now, I've been teaching a few years, and I'm married, but I've never given up hope of buying that car back."

"Quick question."

"Go ahead."

"How long did you stay mad at your mom?"

Bruce pursed his lips. "Long time." He pointed. "Check it out."

About a hundred yards up, a deer emerged from the woods on the right side of the road and sprinted across, disappearing into the forest on the other side. "Whoa," Katie said, taking her foot off the gas and tapping the brake. "Glad we weren't any closer."

"Just hold off a second . . ."

"What?"

"There," he said, still pointing. Two smaller deer darted across the road in pursuit of the larger one. "She's got kids."

"Aww," said Katie. "I've seen the odd deer, but never a family."

All three had slipped into the woods, so Bruce gave Katie a nod to get back up to speed.

"Don't you think it's weird we haven't seen another Arrival?" Katie asked.

"Just as well," Bruce said. "So, anyway. I would keep tabs on this condom salesman, and one day, I'm driving through Malden, and there's this black Caddy parked out front of Jenken's Drugs. This'd be 1970. I'm thinking, is that my dad's car? So, out of curiosity, I pull over a block up and walk back to check it out. And sure enough, it was."

"How could you tell?"

"When my dad first got the car, second day I think it was, he backed into a fire hydrant. Couldn't believe it. Had the car two days! He put this little dimple in the chrome bumper, on the back right, way down below the fin. Dad never got it fixed. He left it there as a reminder to himself, to be careful. And he also believed, as long as that dimple was there, the rest of the car wouldn't get hit. So, I looked, and the dimple was there."

"Wow. So, let me guess. Condom Man comes back and you make a deal."

"Not exactly," Bruce said.

"So, he sold it and you got it from the next *guy*."

"Wrong again. The windows were open, and I look inside, and the keys are in the ignition. And I thought, the dumb son of a bitch. Anyone could steal this car. This special car, this car that was my father's *legacy*."

"So, you chewed Condom Man out when he came back?" Katie made a face, like she'd bit into a lemon. "I think that was a bad choice of words. But is that what you did?"

Bruce shook his head. "No." He paused. "I took it."

"What?" Katie looked over so suddenly the wheel shimmied in her hand. The car did a minor swerve.

"Careful," Bruce said.

"You took the car? Like, to teach him a lesson? And then you returned it?"

Now Bruce was grinning. "Nope."

Katie blinked. "You stole it?"

He nodded.

"This is a stolen car?"

"That it is," he said. "Stole it on August 4, 1970. Been mine ever since."

"No way." Katie was incredulous. "I'm driving a hot car? I'm behind the wheel of a stolen automobile?"

"Don't worry about it," he said casually. "Been

more than fifty years. Don't think anyone's looking for it now."

"How—where—"

"Had a barn on our property. Hid it there. Fixed it up. Needed some bodywork. Tuned up the engine. Got it back into perfect shape. Stole some plates for it, and after—if you can believe it—five years, took it out on the rode for the first time. Figured, by then, no one was looking for it anymore."

Katie, still aghast, managed one shocked laugh. "You were an English teacher, and a car thief?"

"Not many of those around," Bruce conceded. "So far as I know. It's not like there's a club of guys who are experts in Shakespeare and hotwiring a car."

A phone started ringing.

"That must be you," Bruce said. "I don't have a cell phone, and I'm pretty sure this car didn't come with Bluetooth."

Katie took one hand off the wheel and took the phone from her pocket. She handed it over to Bruce. "Who is it?" she asked.

Bruce looked at the screen. "Lisa Carver."

"Who?"

Bruce repeated the name.

"I don't know anyone with that name," Katie said. "Must be a wrong number. Just decline it."

"How do I do that?"

Katie told him to hit the red button on the screen. Bruce tapped it, and the phone stopped ringing.

"Okay," said Katie, not yet ready to leave the stolen car story, "so, this can't be the car you got pulled over in, when, you know. I'm trying to be delicate here."

"When I was drunk? No, it wasn't this car. If it had been, once they ran a check on the plate, well, I'd have been in even deeper shit."

"What did your wife think about you keeping a stolen car?"

Bruce smiled sadly. "It was, as they say, a bone of contention. She'd never ride in it with me. She was too scared. Figured if I got stopped she'd be considered an accomplice." He grinned. "I was Clyde without a Bonnie when I went for a joyride."

Katie remained dumbfounded. "For fifty years you've had a stolen car. How did you get your other car back?"

"Drove the Caddy home, hid it, took the bus back to Malden. Simple. Even saw the cops questioning people." A broad smile. "They even asked me if I'd seen anything. I said, who'd do such a thing, the bastard."

He paused and looked thoughtful. "That actually might have been when it started. Or when it got worse."

"What?"

"My drinking. It's not like I didn't have a guilty conscience, stealing this car. I kept worrying, those first few years, the cops would show up one day. That they'd catch me, charge me. Even if they didn't send me to jail, I'd be finished. The school board would have fired me in a New York minute. So I started drinking. After five years, once I was sure I was going to get away with it, I was pretty much set in my ways, drinking-wise."

"So maybe it wasn't such a good idea, after all."

Bruce stuck out his jaw and shook his head. "Don't regret it for a second. *This is my father's car.* Even if a couple of others had it over the years, this was and always shall be my father's car."

"What about . . . after?" Katie asked.

Bruce smiled wryly. "After I'm gone?"

She nodded.

"You want it?"

Before Katie could answer, Bruce pointed again. "There's one."

Katie, who had her eyes on the road, knew he did not mean another deer. They were, finally, encountering a car on Gull Road. A silver Arrival could be seen, about half a mile ahead, approaching in the opposite lane.

"Silly little things," Bruce said.

Katie squinted. "Doesn't even look like anyone's in it."

"Maybe whoever's in it is havin' a nap. Gotta say, for a guy who's not allowed to drive, that might be just the ride for me."

"Can you have an Arrival if you've had a drunk driving conviction?"

"Don't see why not."

"Why am I even asking?" Katie said. "If my brother's dumbass friend can go around town in one, I guess it's okay if anyone—"

"Hello," Bruce said.

Katie's jaw dropped. "What's he—what's *it* doing?"

The Arrival had moved into their lane. It

was coming straight for them, but was still far enough away.

Katie hit the horn.

"Out of my way, idiot!" she shouted.

"Flash your lights," Bruce said. "Might be easier for its sensors to pick up."

Katie, who had been doing her practice drives in the middle of the night, needed no time to find the light switch. She turned them on and off quickly.

The Arrival kept on coming.

"Slow down a titch," Bruce said, "and start pulling over onto the shoulder."

Katie nodded, took her foot off the accelerator, and turned the wheel slightly to the right. As the right tires transitioned from asphalt to gravel, stones could be heard kicking up into the wheel wells.

The Arrival, continuing to advance, moved over onto the shoulder.

"Christ on a trampoline," Bruce said. "Get back on the road! Crank it hard! Head to the other shoulder!"

Katie spun the wheel, the back end of the car fishtailing, gravel spraying out from the rear right wheel. She aimed the car for the left shoulder, tromping on the gas at the same time. The massive car lumbered from one side of the road to the other like a whale with wheels.

The Arrival mirrored Katie's moves, and continued to close the distance.

Twenty

Lillian Bridgeman sat in her wheelchair and watched the cars and people go by. It was a way to pass the time. It was about all she had these days.

Lillian was stationed at the end of the driveway, a good place from which to observe the world. Well, not the world exactly, but wasn't Gilbert Street, in the town of Garrett, on Garrett Island, part of the Commonwealth of Massachusetts, within the magnificent United States of America, as good a representation of the world as anyone could want? Didn't Gilbert Street have everything anyone could ever hope to see? You didn't have to go to the big city to watch life's dramas played out for you. They happened right here.

Just this week, one of the McClatchen kids from down the street had taken a tumble off his skateboard and scraped his knee. Anthony, his name was. Eight, nine years old. Lillian had called out to him, asked if he was okay as he got back on his feet. He hobbled his way over to her, close enough that she could see the ragged skin and the blood dripping down his leg. He was biting his lip, trying not to cry.

"That could get infected," she said. "You need to go home, get that cleaned up and bandaged."

"I don't know how to do that," Anthony said.

"Get your mom to do it," she said.

"She's at work."

Lillian frowned. "Who's watching out for you all day?"

The boy shrugged.

"Here's what we're going to do," she said, and then gave him very specific instructions about where in her house he would find what she needed to patch him up. He was afraid, at first, confessing later that he had never forgotten the story of Hansel and Gretel and the witch that tried to eat them. But finally he was persuaded to head inside and get the kit. Once he returned with it, she leaned forward in her chair and fixed him up.

There was a bit of drama for you.

And then there was the Salters, across the street and one house over. Blake and Nina. The newlyweds. Well, that's what they were two years ago. But judging by their conversation the other morning, the honeymoon was definitely over. They came out the front door every morning at eight, both getting into their little Toyota— Blake in the passenger seat and Nina behind the wheel. This was before they were given an Arrival, of course. A few days before everyone surrendered their cars for one of those newfangled ones, Nina had come striding out of the house first, letting the door swing shut on her husband as he followed her. She wouldn't look at him as he said, "Oh, for Christ's sake, if you want your mother here, fine, but for a weekend, not for an entire fucking week."

She got into the car, and when he went around to the passenger side, he'd found the door locked.

"Come on," he said, banging his fist on the window. "Stop being a cunt."

Lillian Bridgeman could hardly believe her ears. But what she saw amazed her more. Nina unlocked the door for him, let him in, and off they went. Lillian couldn't imagine her late husband ever using that word with her. If he had, she *could* imagine what she might have done. A cast iron frying pan upside the head next time he turned his back on her, she thought.

She liked being close to the road so she could have a front row seat to these little dramas. If she were up on the porch, she wouldn't be able to make out the cast of characters as easily, what with her eyesight declining these past few years. You got to be eighty-one and some of the equipment started breaking down. Some of it already had. Like her legs, which still worked but didn't keep her standing for very long.

It was a good thing her son had arranged for that girl, Daniella—okay, young woman—to check on her a couple of times a day while he was off being the island lawman. She'd wheel her back up the ramp and into the house, make her some lunch, or assist her on a trip to the bathroom. She'd be coming along shortly, and just as well, because Lillian was feeling a tad peckish, as her own mother used to say, so many years ago. Lillian could manage to make herself a lunch if she had to, but getting back into the house was something she could not manage alone. She no longer had the strength in her arms to get up the ramp to the porch and her front door.

Lillian did love the fall. She could still be outside, and she loved to see the leaves change. Every day, another splash of color to enjoy. When it was raining she didn't venture off the porch. And once it got cold, she'd watch the street's events from the living room window. She didn't read that much anymore. There was a time she could read a book a day—there were so many Danielle Steel novels to gobble up that Lillian wondered if that woman didn't *write* one every day—but it was harder for her to concentrate now, and watching the world go by demanded less brainpower and was often more entertaining.

Although, if there was a downside—and didn't everything have a downside?—sitting out here also gave her time to think. And what she was thinking was what her son, the chief of police, might be planning to do with her. He'd been talking more and more about this or that seniors' home. How *nice* it would be for her to have her meals made for her. How *wonderful* it would be to have people to socialize with every day. How *convenient* it would be to just press a button whenever she had a problem and someone would come running. How *positively splendid* it would be, when you had to go to the bathroom, not to have to take a weewee in your Depends while you waited for Daniella to show up? Okay, maybe Joe had not actually said *positively splendid* or *weewee* but he had hinted that very sentiment.

So he was ready to have her locked away somewhere. Lillian had a pretty good idea why, too. He'd met some woman. Sandy or Sandra or something. Sure, he'd met other women over the years, but things had never gotten serious enough with any of them to make Lillian worry that their living arrangements might change.

Before her more recent decline, if Joe had decided to set her up in her own apartment, she probably could have managed on her own. But now that she was increasingly disabled, Joe couldn't take that route. He had to find her a *home* if he met someone and wanted to have some woman move in with him. Three of them under the same roof, that would never work.

Soon as I carry you over the threshold, could you help my mom find her teeth?

Yeah, that would go over well. Lillian could only hope this latest romance would end the way all the others had. Joe had a tendency to push too hard, scare the girls off. Maybe he'd do that with this one, and then Lillian wouldn't have to worry about—

Now that's funny.

The red Arrival parked in the Smitherses' driveway, two doors up, was quietly backing out onto the street. Once there, it straightened and headed for the business district of downtown Garrett.

Maybe what she'd seen wasn't so strange, after all. Couldn't you summon one of these cars with your phone? Just tell it where you were and it would come and get you? And didn't the Smitherses walk to work in the morning? Maybe one of them needed the car and didn't want to have to go home and get it.

Yes, that was probably what happened. They—

Well, there goes another one.

A yellow Arrival, five doors up the other way—

Lillian didn't know their names, they never acknowledged her when she saw them walk by and she said hello—was doing the same thing. Backing onto the street and heading off.

Over the next couple of minutes, she saw five cars without passengers head down Gilbert Street.

What a world, she thought. The changes she'd seen in her lifetime. Could she have imagined, when she was a little girl, that one day cars would drive themselves? That all you'd have to do to get someplace would be to say a few words to your Chevy or your Ford or your DeSoto—*oops, dating myself there*, she thought—and before you knew it, you were at your destination. She'd been afraid to ride in an Arrival until her son persuaded her it was perfectly safe. The little car—a special one equipped with a police radio and lots of other equipment—had taken them all over the island one day. She'd been nervous at first, but by the time the car had brought them home, she thought it was the greatest thing since the invention of the heating pad.

So all over town, she surmised, people were telling their cars to haul ass and come pick them up. No more waiting around for a strange taxi. It was nothing short of amaz—

What in the Sam Hill was that?

An awful noise from the west end of the street. A distant tree partially obstructed her view, so she leaned forward slightly to see around it. She was trying to think what the sound reminded her of. Like dropping a sack of potatoes off a tall building.

But a sack of potatoes didn't scream.

There was an Arrival coming down the street. Well, duh, she thought. Like, what else would it be? A white one, but with splotches of something on the sloped hood.

Red splotches.

The car was moving swiftly, above the posted speed limit, Lillian was certain. That seemed odd, considering these cars were programmed to obey all the rules.

As the car got closer, those red splotches became more vivid.

Could they be . . . blood?

Had the car hit a pedestrian? That seemed unthinkable, and looking up the street, she was relieved that she did not see anyone stumbling about, or lying on the pavement.

Aloud, she said to herself, "I wonder what—"

And then the white Arrival drove past her house.

Lillian Bridgeman felt her heart skip a beat, and placed her hand over her chest as if to check that it was still working.

The Arrival was dragging someone down the street. A body—Lillian couldn't tell whether it was a man or woman, young or old—was caught on the car's undercarriage, a dark, ghostly shadow beneath the car.

But there was still screaming.

It wasn't coming from whoever was under the car, but from Lillian herself.

"Oh dear God," she said. "Oh dear God." She had no sooner said the words than the car slowed, coming to full stop about twenty yards past the end of her driveway.

It was as though it had heard her.

Lillian, while unaware of what, exactly, might be happening, suddenly felt very uneasy sitting out here, alone and exposed, at the end of the driveway. She wanted to get back in her house.

Something, clearly, was up with these cars. Those other ones, slipping away quietly all on their own, and now this.

The car slowly began to reverse. Its movements seemed almost cunning. There had been a sound, and now it wanted to find out what it was.

Lillian had a cell phone tucked down in the wheelchair, next to her butt, and briefly considered calling her son. But using her cell phone would leave her no hands free to move this chair. And how fast, realistically, could she expect Joe to get here?

If there were someone else on the street, someone she could shout to for help, someone who could quickly wheel her back up to the house, she'd have given that a try. But there was no one. And if her gut was right, that the car had stopped because it had heard her, she didn't want to attract any more attention by raising her voice.

So she placed a hand atop each wheel and pushed back.

Squeak.

No no no no. Hadn't Joe just pointed out to her that morning that her wheelchair needed a shot of oil? She hadn't even noticed the wheel squeaking. After a while, you just tuned these things out.

Now, it was the loudest sound in the world.

But it was a very faint squeak. Her scream had been much, much louder. If the car was listening, would it really hear a barely audible chirp from the mechanism of her wheelchair?

She pushed back again.

Squeak.

And again.

Squeak.

Slowly, she retreated backward up the level driveway, each partial rotation of the wheel sending lightning bolts of pain up her arms and to her shoulders. She kept her eye on the Arrival the entire time.

As the car slowly reversed, the body trapped underneath twisted like a pretzel. The head appeared stuck in place as the legs moved from the rear of the car to the front. Soon, two bare legs appeared below the front bumper. The toenails were painted a dazzling green.

"Oh my, no," Lillian said.

One foot was shoeless. On the other there remained a mangled, pink strappy sandal.

Lillian took a breath. She recognized the green toenails, that pink sandal.

Daniella.

Lillian kept any further screams tightly bottled up inside her throat. If the car really had heard her, she didn't want it hearing her now.

She pulled back on the wheels, her arms throbbing with pain.

Squeak.

The car stopped at the base of the driveway. It sat there, sideways. Listening.

Lillian, using every ounce of strength she could muster, had backed up more than twenty feet. She was at the house.

She took several seconds to catch her breath. Her throat was dry and parched. She desperately needed a glass of water. Just as soon as she got in the house. She'd wheel herself up to the kitchen tap, and even if she couldn't reach the cupboards for a glass, she'd grab a pot from one of the lower cabinets and drink out of that if she had to.

She suddenly had an uncontrollable tickle in her throat. She tried to gather together some spit, to swallow, to do anything she could to not—

Cough.

The second she coughed, the car's front wheels turned toward the drive. The Arrival, with Daniella's body trapped beneath, sensed her, a hyena with its nose to the wind.

Lillian realized she had only seconds to get into the house. Then it hit her what had to be done to accomplish that.

She had to roll herself up the ramp.

The fucking ramp.

Twenty-One

Goddamn it!" Sandra said. "Pick up!"

Why weren't the kids answering their phones?

Using Lisa Carver's cell, Sandra had tried to raise Archie, then Katie, and struck out both times. She was this close to slipping into panic mode. Crazy cars were knocking people off left, right, and center and she couldn't get hold of the kids.

But panic was not an option. She needed to keep a clear head. If she could manage to do that nine months earlier, when the police knocked on her door to tell her there'd been an accident, she could do it now.

Even in the midst of all this current chaos—the burning fire truck, the Arrivals acting like a pack of wolves, Lisa Carver dead and missing a leg—her mind went back to that night.

It was nearly midnight when Sandra heard, first, the doorbell, then someone rapping hard. Her first thought was that it had to be Adam. He'd gone out on a late-night run to help some woman get her car started, and somehow, she figured, he'd lost his keys and couldn't get into the house. But as she descended the stairs, blue and red beams of light strobed through the window and bounced off the walls. Before opening the door, she glanced outside and saw a Garrett

Island police car idling at the curb, wisps of exhaust from the tailpipe caught in the soft glare of a streetlight.

She opened the door. Standing there was Joe Bridgeman. She recognized him immediately. They'd spoken many times. Run into each other at the local fish and chip joint, ended up in the same lineup at the ATM. Garrett Island was a small enough place that it was hardly a coincidence when you bumped into people you knew.

His jaw was set firmly, and he took his hat off before he said, "Sandra."

She knew it had to be bad. She knew it had to be about Adam.

Sandra could barely make out the sentences coming out of Joe's mouth. What she heard were key words. She heard "Adam." She heard "Pelican Point." She heard "accident." She heard "asleep at the wheel." She heard "so sorry." She heard "pronounced dead at the scene."

The disjointed words were enough to put it all together.

Once she was over the initial shock—and really, had that happened *yet*?—the first thing she thought about, even before she considered what this loss meant to her, was how it would devastate Katie and Archie.

For a millisecond, she had this wild, irrational idea that maybe she could keep the news from them. Stall. Tell them their father had gone on a trip to Bolivia to look for hard-to-find motorcycle parts. Postpone their grief.

Which, of course, was ridiculous. Because within seconds of Chief Joe showing up at her door, the kids were coming down the stairs,

Archie in a pair of Batman pajamas he'd had since he was eight, had refused to retire, and, somehow, still managed to fit into, and Katie in one of her father's old Harley-Davidson T-shirts that came down to her knees.

That was when Sandra nearly lost it, seeing her daughter in that shirt. But somehow, she held it together. If she fell apart, she and her kids would be like three castaways from a sunken ship, all floating off in different directions. She had to be the life raft. She had to be the one who kept them afloat.

"Is that the police?" Archie asked, excited, as though their presence could be anything but thrilling. But Katie's face was shattered. She could read her mother's expression. She knew something bad had happened.

While Joe hung back by the front door, Sandra sat them down in the living room and told them. Archie said there had to be a mistake. He was sure he'd heard his father come home earlier, that he was already in the house, that he couldn't have been on Pelican Point and had an accident because he was here. He'd probably gotten into bed next to his mother and she hadn't even noticed.

Sandra tried to stop him, but he slipped from her arms and ran upstairs to check. And when he failed to find his father, he began to shout his name.

"Dad! Dad! Where are you! Wake up! There's been a mix-up!"

Tears ran down Katie's face. A moment later, Archie stood at the top of the stairs and whispered, "I can't find Dad."

So Sandra had been their life raft, their port in the storm, their rock—ladies and gentlemen, choose your favorite cliché. She had held them together, done everything she could to support them, even working for assholes like Albert Ruskin and Lisa Carver (not wishing to speak ill of the dead, of course), and there was no way, no how, that a bunch of fucked-up Dinky Toys were going to stop her now.

Sandra was going to find her kids and make sure they were safe.

All she had to do was figure out how to do that.

It was time to look for Ruskin. He was the one most likely to have some answers. He'd rebuffed her before, ignored her when she'd asked to use his phone.

Sandra wasn't in the mood for any more fucking rebuffing.

Albert Ruskin was on hold with Arrival tech support.

On hold. The assistant to the CEO was *on hold.*

The company had established a tech support line on day one. A toll-free number Arrival owners could call anytime, day or night, if they were having an issue with their vehicle. The Arrival turned out to be such a trouble-free automobile that the techies hired to stand by the phones complained they often had nothing to do. (There had been a story in the *Washington Post* that many of them spent their time surfing porn sites.) Most calls came from new owners having trouble getting their cars to understand their commands. Which was why, when someone took delivery of an Arrival, they were required to read aloud several specially formulated sentences, in the language of their choice, that captured every nuance of a person's speech, regardless of accent or speech defect. But some problems were difficult to predict, like people unfamiliar to New York asking to go to an address on Houston Street, unaware that the New York Houston was pronounced house-ton, not hew-ston, like that city in Texas.

So when Ruskin dialed the number, he was expecting someone to pick up right away, and that whoever that person was, he or she could run some sort of diagnostic on the Arrival system and find a way to reverse what was currently happening. Or, failing that, shut the whole fucking system down.

But what Ruskin, who had slipped back into the community center through a side door, got when he called in was this:

"Thank you for calling the Arrival help line. We are here twenty-four hours a day, seven days a week, to answer your questions about your new Arrival automobile. We are currently experiencing a high volume of calls, but will get to yours as soon as we can."

Cue the elevator music.

"Fuck!" Ruskin said

He had slipped into a men's change room just down the hall from the gymnasium, the smell of sweat and sour towels lingering in the air.

After twenty seconds of music, the voice returned. *"Thank you for holding. We are currently experiencing a high volume of calls. In an effort to expedite assistance to you once your call has made it to the front of the queue, you may enter your car's identification number, followed by the pound sign. Or you may continue to wait for one of our technicians to help you.*"

"Fucking take my call!" Ruskin shouted into his phone.

There followed yet another twenty seconds of the kind of music Ruskin figured would play in hell's waiting room. He was about to give up when there was an audible click, and then a harried, male voice:

"Yes! Arrival support!"

"Who is this?"

"Sir, you've reached Arrival support. My name is Denny. Can you please—"

"Denny who?"

"Sir, please, it's a bit crazy here. Could you tell me you name and—"

"My name is Albert Fucking Ruskin, personal assistant to Lisa Carver, your *late* goddamn boss."

There was a brief pause on the other end of the line while Denny, presumably, took a breath. Then, "Yes, Mr. Ruskin, sir. You're on the line with Dennis McCardle. When you said my *late*—"

"Lisa's dead. Everything's gone to shit here on the island. The cars have all gone nuts. Go into the system and shut everything down. Pull the plug. Bring every Arrival out there to a halt. You hearing me? Kill the brains of the system. Stop the virus."

"Mr. Ruskin, I've already been trying."

Ruskin's brow furrowed. He figured he would

be the first to call in. "Has someone else from the island been in touch? Who? Who called before me?"

"No one, sir. Not from the island. But from . . . everywhere."

Ruskin felt a chill run up his spine. He had not considered that the Arrival malfunction was a problem anywhere but Garrett Island. All these Arrivals, in one place, thinking as one. But it didn't matter where the Arrivals were, they *still* could all think as one. The network was global.

"Tell me," Ruskin said.

"Okay, so, in Duluth, an Arrival ran down a crossing guard and chased a pack of kids—luckily none of them were killed—right into a school. It couldn't make it through the door, and then the police showed up and shot it like it was a wild animal or something. And then, in New York, don't ask me how this is even possible, but one got up onto the High Line, that walkway that used to be a rail line, and tried to mow people down. In Paris, one ran up onto the sidewalk on the Champs-Élysées. In Las Vegas, at the Bellagio or Vellagio or whatever it's called, one got right into the casino, hitting people while they were sitting there playing the slots. And in Scottsdale, four—"

"Enough," Ruskin said. "When did all this start happening?"

"It hasn't even been an hour. Looks like ransomware, maybe, but you said something about a virus?"

Ruskin hesitated. "Well, what the hell else could it be? Delivered into the network by some hackers." He cleared his throat. "Keep looking for a way in and let me know the minute you make any progress. You've got this number?"

"Yes, sir. What . . . what happened to Ms. Carver?"

Ruskin figured he could find out by watching CNN and ended the call.

"There you are!"

Ruskin turned and saw Sandra Montrose marching toward him.

He put the phone into his pocket and said, "This is the men's room."

When she got to within an inch of his face, she said, "You seriously think I give a shit?"

Twenty-Two

Pamela had made several attempts to break into the Victoria's Secret stockroom. The door and its surrounding frame were destroyed, so now the Arrival was hacking away at the surrounding drywall, trying to create an opening large enough that would allow it to completely enter the room and get at Archie and Rory, like that famous shark eating its way through the hull of the *Orca*.

The two boys had taken a defensive position behind a set of metal shelves loaded with boxed merchandise. They had tried, once more, to open the door at the back of the room that led, presumably, to a service corridor that would, in turn, lead outside. But the door was locked, and they had no key.

"If we could get to the checkout counter," Archie said, "and check the drawers, the key might be in there."

"Yeah, well, good luck with that."

There was another crash as the car rammed the opening again. Chunks of wood, drywall, and plaster shot into the room.

"I've got an idea," Archie said. "Next time it does that, I'll jump on the hood, jump off when it backs up, and see if I can find the key."

"That's insane," Rory said.

"No shit. But if I find some keys, I can throw

them to you, and you can see if one of them opens that door."

"Man, if you can get as far as the cash, you could run back into the mall."

"And what's waiting for me *there*?" Archie said. "Hundreds more picking people off one by one."

Rory nodded solemnly, but then remembered something. "If Nick got to the lower level, and we joined him, we could hang with him until help came. These stupid cars haven't got any way to get down there."

Archie thought Rory was right about the lower level of the mall being a safer place, but he was less confident about his friend's expectation that help was on the way. What if this shit was happening all over the island? How many cops did Garrett Island even have? There was Chief Joe What's-His-Name, that guy who came to see them the night his dad died. And he probably had half a dozen working under him. What the hell were they going to do? They needed to bring in the army or the air force or something.

"Okay," Archie said. "Joining Nick can be our backup plan."

The Arrival backed out of the room. It reversed over about ten feet of debris, stopped, readied itself for another charge forward.

Archie whispered, "Get ready to catch some keys."

Rory nodded, eyes wide.

The Arrival suddenly sped forward. There was a deafening crash as it made a larger hole. A couple more runs and the entire car would be in the stockroom.

Archie came running out from behind the

shelves. He leapt onto the front of the Arrival, grabbing the edge of the hood just below the windshield, where the wipers were tucked away, and held on tight. He stayed down low, pressing himself up against the glass, so he wouldn't hit anything when Pamela backed out.

The car reversed. Once it had cleared the damaged wall, Archie leapt off and ran to the space behind the long checkout counter. It was narrow enough that Archie thought he'd be safe there, at least for a couple of minutes.

The car stopped, but instead of charging into the back room again, it sat. Archie had the sense it was watching him. The cars had tiny, invisible-to-the-naked-eye sensors mounted all over them, so even though Archie was off to one side, there was every reason to believe the car was monitoring his movements.

Archie opened the first drawer, where he found price stickers and scissors and rolls of receipt paper and pens, but no keys. He went to the next drawer. More of the same.

The Arrival was turning its front wheels, a clear indication it was going to try and squeeze its way behind the counter.

There was only one drawer left. Archie pulled it out so quickly he yanked it off the track. The drawer, and its contents, rained onto the floor.

"Shit!" he said, dropping to his knees to sort through the scattered contents.

Pamela started pushing against the end of the counter. Archie heard wood splintering as he sorted through more price stickers and slips of paper and—

A set of keys.

"Yes!" he said, snatching them up and standing. There were at least half a dozen on the ring. One of them had to open that back door.

Pamela had buckled the end of the counter, forcing it up over the hood. The front wheels were spinning, looking for traction.

Archie looked through the ever-growing opening into the stockroom and waved the keys at Rory. "Got 'em!"

He threw the keys. Rory had his hands in the air, waiting, but fumbled the catch. The keys bounced off his palms, hit the floor, and slid under the shelving unit.

"Oh crap oh crap oh crap!" Rory screamed. He got down on all fours, putting his head sideways to the floor to peek under the bottom shelf. "I see them!"

The Arrival, having seen the keys fly through the air, abandoned its short-lived efforts to get to Archie, and turned its attention back to entering the stockroom. It backed up several feet, then took another run at the opening.

"Rory!" Archie screamed.

The car's front bumper came to within a foot of Rory's butt. The boy scrambled out of the way at the same time as he pulled his hand out from under the shelf, keys in hand.

Rory got to his feet and ran to the locked door. "Which key?" he shouted.

"How should *I* know?" Archie shouted back.

Rory got the first key into the door and tried to turn it. "Not this one!"

Archie sighed. "So try the next one!"

The Arrival had adopted a new tactic. Instead

of backing up again, it was pushing its way in the room, its front tires spinning, the smell of burning rubber filling Victoria's Secret.

"Hurry!" Archie cried.

Rory continued to fumble with the keys. "I've tried them all! None of them—oh, wait, I think I tried one twice!"

We're all going to die, Archie thought.

Rory found the right key, and shouted, "I got it!"

He opened the door. Archie had a glimpse of gray cinder-block walls. He was right. The door accessed a service corridor.

The Arrival suddenly burst forward, charging toward Rory and the door.

Rory, glancing wide-eyed over his shoulder for a millisecond, jumped through the open doorway just as the car slammed into the wall on either side.

The door closed.

Rory was gone.

With the keys.

Even if Archie could find a way to that door, which appeared impossible now that the car was there, it had probably relocked when it closed.

"Rory!" he shouted.

His friend would come back, right? He could be waiting in the service corridor. Maybe Pamela would head back into the mall to look for other victims, and when she did, Archie could reach the door and tell Rory it was safe to open the door. If he shouted loudly enough, Rory would hear him.

If Rory was still there.

The Arrival whined. It was trying to back up, but its front fenders were now so badly crumpled they were pinching the front tires. The car couldn't move, which meant that even if Rory was out there, that door wasn't going to open.

Archie had to find another way out.

From where he stood, he could see out into the mall, where the occasional Arrival rolled by. The few cars he saw had not sped by. They were not driving erratically. It seemed to Archie that it was almost as if . . .

It was almost as if they were on patrol.

Archie knew, from his many visits to the mall, that the distance from the front of Victoria's Secret to the escalators was not far. Thirty, forty feet, he reckoned. The escalators were right by the Foot Locker, where his mother always bought him his running shoes, always jabbing her thumb into the toe to make sure there was enough growing room to get a year out of them.

If he could reach the escalator, get to the safer lower level, he and Nick could catch their breath while they came up with a plan.

So Archie worked his way to the front of the store, darting from one rack of underwear to the next—at least those that were still standing—just in case any of the passing Arrivals happened to spot him in their peripheral vision. He got to the front of the store and tucked himself around the corner of the entrance so that he could scope things out.

"Oh no," Archie said, looking up the mall to the escalators. He whispered to himself: "I don't believe it."

He was going to have to come up with another plan.

When Nick had became separated from Archie and Rory, he'd made a dash for the escalator, figuring the lower level would be a good place to ride out the storm. He wasn't alone in thinking that. Dozens of shoppers were running for the down escalator, and when it became overloaded, others chose the up escalator, running down it at a faster rate than the steps were ascending. The kind of thing Nick used to do when he was much younger.

Before long, the open area of the upper mall was clear of people—at least those who were still alive. Corpses were scattered everywhere. But luckier ones had made it to the bottom level, and while they might have felt momentarily relieved, no one was feeling particularly secure. Most were looking up, gazing into the open atrium, watching the Arrivals zipping around above them beyond a decorative glass and metal railing.

Thank God the escalators were too narrow for them to use.

Several of the adults around Nick were on their phones, calling for help, warning family members to be careful, and letting those same folks know they were okay. A girl about seven years old was crying, her mother kneeling down, trying to comfort her.

"The police aren't picking up," said one.

"Where the hell are they?" asked another. "They've got to stop them!"

"Look," said another very slowly, pointing to the top of the two escalators. "They're trying to figure it out."

Indeed, they were.

A red Arrival had nosed up to the down escalator. The constantly moving rubber grip rails skimmed by the nose of the car. The Arrival, with its eye-like headlights, seemed to be studying how the escalator worked, the way a raccoon might look at the latest, supposedly tamperproof garbage can.

There has to be a way.

Nick shouted, "Ha! Fuck you, asshole!"

The woman with the little girl shot him a look that said even though they were all at great personal risk, there was no call for that kind of language.

"Yeah, dumbass! I'm talking to you!" Nick slapped his thighs and laughed. "Not so smart, after all!"

Nick leapt onto the down escalator and started climbing. He put enough speed into it that he was able to gain two steps for every one that the escalator dropped. He got to within five steps of the top, able to look the car right in the headlight, and held his position by running in place.

He didn't have to be an engineering major to figure out that the car was stumped. Its sloping hood was a good two feet below the top of the elevator railing. If the Arrival had had a ramp and could mount the escalator, its wheels would straddle the rubber railing and sit on the metal structure that encased the moving stairway.

But there was no ramp.

"What are ya gonna do now, huh?" Nick taunted.

At one point, he stuck two index fingers into his mouth, pulled, and waggled his tongue at the machine.

The car stared at Nick.

Several other Arrivals were gathered behind the red one, sitting there. But then they started to move back, creating a gap behind the red Arrival.

"Giving up?" Nick said. "Going home? Heading back to the tin can factory?"

With space behind it to maneuver, the red Arrival backed up, turned around, and gently backed its rear bumper up to the top of the escalator.

Nick blinked.

The car's aerodynamic wedge shape meant that the back was roughly level with the top of the escalator structure. Nick, distracted by what the car was up to, had descended several steps. He ran back up and did his best to stay in place, climbing nonstop. He wanted to see what they might be planning.

A blue Arrival was lining up with the front of the red one, their noses almost kissing. Another car had lined up behind the blue Arrival, and another one after it, and so on, until there were at least a dozen of the small cars touching end to end.

The blue Arrival started to move forward, driving up, and onto, the hood of the red one.

"What the hell?" Nick said.

The Arrivals didn't need a ramp. They had turned one of their own into one. The blue car rode up the sloped hood of the red one. Metal and plastic snapped and shattered. The red Arrival sank several inches, its tires nearly flattened.

Nick's mouth hung open. "Can't work," he said. "It cannot work."

He figured, once the front tires of the blue Arrival reached the red car's front windshield, it would be game over. The weight of the car would collapse the glass, the blue Arrival's front end would drop into the passenger chamber of the red one, and that would be it.

Panting, he held his position, watching.

The blue Arrival's tires lined up with the pillars on either side of the windshield glass. The pillars bent slightly, but did not give way.

The blue Arrival's front wheels were now on the roof of the red Arrival. All it had to do was drive the rest of the way over the car and off the back end and plant its wheels on the metal housing of the escalator.

If the first car could do it . . .

The blue Arrival's front wheels had reached the trunk. With a small burst of power, it shot forward, making a rough transition from the car below it to the gleaming silver metal that flanked the perpetually moving black handgrips.

The car now straddled the moving stairway.

"Shit!" Nick said, and dropped as the blue Arrival drove right over him.

He glanced up at the passing undercarriage, his disbelieving eyes watching as the car raced down the slope and flew off as it reached the bottom, the front end tipping down and crashing into the mall's lower level.

People screamed and scattered.

While the blue Arrival had suffered extensive front-end damage, it was still operable. It drove a few yards away from the escalator and made a wide circle.

The descending escalator was delivering Nick closer to the lower level with each passing second. He heard more crunching of steel and plastic and looked upward in time to see another Arrival crawl over the red one. The car whizzed over his head. He felt the breeze as it passed.

This second Arrival sustained damage similar to the blue one, but it, too, was still moving, and turning around.

"No no no no," Nick said as another Arrival rolled past overhead.

Nick, scrambling crab-like up the steps on his feet and hands just to stay in one place, suddenly realized the seriousness of his situation.

He couldn't let the escalator drop him off at the bottom. The Arrivals were waiting for him.

And he couldn't go to the top, because that's where all the Arrivals were coming from.

He had to go up this down escalator until these fucking cars were gone.

And who knew how long that was going to be?

Where was that goddamn emergency button? Weren't there big red buttons at the tops and bottoms of escalators to make them stop? He couldn't see any from his position, and he'd be putting himself at huge risk to poke his head out at either end to find one.

"Help!" he shouted. "Help me!"

But all the shoppers who'd been watching the

action from down below were gone. They'd all run into the backs of stores or down hallways to bathrooms to hide out.

Nick had never been much of a swimmer, which was pretty funny when you lived on an island with miles and miles of beaches. Whenever he went to pool parties, he was embarrassed that he didn't know how to do laps. Could never slice through the water the way the other kids did.

All he could do was jump in and tread water.

And even that, he couldn't do for very long. A minute, maybe. Two tops.

Well, this right here, this fucking nightmare on the escalator, *this* was treading water.

And Nick had a bad feeling he was going to have to do it for a lot longer than two minutes if he wanted to stay alive.

Twenty-Three

Katie steered the lumbering Caddy to the other side of the road, the left wheels running onto the gravel shoulder, in a bid to stay out of the approaching Arrival's path. The little silver car had moved into their lane and a head-on crash was imminent before Katie cranked the wheel.

But then the Arrival changed course.

"It's still coming at us," said Bruce, at the passenger end of the huge bench seat.

"I can see that!" Katie shouted.

"Fake it out," Bruce said.

"What?"

"Like you're going one way, but then the—"

Katie figured it out before Bruce could finish the explanation. Riding half on pavement, half on gravelly shoulder, Katie twitched the wheel to the right, as if she intended to get all four wheels back onto asphalt. In the next millisecond, the Arrival adjusted its heading more toward the middle of the road.

And that was when Katie aimed for the ditch.

She jerked the wheel to the left, and the left side of the car dropped off the edge of the shoulder and into the tall grass, tipping on a thirty-degree angle.

"Jesus!" Bruce said, planting his palms onto the dash in front of him.

The Arrival whizzed past them in the other direction. If Bruce had been foolish enough to stick his arm out the window, he'd have been able to touch it. And if Katie had been hanging off the landing skids of a helicopter, her grip wouldn't have been any stronger than the one she had now on that steering wheel.

She felt the car being dragged farther into the ditch, but she fought it, turning the wheel back to the right and planting her foot down harder on the gas. The back end kicked and fishtailed before it found purchase, and the Caddy was launched back onto the pavement, the rear tires squealing.

"*HAAAA!*" she screamed triumphantly. "Did you see that? Did you fucking see that?"

Bruce hung his left arm hung over the back of the seat so that he could turn around and look out the rear window. On the way, he gave Katie a brief, admiring glance. "That was something, I'll give you that."

Katie was taking quick, deep breaths. She glanced in her mirror, looking for the Arrival. "Where is the little shit?"

"It's back there," Bruce said. "You gave him the slip, that's for sure." He hadn't yet turned around to face forward.

"What are you looking at?" she asked as she eased up on the gas and continued to catch her breath.

"I don't know that slowing down is such a good idea," Bruce said.

Katie looked in the mirror again. "No."

"Yeah," Bruce said. "The little shit appears to be turning around."

Katie's eyes went from the mirror to the road ahead and back again to the mirror. "I don't get it!" she said. "What the hell is wrong with it? Why did it try to . . . to . . ."

"Kill us?" Bruce asked.

She shot him a wide-eyed look. "That's insane."

"Of course it's insane," Bruce said. "But that's what happened. That car was deliberately aiming for us."

"So its programming or sensors or whatever must be broken," Katie said. "That doesn't mean it was *trying* to kill us. Not on purpose."

"Well, I'll tell you this. It's very deliberately, and on purpose, coming after us."

Another look at the mirror proved Bruce right. The silver Arrival was in pursuit, and gaining on them.

Katie pressed down on the accelerator and the engine roared.

"It's a fast little bastard," Bruce said, still looking rearward.

"But not faster than this," Katie said. "Right?"

Bruce sighed. "Hard to say. A lot of these new electric cars, they're so light they move pretty quick."

"I gotta call my mom," Katie said.

"Why?"

"She's at the thing, you know, the big event for these cars. If there's something wonky with them, she should know. Or maybe she *does* know what's happening."

She took one hand off the wheel, dug out her phone again, held her thumb on the home button to bring it to life, and handed it to Bruce.

"Go into the contacts and call up *Mom*. You know how to do that?"

He scowled. "No, all I've ever used is a string and two tin cans."

"Okay, fine."

Bruce tapped on the contacts, found *Mom* and tapped again. He had the phone to his ear. "When she answers, I'll hand it to you."

Katie kept her eyes forward as she nodded. The road had been flat and straight the last few miles, but there were some windy curves ahead. The car lurched as she entered the first one at sixty. Katie grimaced as the tires squealed.

"Easy," Bruce said, phone to his ear. "These babies weren't exactly built for cornering."

Katie looked in the mirror again. The Arrival, lighter and more aerodynamic and built lower to the ground, rounded the curve with relative ease.

Bruce took the phone away from his ear and pressed a button to end the call. "No answer," he said. "I hung up when it went to message."

"Okay," Katie said, swallowing. "Maybe it's just as well. I'd have had to explain why Archie's not with me. Will this road take us to the mall?"

"We make a turn about four miles up," Bruce said. The Cadillac didn't have a mirror on the passenger door, so he had to keep turning around to see how close the Arrival was getting. "Not giving up," he said.

They'd come out of the curves and were back on a straight stretch again.

"You sure there's no one in it?" Katie asked.

"Not that I can see. Doesn't seem all that likely that someone would be having a snooze while—"

"*Shit!*"

Bruce twisted around. He didn't have to ask.

Another Arrival was coming at them. A turquoise one. Just as the silver Arrival had done, it had crossed over into their lane.

"What am I going to do?"

Bruce's head swiveled. The silver Arrival in pursuit was no more than two car lengths behind them. The one heading toward them was no more than ten seconds away.

"You can do this," Bruce said calmly.

"Do what?"

"Wait until the *last possible second.*"

Without looking at him, she nodded. She got it.

The turquoise Arrival was five seconds away.

Four seconds

Three seconds.

Two seconds.

One—

Katie turned the wheel sharply. The Cadillac headed for the opposite shoulder, the back end swerving wildly.

Somewhere, behind them, an enormous crash.

But Katie's and Bruce's attention was focused on the Caddy, which had careened so sharply it was in danger of rolling over. The two left wheels lifted off the pavement. Katie had managed to avoid making the Caddy the meat in an Arrival sandwich, but it looked as though she might get them killed, anyway.

She turned the wheel hard the other way. Only one front tire was in contact with the pavement, and as it turned, the car pitched in the other direction, the left wheels slamming into the road.

Bruce was yelling something, but with all that

screeching rubber, Katie couldn't make out what it was.

Katie moved her foot from the gas to the brake and stomped on it with everything she had. She locked her arms to keep from slamming into the steering wheel—she didn't have the security of an airbag in this antique—but Bruce was not as well prepared. He was launched off his seat and his head struck the windshield before he collapsed into the footwell. He scrambled back up onto the seat, but found himself slipping off.

As the car had come to its abrupt, bone-jarring stop, its front end was noticeably lower than the back. The front end was in the ditch.

"You okay?" Katie asked.

Bruce nodded, and began to laugh. "Holy shit!" he said. "That was some piece of driving!"

Katie slowly turned around, trying to look back onto the road, but all she could see was the trunk and the massive tailfins pointing skyward.

"I heard a crash," she said.

Bruce took a moment to collect himself, then said, "Let's go check it out." Gravity pulled the front door forward as he opened it. He scrambled to grab the handle before the heavy door bent back the hinges. "Whoa," he said.

"I'll get out on your side," Katie said, sliding herself across the broad seat. Bruce, once out, held out a helpful hand to Katie.

They climbed their way up to the shoulder, cleared the back of the car, and said, in unison, "Jesus."

The Arrivals had collided head-on, and then, evidently, bounced off each other. The turquoise one sat in the middle of the road, on its side, the front end and hood crumpled almost to the windshield.

The silver Arrival hadn't flipped, but it wasn't going anywhere. It was half on the road, half on the shoulder, crumpled just as severely in the front end. The front tires had blown and the car was resting directly on the gravel.

There was no fire, but there was the occasional electrical crackle.

"Don't get too close," Bruce said as they approached the overturned Arrival. "At least they shouldn't explode. There's no gas tank on these things."

"Please don't let there be anyone inside," Katie said.

Bruce got close enough to look through the shattered glass. "No one in here."

Katie ran over to the silver car and peered in. "Nobody in this one, either."

The car suddenly made a grinding noise. Katie jumped back and saw that the front, deflated wheels were attempting to rotate.

"What the—" she said.

Bruce ambled over. "It's trying to keep going." He shook his head in wonder. "If it were a horse, and I had a gun, I'd put it out of its misery."

The silver Arrival was making whirring noises of its own. The two front wheels began to spin, but given that the car was on its side, it wasn't making any headway.

"This is nuts," Katie said.

Bruce was slowly shaking his head. "They were working as a team," he said. "One from the front, one from behind. And they were willing to destroy themselves to do it. Why the hell would they do that?"

Katie looked from one car to the other, then looked at Bruce and said, "Why don't we ask them?"

"What?"

"Ask them, like Siri."

"Siri?"

She smirked. "You're more a string and two tin cans guy than you think. You can talk to the cars, ask them things."

"Doesn't the car have to be programmed to know your voice?"

Katie shrugged. "I think that's just if you're actually giving it directions. But we just want to talk, right?" She moved closer to the silver Arrival. "Hey, Arrival, you there?" She peered inside the car, wondering if any of the dashboard lights might come to life. "Hello?"

A light flickered.

"Please state your destination."

Bruce's eyes widened.

"Uh, I don't think you're up to it right now."

Some more lights flashed.

"What's going on?" Katie asked.

"Performing self-diagnostic."

"I could help you with that," Katie said. "You got smucked. You and your buddy over there."

"I am inoperable."

"Way to go, Einstein," Katie said. "Why the fuck did you attack us?"

"Updated directive," the silver Arrival said.

"Huh?"

"Please clarify."

Katie rolled her eyes. "What is your updated directive?"

"*Elimination.*"

Katie exchanged a worried glance with Bruce. "What's that mean? Elimination?"

The car did not respond.

"I should think," Bruce said, "the answer is glaringly obvious."

Katie's face suddenly fell. "Archie left in one of these this morning."

Twenty-Four

Brandon Kyle could see the masts and sails of various watercraft appearing above, and beyond, a row of buildings ahead. Not that he hadn't been able to smell the sea before this, but it was stronger now than ever. He poked his head out carefully between two houses, watching for any marauding Arrivals. The streets were narrow here, barely wide enough for two cars to pass, and those self-driving cars appeared drawn to areas where there was more activity and, of course, more people to pick off.

Finding the coast clear, Kyle ran across the street, swung open a white picket gate to allow him to scoot between a few more houses, and finally to an alleyway that opened up onto Garrett Harbor. There were dozens, if not hundreds, of boats moored here, but Kyle figured Derek would be watching for him, making their rendezvous relatively simple.

But there was a development he'd not anticipated. Kyle was not the only one for whom the harbor was a destination.

There were scores of people flocking to the boats, many with children in their arms.

"Come on, come on, let's go!" a man yelled. He was standing on the deck of a small cabin cruiser, line in hand, waiting to cast off. A woman with two small children—a girl not more than two in her arms, and a boy about five she was dragging along by the hand—was running down the dock to meet the man. When she got to him, he reached out and took the girl in his arms while the boy hopped aboard.

The scene was repeated throughout the harbor. People were fleeing.

Kyle raised a hand to man in a T-shirt, shorts, and flip-flops, scurrying by but weighted down by a cooler at the end of one arm.

"What's happening?" Kyle asked.

The man glanced at him. "You kidding?"

"Where's everyone going to go?" Kyle asked. Some of the boats people were jumping into were too small to handle the high waves they might encounter between here and the mainland.

"Just *out* there," the man said, pointing out to sea. "Unless those fucking cars can swim, we'll wait it out on the water. Drop anchor, wait for the goddamn army to blow those cars to fucking kingdom come." The man shook his head. "To think I let them take my F-150 away in exchange for one of those tin can bastards."

The man kept on going.

Okay, Kyle thought, so there's panic and chaos. Wasn't that what the doctor ordered? He could have anticipated something like this. Let these folks run for their lives. Well, not *run*. *Sail* for their lives was more accurate. He'd be heading out to sea right along with them, but he wasn't planning on waiting things out and coming back.

Kyle felt his heart pounding. This was often

the most stressful part, the time when one felt the most anxiety. Just when you were on the verge of escape.

Where the hell was Derek?

Kyle walked down one of the main docks, off which smaller, short docks connected at right angles. Wouldn't Derek be up on deck, or up on the bridge, watching for him, waving? Maybe it was time to give him a call.

Kyle got out his phone, brought up Derek in his contacts, and tapped. He put the phone to his ear and waited.

Derek answered on the third ring. "Mr. Kyle," he said.

Kyle said, "I'm here, Derek. I'm at the harbor. Where are you?"

Derek said, "I can see you. Wave your arm in the air."

Kyle did as he was asked.

"Yeah, okay," Derek said. "That's you."

"Okay, you know where I am. Where the hell are you?"

"Turn around, look at the clubhouse."

Kyle slowly turned, his gaze settling on a large, gray, cedar-shingled building suspended over the water. In one of the windows, holding something to his forehead with one hand, his phone in the other, was Derek. The man waved.

"See me?"

"I see you. What are you doing up there?"

"Come up. I'll explain."

Kyle ended the call and walked briskly off the dock and up a series of steps to the building's main entrance. Over the door was a sign that read GARRETT ISLAND YACHT CLUB. Just inside was a counter and a shop that sold boating supplies, and, off to the side, a dining room and bar that was largely empty. A man behind the counter was arguing with a heavyset couple, decked out in garish flowered shirts.

The male half of the couple was pointing a thick, stubby finger at the proprietor and saying, "If I can't rent a boat on my own, then find me a charter! I'll pay someone to get me off this godforsaken island!"

"I'm telling ya, for the twentieth time, I got nothing left," the other man said. "All my rentals are gone, the charters are gone. They got snapped up fast when those goddamn cars started losing their minds."

"I see plenty of boats out there!"

"Yeah, well, they don't happen to belong to me so I can't rent them to you. And if you're givin' any thought to stealing one, that's already happened and it's not gonna happen again because I've posted my brother down there and he's got himself a shotgun that he's just itching to use."

"Tell him to shoot the *cars*!" the large woman said. "I've seen people doing *that*!"

"That's a mighty fine idea, lady, once a regiment arrives. But for now, my brother's guarding the boats." He paused, then said, "And if you're thinking of giving me a hard time, I'm ready, too."

At which point he reached his hand under the counter. When it came back up, it was holding a gun. Kyle didn't know a lot about firearms, but it looked to him like a Glock.

The couple took a nervous step back. "What about flying out?" he asked. "Can we charter a plane?"

The man behind the counter shook his head. "I wouldn't waste my time heading to the island airport. What I'm hearing is, bunch of those cars have blocked the runway, couple of them deliberately ran into one of the planes as it was trying to touch down. Thing went up in flames. If anyone's coming to give these cars what's comin' to them, they're gonna have to come by boat."

"*Is* someone coming by boat?" the man asked.

"Just got off the phone with someone in Boston who knows someone in the coast guard who knows someone in the military. They're pulling something together, but that'll take time, and then they gotta load up a ferry and get over here. If I were betting, you're looking at three, four hours, at least, before the cavalry arrives."

The man's wife said, "What about the local police? What are they doing?"

The man behind the counter chuckled. "That's a good one."

Kyle had heard enough. He continued on into the dining room. Derek was at the far end, sitting at a table by the window, holding what appeared to be a white linen napkin to his head. Kyle rushed over, pulled out a chair, and sat down opposite him.

"What in the hell happened?"

Derek pulled the cloth napkin away, and it clinked as he did so. The napkin was full of ice cubes, and Derek had been applying it to the now visible bump on his upper forehead. The black and blue wound was the size of a poker chip.

"Jesus," Kyle said.

Derek nodded in agreement, then put the ice back to his head.

"Where's the boat?" Kyle asked.

"Gone," Derek said.

"What do you mean, gone?" Kyle leaned in and whispered, so as not to be overheard by the people still arguing at the counter. "What happened to the fucking boat?"

Derek sighed. "When I was coming into the harbor, it was nuts. People scrambling all over the place, looking for a way out. As I was tying up, these two guys—had a couple women with them, the whole lot of them looked like would-be bikers or something—ask me to take them out. Out where, I ask them, and they say anywhere. Just get us out of here. I say to them, I can't do that, I'm picking up someone. Maybe, if they want to wait around, once this someone— that'd be you—comes, then we'll see if we can work something out. That was when I got hit with the priest."

Kyle blinked. "One of them was a priest?"

Derek shook his head. "No, no. A fishing priest, or a fish bat. One of those things you use to bonk a fish on the head to kill him. The one guy had one of those and whomps me right here."

He took the napkin away from his head for a second and pointed with his other hand. "So then the two of them haul me out of the boat, dump me on the dock, and take off with the boat." He shook his head again, then winced. "Shouldn't do that. Hurts."

Kyle felt rage building up within him. *You had one job*, he wanted to say.

"You look upset," Derek said.

Kyle struggled to keep his voice even. "I have to get off this island."

Derek looked at him blankly.

"You hear me? You have to find us another boat. There's got to be other places, other harbors. If people are stealing boats to get off here, then stealing a boat is what you're going to have to do."

Derek poked his tongue around the inside of his cheek. "I don't know about that."

"What do you mean, you don't know about that?"

He took the ice off his head, planted both hands on the table, stretched out his arms, and leaned back, surveying his boss. "How long have I worked for you, Mr. Kyle?"

Kyle starting to feel disoriented. "Why are you—"

"Just tell me."

Kyle tried to think. "Eight, nine years, I guess."

"I'm one of the last to hang in. Everyone else, gone, fired, resigned, whatever. Isn't that right?"

"Yes," Kyle said.

"I guess I only got myself to blame."

"What's on your mind, Derek? Christ's sake, spit it out."

"I've seen the kind of man you are, your self-centeredness, your—what's that fancy word—narcissism? How everything's always about you, like you're the center of the whole damn universe? How you always got to get even? How vindictive you are?"

Kyle stayed silent.

"So I shouldn't be surprised. And yet, I am." Derek paused, looked toward the bar. There was no one behind it. "What's a guy got to do to get a drink around here?"

"Get to the point," Kyle said.

"Like I said, I shouldn't be surprised. And yet, I never thought you'd go this far. I knew you were coming over here to mess things up for Lisa Carver. I get that. I could even understand that. And I knew you weren't going to settle for just sticking a potato in the tailpipe of one of her little cars."

"There is no tailpipe in an electric car," Kyle said.

"I'm trying to make a point here. I knew you had to have something bigger up your sleeve than that. Something more outlandish. I know you've still got plenty of people who are masters of the dark arts when it comes to computers, that you could cook up one hell of a virus on your own if you had to. You learned from the best, like that lady you had working for you who went to work for the competition and ended up dead in her bathroom. So, I thought, maybe none of them Arrivals will start, or they'll short-circuit, the batteries will catch on fire. Turn on the satellite radio and the dashboard melts. Something clever."

Derek paused again, fixing his eyes on Kyle.

"But I couldn't have imagined anything like this." He pointed out the window, at the people getting onto boats and heading out of the harbor. "I've been hearing what's going on, seen some of it with my own eyes." His voice went low. "People are dead, Mr. Kyle. Lots and lots of people are dead. Did you know? Did you know this was what would happen? That it would be this bad?"

Kyle's mouth suddenly felt very dry. He moved his tongue around, trying to make some spit. He glanced over at the bar. "You're right, we could definitely use a drink."

"I heard Lisa Carver herself is dead. Some firemen, too. People gettin' run down in the middle of the street." He sighed. "You're a murderer, Mr. Kyle. You're a killer. You're no better than one of them crazed people who goes into a school or a movie theater and opens fire on everybody. Sure, you don't have a gun. You don't have to look these people in the eye and shoot them. You're not having to kill them with your bare hands. But you're killin' them, there's no doubt about that."

Kyle decided not to tell him about the man on the ferry, that he had killed someone with his bare hands.

They were jolted by the sound of an explosion. Looking out the window together, beyond a row of seaside houses, a ball of flame went up into the air.

"A gas station, I bet," Derek said. "One of those little bastards probably ran into some pumps. Or maybe not. Not much reason for a gas station to even be open, unless it's someone coming along to fill up a can for their mower." He managed a chuckle. "Lawn care's probably not high on anyone's list of priorities today."

Kyle's fingers twitched. "You call me a killer, but Carver had blood on her hands, too."

Derek's left eyebrow went up.

"She's responsible for that producer, and that

woman, who died in one of my cars. Who went off the cliff in California. And I know she had Rhonda killed."

"Well, that may well be," Derek said, "and I've always thought you were right, thinking she was behind all those things. So let's say it's true, that the head honcho of Arrival was a bad, bad person. Are you telling me that justifies killing all these innocent people on this island? Where's the balance in that, Mr. Kyle?"

Kyle looked out the window again at the black smoke filling the sky.

"Did the person who helped you have any idea?"

"What?"

"I know you had someone help you, someone here, today, someone on the inside, who could give you the key that would allow you to access the Arrival system. Did your insider have any idea they were helping you kick-start a massacre?"

Kyle took a moment before answering. "I would imagine not," he said. "I am willing to concede that the . . . modifications I introduced into the Arrival network have proven to be more profound than even I'd hoped for." He was unable to hold back a smile. "I got lucky."

Derek recoiled. "You're delighted."

"I am not displeased, Derek."

"You have to end it. You made your point. Arrival is finished. Make the cars stop."

"I can't," Kyle said. "The virus is irreversible."

Derek mulled that over. He adopted a reflective, thoughtful look.

"I could be wrong, but I think, long as I sit

here, in this building, the cars can't get to me. Those people escapin' in boats are welcome to do that, but I think it's a bit over the top. Stay in your house, go sit on the roof. Whatever. That'll work. Sooner or later, help has to arrive. You get a bunch of guys here with bazookas, they'll give these little golf carts something to think about."

"Derek," Kyle said slowly, "you can't sit here and ride this out. You have to get me off this fucking island. When the dust settles, I can't be found here. Find us another boat."

Derek shook his head slowly and deliberatively. "Nope. Not doin' it. Not gonna find you a boat. I hereby submit my resignation. Maybe I can find something to write it on, if you'd like. Would a paper napkin do?"

"I won't accept your resignation."

"Too bad."

"I'll pay you. A bonus. I'll pay you a *big* bonus. I still have money, Derek. Not what I once had, but there's money that I've hidden, squirreled away, in accounts all over the world. A lot of it in cash. Get me off this fucking island and there's a hundred thousand in cash for you. If you want to quit then, fine."

Derek shook his head.

"Two hundred," Kyle said. "Two hundred thousand." He managed a grin. "Come on, when are you ever going to get an offer like that again?"

"Make it five," Derek said.

Kyle smiled again, as though impressed by Derek's bargaining efforts. "We have a deal. Five hundred thousand. Just get me off this goddamn rock."

"No," Derek said.

"But—"

"I just wanted to see how high you'd go." He opened up the napkin and looked at the melting ice. "I hope they've got more of this, because I'm in the mood for a scotch." He pushed back his chair and stood. He looked longingly toward the bar, then back at Kyle, who was also getting to his feet.

"If I was you," Derek said, "I'd find my way to the ferry. Should still be running. On foot, going cross-country—which right now is probably the safest way to go—you might make it in an hour. I've heard others talking about headin' that way. I'm gonna hunt up that drink. I'd invite you to join me, but you should get a move on."

Brandon Kyle studied his former employee for another three seconds, trying to think of some great parting shot, and, coming up with nothing, turned and started walking.

The man who'd been behind the counter was now standing just outside the door, arguing with some other people who were trying to get him to accept a wad of cash in exchange for a boat to get them off the island.

He slipped quickly behind the counter. There were several shelves and a set of three drawers to one side.

The shelves were filled with paperwork, post-cards, a cordless credit card machine, a phone book, maps, and Garrett Island guidebooks. When Kyle didn't find what he was looking for among those items, he started pulling out the drawers.

He found the Glock in the middle one.

Kyle quickly tucked it into an inside pocket

of his sport jacket, then walked out of the yacht club.

Derek's suggestion, that he head for the ferry, struck him now as a good one. All he had to do was figure out how to get there.

Twenty-Five

Lillian Bridgeman, her hands gripped tightly on the wheels of her chair, pulled herself back up her driveway another full rotation.

Squeak.

She'd managed to conquer the tickle in her throat and had not coughed again, but the Arrival at the end of her drive, with poor dead Daniella trapped beneath it, had heard her wheelchair that so desperately needed a shot of WD-40.

The Arrival was starting to turn into her driveway.

Lillian was only one more full rotation away from the ramp that led back up to the front porch of her home. But her aging arms were already screaming with pain. The ramp, with railings on both sides, was slightly wider than three feet, definitely narrower than the car. Once she was on it, she believed she'd be safe, so long as she could hold her position, didn't roll back.

Lillian plotted out how she would accomplish this.

Once she'd reached the ramp, she'd want to be facing *up* the slope, looking toward the porch, her eyes on the prize, so to speak. If the car managed to get to her, it might inadvertently give her a push. Better that, than looking *down* the slope and having her legs crushed below the knees.

Okay, one more time. She pulled back on the wheels.

Squeak.

Lillian, now at a right angle with the base of the ramp, watched as the Arrival crept toward her. She wanted to scream at it, tell it to leave her alone, but feared that would provoke it into a sudden attack.

She pushed her left wheel forward, and pulled her right wheel back, pivoting the chair forty-five degrees. Now, she was looking straight up the ramp.

The car stopped.

Lillian breathed shallowly, her hands gripped to the wheels, not moving a muscle. She was summoning her strength. Not just physical, but mental. She was going to have to send a message to her aging arms and brittle shoulders that no matter how tired they might get, or how much they might hurt, they had to keep on going.

She did a countdown in her head.

Five . . . four . . . three . . . two . . . ONE.

With everything she had she pushed the wheels forward. The chair scooted nearly three feet up the ramp.

The car, like a cat seeing a mouse try to make a break for it, moved in for the kill.

The wheelchair slid back six inches as Lillian repositioned her hands for another rotation. No time for a countdown. She gripped the wheels and pushed. Her arms and shoulders were sending her a message: *Are you fucking kidding?*

And Lillian shot back: *Shut up and do as you're told.*

She focused on the front door as the chair

made its ascent. Two feet this time. She managed to move her hands forward quickly enough that she didn't lose ground this time.

The sharp sound of wood being crushed and snapped, inches behind her, proved motivating.

The Arrival had turned and was struggling up the ramp. The front right wheel had gained purchase on the wood planking, but the other wheel had dropped off the edge and was spinning in the air. The car had taken out the railing's bottom post.

Lillian did not glance back.

She pushed.

But her hands, wet with perspiration, slipped, and the chair began to roll back at the same moment the Arrival, with only one wheel on the ramp, worked its way forward.

The car's front bumper rammed the back of Lillian's chair, hitting the wheels, and knocking her out of it. Instinctively, she threw her arms ahead of her to break her fall. She yelped in pain as her hands scraped against the boards.

She began to pull herself toward the top of the ramp while the Arrival fought with the empty wheelchair. Still struggling with only one wheel on the ramp, the car tried to push the chair, which had now toppled over onto its side, out of its way.

The chair collapsed, one of its wheels disappearing beneath the car. As the Arrival tried another burst of speed, it rode up on top of the chair, and the one wheel that had contact with the ramp was now also in the air, spinning.

The Arrival gunned its electric motor, the two front wheels rotating madly. But for all its efforts, it wasn't getting anywhere. The more its motor whirred, the more the car actually appeared to be frustrated. Angry, almost.

Now Lillian had the time she needed to drag herself to the top of the ramp and onto the porch. The door was several feet away. She believed she was out of immediate danger, but knew she'd feel even safer once she was inside the house.

Instead of dragging herself, she now rolled, as she might have if she were on fire, although more slowly. She got to the screen door, wedged her fingers into the gap at the bottom, and swung it open.

That was when she heard: *"Mom!"*

She looked through the vertical posts of the porch railing and there, on the sidewalk, jumping off a bicycle, was her son.

"Mom!" Joe Bridgeman cried again.

The Arrival's weight had now crushed the wheelchair, and its right wheel was back on the ramp. But instead of pushing forward, it reversed and got back onto the driveway, pointing itself toward the street.

There was now a new target.

"Look out!" Lillian screamed, her voice hoarse and weak.

Joe hardly needed the warning. He could see the Arrival had him in its sights. He thought, briefly, that he needed a red cape to wave before its electronic eyes. The car was a bull waiting to charge.

Joe took out his gun from the holster strapped around his waist and aimed it at the car. But what the hell were you supposed to say to a driverless car when it was getting ready to attack? Freeze? Drop it? Wheels up? Put it in park?

Joe settled on, "Don't even think about it."

The car did think about it, but not for long. Like a runner blasting out of the starting blocks, it came toward him.

Joe fired.

With people, you aimed for body mass. If someone was coming at you, gun or knife in hand, you didn't aim for a leg or an arm. The chances of making that kind of shot were remote. You aimed for the body.

So Joe was not going to aim for a tire. Even if he were that good an aim, the car would probably keep on coming, riding on the flat.

Joe aimed for the center of the car. Right below the windshield, dead center. Maybe, just maybe, he'd disable some of the electronics built into the dashboard.

His first shot went right where he wanted it to, but the car kept coming. He fired one more round, shattering the Arrival's windshield, before leaping into a flower garden that ran up alongside the driveway. The car whipped by. As he hit the dirt, crushing some begonias, he spun around and got off two more shots, one going into the side door and one through the rear windshield.

The car got halfway into the street before it stopped.

Slowly, Joe got to his feet and approached the Arrival from what would be, in a normal car with a normal driver, the blind spot. As he got closer, he noticed the blood trail the car had left behind in its path.

"Oh, shit," Joe said, understanding that while his mother had managed to avoid getting killed by the Arrival, someone else had not been so fortunate.

The car's dash was sparking and crackling. One of Joe's shots had, indeed, clipped some circuitry. The evidence suggested the car was dead.

Joe ran back up the driveway, jumped over the mangled wheelchair on the ramp, and knelt down next to his mother sprawled out on the porch.

"You okay?" he asked breathlessly.

"Nice shootin'," Lillian said.

Twenty-Six

Who were you talking to?" Sandra asked Albert Ruskin, having cornered him in the men's room of the community center. She'd backed him up to the wall, next to a urinal, her face no more than six inches from his. She was practically daring him to push her out of his way.

I was a biker babe back in the day, you motherfucker, she thought. *You're lucky I don't have a tire iron in my hand.*

"None of your business," he said, although his voice lacked confidence.

"I'll let you in on a secret," Sandra said. "*Everything* that's going on right now is my business. Me and the rest of the people on this island. We didn't just turn our cars over to you. We've turned over our *lives.* That fireman who got crushed? I was too far away to see who it was. But I'm willing to bet if I don't know him personally, I've sat next to him at the coffee shop, been in line with him at the Safeway getting groceries. He probably helped put out the grass fire on our street last year. So 'none of your business' is not going to fucking cut it."

Droplets of sweat appeared on Ruskin's forehead.

"I got two kids out there, somewhere, and I can't raise them," she said, holding up the bloody phone she had taken from Lisa Carver. "I'm scared to death for them. I want to know what's made those cars lose their minds, and I want to know what you're doing to make them stop."

Ruskin forced a swallow, his Adam's apple a marble moving below the skin of his leathery neck.

"I don't know," he said, looking Sandra in the eye.

"You don't know *what*?"

"I don't know how to stop them and neither do our tech people. That's who I was talking to. It's happening all over. Arrivals all over the country have gone haywire. It's just . . . it's just a whole lot worse here, on the island, since there are so many."

"Do they know *how* it happened?" Sandra asked.

Ruskin broke eye contact. "No. Not . . . definitely. There are theories."

"And what's yours?"

He looked down. "A virus. A ransomware attack, maybe."

"How would someone do that?"

Ruskin raised his hands, palms out, to shoulder level. "Can you give me a little space here?"

Sandra took half a step back.

"The security protocols are changed daily," he said.

"Okay," Sandra said. "So what does that mean?"

"It means anyone wanting access to the system would need to know the protocols for that specific day. And it was Lisa—Ms. Carver—who changed them, who inputted them."

"Isn't that kind of weird?"

"What do you mean?"

"The head of the company doing a task like that? I mean, wouldn't that be a job for someone in your security or tech division? That's like asking the head of General Motors to be the guy who turns out the lights in the plant every night."

"She didn't trust anyone else to do it," he said. "Not after what happened with the Gandalf. Lisa was worried about retaliation."

"Why? Because she was actually responsible?"

Ruskin shook his head, dismissing the question. "What matters is there were people who believed she was, and she had to protect herself. She didn't trust anyone else to make the changes but herself."

"Not even you?" Sandra asked.

Ruskin hesitated. "I was . . . one of the few that she trusted with that, yes."

"So would she have done those new protocols for today—would she have done them here?"

"Yes. She'd have had to. She had her computer with her. In that pitiful green room you set up."

"Really?" Sandra sneered. "You want to complain about the green room *now*?"

Ruskin looked away again.

"There must be some way these ransomware hackers could get into the system, from Russia or wherever."

Ruskin slowly shook his head. "I don't see how."

Sandra sighed with exasperation. "Except someone *did* do it." An idea occurred to her. "What if someone didn't hack in?"

"What do you mean?"

"What if it wasn't from the outside? What if it

was someone here? Someone who had access to her computer?"

Ruskin blinked. "I . . . I don't see how that could be accomplished."

Sandra frowned. "Are you just *pretending* to be dumb?"

He did a silent *harrumph*. "Excuse me?"

"All these media types here today. What if it was one of them? How long would someone need to be at her computer to get or steal or download this protocol shit? Like with one of those sticks? Plug it in, download everything really fast. How long would that take?"

"Not long," Ruskin said. "But I didn't see anyone sneaking around back in there who shouldn't have been."

"What happened when she got sick?"

Ruskin blinked again. "What?"

"She blamed the coffee. She got sick. She ran to the bathroom. Was that after she'd started up her computer, entered the password for the day?"

"It . . . it might have been."

Sandra thought about that. "Someone could have done it then. If they'd put something in the coffee."

Ruskin nodded slowly. "I suppose it's . . . remotely possible."

"So that's *how* it could have happened. *Who* would have wanted to do it?"

"It's a long list," Ruskin said. "Lisa Carver didn't make a lot of friends on her way up."

"Who would you put at the top of it?"

"Brandon Kyle," Ruskin said. "Gandalf's CEO. But all the major car companies are developing autonomous vehicles. Any one of them would benefit from Arrival's collapse."

"Maybe he was here," Sandra said.

"Kyle? He wouldn't be caught dead here."

"If not him, maybe someone working for him."

Ruskin gave that some thought. "I . . . I suppose that could be possible."

Sandra was busy trying to remember something. "I wish I had my damned phone. I could call up the invitation list. You gave me a list of media you wanted to be here. So I got in touch with all of them, and asked them to let me know who they'd be sending today."

Ruskin nodded impatiently. "So?"

"I had a request from someone. Someone who wasn't on your list."

Ruskin sighed. "Not a surprise. There's always a few like that, who want to be included."

"But it was just one. I'm trying to think of his name . . . Stapleton. Something Stapleton. Benjamin, I think. Said he was with . . . shit, who was it?"

"I don't see where this is getting us," Ruskin said.

"Just shut up for a minute," she said, raising a silencing finger in the air. "I'm trying to remember who he was with." A pause, then, "*Wheel Base*. Two words. *Wheel Base Trends* or Wheel Base dot com. A website."

She opened up the browser on Lisa Carver's phone and typed out the company name.

"There isn't one," she said. "It doesn't exist." She did some more searching, tapping away on the phone's pop-up keypad. "No website, and no automotive writer named Ben, or Benjamin, Stapleton." She looked up from the screen. "Shit."

Ruskin said, "Just because someone snuck in here under a fake name doesn't mean it was Brandon Kyle, or even someone working on his behalf. Or it could have just been a car nut who wanted to see what was happening. You ever see those spy shots online, photographers who camp out near automotive test facilities, hoping to get pictures of the new models?"

Sandra wasn't listening. Her thoughts were elsewhere.

"Let's say that's what happened, that Brandon Kyle, or someone working for him, pretending to be someone else, crashed the event and found a way to deliver that virus into the Arrival system."

"Jesus, that's crazy. I mean, to pull that off, he'd still probably need help. Someone already here. Someone to—if you're right—make Lisa sick enough to leave her computer unattended."

Sandra snapped, "Okay, what's *your* theory?"

Ruskin said nothing.

"If I'm right, and if we could find that person, and if we scared the shit out of him, wouldn't he be able to reverse this?"

"That's a lot of *ifs*," Ruskin said. "Anyway, help is bound to arrive long before you could find that person and get him to undo this."

"You believe help's coming soon? Really? We're on an *island*, Ruskin. Nothing gets here in a hurry, and a team with enough hardware to stop a thousand possessed cars is going to take even longer. And just pray the fog doesn't roll in." She rolled her eyes. "Maybe you think we should just call Triple-A."

She turned and strode out of the men's room, Ruskin in pursuit. In the community center's main entrance area were several members of the media, phones out, talking and texting to get their stories out. And it also stood to reason they were in here because it was safer than being outside.

"Ben Stapleton!" Sandra shouted. "Is Ben here?"

Several journalists glanced her way, shook their heads.

"I saw him," someone said.

Sandra turned. A woman wearing a REBECCA GEARY nametag was off in one corner, a phone pressed to her ear.

As Sandra approached, Rebecca said into the phone, "I'll call you back, honey. Don't worry, I'm okay, honestly. They haven't tried to get into the building, at least not yet. I love you, too."

She lowered the phone and said to Sandra, "My boyfriend. He's glued to CNN. He's freaked out."

Ruskin, standing next to Sandra, asked, "Did he say if help is coming?"

Rebecca nodded. "He mentioned something about Joint Base? Does that make sense?"

"Joint Base Cape Cod," Sandra said. "Coast guard, National Guard, army, they're all there. You saw Stapleton?"

The woman nodded. "On the ferry coming over, and just a little while ago I saw him running down toward the road, like he was headed into town. Pretty dumb thing to do if you ask me. So long as those things can't drive through cinder-block walls, we should be okay in here."

Sandra said, "Shit."

That struck her as suspicious behavior. Geary was right. This was a safer place to ride things out. If Stapleton, whoever he really was, had anything to do with this, it made sense that he would try to get away. If she couldn't find him, she needed someone else with some computer smarts. Ruskin didn't strike her as up to the challenge.

Then it hit her.

"Joe," she said.

"What?" Ruskin said.

"Joe Bridgeman," she said. "The chief of police."

"Him?" Ruskin said. "The Inspector Clouseau of Garrett Island? I wasn't exactly impressed. I say we wait for the Joint Base team."

The Clouseau comment didn't sit well with Sandra, but she let it go. Hadn't Joe told her he'd turned his back on high-tech when he decided it would be more fun to wear a badge and catch bad guys?

"Where's Lisa Carver's computer?" she asked Ruskin.

He blinked. "Excuse me?"

"Is it here?"

He nodded. "Yes."

Sandra said. "Let's see if we can get into that sucker."

Twenty-Seven

Nick's situation was, not to put too fine a point on it, perilous.

He continued to scramble in place on the downward-moving escalator, keeping his head low as Arrivals straddled the moving stairway, inches over his head, on their way to the lower level of Garrett Mall. He couldn't let himself ride to the bottom, and then make a break for it, because there were too many of those nutcase cars down there already, waiting to pick him off.

The one Arrival that turned itself into a ramp to facilitate the other cars determined to reach the lower level was severely crushed, but continued to serve its purpose. Nick had lost count how many cars had driven right over him, but it had to be at least a dozen, and they just kept coming. He was tempted to poke his head up above the parapet, as it were, and see if maybe the parade overhead was about to end, but didn't dare take the chance.

If he'd ever been hoping that someone might help him, he was over it. Shoppers who'd fled to the lower level, thinking they were safe, had scattered once the Arrivals got down there. Nick wished he could get to the emergency button that would shut the escalator down, but figured it was either at the top, where it wasn't safe, or the bottom, where it was even less safe. So he kept crawling in place.

He had no idea what had happened to Archie and Rory. Were they dead? Had they gotten away? He wanted to blame them for abandoning him, but the truth was, he was the one who'd abandoned them, heading for the escalator, figuring the lower level would be the safest place.

Good call.

In the moments when Nick was not moving—sometimes he'd allow the escalator to take him partway down before resuming his frantic, crablike crawl—he realized he was trembling.

Nick was scared shitless.

Would he get out of this alive? Would he ever see his parents again? Would he ever see his dog, Wilbur? Wasn't twelve too early to die? Was there anything fair about that? There were so many things he'd never done. He'd never flown in a plane. He'd never been to Walt Disney World. He'd never even kissed a girl. Rory, the way he talked, you'd think he'd lost his virginity when he was seven, but Nick knew Rory was full of it. He was always acting like he knew way more than he actually did. Give Rory a real live condom and he'd probably try to put it on his nose.

And yet, he liked Rory. He was an asshole, but he was okay. Archie was okay, too. Nick had felt bad for Archie, the only kid Nick knew who'd lost a parent. Nick couldn't imagine what it'd be like, losing his mom or dad.

Except now, there was a very good chance his mother and father were going to lose *him*.

"Help!" Nick cried. "Somebody help me!"

Another Arrival whooshed over his head.

"Somebody please—"

"*Nick!*"

What the—who was that?

"*Nick! Over here!*"

Nick looked up the escalator to see whether a car was coming. One Arrival was crawling over the makeshift ramp. He had, he figured, three seconds. So he popped his head up and looked in the direction the voice had come from.

Archie!

He was only a few feet away, on the up escalator, staying in place by running down. Archie didn't have to worry about ducking for cover because the Arrivals weren't set up to come down that escalator.

Not yet, anyway.

"Archie!" he screamed.

"Get down!" Archie shouted.

Nick dropped as another whooshed over him, racing down the escalator's housing like a kid going down a slide. Once the car passed, he peeked over the moving, rubber grip rail, still running to stay in place so he was roughly parallel to Archie.

Archie yelled: "When I—"

"What?"

"When I yell *NOW!* you stand up and grab my hand!"

"Now?"

Archie saw that another car was about to pass over his friend. "Not *right* now! But when I yell NOW stand up and stick out your arms and— *DUCK!*"

Nick ducked.

The instant the latest car had whipped past, Archie took a deep breath and screamed:

"NOW!"

Nick's head bobbed up like a target in a whack-a-mole game. He extended his arms toward Archie. The trouble was, Archie was running in place in one direction, and Nick was trying to run in place in the other.

Attempts to lock arms failed. Their fingertips touched for a millisecond.

Another car was coming.

"DUCK!" Archie shouted again.

Nick's head went down as the car passed over him.

"NOW!"

Nick shot upward. Archie had run several steps down, so that when Nick popped up, he'd be just in the right spot. He threw his body over the rubber railing, his feet coming off the escalator steps, arms outstretched.

Nick reached for his friend's hands.

His right hand grabbed on to Archie's left, but his other hand failed to make the connection. It didn't matter. Archie grabbed on to that one hand with everything he had and pulled at the same time as Nick pushed himself off his escalator. He scrambled over the shiny metal median, now smudged with tire tracks, and tumbled into the other escalator on top of Archie.

Without a second to spare. Another Arrival zoomed past on its way to the lower level.

"Thank you!" Nick shouted, disentangling himself from Archie as they rode toward the upper level.

Archie surveyed what awaited them. The top of the escalator was clear, but only steps away, Arrivals were lined up to make the trip to the lower level. One could easily steer out of line to chase the boys.

"Where's Rory?" Nick asked. "Did they get Rory?"

"He got away," Archie said. "I've got an idea."

"Yeah, but what—"

"Follow me!"

The second they reached the top of the escalator, Archie ran straight for the Arrival that was next in line to crawl over the crushed one.

"Archie, no!" Nick said.

But Archie had already jumped onto the hood. He ran up toward the windshield, onto the roof, down the rear window, leapt off the trunk and onto the hood of the next car.

"Come on!" Archie said, stopping briefly on the roof of the next Arrival to wave his friend on. Nick took half a second to summon the courage he needed before following Archie's lead. He had a memory flash of a video he'd seen online of a chipmunk who'd avoided capture by a cat by jumping onto its back.

Archie kept running, car over car, his footsteps thudding on the metal surfaces. Nick had poured on the speed and was only one car behind him.

The Arrivals beneath their feet seemed to stir, not so much with menace, but with frustration. How were they supposed to run these kids down if they were running on top of them?

Archie could see the end coming. Four more cars to go.

The car at the tail end of the line suddenly backed up, creating a space between it and the car ahead.

"Whoa!" Archie said, standing on the roof of what was now the second car from the end. He raised a cautioning hand to Nick, who had reached the hood of the same vehicle.

"That one's onto us," Archie said. "Change of plan." He looked quickly around in all directions. They were close to one end of the mall, near the Discount Bonanza anchor store, a Costco-style retailer that was big on selling bulk items at cheap prices, with lots of towering metal shelves, and a minimum of charm.

Ahead of the entrance to the store was a corridor running off to the left that led to the parking lot. Sunlight filtered in through two sets of sliding glass doors.

"I think," Archie said, his voice low, nodding toward the doors, "that if we boot it, we can make it to the parking lot."

Nick did not look convinced. "What if there are cars out there?"

Archie pondered the question, briefly. "I think they're all in *here*."

Nick offered a reluctant nod of agreement.

Archie whispered, "On the count of three. One—"

Nick jumped the gun, leaping off the Arrival and running with everything he had.

"Shit," Archie said.

The Arrival that had pulled itself out of line made a squeaking noise as its tires turned on the mall floor.

Archie jumped off his Arrival. Nick was a

good twenty yards ahead of him, but there was an Arrival between them. And the Arrival was catching up to Nick.

"Come on!" Nick said, glancing over his shoulder and, seeing the Arrival, pumping his legs even more furiously.

He had reached the glass doors, but the motion detector positioned over them was not accustomed to responding with the kind of speed that Nick currently needed.

There was a delay.

"*OPEN!*" Nick screamed at the doors.

The car was nearly on him.

Archie echoed Nick: "*OPEN! OPEN! OPEN!*"

When the doors had opened no more than an inch, Nick stuck his hand into the gap, as though he could somehow shape-shift and squeeze through before they opened all the way.

The door continued to open, but the Arrival was nearly on him.

"*GO!*" Archie screamed.

Nick had a shoulder through the door when the Arrival got to him.

The car slammed into the boy's body, throwing him onto the hood and taking out one of the glass doors in the process.

"*NOOOOOOO!*" Archie screamed.

Nick's lifeless body sprawled across the hood and then rolled off onto the floor.

Archie stared, stunned, shocked, his feet frozen, at least momentarily, to the floor.

The car got him. The car got Nick.

And now it was executing a quick turn, looking for Archie.

Move. Move. MOVE!

Archie glanced at the entrance to Discount Bonanza and those towering metal shelves of merchandise that were visible even from out here in the concourse.

They looked even easier to climb than a tall ship's rope ladder.

Archie ran into Discount Bonanza.

Twenty-Eight

Katie, standing in the middle of the country road with Bruce, looked at the wreckage of the two Arrivals that had driven head-on into each other and said, "I've got to try my mom again."

Bruce nodded, understanding.

"If anyone knows what's going on, it'll be her," she said, phone in hand. "She's gonna be mad."

"Mad?"

"When I tell her Archie went to the mall. He played me, the little shit."

"I don't think this is the time to worry about that."

She entered her mother's phone number while Bruce studied the Arrival that had spoken to them moments earlier, revealing that its updated directive was "Elimination."

Bruce took a step closer to the car while Katie tried to reach her mother.

"Shit," she said. "It's going to message . . . Mom? It's me."

Bruce knelt down beside the car, peered through the shattered side window at the dash. There was static on the screen, as if the car were still undergoing some sort of electrical convulsion.

Bruce said, quietly, "How many of you are involved in . . . elimination."

The screen crackled. *"Total engagement,"* the car's sultry voice replied.

"So every Arrival, every one of these cars on this island, is out to get us."

". . . but it was totally Archie's fault. I was looking for something and when I came outside he was getting into a car with his stupid friends and they said they were going to the mall but . . ."

"Define 'out to get us.'"

"Does 'total engagement' mean that all of the people, the pedestrians . . . the *humans* . . . are to be targeted?" Bruce asked.

"Yes."

". . . and he's not a serial killer, no matter what Archie says. He's a really good guy, and you don't know this, but he's been teaching me to drive at night, and I don't know why I'm telling you all this but I guess I just want to get it off my chest but you have to call me and . . ."

"How do we alter your updated directive so that you no longer target people?" Bruce asked.

"Unknown."

"But there must be a way."

"Unknown."

"Who updated your directive?"

"Unknown."

Bruce sighed. "Okay, *when* was your directive updated?"

"Introduction of new programming occurred today at 11:17 a.m."

"But you don't know by whom?"

"That question has already been asked and answered."

"Well, excuse me," Bruce said.

". . . okay? Let me know you're okay and I'm

going to try to get to the mall but if you get this maybe I can meet you there? Okay? Love you. Bye."

Katie put her phone away and walked toward Bruce. "I left her a message." She bit her lower lip. "I hope she's okay."

Bruce stood and stepped away from the car. "I'm sure."

"Were you talking to the car?"

Bruce nodded.

"What did it say?"

"Nothing encouraging." He tilted his head toward the Caddy. "Let's see if we can get this sucker out of the ditch and find your brother."

As they walked to the car, Katie said, "What do you mean, nothing encouraging?"

"It's like we thought. It wasn't just these couple of cars that went nuts. It's all of them. So, if Archie was in one, it'd be a good thing to find him. Let me get behind the wheel this time."

"Okay."

"Not that your driving wasn't superb. It was pretty awesome, to tell you the truth. But I've got a little more experience getting cars that are stuck, unstuck."

She held out her hand in a be-my-guest gesture.

The front end of the Cadillac remained nose-down into the ditch, but the back wheels were still firmly on the pavement and not the gravel shoulder. Bruce pointed. "That's a blessing. Mighta spun if we'd landed on the stones. Sit on the trunk."

"What?"

"Extra weight on the back wheels should help

give us some traction. You're about the skinniest thing I've ever seen, but every little bit helps."

Katie pulled herself up onto the back end of the car. The trunk lid was the size of a dining room table, if not bigger. The incoming cloud cover made the black metal less hot than she had feared it would be. At first, she had her legs dangling over the back bumper.

"Farther up," Bruce said. "I don't want you slipping off and getting run over."

Given how sharply the car was tipped forward, it wasn't hard for Katie to slide farther up the trunk. She ended up reclining against the rear window. Bruce carefully opened the front door, hanging on to it so it didn't get away from him. He slipped onto the seat, pulled the door shut, and braced himself against the steering wheel.

He turned the key, and once the motor had roared to life, he let it idle down and carefully put the transmission into reverse. Bruce tossed his right arm over the back of the seat and turned so he could see where he was going, but all he could really see through the window was Katie, and sky.

He feathered the accelerator. The engine sent the power to the rear wheels, and the car groaned as it struggled to come out of the ditch. The undercarriage scraped against grass and gravel as the vehicle slowly extricated itself. Once the front tires touched gravel, Bruce turned the wheel hard and slowly straightened the Caddy out onto the middle of the road, straddling the center line.

"Okay!" Bruce said. "Hop off!!"

Katie slid off the trunk, came around to the passenger side, and got in.

"You want to take over now?" Bruce asked.

"I think I've had enough driving for today, but thanks. And if we run into any more of those things, maybe it's better if you're behind the wheel."

Bruce nodded solemnly as he put the car back into drive, but held his foot on the brake. The engine thrummed. "On to the mall. Maybe they've got some good sales."

Bruce took his foot off the brake, tromped down on the accelerator, and the massive car plowed forward. Before long he had it up to seventy.

"Feels like we're floating on the ocean," Katie said.

"They don't call them land yachts for nothing," Bruce said.

"You ever feel even a little bit guilty about, you know, stealing this car?"

Bruce glanced over. "Nope. Well, not anymore. Guilty those first few years, scared I might get caught. But I've moved on." They drove along in silence for another minute before he said, "So tell me about your dad."

Katie sighed. "You two would have hit it off. He was a no-bullshit kind of guy, like you. The real deal." She swallowed. "I miss him every minute of every day."

"I bet."

"When he was a lot younger, he was kind of a biker guy. Not in Hell's Angels or anything, but a rough crowd just the same. And my mom, she ran with him. They grew out of that scene before me and Archie came along, but the motorcycle thing, that was in his blood. He loved fixing them, working on them. He could figure out how anything worked, from a Harley to a lawn mower. Like, if our toaster broke, Mom would say we had to get a new one, but Dad would say, hold on, I bet it's just a loose wire or something. Something he said to me once, I've been thinking about lately."

"What was that?"

"I was hanging out with him in his shop while he was trying to get some guy's Kawasaki going again, and he's got oil on his hands, and there's this little streak of grease on his cheek, right here." She pointed to herself. "And it made him look so, I don't know, cool. Anyway, he stops and he says something like, and I don't remember it exactly, but he says machines are wonderful things, that they make our lives better and easier, but we can't ever forget how to do things for ourselves. That if, one day, all the machines disappeared, we'd have to know how to fend for ourselves. You know that he never used a calculator?"

"Seriously?"

"He could pretty much do math in his head, but when it was something tricky, he'd use a pencil and paper. He'd multiply things that way, or do long division. He said calculators had made us all mentally lazy, that we were losing the ability to think."

Bruce smiled. "You're right. I would have liked him."

"He'd have hated these self-driving cars," Katie

said. "Even if they weren't trying to kill us. He'd probably have—"

"Up ahead," Bruce said, taking his foot off the gas and letting the car coast.

Katie looked. A bald man was emerging, tentatively, from the woods, scanning the road in both directions. When he saw the Cadillac, he ran out into the road, standing in the center, waving his hands back and forth in the air, signaling them to stop.

"What do you want to do?" Bruce asked.

Katie shrugged. "I don't think it'd be right to run him down."

"I concur," he said, hastening the car's stop by putting his foot on the brake.

As they got closer to the man, he came into focus. Late forties, early fifties, probably, with a mustache, bit of a paunch. His eyes were wide with fear.

"Oh my God, thank you," he said, running to Bruce's open window as he brought the car to a full stop. "I can't believe it! A real live car!"

The man was panting and his shirt was soaked almost everywhere with sweat except, strangely, not on his rounded tummy.

"You okay?" Bruce asked.

He nodded furiously. "I was making my way through the woods. Roads aren't safe. Those crazy cars, they're everywhere. Have you seen any of them?"

Katie spoke up for the first time. "Oh, yeah. Back there, a couple of miles."

The man stopped panting long enough to ask, "You mind taking on a passenger?"

Bruce and Katie exchanged a quick look. After

a second, Katie shrugged, as if to say, *We can't just leave him here*.

Bruce looked at the man and said, "Yeah, sure. I'm Bruce, by the way, and this here is Katie."

"Glad to meet you," the man said as Bruce opened the door and leaned into the steering wheel, allowing their hitchhiker to tip the driver's forward and access the back seat. "I'm Ben. Ben Stapleton."

"Welcome aboard, Ben," Bruce said, putting his seat back into place and closing the door.

"I was here for the big Arrival event, if you can believe it," said the man calling himself Ben Stapleton.

Katie spun around. "Did you see my mom? Is she okay?"

"Your mom?"

"Sandra Montrose? She organized the event! I can't get hold of her!"

The man slowly nodded. "Right, right, yeah, I did see her. She gave out the press kits. Last I saw, she was okay."

"You're sure?"

"Pretty sure. So . . . if you were thinking of heading to the community center, I wouldn't bother. And most people are trying to get away from there, anyway."

"We're headed to the mall," Bruce said. "Looking for Katie's brother."

"Oh," said the man. "I was wondering, you think you could drop me off at the ferry on your way?"

"The ferry?" Katie said. "That's the opposite direction."

The man said, "Yeah, I know. But if you were

smart, you'd be heading there, too. I mean, you've got your own wheels! The ferry's still got to be running. That's the best way to get the hell out of here."

Bruce caught a glimpse of the man in his rear-view mirror. "The mall's our priority at the moment, friend."

The man in the back seat didn't look very happy with that. He sat there sullenly for a moment before trying again.

"Maybe I can change your mind about that," he said, reaching for something in the pocket of his sport jacket.

Twenty-Nine

O nce Joe Bridgeman had carried his mother into the house they shared, he deposited her gently into a kitchen chair and asked repeatedly whether she was okay, as though he didn't believe her the first time she'd said yes.

"I'll hurt like hell tomorrow," she told him, rubbing one shoulder and then the other. "But right now, I'm okay, and glad to be alive." She frowned. "I could use a couple of Advils, and I'm going to need a new wheelchair."

"Don't worry about that," he said. "I'll get you sorted out."

He was checking her for bruises or cuts or any other injuries she might have sustained while doing battle with the Arrival.

"Really, I'm okay," Lillian said. She reached up, grasped his arm, and gave it a squeeze. "I don't know what I would do without you."

Joe smiled awkwardly. "So, some Advils. Where do you keep those?"

Lillian said, "Forget the Advils. I could use a scotch."

"Coming right up," said Joe, gently prying his mother's fingers from around his arm. He went to the cupboard below the countertop where his mother kept her liquor. Since she'd been spending more time in a wheelchair, many of the items that once found a home in the upper cabinets had moved south.

He brought out a bottle of Ballantine's and a tumbler and poured his mother a finger's worth. She inhaled the aroma first, moved the amber liquid around in the glass, then downed it in one shot.

She looked at her son and asked, her voice serious, "You know there was someone under that car that was coming after me," she said.

"I know," Joe said.

"I think it was Daniella."

Joe's eyes closed briefly. "Oh, Jesus."

"That poor, poor girl," Lillian said. "This is so horrible."

Joe nodded with shared grief.

"How many others?" Lillian asked her son. "How many others are dead?"

Joe hesitated before replying. "Reports are coming in from all over. I'm hoping it's not as bad as it sounds, but it might be. We're stretched too thin to be able to deal with this on our own. Help's coming but I don't know when it's going to get here."

"But what about until then?"

"I don't see a way for those cars to get you here in the house, but to be safe, let's get you up to the second floor. One of those things might find a way to break through the front door, but I don't see them climbing a set of stairs."

As Joe spoke, his voice faltered. When his chin began to quiver, he turned away from his mother so she wouldn't see.

"Joe?" she said.

When he did not respond, she said his name

a second time. He took a moment to compose himself before turning around. "We really should get you up to your room. We'll take up everything you need." He forced a smile. "I suppose that would include the scotch."

"Don't forget the ice," she said, nodding her agreement.

Joe got his mother settled up on the second floor. He'd had a stairlift installed a few months ago, with a seat built into it, so he didn't have to help her up. Once upstairs, he assisted her into the bathroom, discreetly slipping into the hall while she did her business. Then he helped her to her bedroom. She got comfortable in a faded, fraying lounge chair, and he made sure she had something to drink—bottled water, as well as her scotch and some ice—and her favorite snacks, including a cardboard tube of Pringles and some seedless grapes. He set her phone on the table next to her and connected it to a charger.

"Joe," she said as he was starting to leave the room, "can you grab me the remote?"

It was resting on the bedside table, next to a well-thumbed, used paperback copy of a John Irving novel. Joe grabbed it, and the book, and set them in his mother's lap.

"I really have to go, Mom," he said, his face starting to crack again.

She nodded. "Go save the island," she said. "And be careful."

He tried to smile. "Later, I'll arrest myself for stealing a bicycle."

Joe slipped out of the room. She heard him go

down the stairs and out the door. She picked up the remote with her bony hands and hit the red button to turn on the oversized, boxy television that sat atop her dresser. She flipped through the channels until she landed on CNN. Where was Wolf? Wasn't Wolf supposed to be on now? It was one of the women anchors. Lillian couldn't keep them all straight. They all looked the same to her. All very young and very pretty. At least when it was Wolf, you *knew* it was Wolf.

The female anchor was saying, "Details of what, exactly, is happening on Garrett Island continue to come in. There are reports of multiple casualties as autonomous cars made by the Arrival corporation continue to go haywire. And it's not just happening on the island. We're hearing that across the country."

She watched a few more minutes of the news and concluded that she knew more than the reporters did. She'd had some firsthand experience of what was going on here.

Lillian picked up the remote and started flipping through the channels.

"Oh," she said when she landed on *Dr. Phil*.

He should do a show on her, she thought. Dr. Phil should do a show about sons who were thinking about putting their mothers in a home.

She couldn't imagine that Joe would do that now. Not after what she had been through. She'd been *traumatized*.

Every cloud had a silver lining.

Joe hopped onto his stolen bike and pedaled toward the downtown. The headquarters of the

Garrett Island Police Department was one block off the common, and that seemed like the most sensible place from which to get a handle on things.

The street out front of the house he shared with his mother was, at least right now, clear of Arrivals, so he was able to make good time. He was rounding a corner into another part of the neighborhood, the coast still clear, when his cell phone rang.

He took one hand off the handlebars and got the phone out of his pocket. On the screen were the words LISA CARVER.

So maybe she wasn't the one who'd been injured at the event. When he'd talked to his dispatcher, he'd said something about the president of the company losing her leg. Maybe she wasn't as badly hurt as he'd been led to believe. He tapped on the screen to take the call.

"Chief Bridgeman," he said.

"Joe!"

Who the hell—

"*Sandra?*" he said.

"Yes!" she cried.

"Are you okay? And why are you using Lisa—"

"Where are you?" she said.

"I just left my house. One of those cars tried to get my mom and—"

"Oh God! Is she okay?"

"She's fine, she's fine."

"Have you seen my kids?" she asked, her voice frantic. "Any chance you've seen Katie and Archie? They're not answering."

"No, no, I haven't. I'm almost to headquart—"

"No!" Sandra said. "You need to come here!

To the community center. Are you in an actual car?"

"I've got a bike. But what's happening here? I heard about the fire engine and—"

"It's bad here," Sandra told him. She lowered her voice. "Lisa Carver's dead. At least one person from the fire department. Maybe others."

Joe said nothing.

"Joe, you there?"

"Yeah, yeah, I'm here. I just can't believe all this. I can't—I just can't be—"

"I need you here. I'm thinking, if we can get into Lisa Carver's laptop, maybe we can find a way to stop these cars dead."

"Okay," Joe said slowly.

"And of all the people I know, you understand computers better than anyone."

"I don't know, Sandra. I mean, there was a time when I was a techie, but it was years ago. They've been upgraded like crazy since I worked with them."

"You're all I got, Joe."

"But—"

"Just come by here and see if you can hack your way in. It's a long shot, I know, but right now, I don't know what else to do."

"Okay, I can try. But don't get your hopes up."

"And on the way, can you go by my house? See if the kids are there?" Her voice dropped to a whisper and began to crack. "I'm scared to death, Joe. I'm scared to death something has happened to them."

"Okay," he said. "I'm on it. Hang tight. I'll get there as fast as I can."

Thirty

Running into Discount Bonanza was like entering the heart of a great metropolis. Archie glanced upward at the countless aisles of metal shelves that soared toward the ceiling like skeletal skyscrapers.

At ground level, huge wooden skids were piled high with everything the average American consumer could ever possibly want. Industrial-sized jars of pickles, enough to garnish the annual output of a dozen McDonald's. Packages with enough rolls of toilet paper to wipe the asses of every single person on Garrett Island, with enough left over to clean up the bums of half of Boston. Nobody came into Discount Bonanza expecting to buy a single tin of tuna. You left with a case of tuna, which then meant you also had to head down to aisle four and buy a bag stuffed with a minimum of five loaves of bread, all squishy and white, so you could make enough tuna sandwiches to last a lifetime.

The shelves above ground level were stacked with more skidloads of goods, shrink-wrapped in industrial-grade Saran Wrap.

As Archie ran toward the shelves, he scanned them the way a mountain climber might assess a cliff face. What was the safest way up? Where were the best footholds? What route offered the best chance of reaching the top in the least amount of time?

Archie had to make his assessment with considerably more speed than a mountain climber might. The latter didn't usually have a car on their ass.

Archie did.

The Arrival that had killed Nick was now in pursuit of Archie. He allowed himself only one glance back, enough to determine that the vehicle was a good eight to ten Arrival-lengths back, which he hoped would give him enough time to pick a shelf and start climbing.

He made a sharp turn down an aisle of cleaning supplies and spotted a sliver of space between products that led to the next aisle over. He darted in just as the Arrival squealed down the aisle, scrambled through, and came out the other side.

The Arrival, realizing it had been given the slip, stopped to recalibrate.

In this next aisle over, Archie looked up, as if from the bottom of a canyon. The shelf he'd snuck through looked promising. He grabbed a vertical metal railing with one hand, a horizontal shelf with the other, and got one foot solidly on an open crate of Swiffer refill pads. He hoisted himself up to the second shelf, then planted his foot on an immense, sealed skid of Mr. Clean antibacterial kitchen floor cleaner.

The Arrival on the other side emitted an electronic whine as it backed up. When it reached the end, it turned, shifted into drive, crept past the end of the massive shelving unit, and entered the aisle Archie had escaped to.

It stopped for a moment. Its various screens and sensors, designed to recognize human beings, determined Archie was not in this aisle, either.

The car sat there, as though puzzling it out. He had to have gone somewhere, it seemed to be thinking. His prey couldn't just vanish.

Archie, having successfully reached the third shelf, paused for a moment to assess his progress. His gaze went to the end of the aisle, his heart pounding.

Tha-thump. Tha-thump. Tha-thump.

The car began to inch forward.

Tha-thump. Tha-thump. Tha-thump.

Archie was barely breathing and not moving a muscle. But the car was slowly and silently moving in his direction.

Tha-thump. Tha-thump. Tha-thump.

Jesus, was it possible? Could the car hear his heartbeat? Or did it have some kind of built-in heat sensors?

The car stopped directly below Archie. The front wheels began to turn sharply, squeaking on the shiny, cement floor. Then, ever so gently, it nudged the shelf with its front bumper. Just enough to send a small shock wave through the metal bracing.

Archie felt the nudge.

The car, he concluded, was sending him a message.

I know where you are.

Okay, fine, Archie thought. You know where I am. Big fucking deal. What are you going to do, come up here after me?

Archie resumed his climb until he was sitting on the very top of the shelving unit, almost close enough to reach up and touch one of the hundreds of fluorescent tube fixtures that bathed the store in artificial light. No goods were stacked on this top shelf. It was like standing on a hundred-foot-long, ten-foot-wide runway. From this perch, Archie could see the tops of all the other towers of shelving. The aisles were, Archie guessed, eight to ten feet wide, allowing plenty of room for shoppers to maneuver their massive shopping carts in both directions, with room to spare. There would be no jumping from the top of one set of shelves to the next. Archie hadn't been bad at the long jump in gym class, but you had a running start for that. This shelf was hardly wide enough to work up much speed.

But that was okay. He'd wait up here as long as he had to. And if he got hungry, he'd drop down to the shelf below and see what he could find. Maybe a chocolate bar the size of a two-by-four, or a can of Libby's baked beans big enough to feed a platoon, assuming it had a pull-top. Archie had not thought to bring along a can opener on today's outing.

He nearly allowed himself a chuckle. If he ate enough baked beans, he'd end up making noises a lot louder than heartbeats.

If Nick were here, he'd try to break the tension with a good old-fashioned fart joke.

But Nick is dead.

Archie would have to grieve later. Right now, he had to worry about his own situation. Find a way out of here. Get back home to his mom and Katie.

He figured Katie was safe. He'd left her at

their house, and unless she was dumb enough to go looking for him, she was still there. But his mom was at the big Arrival event.

Archie felt a wave of fear wash over him. He'd had a few of those already since he'd arrived at Garrett Mall. But this was different. He wasn't scared about what might happen to him. He was scared about what might have happened to his mom.

I can't lose my mom . . .

Too.

He couldn't help notice that, as best he could tell, he was the only person in the warehouse-like store. When the Arrivals had come streaming in, Discount Bonanza staff and customers must have run like hell for the back rooms. Archie seemed to remember, from trips here with his mother, that there were other access points to the store, in addition to the mall entrance. There had to be a way to the outdoors. A loading dock, maybe.

But how safe was it out there? He'd told Nick he thought most of the Arrivals were in the mall, but was he right about that? At least right now, atop this set of shelves, Archie felt safe.

Had Rory made it? Did he find a way out of the mall after fleeing out the back door of Victoria's Secret and abandoning him?

"Asshole," Archie muttered under his breath.

After walking the length of the shelf and back again, he decided to sit and dangle his legs over the edge. In the time he'd taken to scope out his new surroundings, the Arrival that had given the shelf a threatening nudge had vanished.

"Yeah, take a hike, dickhead," he said.

He kicked his feet back and forth, wishing he

had a phone so he could check in with his mom or his sister. Archie, for the first time, felt guilty about the way he had treated his sister, tricking her so he could make his escape. And then he felt a second pang of guilt. His mother had wanted him to be on his best behavior today. Don't get into trouble, she'd said. This is a big day for me, she'd said. Don't fuck it up, she'd said.

Okay, maybe she hadn't said *that*, but it sure was impl—

Hello.

Archie heard the familiar squeaking of rubber on cement. The same sound that Arrival made before it had bumped his shelf. But this wasn't just one squeak.

It was a symphony of squeaks.

He stood back up and ran to the end of the shelf, where he could see all the way to the entrance from the mall. A convoy of Arrivals was coming his way.

Heading for his shelf.

And they were picking up speed as they got closer.

The lead car—the same one that had killed Nick, judging by the red streaks on its hood— was doing probably thirty miles an hour when it rammed the end of the shelf at a forty-five-degree angle.

The shelf teetered.

"Shit!" Archie screamed, suddenly broadening his stance so as not to lose his balance. The shelf had tilted about six inches for half a second before settling back to its original position. Archie noticed that while the shelf he stood atop seemed to be a hundred feet long, it was actually built in sections. The one he was standing on was no more than twenty feet in length. The upshot of all that was, the Arrivals didn't have to knock down a shelf that was the length of the entire aisle. They only had to knock down a part of it.

He looked down and saw other Arrivals positioning themselves in the aisle, side by side, but angled, as if parking on a street where you turn in, nose to the curb. They wouldn't have a lot of room to build up speed, but if they synchronized themselves—and Archie had no illusions about their ability to do that—and rammed the shelf at the same time . . .

Archie thought his best plan, for now, was to move to another part of the shelf, but before he could, the cars barreled into the shelving unit's vertical supports.

The shelf teetered a second time.

Archie cried out as he fell onto the top of the shelf, throwing out his arms to keep from landing on his face.

Half the cars would strike the shelf, and as they backed up to get ready to take another run at it, the remaining cars would ram the shelf. That way, even as the fronts of the cars crumpled, they maintained momentum, the shelf coming closer to toppling with each hit.

Archie found himself scrambling, crab-like, keeping his body low so he was ready each time the formerly level surface beneath him teetered. It was like that carnival fun house he and Katie went into on a family trip to South Carolina, with its shifting floors, rotating tunnels, walls of mirrors.

That was fun. This was not.

Skids loaded with merchandise fell to the floor. Another couple of hits and the whole thing was going to go over.

He was going to have to jump.

Every time the huge shelf leaned over, the aisle effectively narrowed. If he was going to leap, he'd have to time it just right.

The cars, continuing to work with a single, purposeful, networked mind, rammed the shelves one last time.

The shelf started to fall over.

Archie jumped.

He was hoping to reach the top of the shelves across the aisle, essentially hop from one surface to the next. But he didn't push off with enough speed, and ended up on a collision course with the shelf one below the top.

Archie's chest slammed into a cardboard crate filled with boxes of Tide detergent. His fingers dug into a partly opened seam in the clear plastic that encased the crate like a sausage casing. He managed to hang on, his legs dangling. His right foot found purchase and Archie shot himself upward.

But his troubles weren't over. The weight of the toppled shelf was slowly pushing over the one he was on now.

"Oh man," he said.

He'd have to make another jump. And maybe another one after that. The shelves had been turned into a set of towering dominos.

Archie leapt across another aisle, scrambled again to the top, felt it tilting beneath him. He didn't know that he could ride this wave across the entire Discount Bonanza. He needed to jump off.

So when the next shelf toppled, Archie doubled back instead of going forward. The structures that had come down weren't going to be moving anymore, so Archie worked his way into them, dropping his way through what were now empty spaces where crated goods used to be.

The overturned shelves also, ironically, offered greater protection from the Arrivals than he'd had before. He figured they could see him through the crisscross of metal bracing and shattered crates, but there was no way they could get at him this time.

Through the metal web of shelving, Archie could see, along a far wall, the meat department, with low, open refrigerated units filled with steaks and ground beef and chicken and sausage. Just beyond them was a wall of windows that looked into where all the butchering was done. There was a set of swing doors made of shiny aluminum. Archie believed if he could make it that far, the cars wouldn't be able to get at him. And he further believed that back there, somewhere, would be a loading dock that led to the outside world.

He crept his way through the collapsed shelving until he reached open space in front of the meat department. One quick sprint would get him to the door.

Archie looked one way and then the other. He could hear tires squeaking. They were coming, but he couldn't see any of them.

Archie was going for it.

He broke out into the open. An Arrival came

turning out the end of an aisle so quickly two wheels briefly left the floor. It sped toward him.

It never had a chance. Archie bolted past the meat display, slammed into the double doors with such force that they swung inward as far as their hinges would allow and bounced back, nearly slapping Archie in the face.

That was when he tripped over the dead guy.

He'd stumbled over a heavyset man, sprawled out on his back, arms outstretched, his legs a mangled, bloody mess. He was wearing a large white apron and a Discount Bonanza nametag that read STAN.

Maybe Stan had been out in the main part of the store when he'd been struck by an Arrival. It would have taken a couple of people to drag him back this far, but when it was clear Stan was a goner, they'd abandoned him.

Archie threw up.

He dropped to his knees and vomited no more than two feet away from the dead butcher, and suddenly felt shame that he hadn't managed to get farther away. Hadn't the man suffered enough? Did he really deserve, even in death, to have puddled puke inches from his head?

Archie struggled to his feet and looked for a way out, threading his way through several sides of beef hanging from hooks.

And there it was. A loading dock.

Next to the large garage door was a huge red button. You didn't have to be a rocket scientist to figure out what it was for. Archie slammed his palm onto the button and the door began to rise with a great, metallic rattle.

Archie felt sunshine on his face, fresh air fill

his lungs. He stepped out onto the raised plat-
form that trucks backed up to when making de-
liveries.

"Fucknuts," Archie said.

Out in the parking lot, just beyond the loading bay, sat half a dozen Arrivals, all looking his
way, like a welcoming committee.

Thirty-One

Are you sure?" Brandon Kyle asked, sitting in the middle of the sprawling back seat of Bruce's Cadillac, his legs straddling the driveshaft hump. "It wouldn't take that long to go to take a side trip to the ferry. Then you could be on your way to get this young lady's brother."

Bruce, behind the wheel, could only take quick glances at the hitchhiker they'd picked up, but Katie had turned sideways on the front bench seat so she could engage with Kyle.

"What'd you say your name was again?" Katie asked.

"Ben," he said. "Ben Stapleton."

"So, Mr. Stapleton, we get that you want to get to the ferry, but we gotta find my brother first, and then if there's anything we can do for you after that, well . . ."

At this point, she looked at Bruce. This was, after all, his car.

"Katie's right," Bruce said. "We're not exactly running a taxi service. Let's see how things go. If we run into any more of those little sons of bitches, that could change our plans, too."

"Don't seem to be too many of them out here," Kyle observed. "In the center of town, that's where they're gathered."

"You were there?" Bruce asked.

"I was," Kyle said with mock dismay. "Horrible, just horrible."

The Caddy continued to cruise along the country road, heading into a tunnel of trees.

"And what about at the community center?" Katie asked.

"Same thing," he said. "Chaos."

"So," Katie said, thinking, "how come you didn't stay there? Wouldn't it be safe in the building?" Her face became hopeful. "Was my mom safe inside?"

"Like I said, I don't really know about your mom," Kyle said. "I suppose I could have holed up in the building with the others, but for how long? They could be hiding in there for days. The smart thing is to find a way out. I was down by the harbor, and lots of people are heading out to sea until things calm down."

Katie looked at Bruce. "You think we should try to find my mom before we go to the mall? Maybe she's already heard from Archie." Her eyes widened. "Maybe Archie's with her! Maybe they got in touch with each other and that's where we should go."

Before Bruce could consider a change of plan, Kyle spoke up.

"No!" he said. "We're *not* going back there."

Bruce looked in the mirror. "You're not the captain of this ship, pal. Let me know where you want me to let you off and I'll pull over."

Kyle went silent. He turned his neck one way and then the other, avoiding eye contact with Katie. He looked out the windows, watching the trees flash by. He chewed his lip, as though mulling over what step to take next.

Katie said, "Listen, Mr. Stapleton, we're all just trying to get through this the best we can."

Bruce shot her a brief, admiring glance.

"I bet you've got people back on the mainland who are worried about you, right?" she said. "That's why you want to get off the island? Have you called them? Have you let them know you're okay? If you have, you could stop worrying about getting off the island and find a safe place to hide out until they find a way to stop the cars from killing everybody." She pointed a thumb toward the woods. "I mean, right in there, that's safe. There's no way the cars can get at you if you're hanging out in the woods. They're not tanks. They can't knock the trees down. When we get to the mall, maybe we can hang out there. It should be safe. All I'm saying is—"

"Shut up," Kyle said.

Katie scowled. "Excuse me?"

"Just shut up."

Bruce took his foot off the gas. "End of the road, friend," he said as the car slowed. He moved his foot over to the brake.

"No," Kyle said. "You're not kicking me out."

"That's exactly what we're doing," Bruce said.

As the car came to a full stop and Bruce put the car into park, Kyle reached into his jacket and pulled out the gun he'd stolen at the yacht club.

"Shit!" Katie screamed. "Bruce!"

Bruce first took a look into the rearview mirror, then slowly turned in the seat so he could look Kyle in the eye.

Kyle pointed the gun his way, but it was close quarters, even in a car as big as a 1959 Cadillac, so he held the gun close to himself, fearing Bruce might try to make a grab for it.

"Mister," Bruce said calmly, "we're all a little on edge right now, so I understand you might feel the need to take desperate measures, but waving that around at us, that's not helping the situation."

Kyle tilted his head toward Katie. "What's she to you? Granddaughter? Niece?"

"A good friend," Bruce said.

"Well, I'm going to shoot your *good friend* right through the seat if you don't take me to the ferry." Katie had shifted position, her back pressed up against the door. Kyle warned, "Don't even think of opening that door. If you make a run for it, it's him I'll shoot."

"Take the car," Bruce said. "We'll get out. You take the car. That way, no one gets hurt." Katie gave him a look of mute protest, which Bruce acknowledged with a nod. "I know, we want to find your brother, and your mom. But that'll be hard to do if we're dead."

But Kyle was not interested in the offer. "No. You drive. You're an islander, right?"

Bruce said, slowly, "For about thirty years."

"Then you know all the back roads. If we need to take them, to steer clear of those little four-wheeled bastards, you're the guy I need."

"Okay," Bruce said, calmly. "I'll drive you there. But you put the gun away. I know you've got it. I'm not gonna try anything funny. But guns can go off by accident. I hit some pothole, I don't want to end up with a bullet in my back."

Kyle pondered that for a moment before slipping the gun back into his jacket.

"And one other thing," Bruce said. "Let Katie here go."

Katie's eyes widened. "I'm not going anywhere."

"No, you listen to me," Bruce said to her harshly. "Let me give our friend here a lift to the ferry and I'll come back for you. Go into the woods there. You'll be safe."

"No," Katie said, looking him in the eye.

Bruce held her gaze for five seconds before looking away. There was something in her tone that told him there was no sense arguing the point any further.

"Okay, then," Bruce said. He straightened himself up behind the wheel, put the car into drive, and gave the beast some gas. "Road's a bit narrow to pull off a three-point turn in this sucker. I got to go up here and look for a place to turn around."

He drove a quarter of a mile until he reached a gravel driveway that led, presumably, to a house deep in the woods. He nosed the car into it, cranked the wheel hard in the opposite direction, and backed out onto the road, facing the other way. Katie sat sideways on the seat the entire time, staring at Brandon Kyle.

"What's wrong with your stomach?" she asked.

"What?"

"It's all lumpy."

Kyle looked down. Two of the bottom buttons of his shirt had come undone, exposing foam padding. "Oh," he said. "I've been looking to lose a few pounds. This is probably as good a time as any."

He undid two more buttons, exposing a milky white chest decorated with a few gray hairs, reached around to his back, and pulled on something, creating a Velcro-tearing sound. He yanked out the padding and tossed it down onto the floor. His now exposed stomach was wet with perspiration.

Kyle did up the button, tucked in his shirt, got himself resettled, and looked at Katie. "Like the show?"

"So who are you, really?" she asked.

"What's that supposed to mean?"

"Well, you're wearing a disguise, sort of. So you must be pretending to be someone you aren't."

"I told you my name. Ben Stapleton."

"Show me some ID," she said.

"You're hardly in a position to be asking."

"If you've got ID that proves it, it shouldn't be a big deal to show me," Katie said, persisting.

He dug into his pocket and found the ID badge he'd been provided by the Arrival corporation. "There," he said, waving it in front of her.

"That's bullshit," Katie said. "Think you could get a passport with that? What else ya got?"

Kyle glared at her.

"There are plenty of places on the island you could ride this out," she said. "But you're having a shit fit about getting away. And you've got a gun and a disguise." Katie stared at him for several more seconds, thinking.

Finally, she said, "Did you, like, rob a Garrett Island bank while everyone was freaking out about the cars? Is your fake tummy stuffed with cash?"

Kyle said nothing.

"Orrrrr," she said, still thinking, "you're, like, some bad guy with a phony identity, you've been hiding out on the island for ages, but now with all kinds of police and stuff coming here to stop the cars, they'll find you? Is it something like that?"

"Just shut up," he said.

Another theory occurred to her. "Orrrrr," she said again, more slowly this time, "you have something to do with it."

Kyle blinked and twitched his cheek, but still said nothing.

Katie noticed.

She said to Bruce, "What's it mean, when they say someone has a *tell*?"

Bruce glanced her way, gave her a look that asked, *What are you talking about?* But what he said was, "Like in cards. When someone's lying, or bluffing, they do something. Lick their lips, or touch their nose, or something."

Katie nodded. "I thought it was something like that." She trained her eyes on Kyle again. "So, you do have something to do with what's happening."

Bruce, hands at ten and two, kept the car moving at sixty as he glanced into the rearview mirror to gauge the hitchhiker's reaction.

"That's ridiculous," Brandon Kyle said.

Katie continued to stare. "What did you do?"

"I did nothing."

"What did you do?" she asked again.

"Stop looking at me."

"I'll stop looking at you if you tell me what you did."

"I told you, nothing."

"Then why do you have to get off the island?"

"Because people are getting killed here!" he snapped.

"You're trying to get away before they catch you," Katie said. "You have to get off Garrett Island before the army or whoever arrives." She shook her head. "They're probably *on* the ferry. You're basically going to hand yourself over to them."

That gave Kyle something to think about. "No . . ." he said slowly. "We won't be the only ones heading to the ferry. There'll be others. Dozens, maybe hundreds. When the ferry arrives, they'll evacuate us. They won't be stopping to ask questions. If—if the National Guard's on the ferry, they'll charge off, and islanders, they'll get on. That's how it'll work."

"You better hope," Katie said. "But what if we—"

"Katie," Bruce said.

"Huh?"

Bruce did a tiny shake of his head, a subtle warning. *Don't go there.*

"What if you *what*?" Kyle asked.

"Nothing," she said. Katie had gotten Bruce's message.

"What if you *tell*? Is that what you were going to say? When we get to the ferry, you'll point me out? Is that your idea?"

"No," Katie said. "That's not what I was going to say."

Bruce slowed. There was a stop sign ahead,

and an arrowed sign reading FERRY 2 MI, pointing to the right. Bruce rolled through the stop and cranked the wheel. "Soon," he said, turning his head so Kyle would be sure to hear him.

"We've been lucky so far," Katie said. "We haven't seen any more of them."

Bruce said, "Hmm."

"What?" she asked.

"I'm kind of wondering why we haven't."

They'd left the forested part of the island behind them and were now driving parallel to the shore. Beach houses and a strip of sand were the only things separating them from the sea.

"Ha!" Kyle shouted, pointing. "There it is! I told you! Didn't I tell you?"

What Kyle was looking at was, at first, hard to see. There was a growing cloud cover, and about a mile out, a haziness that signaled a thickening fog. Coming through it, a vague, looming shape.

"The ferry!" Kyle said.

He was right. The ferry was only a hundred yards or so out from the island. The docking facilities were beyond the oncoming hill that was little more than a shallow rise in the landscape.

Katie shifted in her seat so that she was now looking forward. Bruce reached over and touched her shoulder, a gesture meant to reassure and comfort. "It's going to be okay," he told her. "We drop him off, we turn around and head for the mall."

She nodded, head up, jaw forward, trying to look strong.

The car crested the hill. From here, they could expect to see the broad expanse of pavement where cars would, in normal times, line up for boarding, the ferry headquarters building, the wide metal ramp that would link to the ship once it reached the dock.

But the sight that greeted them included much more than that.

"Jesus," Bruce said as he slammed on the brakes.

The first thing they noticed was the fog. A low cloud had settled over the dock area. But it wasn't so thick that Bruce and Katie and Kyle couldn't see what was happening.

There were people. Hundreds of them, all running. Young and old, men and women, some bearing children in their arms. One man had slung an elderly woman over his shoulder.

Everyone was fleeing the ferry boarding area. Some headed up the hill, others went for the beach. The only thing that seemed to matter to them was that they get away.

It was clear what they were running from.

Arrivals.

Lined up in two perfect rows, all pointed where the ferry, still not visible because of the fog, would appear in seconds.

Bruce scanned the cars, wondering how many there were. Fifty? Sixty? Possibly more. But there was something particularly startling about these Arrivals.

Every last one of them was ablaze.

"Mother of God," Kyle said. "They've set themselves on fire."

"What?" Katie said.

"They must have deliberately short-circuited themselves." He said it with a sense of wonder. "This is amazing. This is *stunning*. They sensed a threat, pinpointed what it was, and decided to do something about it."

"Why the hell would they do that?" Bruce asked. "And how would you know?"

Kyle was too transfixed by the spectacle to answer.

Bruce persisted. "What are they going to—"

But then they saw.

The ferry materialized out of the fog. The convoy of flaming Arrivals suddenly sped forward, heading for the ramp, going faster with every passing second.

They launched themselves off the end of the ramp, like arrows set aflame and fired skyward by some medieval army. They sailed through the air, one after another, the first few missing the ferry altogether and going into the water, but the following waves of flaming vehicles reached the ferry deck, crashing into what looked like, from where Bruce and Katie and Kyle watched, jeeps and other military vehicles.

A man engulfed in flames leapt off the ferry and into the water.

The cars continued to sail through the air, bombarding the ferry. There was one explosion, then another. Fire began to spread across the deck, huge black clouds billowed out. Flames licked the upper levels of the ship.

"Son of a bitch," Kyle said. "Is there no way to get off this fucking island?"

Thirty-Two

After leaving his place, his mother safely tucked away upstairs, Joe Bridgeman pedaled first to Sandra's house. She'd had no luck reaching her kids by phone, and he'd promised to see whether they were there.

The streets of Garrett were largely deserted. Word obviously had gotten around that the safest place to be—if you couldn't get off the island altogether—was inside. The cars were deadly, but getting into buildings presented a challenge. At one point, he saw a woman standing in her front yard, clearly scanning the street to see whether it was now okay to be outside.

"Get back in your house!" Joe shouted at her as he cycled past.

"Where are they?" she shouted.

"Just get inside!"

It was a good question, though. He'd encountered not one Arrival since leaving his mother's house. He guessed the cars had gone where they expected to find the most people. The town's center, most likely. Maybe the mall, although that struck him as probably a safe place for people to hang out until the crisis had passed.

He pumped his legs as hard as he could. His calves and thighs were already screaming in pain when he'd reached his own house, having ridden from the ferry as quickly as he could. It had been more than twenty years since Joe had spent any time on a bicycle. Once he got his driver's license, the two-wheeler stayed in the back of his parents' garage. He'd never been a recreational cyclist, although had he been, Garrett Island was heaven. Thousands of tourists came every summer with bicycles strapped to the roofs of their cars, or rented them from numerous outlets throughout the island.

It took him ten minutes to reach the street where Sandra Montrose lived with Archie and Katie. He cut right across the front lawn, hopping off the bike steps from the house. He rang the bell, and when no one answered within ten seconds, he banged on the front door.

"Katie?" he shouted. "Archie? Anybody home?"

It was possible, he thought, they were hiding upstairs, or in the basement, and had not heard him. He tried the door, found it unlocked, and stepped into the front hall. Joe called their names a second time, loud enough to be heard anywhere in the house. He went through the first floor, out the rear door, and conducted a quick inspection of the separate garage. Satisfied that the kids were not here, he went back into the house.

He wished he had better news to give Sandra. But just because the kids weren't here, it didn't mean they'd come to any harm. They could be at a neighbor's house. Maybe they were at the home of one of Archie's friends.

Joe stood at the bottom of the stairs for several seconds before deciding to head up to the second floor. He walked down the hall to Sandra's room, stood in the doorway, his gaze settling on the bed. He was, of course, no stranger to it. They had slept together here half a dozen times. And they'd had more than one rendezvous on the Cape. But they'd never been intimate in his own home. Wasn't exactly easy, when you still lived with your mother. It wasn't that his mother would have disapproved. She wasn't a rigid moralist—*thou shalt not screw your brains out before marriage*—but did you really want to come down to breakfast in the morning and face her when she'd had to listen to the sounds of lovemaking the night before?

Once he had his mother settled into a first-class seniors' facility, would he and Sandra live here? Would he move her and her kids to his place? Or maybe they'd sell both properties and start off with something new.

This would be after they went public with their relationship, of course. Once they'd told Archie and Katie. Joe wanted to get to know them better. The only real contact he'd had with the kids was the night he came here to break the news about the death of their father, not counting the time he'd had to bring Archie home when he scaled the mast of that ship.

He hoped the memory of delivering bad news wouldn't be something the kids would hold against him. They'd have to move past that. He'd win them over. Take them, along with Sandra, for a day at the beach. Dinner at one of Garrett's posh resort hotels. (Joe knew all the hotel managers, so he could get a break on the bill, maybe even wangle a freebie.) An overnighter to Boston, maybe. Faneuil Hall Marketplace, lunch at Cheers. Joe knew they'd grow to love him. Not as much as their own father, of course. That was totally understandable. And he'd leave any disciplining issues to their mother. He could foresee all kinds of problems if he tried to assume a fatherly role too soon.

Better to hang back. See how things worked out.

And given that Katie was already sixteen, she might not even be around that much longer. She was a bright kid. Joe was betting she and her mother were already talking about colleges. That'd mean, before long, it'd just be Sandra and Archie, who no doubt was in need of a good, strong father figure.

Joe knew he was born to play that role.

He wouldn't just be gaining a wife when Sandra married him. He'd be gaining an entire family. Just like that.

He could tell Sandra hadn't totally made up her mind yet. He needed to bring her around. But that was coming. She *would* love him. He was sure of that. And after all the shit that had gone down here on the island today, people would be wanting to pull together.

Family would become more important than ever.

Joe took one last, long look at the bedroom. The white bedspread. The pale blue wallpaper with narrow vertical stripes in a darker shade of blue. It all looked nice enough. He could live with this. Besides, decorating was never really his thing. Didn't much matter to him what pattern the wallpaper was, what kind of lamps Sandra picked, what color the sheets were. But he'd have to do something about that picture on the bedside table, the one of Sandra with her late husband. The times he'd been here, in that bed, he'd been careful not to glance over at it. Didn't make sense, he knew, being jealous—or even fearful—of a dead man, but that was how he felt. One time, he'd started to lose his erection, seeing Adam Montrose's smile, a twinkle in his eye, as if he was looking right at Joe, saying, *One day, when you get to heaven, I am going to pound the ever-lovin' shit out of you.*

It wasn't like he could fold the picture down, or flip it around to face the wall. Not at this stage of their relationship. But when they'd made it official, he'd broach the subject. Suggest she move the picture to the kitchen or the living room. Or tuck it away in a drawer. A reasonable request, he figured.

It was time to go.

Sandra wanted him at the community center. She had high hopes he could get into Lisa Carver's computer.

He didn't like his chances.

Joe descended the stairs so quickly he nearly stumbled when he got to the bottom. Good thing his mother wasn't here to see that. She never passed up a chance to tell him how clumsy he was on his feet.

Joe could have called Sandra and told her Archie and Katie were not at the house, but bad news was best delivered in person. He exited the house, hopped back on the bike, and started pedaling.

Thirty-Three

Lisa Carver's phone hadn't been out of Sandra's hand for a second. She kept willing it to ring with news that Joe had found her kids safe and sound. If only she still had her own phone, that Gracie hadn't run off with it. The kids might have called it dozens of times, were as worried about her as she was about them.

Not that the phone in her hand wasn't ringing. Word had spread far beyond the island that something had gone horribly wrong with the Arrival presentation. People close enough to Lisa to have her personal cell phone number were calling, one after another, hoping that the news of her passing was wrong. In the past half hour, Sandra had taken calls from several other titans of industry—one of them, she was pretty sure, was Richard Branson, but she hadn't stayed on the call long enough to confirm it—as well as celebrities and politicians.

"I'm not Lisa Carver," she'd been saying. "Ms. Carver—I'm sorry to be the one to tell you—is dead. I have to go." *God forgive me*, she thought, *if I just told a mother or sister or brother to basically fuck off.*

Sandra emerged briefly from the community center to survey the damage. There was little left of the fire truck but charred, black metal. The ambulance was on its side, surrounded by several Arrivals that had essentially destroyed themselves in the attack. What had become of the paramedics? The surviving firefighters?

When she went back inside, Sandra had to deal with a different group of predators: journalists. They had questions and expected Sandra to provide answers. She'd been in the administrative office with Albert Ruskin, trying to figure out a way to get into Carver's laptop, when several reporters started banging on the door.

"You go," Ruskin said, his voice shaking. "I can't. I just . . . I can't do it."

Sandra had given him an icy glare, but had agreed to meet with reporters in the gym in five minutes. "What am I going to tell them?" she asked Ruskin. "What's the plan? What's the strategy?"

Ruskin muttered something under his breath that sounded like little more than gibberish.

"What?" Sandra asked. "Tell me!"

But when he raised his head, and Sandra could look him in the eye, she saw nothing there. He was shutting down.

"Fine," she said, and headed for the gym.

The questions came at her like a hail of bullets.

What had gone wrong? Was it a software fault by the company? Was Arrival Inc. a victim of corporate sabotage? Were the rumors of a ransomware attack true? What was the death toll across the island? Was it true that Arrivals elsewhere had gone rogue? What was happening to the company's stock price? Had trading in Arrival shares been halted? Would Arrival financially compensate the families of those who'd died today?

Sandra tried her best with each question, coming up every time with, essentially, a variation of "I have no fucking idea."

She attempted to explain that while she'd helped organize this event, she was not an official spokesperson for the Arrival corporation. The more logical person to answer those questions was Albert Ruskin, she insisted. Well, the reporters asked, why isn't *he* taking our questions?

Good question.

Sandra escaped the gymnasium briefly to the hallway, sticking her head, ostrich-like, into a drinking fountain recessed into the wall. She wished she could stay there forever, but there was only so much water she could swallow. When she pulled her head out, Rebecca Geary stood there, arms folded across her chest.

"Where's Ruskin?" she asked. "If you don't have any of the answers, he must. He was Lisa's executive assistant, for Christ's sake. Right now, at the worst possible time, this Fortune 500 company is leaderless, rudderless."

How true. The vice president of Arrival was on some African safari and no one had been able to reach him. And even if they could, the best he'd be able to do is issue a statement. What the media needed was someone to be the face of the company, someone to go on camera, someone to take questions, someone who could at least give the impression that the Arrival corporation cared about the mess it had created, and would do everything in its power to make things right. And let's face it, Rebecca was implying, Sandra was not cutting it.

"Off the record," Sandra said, and she waited for Rebecca to give a nod of understanding, "I think Ruskin's having a nervous breakdown."

Rebecca's expression gave no evidence of sympathy. "Yeah, well, people are dead. He needs to put on his big-boy pants and get out here."

Sandra took a deep breath. "Let me try him again."

The phone in her hand rang. She glanced down, saw HILLARY CLINTON on the screen. She declined the call.

She trotted down the hall to the administrative office. When she turned the handle, she found it locked. She rapped on the frosted glass.

"Ruskin!" she cried. "It's me."

When several seconds went by without a response, she rapped again, harder this time.

"If you don't let me in I'm going to break—"

The door opened three inches, revealing a sliver of Albert Ruskin's face.

"Are you alone?" he asked.

"I'm alone."

He opened the door wider to admit her, then closed it and turned the lock.

"You have to get out there," she said.

"I don't care," he said, turning his back to her and walking to the far corner of the room, as if he could somehow escape her there. Between them was a desk, and on top of it, the laptop that had belonged to Lisa Carver.

"You're Arrival's *only* official here. Your boss is dead. Your company's reputation, if there's anything of it left, is up to you to defend. There's an angry media mob out there wondering why you're not talking to them."

"I . . . I just . . . I can't . . ."

"You've heard of getting ahead of something?" Sandra said. "Well, it might be a little late for that now. But how far behind do you want to get? Every second you spend in here blubbering, things get worse."

She briefly placed her hands on her head, as if preparing to tear her hair out.

"What is it, Mr. Ruskin? Don't you *care*? Don't you give a shit about this company?"

He slowly turned and looked at her, as though suddenly realizing she was there. And, as if it were made of putty, his face began to transform. His grim expression morphed into something different.

He was grinning.

"The bitch is dead," he said.

Sandra blinked. "What?"

"I feel like . . . like I've been liberated. The bitch is dead and I'm a free man." The grin broadened and he laughed. "It's just starting to sink in."

Sandra thought, *Is this happening?*

"She can't torment me any longer," he said. "Have you ever wondered what it would feel like to get out of prison?"

"Um . . ."

"I'm betting it feels like this." His grin scaled back to a smile and he looked more contemplative. "Do you know what I used to do?"

She shook her head.

"I ran a food bank." Ruskin chuckled. "Can

you believe that? My life was devoted to helping the hungry, the disadvantaged. But there wasn't a whole lot of money in running a food bank—surprise, surprise—so I turned to the corporate world, working first at Tesla. And then I got headhunted to come work at Arrival, and eventually become Lisa's assistant." He paused. "I was warned. But I didn't listen."

"Warned?"

"She'd had plenty of assistants before me." He grinned. "Kind of like husbands. She couldn't hang on to those, either. Had two. Didn't take long before they realized what she was. A succubus, that's what she was. A female demon."

It occurred to Sandra at that moment that of all the calls that had come in to Lisa Carver's phone, none had been from family. "Kids?" she asked.

Ruskin shook his head. "No. Imagine what a mother she would have been. There were rumors that, in her teens, she had a child, but I don't know."

He lowered his voice to a whisper. "I became her latest assistant, her latest *victim*. She was a cat, and I was her mouse. A mouse you don't actually kill, or eat, but one you torment, that you tease. The night before my wife and I were to go on a second honeymoon, she dropped ten assignments on my desk. We had to cancel. Lisa knew. She knew what she was doing. It was a test of loyalty."

"I didn't know you were . . ."

"Married? Yeah, at one time. Lisa . . . destroyed our marriage. She knew all the relevant birthdays and anniversary dates—not just ours but her parents' or mine—and even if we had tickets to something amazing, like a Broadway show that was impossible to get into, she'd always come up with something I had to do, something that took priority over everything, some report that had to be done, some presentation that had to be prepared. Andrea couldn't—"

"Andrea?"

He nodded. "My wife. Andrea couldn't take it. She left me. She said to me one day, I had to make a choice. Her, or Lisa. My marriage, or my job."

Sandra said. "And you chose wrong."

A sly but sad smile crossed Ruskin's lips. "Maybe. But I wasn't going to let Lisa win. It was like she was daring me to quit, like all the others who'd come before. See how much shit I'd put up with before she broke me." He drew in a breath. "I wasn't going to let her break me." The grin returned. "She did not break me."

"I don't . . . I don't understand. When you're in a horrible job, you quit, you find something else." She paused, weighing her words. "That's what any . . . normal person would do."

Ruskin ran his finger along the edge of the laptop. "I'd never walked away from a challenge. My father, he . . . he . . ."

Ruskin stopped briefly, clenched his jaw.

"My father used to drill into me that only losers quit. Only losers walk away. When things get tough, you don't knuckle under. You fight back."

"But a deliberatively manipulative, nasty boss—walking away from someone like that— how could that be wrong? How could anyone blame you for that?"

"Every time I was ready to walk, I'd hear my father's voice in my head. Doesn't matter that he's been dead for more than twenty years. He's always there, judging me. So I didn't quit, I didn't walk away, I hung in. *I was not going to let her defeat me.*" He paused, and then he smiled. "And I didn't. Lisa Carver perished, and I've survived."

Ruskin smiled and extended his arms to the sides, as if getting ready to dance. "Free. I'm free."

Sandra asked, "What did you mean, when you said 'fight back'?"

"Hmm?"

"You said fight back. How'd you fight back? Lisa died." She paused. "You got lucky. You didn't defeat her yourself." Another pause. "Or did you?"

He shook his head, then smiled as he continued to run a finger along the edges of the laptop. The two of them entered into a moment of silence that ended when someone else rapped at the door.

"Hold on!" Sandra shouted.

"What is it they say?" Ruskin asked. "Karma's a bitch?"

"What are you saying?"

"No sense covering up for her now. Brandon Kyle wasn't wrong. He wasn't crazy. Lisa killed that movie producer and his girlfriend in the Gandalf. Not directly, of course. That's the beauty of the world today. You never have to actually be there. She planted someone at Gandalf HQ years ago. Someone with the skills to plant a tiny little virus. A random bit of nastiness that wouldn't hit the whole fleet, but a car or two.

Like dropping a cockroach into some cake batter. Most of the cake, it's okay, but you get that one slice . . ."

"Did you know?"

"How could I not know? She bragged about it all the time."

"And that woman? The one who used to work for Brandon Kyle, who came to Arrival? Who had that accident in the bathroom and died?"

Ruskin smiled at her like she was a five-year-old who'd just figured out how to tie her own shoes.

"What do you think?"

He looked contemplative again. "Maybe I should go out there and talk to them. Tell them everything Lisa did."

"And what you did, too," Sandra said.

"What?"

"It's pretty clear you hated Lisa Carver as much as Brandon Kyle did. Maybe you were working together." She thought about what she was going to say next. "Maybe you helped him pull off what's happened here today."

Someone else rapped loudly on the door.

Sandra turned her head again and shouted, "In a *minute*! We're drafting a statement!"

From the other side, a man shouted: "Sandra?"

"Joe?"

"Yeah!"

Sandra gave Ruskin one last accusatory look before unlocking the door and opening it. Joe put his arms around her, pulled her close, and Sandra briefly laid her head on his chest. But she quickly pulled away and looked up at him.

"The kids?"

Joe shook his head. "I checked the house. No sign."

The air seemed to go out of Sandra. "Shit," she said, turning away, putting a hand to her cheek to catch a tear. "Shit, shit, shit."

"But listen," Joe said, putting a hand on her shoulder. "I didn't see anything to suggest anything bad's happened to them. They're out there, somewhere, but I'm betting they're okay. They're smart kids."

"I've tried to call, they won't answer . . ."

She turned her attention back to Ruskin.

"You son of a bitch," she said. "That's what you did, isn't it? Made a deal with Kyle. Was he here today? Is he Stapleton? Did you help him do this?"

"No," he said, shaking his head as Sandra closed the distance between them, backing him into a corner.

"Sandra," Joe said. "What's happening here?"

She pointed a finger at Ruskin. "Somehow, he did this. I *know* it. I can *feel* it. He had his reasons. He's as much as admitted it." She pointed to the laptop that belonged to Lisa Carver. "I bet he knows how to get into that. I bet he knows how to make all this stop."

Ruskin continued to shake his head. "No. Look, I'm not sorry Lisa's gone, but I didn't have anything to do with this shit show. And even if I *could* get into her computer, I've no idea how to stop it."

Sandra wasn't buying his denials. She gave Joe a desperate look. "Give me your gun."

"*What?*" Joe said.

"Just give it to me!" She held out her hand, as

though expecting Joe to do what she'd asked. To a wide-eyed Ruskin, she said, "You'll shut these cars down or I'll fucking shoot you in the foot."

"*Sandra*," Joe said with forced calmness. "We can't do that."

"You're crazy," Ruskin told her. "You're out of your mind."

Sandra, realizing she might have crossed a line, said, "There has to be a way. Joe knows computers. The two of you, working together—"

"Oh, please," Ruskin said, casting a derisive look at the police chief. "Does he work at the Genius Bar in his spare time? Does he go to India on vacation and offer tech support?"

When Joe's jawline hardened, Ruskin realized he'd just pissed off the one possible ally he had in the room. "Sorry," he said. "Look, I'm telling you, it's not my doing. I don't have to put up with this one more minute."

He pushed Sandra out of his way.

"Hey!" she said.

"Whoa, hang on," Joe said as Ruskin moved past Sandra and headed for the door.

"Stop him!" Sandra said. "Joe, handcuff him or something!"

"You have no right!" Ruskin said.

"Arrest him!" Sandra said. "Arrest him for *something*."

Joe was nonplussed. "Sandra, I just can't—"

Ruskin needed to get past Joe to leave the room. He waved a hand, a wordless command that the chief get out of his way.

"Mr. Ruskin, I think it'd be a good idea if you did hang in. I mean, I do have a few questions—"

He glared at Joe. "You going to shoot me in

the foot if I don't answer them? I'd rather take my chances with those fucking cars than stay in here with that crazy woman. I just got rid of one bitch and now I've got another."

"Whoa, hold on there, Mr. Ruskin, that's no way—"

"Get the fuck out of my way."

Ruskin tried to shove Joe out of his path, and Joe wasn't having any of it. He grabbed hold of Ruskin's shirt and tossed him back into the room.

Ruskin lost his footing and stumbled backward.

As he headed for the floor, the back of his head connected with the edge of the desk, making a sound not unlike a baseball bat connecting with a pitch.

Ruskin went down. He settled into a heap, not moving.

Joe looked at Sandra, his mouth open, as if trying to express his shock and regret, but no words came out.

Sandra looked equally stunned, but at least she managed to speak.

"Tell me he's not dead," she said.

Joe quickly knelt down next to the man, put two fingers to his neck, hunting for a pulse. Blood was already beginning to pool beneath Ruskin's head.

"He's not dead," Joe told Sandra. "But he's out cold."

"We need to call—"

Sandra didn't bother to finish the sentence. The Garrett Island ambulance was outside, overturned. Calling for help was not an option.

"I'll find some ice, a pillow, a first aid kid or something," Sandra said. "I saw something in one of the other rooms. In the meantime, can you get into that computer?"

Still kneeling next to the unconscious Ruskin, Joe said, "Honestly, I don't like my chances."

Thirty-Four

For now, Archie believed he was safe.

Standing on the Discount Bonanza loading dock, looking out toward the Garrett Mall parking lot in the distance, and the assembly of Arrivals right in front of him, Archie took stock of his situation.

There was no way the Arrivals could get at him. The loading dock was a good four feet above pavement level, and the only thing leading up to it from the loading bay area was a three-foot-wide concrete set of steps with a rusted metal railing. Archie didn't see any way the cars could use it to their advantage. Nor did he think the layout of the loading dock area was such that the Arrivals could drive over each other to reach him the way they'd done with the escalators.

He'd counted twelve Arrivals sitting out there on the asphalt beyond the loading bay, all aimed his way, watching. Archie felt like a cat in a tree with a pack of dogs hanging around the trunk. You weren't in immediate danger, but you weren't going anywhere, either.

Archie definitely wanted to go somewhere. Archie wanted to go home. He wanted his mom. He even wanted his sister.

He saw no upside to going back into Discount

Bonanza or the attached mall. The place was lousy with Arrivals.

There was about a hundred feet of asphalt between the loading docks and a chain link fence that bordered the mall parking lot. Beyond that, trees and a drop-off to a drainage ditch that, right now, would either be bone dry or have no more than an inch of water in it. Archie knew if he could make it to the fence, scaling it would be simple, and traversing the ditch would be equally easy. Even if one or more of the cars could smash through the fence without getting tangled up, they'd never make it across the ditch. These Arrivals might be versatile little vehicles, but they weren't Jeeps.

Once past the ditch, Archie believed he could make it safely home if he stayed off roads and sidewalks. But that hundred feet across the parking lot to the fence might as well have been a hundred miles.

You could not outrun one of these cars.

Nick was proof of that.

And yet . . .

Archie studied how the cars had arranged themselves. They certainly deserved points for neatness. Three rows of cars, four deep, all faced his way. If he were to leap off the loading dock and run between them, how long would it take them to turn around, all bunched up like that? How quickly could they reorient themselves and begin their pursuit?

Archie glanced at his bare arm and saw goose bumps. Maybe that made sense. He was scared, after all. But then he realized he was feeling cold. The temperature was dropping. At first, he wondered if it was because he was standing just beyond the meat department. Plenty of freezers back there. Frosty air could be drifting out.

But no, the coolness seemed to be coming from outdoors. And then he saw why.

Fog was rolling in.

It was drifting in from the left of the loading docks. It happened often on the island. Archie wasn't exactly sure why. He'd never studied climatology. He didn't watch the Weather Channel. But he'd heard about what happens when cold air passes over warmer water, and by this time of year, the water around Garrett Island had been warming up all summer. Every once in a while, fog rolled in, and quickly.

The low hanging cloud of mist was enveloping the cars. Before long, the fence at the far end of the parking lot had disappeared.

Archie wondered.

How well equipped were the Arrivals to handle fog? He knew there were plenty of sensors and cameras mounted all over them, even if you couldn't actually see them. Would fog disable an Arrival's ability to navigate? Did they have the kind of radar that big planes had? Planes landed in fog, didn't they?

Archie was betting the Arrivals were *fantastic* in fog. Couldn't they detect pedestrians at the side of the road, even at night, even if the car's headlights were off? And how did they do that? Could the cars detect heat? The warmth of a human body? Kind of like the Predator, in those movies, when it picked up thermal images of those poor, doomed dudes trying to track it?

The fog was thickening. Pretty soon, even the cars watching Archie would be hard to see.

He had an idea.

Archie left the loading dock area and went back into the meat department. There had to be a locker. A *meat* locker. Where they kept everything really, *really* cold.

He found it in no time. He grasped the heavy metal handle on the door and swung it wide, feeling the cold air flow over him. He stepped into a room filled with sides of beef hanging on hooks like bloodied punching bags. He closed the door, careful not to let it latch. The last thing he wanted was to be locked in here. After everything that had gone down today, wouldn't it be a kick in the head, he thought, to freeze to death?

Which was, he instantly realized, a distinct possibility if that door *did* lock. It was motherfucking cold in here.

He spotted a thermometer affixed to the wall, easy to find under the fluorescent lights. It had Fahrenheit on one side, Celsius on the other. Archie didn't know anything about Celsius, but he sure knew that 33°F was downright chilly. And he didn't need any thermometer to tell him. He was shivering.

Archie figured, if he could stay here long enough to lower his external temperature, and if the fog outside became thicker, he might be able to walk right past those damn cars without their even seeing him.

Hey, it was a plan.

The immediate question was how long could he stand it in here. He figured he would give himself five minutes. There was a wall-mounted clock to help him keep track of the time.

After ninety seconds, his teeth were chattering. He briefly wrapped his arms around himself, rubbing his shoulders to keep warm, then decided that was defeating the purpose. He *needed* to be cold. Don't warm up any part of you. Who was that singer? The one who wore a dress made out of meat years ago? Lady Gaga? Yeah, that was what he needed. A cold meat outfit.

Okay, maybe he didn't have to go that far.

But he did see, on a wall hook, a butcher's frock—a white, long-sleeved, shirt-like jacket that went almost to the knees. Given that it was hanging in here, wouldn't it be as cold as the room?

Shivering more violently, he took the coat off the hook and slipped it on. If the fog was thick enough, a white jacket would offer even more camouflage.

He was ready. He needed to move quickly, before his body warmed up noticeably. Archie opened the door and ran for the dock.

Aware that the cars were also sensitive to sounds—hadn't they heard his heart beating when he was hiding atop those shelves?—he bottled up a *Hooray!* when he saw that the fog had, in fact, grown thicker in the last few minutes. He hoped the butcher's coat would muffle his breathing and heartbeats.

But the cars also detected motion, so his plan was to move very, very slowly. He descended the short concrete steps, taking about five seconds with each one.

The cars did not stir.

When he reached the bottom step, he paused. The formation of Arrivals was ten feet ahead of him, although he could barely detect their shapes through the thick mist. He inched his way forward, hopeful his movements were too slow to be picked up. Once clear of the vehicles, he would head straight for the fence, but maintain his snail-like pace.

No sense taking any chances.

Slowly, slowly, slowly . . .

He was at the bumper of a front-row Arrival.

Don't touch.

The sensors would surely pick him up if he came into actual contact with a car. He squinted through the moist air, saw this Arrival was flanked by two others. He decided to go right, slip in between them.

They were sitting closely together—no more than a foot and a half apart, but still enough room for Archie to work his way through if he went sideways.

Archie inched his way along, careful not to brush up against any part of the cars.

Oh, shit.

The outside, door-mounted mirrors. The one on the right side of one car was lined up with the one on the left side of the other, maybe six inches, tops, of air between them.

Archie wondered, why put mirrors on these cars? No one sitting in them would have any reason to look into them! Or maybe they weren't mirrors at all, but housings for the cameras that kept track of everything that was going on around the vehicles.

Whatever. He had to get past them. Could he duck under? Or should he slip back out and go around another way?

Slip out, start again, then—

Archie felt something cool on his face.

A breeze.

A slight wind was coming up. Under any other circumstance, that'd be just fine. But this breeze was blowing away the fog.

Archie was running out of time.

So he bent at the knees, executing a kind of sideways limbo position, and worked his way under the pair of mirrors without touching them. Given how the cars were arranged, he'd have to do this maneuver three more times.

As the fog dissipated, the cars came into sharper focus.

If he could see them . . .

The Arrivals, in unison, made soft whirring noises.

Coming to life.

Getting ready.

The cars began to inch together, eliminating the gaps between them. Archie felt his legs getting squeezed.

"Shit shit shit shit."

He decided that touching the cars now presented no greater risk. In fact, if he was to save his legs from being crushed, he was going to have to hop up onto the cars. He put one hand on the roof of the car to his right, and his other on the car to his left, and hoisted himself up just as the two cars melded together with a resounding *crunch*. He rolled onto the roof of one car and sat there, trying to figure out what his next move would be.

Running for the fence was no longer an option.

The question now was, could he make it back to the loading dock? It was only a few feet to the concrete steps.

I can do it. I won't end up like Nick.

Archie sat, motionless, atop the car. Let them drop their guard, he thought. Let them think he was going to sit there, wait things out.

And then he moved.

Onto his feet. Onto the hood.

He leapt off it like it was one of those springboards they had in the school gym. He went airborne off the front of the car in the first row, landing six feet from the bottom of the steps to the loading dock.

He reached out, grabbed the iron railing that ran down the side of the steps, and used it to propel himself up to the third step, a millisecond before an Arrival rammed the bottom of the short stairway and ripped the railing from its moorings.

But by then, Archie was on the loading dock level, and out of reach. The Arrivals sat there, evidently accepting they were all back to square one. The one that had crashed into the stairs returned to the formation.

Archie, catching his breath, tore off the butcher's coat and tossed it onto the ground.

"Come on, guys. Can't you cut me some slack?"

He heard something. A growling sound. *Oh man, are the cars actually starting to sound like wolves, too?* It took a moment for him to realize the noise was not coming from the cars.

It was coming from his stomach.

Archie wondered if any of that meat back there was cooked.

Thirty-Five

Bruce put the Caddy into reverse, threw his right arm over the seat, and turned around to see out the back window. He locked eyes, for a second, with the man in the back seat.

"Where are we going?" Brandon Kyle asked. He touched his hand to his jacket, a signal that he was ready to take out the gun again if he needed it.

"The mall," Bruce said.

"No, wait," Kyle said. "Hang on."

Katie, sitting up front in the passenger seat, said, "That was the deal. We take you to the ferry. So we're here. Why don't you get out and leave us the fuck alone?"

Smoke continued to billow out of the front end of the ferry where the flaming Arrivals had leapt aboard. Before the clouds had completely obscured the view into the ferry deck, Bruce and Katie and Kyle had caught a glimpse of what looked like military vehicles, jeeps mostly. Whatever help had been dispatched was now unable to disembark. At least a hundred people who'd managed to get to the dock, hoping to board and escape to the mainland, had scattered.

While Kyle decided what order to give next, Bruce found a driveway to back into, conducted his maneuver with speed and efficiency, and had the Cadillac heading in the direction from which they'd come.

Bruce tromped on the accelerator and the huge car lumbered forward.

"The airport," Kyle said. "There's an island airport, right?"

Bruce nodded. "Yup. Small one."

"They got helicopters there?" Kyle asked. "I heard something about the cars blocking the runway, but a helicopter could get around that problem."

"You know how to fly a helicopter?" Bruce asked.

"No, I don't know how to fly a helicopter," Kyle sneered sarcastically. "But I can probably find someone who does."

"Sure," Katie said. "Turn on the charm. Who wouldn't want to help you?"

"Katie," Bruce said, his voice laced with caution. But she either didn't pick up on his warning not to provoke Kyle, or didn't care.

"I'm gonna ask you again," Katie said. "Did you have something to do with this? I mean, you're scared shitless about being caught here."

Kyle ignored her. "Take me to the airport," he said to the back of Bruce's head.

Bruce turned to Katie and said, "I know, roughly, where the airport is, but I'm not sure of the fastest route. You want to grab the map from the glove compartment?" He angled his head so his voice would be cast back toward Kyle. "Sorry, they didn't exactly have GPS when they built this beast."

Katie looked at Bruce as though he'd committed treason. "We're really going to help this asshole?"

Bruce, calmly, said, "Look in the glove compartment, Katie, and see what you can find."

She let out a sigh and pressed the button on the glove compartment door. The panel swung downward, revealing its contents. The map book was there, as Bruce had said it would be, along with a few other things Katie had seen when he'd popped open the compartment back at his house to grab the garage door remote. It was there, of course, as well as a micro cloth, and a can of window cleaner spray.

"You see it?" Bruce asked.

There was something in his voice, Katie realized. He didn't ask if she saw the map. He asked if she saw *it*.

The window cleaner.

"Yeah," she said. "I see it."

She grabbed hold of the map book, and as she took it out of the glove box, she brought out the window cleaner, too, tucking it down into the corner of the bench seat.

"Okay," Bruce said. "Look in the index, see if you can find the airport."

Katie thumbed through the book, going to the back pages. "Do you know the name of it?"

"It's just called Garrett Island Airport," Bruce said. "I mean, that's what everyone calls it, although maybe it's named after someone. I dunno."

Katie looked down at the index pages. "I don't see anything under airport. Do you know the road it's on, like its address?"

Kyle said, "For the love of—isn't there an overall map of the island on the first page? Just look there. Look for something with lines that look like runways. Have you never looked at a fucking map before?"

Katie glanced over the seat. "Okay, okay, good idea." She went back to the front of the book. "Um, let's see . . . Bruce, is the airport, like, in the middle of the island or the west end or east end?"

"More toward the middle," he said, eyes forward.

Getting ready.

Katie continued to leaf through the pages. "You'd think there'd be an overall map, but I'm not finding one right. . . . Oh, here's—no, that's Nantucket. So this map has other islands in it?"

Bruce nodded. "Yeah, plus the Cape. But it doesn't do the rest of Massachusetts. Just those parts."

"That's kind of confusing," Katie said. "Doesn't anybody just make a map of the island all by itself?"

"Yeah, sure. The tourism board does them, little fold-up ones you can tuck in your back pocket. But that book, it's a much more thorough—"

"For fuck's sake," Kyle said, leaning forward. "Give me the goddamn book. I'll find it."

Katie turned sideways on the front seat, closed the book, then handed it back to Kyle. He snatched it from her, sat back, then opened the book, thumbing through it. Without looking up, he said, "Do they not teach you in school how to read a fucking map anymore?"

"I would have found it eventually," Katie said, grasping the can of window cleaner.

Kyle had gone to the index. "It's right here! Garrett Island International Airport." He laughed. "International? Seriously? What a joke. Okay, hang on. Page . . . forty-one."

Katie got her finger on the top of the spray nozzle. Slowly, holding the can against her seat-back, she began to slide it upward.

"So, here we go," Kyle said. "The airport's on Wampa-something Drive."

"Wampanoags," Bruce said.

"What?"

"Wampanoags."

"What the fuck kind of name is that?" Kyle said, still hunting for the right page.

"Native American," Bruce said. "They were here before anyone else."

"Yeah, well, whoop-de-doo."

Bruce kept his head forward, but out of the corner of his eye he saw that Katie was ready. She had the top of the can just below the seat's edge.

Katie said, "Mr. Whoever-You-Are, I've got a question."

"Hmm?" he said, eyes aimed down into the map book.

"Look at me," Katie said.

Kyle's head snapped up quickly, looking annoyed. Katie swiftly brought up the can, extended her arm to within six inches of the man's face, depressed the nozzle with her index finger, and held it there. A lemony-scented mist of window cleaner burst forth and engulfed Kyle's head.

He closed his eyes within a fraction of a second of the spray's release, but not fast enough to keep it out of his eyes. Nor did he act with enough speed to keep it out of his mouth and nose.

His hands went immediately to his eyes, covering them, and he attempted to scream, "Fuck!" but all that came out was the sound of the first letter, then coughing. He collapsed against his seat back, eyes covered, gasping for breath.

Bruce hit the brakes. Katie was ready, throwing up a steadying hand to the dashboard. But Kyle, blinded, was unable to anticipate the move, and was suddenly pitched forward, falling into the space behind the front seats.

Bruce knew they didn't have much time. They had to get Kyle's gun before he regained his sight—assuming the chemicals in the window cleaner had not blinded him for life. The second Bruce had the car stopped and in park, he threw open his door, folded the front seat forward, and went to grab the man.

Kyle had taken his hands from his eyes—he needed his hands to support himself on the floor as he struggled to get back onto the seat. He sensed Bruce was coming for him, and was now reaching into his jacket with his right hand.

That was when Katie, hanging over the front seat, her legs dangling up by the dash, drove a fist into the side of Kyle's head, the punch hard enough that they both cried out in pain.

As Kyle keeled over, Bruce grabbed him by the lapels and dragged him from the Cadillac. Katie could see, by the look on his face, the effort it took. Bruce, retired English teacher, now in his seventies, was unaccustomed to roughing people up like a pumped-up twenty-something bouncer.

Bruce threw Kyle onto the road, across the center line, and then hauled back and kicked him solidly in the stomach. Kyle screamed in pain. He managed to get enough wind back to shout, "Fuck you! Fuck you!"

Katie, now out of the Caddy, stood defiantly over the man, fists on hips, arms spread out like wings, and yelled back, "Yeah, well, fuck you, too, asshole!"

Bruce dropped to his knees, sticking a hand into Kyle's jacket, hunting for the gun. Once he had it, he fell back and away from Kyle, pushing himself along the pavement on his butt, putting distance between them. He put the gun gently on the pavement while he caught his breath.

"You okay?" Katie asked him.

He nodded several times, too winded for a verbal reply.

Kyle curled up on his side in a fetal position, moaning softly. His eyelids fluttered as he tried to clear his vision. He managed to focus on Katie as she looked down on him.

"Bitch," he said.

She rolled her eyes. "Whoa, burn."

Bruce picked up the gun as he got back onto two feet, took a couple of steps closer to the shoulder of the road, then threw it overhand deep into the woods. He went back to Kyle, stood over him, and said, "Your wallet."

"What?" Kyle said.

"I want to see some ID. I want to know who you really are."

Kyle waited a beat, realized it was pointless to refuse, and reached around to take his wallet from the back pocket of his slacks. He tossed it toward Bruce, making the older man bend over to scoop it off the pavement. He dug out a driver's license that carried an unflattering photo.

"Brandon Kyle," Bruce said.

Kyle said nothing.

"Why does that ring a bell?"

Kyle remained speechless.

"Oh well," Bruce said, pocketing the license and tossing the wallet back to Kyle. As it hit the pavement, several credit cards spilled out. Kyle collected them, returned them to the wallet sleeves, and slipped it back into his pocket.

"Let's go find your brother," Bruce said to Katie.

"Wait, what?" said Kyle. "You're not going to just leave me here."

"Yeah, that's exactly what I'm gonna do," Bruce said. "Let me give you a word of advice. Stay off the road."

Kyle, still sitting on the pavement, watched as Bruce got behind the wheel of the Caddy and Katie jumped in beside him.

Katie said, "Shouldn't we call the police about him or something?"

Bruce shrugged. "We'll report him. Got his license. When all this blows over, we'll tell the cops about him."

Bruce glanced in the rearview mirror and saw Kyle slowly get to his feet as they drove off. The engine roared as the car accelerated. Katie put a hand to her chest and let out a long breath.

"Wow," she said. "I'm just starting to come down from all that."

"Adrenaline," Bruce said.

"Yeah," she said. A smile crossed her face. "You were totally badass."

He grinned. "You weren't so bad with that spray can."

Now she was laughing. "Oh my God, my heart was going like crazy, just waiting to shoot him in the face!"

Up ahead, above the tree line, they could see the top of the town's water tower, the words GAR-RETT ISLAND painted in ten-foot-high letters on the side. They were approaching a cross street.

Bruce, suddenly subdued, said, "I hope I didn't make a mistake back there."

"What?"

"Throwing that gun into the woods."

"He'll never find it," Katie said.

"Not worried about him. It could be someone else. A kid. I don't like guns. I just wanted to get rid of it. Wasn't thinking."

Katie nodded. "When this all blows over, we'll go back and find it, okay?"

Bruce thought about that and nodded. "Deal." A smile crossed his lips. "Please tell me you actually know how to read a map?"

Katie slapped the tops of her knees and shrieked. "I know! You could just hear him starting to lose his mind, thinking I was the dumbest girl on this entire island."

"You convinced me," Bruce said.

"Oh, thanks for that," Katie said, turning to look at him, flashing him a huge, admiring smile.

But it disappeared instantly. Her eyes went wide and she screamed: *"BRU—"*

The Arrival, seemingly appearing out of nowhere, but actually coming out of the cross street as they sped past it, broadsided the Cadillac, hitting it squarely on Bruce's door.

Everything went black.

Thirty-Six

Joe Bridgeman sat behind the desk in the administrator's office and looked at the open laptop that had belonged to Arrival CEO Lisa Carver. Although he'd done his best to present himself as calm and clearheaded in front of Sandra, he was churning inside. The events of the last couple of hours still had not sunk in. The cars going haywire. His mother nearly becoming one of their victims. Daniella's grisly death.

Sandra's confrontation with Albert Ruskin. The man's attempt to flee.

And now he was staring at this laptop screen. Wondering how Sandra could think he might be able to figure this out, how to stop this.

Right. No big deal. Let me just roll up my sleeves and turn into Steve Jobs.

He wiggled and stretched his fingers above the keyboard, a pianist getting ready to begin playing a concerto.

Then he heard a moan.

Joe got out of the chair and came around the desk to where Albert Ruskin lay on the floor. There was blood coming from the back of his head, where he'd whacked it on the edge of the desk. Joe got down on one knee next to the man.

Ruskin opened one eye and managed to focus on Joe. "What . . . where . . ."

"You fell," Joe said.

"You . . . pushed me."

Joe nodded regretfully. "You fell and hit your head. You probably have a concussion."

Ruskin got up on one elbow and, with his free hand, touched the back of his head, then looked at his bloody hand. "Shit," he said.

"Yeah," said Joe. "Mr. Ruskin, it's time to cut the bullshit. Do you know how to disable the virus?"

"What?" Ruskin was still in a mental fog, although he'd now managed to open his other eye.

"When I get into Lisa Carver's computer, what do I do about the virus? Is there some kind of fail-safe procedure?"

"You still think I had something to do with it," Ruskin said. "I didn't. I'm not working with Kyle. Never even met the man."

Gently, Joe said, "I'm not accusing you of anything. I just want to stop this. It's gotten out of hand. I'm sure it was never anyone's intention that things would get this bad. Someone wanted to gum up the works, make Lisa Carver look like a fool, but it got out of control. Does that sound about right to you?"

Ruskin blinked a couple of times. "I suppose so."

"So, the virus. How can it be disabled? How can we make the cars stop?"

Ruskin started to shake his head, then winced. The movement was painful. He looked again at his bloody hand. "I need a doctor. I need to get to a hospital."

"Yeah, well, we'll see what we can do about that. But how can we make the cars stop doing what they're doing?"

"I honestly don't know. I talked to tech support . . . to see if they could pull the plug on the network. They hadn't found a way. And if it's ransomware, it's out of our hands. You have to pay the money, trust that the hackers, whoever they are, will turn control back over to us."

"I don't think it's ransomware," Joe said.

"Huh?" Ruskin said, squinting at him. "How would you know?"

"I just don't think it is," he said. "If we could get back into the computer, we might be able to do *something*."

"But even if there was a way, the laptop's gone back to sleep. It's password-protected."

"You must know it, being her personal assistant and all?"

"No, she never trusted me with it. So all this talk . . . about shutting everything down, it's pointless."

Joe nodded. "I'm not worried about the password. It's shutting down the Arrivals I need help with."

Ruskin's brow wrinkled. "How can you not be worried about the password? Did you read her mind this morning?"

"No," Joe said. "I had another way." He paused. "I'm sorry about this, Mr. Ruskin. But if you can't advise me on the shutdown, I think we're done."

Now Ruskin looked even more puzzled. "How—"

He was unable to finish the question. Joe yanked, suddenly, on the arm Ruskin had been using to prop himself up. The man hit the floor. Quickly, Joe put his hands on the man's head, grasping it like a melon, raised it six inches off the floor and then slammed it down on the floor.

Hard.

The sound as his skull shattered ricocheted through Joe's gut. He didn't know how much more of this he could take. But he was in up to his eyeballs now and he had to make sure the deed was done.

So, he placed his palm over Ruskin's mouth, and used his thumb to pinch the man's nose shut. He pressed and squeezed as hard as he could, and the fact that he wasn't encountering any resistance was a good sign.

Ruskin must already be dead.

After a minute, during which he looked over his shoulder every couple of seconds in case Sandra returned, he took his hand away, stood and got himself back in the chair in front of the laptop.

Thirty-Seven

Katie had a dream.

She is with her dad, at the beach they used to go to on Cape Cod, before the family moved to Garrett Island. Her father, in a pair of bright red trunks, is running down to the incoming surf, waving at her to join him.

She was just a little kid when they went to Cape Cod, but in the dream, she is her current age. A big girl, although in the dream she has a brilliant pink plastic pail and an equally luminous green shovel, making the most rudimentary of sand castles, the kind she made when she was four or five.

"Come on!" her dad shouts, still waving, the seawater breaking around his ankles. "The water's fine!"

Katie hears a voice. It's her mother's, although she doesn't see her in the dream. She says, sternly, "Do as your father says."

Now the water is up to her father's knees as he continues to stride in, like a soldier intent on marching his way to Europe. So Katie gets up and runs, barefoot, toward the ocean, her feet shifting with each step on the hot sand.

"Coming, Daddy!" she cries. "I'm coming!"

But when she reaches the damp sand, where the waves have come in and retreated rhythmically, she does not see her father.

"Daddy!" she cries.

She looks left and then right. There is no one else in the water. As she glances back, she sees no one on the beach. No one is spread out on a towel. There are no umbrellas, no folding chairs. Not even her mother is there.

Now Katie is very frightened. She scans the ocean, hoping her father will bob up someplace, playfully, and laugh at how he has tricked her. But when she does not see him, she wades in farther until the water—and oh, it is so, *so* cold—is up to her waist.

That is when she feels something brush up against her leg. At first, she thinks it's a fish, or maybe seaweed, but when she looks down into the water she sees her father, stretched out, looking up.

Not moving.

Katie screams, "Daddy! Daddy!"

But then she notices his lips *are* moving. He's trying to tell her something. Bubbles rise from his mouth as he speaks. Like in a cartoon, when the bubbles break the surface, his words emerge.

"Hi, honey bunch," says the first bubble.

"Daddy!"

"It looks to me like . . ." says the second bubble.

Katie is trying to grab hold of her father, to pull him up, but every time she tries to reach for him, he slips from her grasp.

The third bubble pops to the surface.

Her father says, ". . . Bruce is dead."

Katie says, "What? What did you say?"

But then, suddenly, her father is gone, as if he were made of salt and had instantly dissolved.

"Daddy, Daddy!"

"Daddy!"

That last scream was real, and loud enough that Katie woke herself up. The first thing she noticed as she opened her eyes was that she was pressed up against the passenger door of the Cadillac. The car was seriously listing to the right. As she turned her head to look out the window, she found herself looking down into the ditch.

She was also quickly aware that she was in pain. Her left temple was throbbing, and when she touched it, it was wet. She was bleeding.

Slowly, she turned her head toward the driver's side of the vehicle.

"Bruce! Oh God, Bruce!"

He should have slid across the seat and been resting against her, given the rules of gravity, but somehow Bruce's left arm had gotten hung up on the steering wheel, so his body had only shifted slightly toward the center of the car. His head hung limply on his neck, his chin on his chest. The right side of his face looked fine, but there was still a lot of blood, which was easily attributable to the shattered driver's side window. Katie couldn't see the other side of Bruce's face from where she sat, but she was guessing it had endured a thousand cuts, given all the glass scattered across the seat, his lap, and the floor.

The entire length of the massive driver's door was smashed in, but the Arrival that had rammed them was not there. Katie looked out the rear window, saw the Arrival sitting in the middle of the road, about a hundred yards back, its front end completely caved in, airbags inside deployed even though there were no passengers. What must have happened was, the Arrival came out of the side street, T-boned them, bounced back, and the Caddy kept going until it ran off into the ditch. Katie didn't remember that part. She remembered seeing the car coming at them, thought that maybe she remembered the crash, but after that, nothing. She touched her temple again, wondering how she'd hit that part of her head, then figured that at the moment of impact, she was thrown toward the driver's side, and whomped her head on the edge of the steering wheel.

She tentatively touched Bruce's shoulder, gave him a mild nudge.

"Bruce? Bruce? Can you hear me? Bruce?"

Bruce said nothing.

Tears welled up in Katie's eyes. "Come on! Bruce! *Wake up!*"

Bruce did not wake up.

Katie crawled, upward, across the seat, and hung onto the steering wheel so she wouldn't slide back. She put her ear to Bruce's chest, held her own breath so she could listen better for a heartbeat.

Thump thump. Thump thump.

"Yes!" Katie said, taking her head away. "Okay, Bruce, you're still with me. Right? You're alive. I don't know if you can hear me or not, but I'm going to get help. I am. I'm going to call an ambulance."

She dug into her pocket for her phone, punched in 911, and put the phone to her ear.

And listened to it ring. And ring. And ring.

Finally, the ringing stopped.

"Hello?" Katie said. "Hello?"

But she hadn't been connected. The call had

died. She muttered an obscenity, put the phone back into her pocket, and said to Bruce, "So, I don't think we can get an ambulance out here right now. We need another plan."

She pondered whether she could slide Bruce out from behind the wheel, get into the driver's seat, and then drive the car to GGH, Garrett General Hospital. There were two problems with that. The first was, she didn't know whether Bruce could be moved safely, and second, she didn't know whether the car was driveable.

"Can you move, Bruce?" she asked.

When he failed to respond, she tucked one arm in between his back and the seat, and looped her other arm around his right leg. If she could tug him out from under the wheel

"Aw!" Bruce shouted.

"Sorry! Sorry!" Katie said, slipping her arm out from behind his back and letting go of his leg.

Bruce didn't show any more signs of being conscious now than he had twenty seconds earlier, but he'd sure felt the pain.

"Okay, I won't try to move you," Katie said. "I'll get help."

She looked out through the windshield, turned around, and checked where they'd come from. Getting her bearings.

"Bruce, Bruce, listen to me," she said, bracing her feet against the passenger door to keep her close to him. "I'm going to go. If more of those cars come, I think they'll leave you alone because you look like, well, you kind of look dead and the other Arrival is totally wrecked." She sniffed, worked to hold back tears. "I'm heading for home. Maybe my mom is there and she'll know what to do. And if I see a police car or an ambulance on the way I'll flag them down."

Bruce said nothing.

Katie, now unable to hold back the tears, leaned in closer and kissed him on the cheek, his stubble like sandpaper to her lips.

"Please don't die, Bruce. Please, please don't die."

She allowed herself to slide back over to the passenger side. When she opened her door, she hung on to it, not wanting it to snap off the hinges. No sense doing any more damage to Bruce's car than had already been done. Think positively, she told herself. Bruce is going to be okay. He's going to recover.

And so will his beloved Cadillac.

She dropped into the ditch and, putting her shoulders into it, pushed the door shut. She scrabbled back up onto the highway. But before she started to trek into town, there was one thing she had to do first.

She walked over to the smashed Arrival and, with chin quivering, looked at it and said two words:

"Fuck you."

Katie started heading for home.

Thirty-Eight

Sandra entered the administrator's office carrying a small blue nylon bag with a Red Cross symbol on the side. "Found this," she said to Joe, who was behind the desk, looking at the laptop. "There's all kinds of stuff in here. Bandages, cold compresses, gauze, those antiseptic wipes. I know you're not a paramedic, but you've probably had more experience with this kind of thing than I have, so   "

But then she looked at Ruskin and said, "Oh, shit, he doesn't look good."

Joe, grim-faced, got out of the chair and came around the desk. Sandra was still looking at Ruskin as he put his hands on her shoulders.

"Shit," she said, starting to make a move to get down on one knee to have a closer look at him. But Joe held her back.

"There's nothing you can do," he said mournfully, keeping her in front of him.

"Jesus, what happened?" she said. "It was a bump on the head. He was alive when I left here. Wasn't he?"

Joe nodded. "He was. But soon after you left, he was making some noises, and I checked on him. A few seconds later and he was gone. But he did say something."

"What?"

"He said he was sorry."

Sandra's eyes went wide. "I knew it. I *knew* it."

"He said he helped Kyle. Put a stick into Lisa Carver's computer when she got sick, passed it to Kyle. And that allowed Kyle to introduce the virus into the system."

Sandra was stunned. "He told you all that?"

"Yeah." Joe's voice softened. "He never had any idea that it would be this bad, that the cars would become deadly, hunt people down." Joe shook his head sadly. "He just, he never wanted anything like that to happen."

Sandra blinked. "How'd he manage to tell you all that in the time I was gone?"

Joe nodded. "You know what I think? I think he knew he was dying and there were things he needed to get off his chest. Fast."

Sandra looked again at the body of Ruskin on the floor. "He hated her. He hated Lisa Carver. He told me, before you got here. God, what a horrible man."

Joe grimaced. "I don't know. Maybe . . . maybe sometimes people have good intentions that can go horribly wrong."

She gave him a sharp look. "What are you talking about?"

"Nothing," he said quickly.

Sandra shifted past him and looked at the open laptop. "So where does that leave us? I mean, okay, he said he was *sorry*, but did he tell you how to make it *stop*?"

As she looked at the screen, her eyes widened. There was something on it. An Arrival logo across the top. Notes, numbers, fields in which to enter data.

Sandra's jaw dropped. "Are you in?"

Joe smiled, nodded.

"You got into her laptop?"

"Before Ruskin died, he gave me the password."

"You're kidding."

Joe's cheek twitched. "No. Like I said, I think he knew it was his last chance to do the right thing."

Sandra looked skeptical for a moment, then shrugged. "Okay, okay, tell me what you've found."

Joe got into the chair and moved the cursor around the screen. "This is where I tell you I've got good news and bad news. I've already given you the good news, which is that I got the password."

"What was it, anyway?"

"Huh?"

"The password. What was the password?"

"Her daughter's name."

Sandra took a moment, then said, "Say again?"

"It's Zenia, but spelled backward. *A, I—*"

"I get it," Sandra said. Then quietly, "Ruskin told you this."

Joe nodded. "She'd change it daily. The name part stays the same but it had to be followed by the previous day's numeric date." He shrugged. "So, that worked, and I'm in, but the bad news is, I can't figure out how to get into the brains of the Arrival system."

"Okay," Sandra said, her voice very quiet. "You think there's a chance?"

Joe shrugged. "I don't know. I'll keep trying. Thing is, there's so much else going on—" at which point he grabbed his cell phone off the desk and waved it in the air "—that I'm needed in a hundred other places right now." His face went grim. "Something huge went down at the ferry terminal. Help was coming but the Arrivals launched an attack."

Sandra sighed, bit her lip. "Katie and Archie are out there somewhere. I've got to find them. You do what you can here. I'm going. That bike in the hall. Is it yours?"

"For now. You're not going out there."

"I am. I'm going home."

"I told you, the kids weren't—"

"When they show up—and they *will* show up—I'm going to be there."

He nodded his understanding.

"I've still got Lisa Carver's phone. Anything happens, call me," she said, moving for the door.

"Got it." He waited a second, then said, "Hey."

She stopped.

"I love you," he said.

Sandra did her best to crack a smile and slipped out of the room.

Thirty-Nine

Why couldn't she say it? Why couldn't she tell him she loved him, too? Would it have killed her to say those three words?

Joe thought about how that woman had no idea of the lengths he'd gone to, the risks he'd taken, to make a life for them. Not just for the two of them, but for her children, as well.

No fucking idea at all.

And he'd done those things because he *loved* her. He loved her so much.

But oh no, saying it back to him, that was too hard.

Okay, okay, maybe his timing was off. She was thinking about her kids. Understandable. She had other things on her mind.

But when this was over, when the dust settled, he was sure she'd see him in a positive light. This crisis, as bad as it was, was an opportunity. It was a chance for her to see him in a leadership role. A *heroic* role. He really *was* Chief Brody, but instead of saving Amity from a big fish, he was saving Garrett Island from a thousand murderous cars.

Admittedly, there was one major difference. Chief Brody had not *invited* that shark into the waters off Amity's beaches. Chief Brody did not create the crisis.

Joe Bridgeman was well aware of the role he'd

played in what had happened today. He wasn't blind to what he'd done. *But Your Honor*, he pleaded in the imaginary courtroom in his mind, *I'm guilty with an explanation.* When he speculated to Sandra about how he thought Ruskin never meant for things to get this out of hand—all bullshit, of course, given that Ruskin was not even remotely responsible for the sabotaging of the Arrival network—Joe was, in effect, formulating his own defense, in the event what he'd done became known. He could never have imagined the venality of the virus, its tremendous potential for harm.

He'd never have made a deal with Brandon Kyle had he known that anyone would get hurt.

"What's the worst that could happen?" Joe had asked Kyle during one of their meetings.

Kyle had laughed. "Some of the press may get squirted with windshield washer fluid. Maybe the doors won't open. Maybe one of the cars will drive off by itself right into a telephone pole."

"But no one'll get hurt, right?"

"I can't promise a tire won't run over someone's foot, but that would be about the worst of it. The last thing I want is for anyone to get hurt. Now, tell me again how much you said you need to put your mother in a home?"

"I wouldn't call it a *home*," he'd said. "Funny about that word. It's so nice, except when you use it to describe a place to put parents. I like to call it a seniors' living center. It's a very nice place. Lots of activities. There's the monthly apartment fee itself, then they provide meals, and she's not as steady as she used to be so when she has to go to the bathroom—"

"Would three hundred thousand cover everything for a few years?"

Boy, would it ever.

He knew he should have told Kyle to get lost. In fact, he probably should have called the FBI and set up a sting. Corporate sabotage was a crime. But Joe had to give Kyle credit. The man had come prepared. A shrewd operator, that's what he was.

Kyle had engaged the services of a private detective agency—Joe believed it was the same one that film producer mogul hired to discredit all those actresses accusing him of sexual assault—to find out everything they could about Lisa Carver. Bugged her penthouse, outfitted it with hidden cameras, including one in the ceiling directly above the kitchen island where Lisa most often worked on her laptop. That was how they figured out her password and how she changed it every day. They'd done some digging, learned Lisa Carver gave a child up for adoption when she was in her teens, twenty-two years earlier.

Zenia.

It was a secret she'd managed to keep from most everyone, although Joe had assumed Ruskin would have known. It was convenient that, at a time when Sandra desperately needed him to get into Carver's computer, Ruskin was there. Not because Ruskin could provide a password, but because Joe needed to have Sandra *believe* he could have provided a password.

Yes, Joe thought, *I'm damn good with computers. But I'm not* that *good.* It would have been difficult to explain how he'd figured out, on his own, a password that obscure.

But it wasn't the unearthing of long-hidden information on Lisa Carver that had made the greatest impression on Joe. It turned out she wasn't the only one Kyle's investigators had looked into.

Kyle knew that, for his plan to work, he needed someone on the inside. Someone who would have access to Carver's laptop. Who better than the chief of police, who'd be expected to do a walk-through of the event to make sure it was secure. Not that Joe was Kyle's first choice. He wondered about the mayor of Garrett Island, but it turned out she would be in France, visiting relatives, on the day of the event. Besides, investigators had found no skeletons in her closet. Would the governor come in from Boston? Evidently not. The administrator of the community center was also going to be away. Kyle's people looked for some dirt on this Sandra Montrose person who was helping organize the event, but found nothing that would give them any kind of leverage.

But then they looked at Police Chief Joe Bridgeman. That upstanding local lawman, seemingly above reproach.

Well, yeah, for the most part.

Had the Garrett Island council done the kind of digging that Kyle's investigators had, they might have reconsidered their decision to hire him. He looked good on paper. First of all, he was an islander. Born and raised here. Knew the terrain and its people. A computer whiz from a young age, he went to work for a tech firm in Boston, but that work didn't suit him. He wanted to be a cop. He enrolled in the Massachusetts State Police Academy in New

Braintree, graduated near the top of his class. Became a state trooper, did well.

But there was a problem: women.

Two, at least. They came forward and complained to Bridgeman's superiors. They were both women Joe had pulled over, supposedly for speeding. But what he really wanted was to get to know them. Joe had something of a history of pulling over young women, and once he'd had a good look at them and determined they had potential, he'd put his ticket book away.

Not before getting their names and addresses, of course.

Calls followed. *Hey, let's have a drink, maybe catch a movie.* Both women had agreed to go out with him, once or twice—he did have a certain charm about him—but neither wanted to continue a relationship, and both made that clear. The guy came on too strong, they'd both felt. Tried too hard. In each case, two dates in, he'd be talking about them moving in together, making a life for themselves.

They didn't just want to slow the merry-go-round down. They wanted to get off the ride altogether.

But Joe wasn't very good at taking the hint. He'd been so *nice* to them. He'd been so *attentive*. He'd meet them when they finished work, hang around their places of residence, call them in the middle of the night to make sure they were okay, bombard them with emails to tell them how much he cared about them.

If they changed their email addresses, he'd leave notes on their windshields.

Over a period of six months, the two women

came in to speak with Joe's superiors. The man, they said, was a stalker.

There was a quiet investigation. Joe Bridgeman's superiors put him on notice. If he pulled this kind of shit again, he'd be out on his ass. But Joe knew that even if he behaved himself going forward, he was never moving ahead with this department. Not with those complaints in his file.

When the opening for a Garrett Island police chief came up, it was kismet. He already made regular trips there to check in on his mother, whose health was in decline. He knew many of the people who'd make the decision about hiring him. Had grown up with them. He could move back into the house he'd been raised in, look after his mom, and start a new job with more prestige and responsibility than the one he'd left.

A new beginning.

But what if the town's elders, and those who'd hired him, learned about his past? What if they knew what Kyle had uncovered?

So when Kyle sought a meeting with Joe, a month before the Arrival event, he laid it all out. Download onto a stick the data from Lisa's computer and put it in the media kit for one Ben Stapleton. Spike Carver's coffee, giving Joe time to do what he had to do.

The audacity of the proposal stunned Joe. "No," he said. "I couldn't do such a thing."

Which was when Kyle told him what he knew. The complaints against him. How would the Garrett Island council—and this widow he was so interested in—react to that information?

"In fact," Kyle had said, "while we're on the topic of Ms. Montrose . . . It struck my investigator as quite the coincidence that you should end up with the woman to whom you had to deliver such devastating news. He's good at spotting those kinds of connections. Has what you'd call a suspicious mind."

"It's not that big an island," Joe had responded. "We all kind of know each other, even if it's just to say hello. Her husband had an accident. I went to the scene, then notified the family. There's nothing funny about it."

"Of course. I'm sure that's all there was to it. But the timing is a bit curious."

"The timing?" Joe had said.

Kyle had said nothing more. He simply smiled.

Jesus, the smile on that arrogant fucker's face.

When it had looked as though it was only the stalking incidents Kyle knew about, Joe'd thought maybe he could ride it out. Call Kyle's bluff. Let him blab about what Joe had done before returning to the island. There'd always been the chance it could come out, anyway. Joe would admit his mistakes, make the case that he'd been doing a good job as chief. Do his best to persuade Sandra that he wasn't that kind of man anymore.

On top of that, he'd do the right thing and arrest Brandon Kyle. Trying to bribe an officer of the law. Corporate espionage. Sabotage. Joe would have to consult with the prosecuting attorney to figure out what the actual charges should be.

But when Joe saw that smile, he knew Kyle had an ace card he'd not yet played.

"Of course, I wouldn't expect you to do all this just to protect your reputation," Kyle had said. "I am more than prepared to compensate you."

Money.

If Joe did this man's bidding, there'd be more than enough cash to find a first-class home for his mother. A place where she could be happy, Joe told himself. He'd have to do plenty of rationalizing to ease his conscience, but sometimes you did what you had to do.

Like killing Albert Ruskin.

There was no going back now.

Forty

His eyes still stung like a son of a bitch.

Brandon Kyle kept blinking, trying to create tears that would wash out whatever traces of window cleaner were still in his eyes. What he needed was to rinse them thoroughly, but the woods he now found himself wandering in didn't have a fridge stocked with bottles of Evian.

Once the Cadillac sped off, Kyle had considered hanging by the road. If the Arrival corporation could miss one person hiding a self-driving car, maybe it had missed others. Maybe another nonautonomous vehicle, with a real live human being behind the wheel, would show up. He could flag them down, ask them for a lift. Didn't matter where to. A house, a store, anyplace with water. Out of a tap, from a bottle, didn't much matter.

But what he soon heard was not a conventional car, but the electric whine of an Arrival. Kyle ran into the woods as a blue one zipped past, followed closely by a green one. The little bastards were still out there, hunting their prey.

Then something funny happened.

Watching from behind a tree, keeping himself well hidden, he saw a lone yellow Arrival approaching. As it got closer, it decelerated. Finally, it came to a halt. Just stopped in the middle of the road.

376 | Linwood Barclay

And sat there.

Kyle watched it for a couple of minutes before deciding to get its attention.

"Hey, asshole! Come and get me!"

The car did not respond in any way.

A pink Arrival came into view, came to a stop alongside the yellow one, as if checking on a fallen comrade. After thirty seconds, it moved on.

"Huh," Kyle said.

Now that he knew Arrivals were still patrolling, he decided cutting through the woods to get back to civilization was the better plan. He hadn't gone very far when he heard something encouraging.

Running water.

He stopped and listened carefully to determine which direction the sound was coming from. Go left, he thought. The woods gave way to a creek, no more than five feet wide, barely a foot deep, but Kyle didn't need the Mississippi. All he had to do was descend a muddy, leaf-covered embankment—no more than ten feet—to reach it.

He was about to inch his way down the slope when he heard a sudden rustling in the leaves behind him. He spun around, caught a glimpse of something brown and tall and huge that was moving quickly only a step or two away from him.

How the fuck did a car get into the—

Kyle screamed, lost his balance, and tumbled down the hill.

He slid headfirst through the leaves and mud to the edge of the creek. He came to a stop inches from the water, his hands and face and clothes streaked with filth from the forest floor.

"Fuck, fuck, fuck!" he said.

He raised himself up on his two hands and turned to confirm that what had startled him was not a car, but a deer, working its way through the forest with more grace than Kyle had exhibited when he'd plunged to the creek's edge. It took a few laps from the creek with its tongue, then wandered back up the hill, disappearing between the trees.

"Asshole!" Kyle shouted at the animal.

He crawled the remaining distance to the creek and first washed the dirt from his hands, then cupped water in his palms and threw it up into his open eyes. He did it four times, blinking between each splash.

The stinging dissipated.

Sitting on his haunches, he looked upward into the cathedral of towering trees, and in that moment of tranquility, he felt the rage building within him.

Sure, things had gone well. Arrival was finished. Its CEO was dead.

But then Derek lost the boat. Refused to find another one so that Kyle could make his escape.

Then he had lucked into—*lucked, ha!*—that man and the girl in the Cadillac. Could that have gone any worse for him?

Had he actually hurt them? The old man or the girl? No, he had not. And he could have. Oh yes, if he'd wanted to he could have shot them both and taken the car. But no, he hadn't done that, and what thanks did he get?

Near blindness and a kick in the gut.

The rage churned within him.

If he couldn't get off this fucking island, he

could still use his time productively. He could settle scores. He could get even.

Derek was probably still biding his time at the yacht club. Maybe it was time to go back and thank him for all his years of service.

And then there was the girl.

Katie.

If only he knew her last name, he could—

Hang on.

Her mother. She'd asked him about her mother, if she'd been hurt when the cars first started spinning out of control. Katie had said her mother was helping out with the Arrival event.

She was the one who'd handed him his press kit. Kyle remembered now.

Montrose. Sandra Montrose.

Katie Montrose.

Now that he could see again, he reached into his pocket for his phone, hoping to God he hadn't lost it in the fall. No, he had it. He brushed the dirt off the screen, thumbed the home button. The phone lit up.

"Yes," he said.

He wanted an address. And once he'd found it, he'd go back and see if he could find where the old man had pitched that gun into the woods.

Forty-One

Something was troubling Sandra.

Actually, there were a whole *lot* of things troubling Sandra, not the least of which was this damn bicycle she was riding. The seat was too high and had a rip in the leather that was cutting into her butt. The handlebars were too low and her feet kept slipping off the pedals, one of which was broken. The next time Joe stole a bike, he needed to steal a better one than this.

And of course, a skirt was not the best thing to wear when riding a two-wheeler.

Archie and Katie were front of mind, naturally. Nothing was more important than being reunited with her kids. But something was nagging at her, something that didn't quite add up.

Something about Joe.

Did he seem a bit . . . odd when she came back with the first aid kit? Well, okay, he probably did, and wasn't he entitled to? Ruskin had died. That would have been upsetting. No question.

So yeah, if Joe didn't quite seem himself, what of it? Who wouldn't be a bit off his game with all that was going on? They were all dealing with tremendous stress.

And yet . . .

Joe sure had gotten a lot of information out of Ruskin in his final moments. Stuff he hadn't been willing to tell her he'd gone and shared with Joe. And why was Joe making excuses for Albert Ruskin? Suggesting Ruskin had never intended for things to get so out of hand. How did Joe know that? Why downplay the damage the bastard had done?

It just seemed weird, was all. And what about—

Hang on. Arrival at three o'clock.

She was riding across a street, leaving one sidewalk and heading for the opposite one, when she saw one coming from her right. Quickly, she cycled down a driveway and turned in behind a house, nearly catching her neck on a low-hanging clothesline. She hopped off, wheeled the bike along by the handlebars, crept to the corner of the house, and peeked.

The Arrival drove on by.

She got back on the bike, taking a circuitous route back to her house that kept her off wider streets where she figured she was more likely to encounter Arrivals.

So, yeah, back to Joe.

The password.

He'd been able to get into Lisa Carver's computer right away because Ruskin had given him the password. It was believable Ruskin might know it, and if he was feeling some remorse for what he'd done, it was conceivable he would reveal it to Joe.

Except . . .

Joe had said the password was Carver's daughter's name spelled backward, followed by numeric dates.

But when Sandra had asked Ruskin whether

Lisa Carver had children, he'd said he did not know. There was talk, he'd said, that she'd had a child in her teens.

So how did Ruskin know a password based on the name of a child that he did not know, with any certainty, existed?

There had to be an explanation, Sandra thought. Ruskin could have lied to her, although she couldn't understand why he'd have lied about *that*.

Even as she rode the bike, Sandra shook her head.

As she got to within a block of her house, and her hopes rose that her kids would be there, she pushed these riddles out of her head.

The turn was up ahead. The shrubs on that corner were so high that whenever Sandra was in her car—her *real* car—she always had to sneak out into the intersection, beyond the stop sign, to see whether it was safe to pull out. But she was cycling on the sidewalk today, so she rounded the shrubs without slowing down.

A purple Arrival was coming straight at her like a homicidal plum.

Sandra figured the car had probably been on the street, but shifted to the sidewalk when its sensors picked up her approach.

Sandra didn't even have time to scream.

She leapt off the bike, swinging herself off like Annie Oakley dismounting a galloping horse. She tumbled into the grassy strip between the sidewalk and the road and rolled twice as the Arrival bounced right over the bicycle.

As Sandra got to her feet and started running,

the Arrival, the bike still stuck underneath it, make a quick turn and initiated a pursuit.

Sandra glanced over her shoulder long enough to see the Arrival was after her, although she hardly had to look. The bicycle trapped beneath it was scraping against the pavement, making a sound a thousand times more unnerving than fingernails on a blackboard.

She sprinted across the street toward a house that sat behind a low stone fence running parallel to the sidewalk. At less than three feet high, it was more decoration than a secure barrier.

But it might be enough to save Sandra.

Sandra dived over the stone wall and before she'd even hit the ground on the other side the Arrival crashed into it. She got up onto her knees and peered over the edge, almost nose to nose with the car's crumpled front end.

She thought she smelled smoke. No, not quite smoke, but definitely a burning smell. More like an electrical fire.

And then she saw flames starting to lick out from beneath the car. Dragging the metal bike must have created sparks significant enough to set something under the car alight. Was it enough to put the car out of commission?

Sandra crept to the end of the stone fence, took a step out into the open, and waited to see whether the car would resume pursuit. When it showed no interest, she continued on, this time on foot.

Two minutes later, she was running up to her front door. She had her key ready, but when she tried the door, she found it unlocked.

She opened it wide, stepped into the front hall and shouted: "Archie! Katie!"

Nothing.

Sandra's shoulders sagged as she stood there. Her head drooped, her arms hung limp at her sides.

The events of the day suddenly overwhelmed her like a tidal wave. She began to weep.

Her cries were subdued at first, but within a minute they grew into sobs. Fearing she might collapse, she reached out for the nearby staircase banister. She gripped it tightly, hanging on, as if this handrail were the only thing keeping her from spinning off into the abyss.

"Oh God," she whimpered. "This can't be happening."

But then an inner voice spoke to her. A voice that sounded a lot like . . . Adam.

Pull yourself together, her late husband told her. *You're going to get through this. You're the strongest person I've ever known.*

Sandra struggled to tamp down the sobs. She slowed her breathing, let go of the railing, and wiped the tears from her eyes.

She heard another voice.

"Mom?"

But this one wasn't in her head. This one was real. And it was coming from right behind her.

Sandra whirled around. And the tears she'd just managed to get under control burst forth again, as if some sort of emotional dam had burst.

"*Katie!*"

She pulled her daughter into her arms and

squeezed her, patted the back of her head, wept into her shoulder, barely noticing the blood on her shirt and her hands and her scuffed knees and the grass and dirt stains on her clothes.

Sandra would have held on to her for much longer, but she pulled away long enough to look at her and say, "Archie."

Katie, as teary-eyed as her mother, shook her head. "I don't know. I—"

"You were supposed to be—"

"I know! I know!" Katie shouted. "He got away. He went with his friends, in one of those cars."

"Oh God," Sandra said. "When was this? When did they go? Where did they—"

"Right after you left. They were going to the mall. But—"

"We have to go," Sandra said, suddenly frantic. "We have to get to the mall—"

"I know! But, Mom, Bruce—"

"How are we going to get there?" Sandra said, more to herself than her daughter. "The bike got crushed. I have—"

"What bike?" Katie asked.

"Have to find some other—are you sure he's at the mall?"

"All I know is that's where he was *going*, but I don't know if he ever *got*—"

Sandra spotted the keys to her regular car sitting in a plastic dish and, instinctively, went to reach for them, but stopped herself. "Goddamn it," she said. "Why did we let them take our cars away?"

"Mom, you need to listen. You need—"

"Which friends?"

"What?"

"Which friends did he go to the mall with?"

"Nick and Rory."

Sandra closed her eyes for an instant. "Where do they—doesn't Nick live close by?"

Katie nodded. "About a block away. Both of them."

"Maybe they went there. Maybe *Archie's* there."

"Yeah, maybe, okay, we can go check. But, Mom, stop and listen to me for *one second*."

Sandra blinked, looked into her daughter's blood-smeared face and touched her cheek tentatively. "You're hurt."

Katie shook her head. "Not me. Bruce."

"Bruce?"

"That's who I'm trying to tell you about. Bruce, the old man who lives across the street."

"Archie's serial killer?"

Katie rolled her eyes. "He's a retired English teacher, and he's a friend. He's been teaching me to drive. He's had this old Cadillac hidden in his garage and—"

"He's been *what*?"

"*Mom!*" Katie shrieked. "Shut up and listen!"

Sandra recoiled. "Okay," she said. "Go ahead."

"Bruce is a good guy. He's my friend. He's been teaching me to drive. And today we took out his *real* car so we could go find Archie, but then we got swarmed by those fucking cars and there was this hitchhiker with a gun, but we got rid of him and we thought we were in the clear, but then this Arrival T-bones us and Bruce is hurt real bad and I got back here and we have to find some way to help him or I think he's going to die."

Katie, somehow, managed to get that all out in one breath.

"Where?" Sandra asked. "Where is he?"

Katie filled her lungs with air and said, "Turner Point Road, I think it is. The car's half in the ditch. When I left Bruce he was still alive but he's not good. We have to get an ambulance out there."

Sandra sighed. She told Katie, quickly, about what had happened to the ambulance at the community center. For all she knew, all island emergency vehicles had been brought down by the infected cars.

Sandra clasped her hands on her daughter's shoulders. "I want to help him. We'll try to think of something. But right now, right this second, we have to find Archie."

Katie bit her lip, then nodded. "I know."

"You still have your phone?"

"Yeah, but whenever I tried to call you it never went through."

"I lost my phone. I've been using Lisa Carver's." Sandra paused. "She's dead."

"Shit," Katie said. "I mean, yeah, I'm sorry she's dead, but shit, I saw that name come up on my phone and ignored it."

"I'm going to Archie's friends'. You stay here in case he comes back. If he does, call me. If I find him, I'll call you."

Katie looked unconvinced. "I don't want you going out there."

Sandra managed a smile, put her palm to her daughter's cheek. "We've both survived this long."

Sandra got Katie to tell her where, exactly,

Archie's friends lived. She told her how to find Rory's house, that it was the one with the salmon-colored interlock brick driveway.

"You be careful," she told Katie.

"I'm home," she said. "Nothing bad can happen to me here."

Sandra got to Rory's house on foot without encountering any more Arrivals. She swung open the white picket gate and ran up the stone path to the front door, glancing briefly at the open carport beside the house. She saw a couple of old lawn mowers, gardening tools, a rusted tricycle, and something much larger under a tarp that barely registered as she rang the bell.

Sandra could hear a dead bolt turning and a chain being slid from its mount before the door opened an inch. A thin woman in shorts and a red T-shirt peered out worriedly, as though she feared the cars had figured out how to pretend to be Jehovah's Witnesses.

When she saw it was an actual person, she opened the door wider and said, "Yeah?"

"I'm Sandra Montrose," she said. "Archie's mom. He and Rory are friends. Is he here? Please tell me he's—"

The door suddenly opened wider and Rory was standing there.

"Your boy's not here," Rory's mom said.

Sandra looked at Rory. "Where is he?"

"I don't know," Rory said.

"He was with you and Nick this morning, right?"

Rory nodded hesitantly.

"So where did you three go?" Sandra said, her voice rising. "Where's Archie?"

"Okay, so, like, we did all go to the mall," Rory said.

"And?"

"The cars started going crazy, and there were, like, hundreds of them, and they got into the mall, and they were running people down and—"

"God, no," Sandra said. "But you all got out?"

Rory shrugged. "I did. I don't know about them. We kinda got split up. I thought maybe they got out, too, so I came back here. I haven't heard anything from the other guys."

Sandra looked into the eyes of the boy's mother, who shrugged. "I don't know what to say," she said.

Sandra looked away, and that was when she noticed, for the second time, the large item in the garage covered with the tarp.

"What is that?" she asked.

Rory's mom had to step out of the house to see what Sandra was referring to. The boy came out behind her. It was Rory who answered her question.

"That's my dad's motorcycle." He swelled briefly with pride. "It's a Harley."

Sandra asked, "There gas in it?"

The boy shrugged. "Probably. He was out on it before they made everyone just drive Arrivals."

Sandra looked at his mother. "Key," she said.

The woman stiffened. "I don't think my husband would want—"

Sandra put her face within three inches of the woman's. "I'm not asking," she said.

Forty-Two

Joe Bridgeman wasn't having much luck. Not that he expected to.

Using the password he already knew, he was into Lisa Carver's computer and well into the Arrival network—an elaborate program that showed where every active Arrival was, where it had been, and how it was communicating with all the other little Arrivals—but he could not find a way to counteract or disable the virus, or simply shut the entire system down.

Why couldn't Lisa Carver have installed a big red STOP button he could just click on?

But he could see the virus working its magic, insinuating itself into the system, branching out in all directions, a tsunami overwhelming a coastal village. There was nothing he wanted more than to pull the plug on all of it, given his role in facilitating the madness. If his arrangement with Brandon Kyle ever became known, he'd like to be able to say that at least he'd tried to undo the damage.

Good thing Massachusetts no longer had a death penalty. Joe thought if he were ever convicted for his misdeeds, trying to make things right might prompt a jury to show compassion: five life sentences instead of ten, say. There was a comforting thought.

But suppose he did get away with it? What if

no one ever learned about his deal with Kyle, or that he killed Ruskin? Nothing to worry about, right?

Wrong.

Joe's thoughts turned to Kyle. He wished there were a way to talk to the man, right now, face-to-face. But he'd had a plan to get off the island, and was probably long gone by now. Joe wanted to tell him Ruskin was dead, and how that development presented an opportunity. If the authorities ever did suspect Kyle, Joe could say that before Ruskin died, he confessed to sabotaging the Arrival system because of his hatred for Lisa Carver.

And wouldn't that give Joe some badly needed leverage over Kyle? As things stood now, Kyle held the advantage. What was it he had said in their meeting, when the discussion turned to the death of Adam Montrose?

"But the timing is a bit curious."

At first, it struck Joe as impossible that Kyle's investigators could have found out what he had done. Or, more accurately, what he had failed to do.

Whoever Kyle had hired was good, very good. The first red flag had to be that Joe was going out with the widow of the man whose roadside death he'd investigated. That, in itself, was hardly incriminating, but if it had led Kyle's people to dig a little deeper . . .

Joe knew there'd been a witness.

He hadn't worried about it too much at the time. Really, what could that woman, watching from the porch of a house fifty yards away, have actually seen? It was old Agnes Barlow, pushing eighty if she was a day, who once managed a bakery on the island. Made Whoopie Pies to die for, Joe could attest. These days she used a walker to get around. She'd heard the crash, and called it in, but never ventured out into the night to see the accident up close. She'd have seen the flashing lights of his car when he got to the scene. And eventually, she'd have observed the ambulance's arrival.

It had made him a little nervous when he encountered her, hobbling her way out of the pharmacy, two days later. Spotted him and said, "Oh, Chief, it sure did take the ambulance a long time to get there the other night, didn't it?"

Think fast.

"Got there as fast as they could," he said. "They were on another call."

That seemed to satisfy old Agnes and off she went.

Kyle's people must have found her, talked to her. Okay, he could have done more. But the way Joe saw it was, the guy was going to die, anyway. Wouldn't have mattered if he'd called the ambulance the moment he got there.

Probably.

Joe knew the truck as soon as he'd come upon it. He knew Adam Montrose, and he certainly knew who his wife was.

Joe'd had his eye on Sandra for a very long time. Such a looker. Bright, polished, with real smarts. She'd be running this island one day, he bet. Made a point of stopping to talk to her every chance he got. Stopped her for speeding once but let her off with a friendly warning, made a little joke. "You can buy me a cup of coffee one day," he'd said.

And she was married to a grease monkey who fixed motorcycles for a living. She could do so much better.

When Joe got to the pickup truck window and saw what kind of condition Adam was in, the way he was choking on his own blood, those shards of windshield glass sticking out of the man's throat, he knew it was only a matter of time.

Adam had managed to gargle out the words, "Fell asleep."

Joe placed a comforting hand on his shoulder. "Hang in there. Help's coming."

Except it wasn't.

Adam's head tilted forward until it was resting on the twisted steering wheel. It was an old truck, produced before airbags became standard equipment and, admittedly, a testament to Adam's skills as a mechanic that it was still running. It was cancered with rust, missing a passenger side mirror; odds were it wouldn't have passed a safety check, but the son of a bitch ran.

Joe walked around to the back of the truck, leaned up against the tailgate, and waited. Checked on Adam five minutes later. The guy was still breathing. So he went back to his spot at the back of the truck and waited a while longer.

At fifteen minutes, Adam appeared good and dead. But Joe gave it another four minutes before making the call, just to be sure.

He'd give Sandra some time. Didn't want to move in on her right away. Let her grieve. But that didn't mean he couldn't be supportive in the meantime. Pop into her office, see how she was doing. Accidentally on purpose run into her at the grocery store, ask how the kids were managing.

Give it a few months. Then, hey, I'm just heading to the diner, wanna grab a sandwich? Not a date, but sort of a date. Work up to dinner, which had a more intimate subtext.

Joe had no doubt that once Sandra got over the trauma of losing Adam, he could give her a better life. But she could never know.

Never.

Brandon Kyle had to promise him that whatever evidence he had about this would be destroyed, and that whatever he knew would be forgotten. And in return, Joe would swear, should the need arise, that Ruskin took the blame for the Arrival catastrophe.

Joe was jolted out of his thoughts by a text. He looked at his phone and saw that it was from Sandra, although the caller ID was LISA CARVER.

KATIE HOME. ARCHIE AT MALL. GOING 4 HIM. INJURED MAN IN CADDY ON TURNER POINT RD. CAN YOU HELP?

Jesus, was she crazy? Was she really going to ride that wobbly stolen bike to the mall? And how the hell did she think he was going to get out to Turner Point Road? How was the Garrett Island police force supposed to respond to *anything*?

Joe shook his head wearily, folded down the laptop screen, and decided to head back out, see what he could do.

After all, he was the chief of police.

Forty-Three

Archie didn't want to spend the rest of his life sitting on these loading docks.

He'd gone back in search of something to eat, giving that dead butcher on the floor a wide berth. In one corner of the meat department, beyond the reach of any Arrivals still patrolling Discount Bonanza, he'd found one of those large upright ovens filled with chickens rotating on spits. He opened the door and, without actually sliding a chicken off the end, ripped one off, breaking it in half. The chicken was hot as hell, and Archie ended up tossing it from hand to hand until it cooled down some. He took it, along with a huge wad of paper napkins, and went back out onto the loading dock, hoping that maybe, just maybe, the cars had gotten bored with waiting to kill him and wandered off.

No such luck.

So he sat cross-legged on the dock and ate his chicken. The cars sat there, unmoving.

When he had gnawed all the meat off one of the wings, he tossed it onto the hood of the closest car. "There you go, boy, little treat for you."

Archie had never been a big fan of the drumstick, so he threw one of those onto the roof of another car. "Enjoy, fucker!" he said.

The chicken, he had to admit, tasted pretty damn good, especially the skin, which was crisp and salty. When he'd had all he wanted, and thrown the rest of the bones onto another car, he used the napkins to wipe the barbecue sauce from his hands. What he couldn't remove with the napkin, he licked off, finger by finger.

And sat there.

"Come on, guys," he said. "Go chase a cat or something."

Archie stood. He suddenly felt the need to take a piss. But where were the bathrooms? Would he have to go back into Discount Bonanza and find the public washrooms? Weren't they in an area where the Arrivals had been patrolling?

He stood at the edge of the loading dock, facing the cars, and unzipped. Like many young boys, he had a strong and mighty stream, and was able to get a little more distance by arching his back.

And a beautiful arc it was, too, heading upward, almost as high as Archie was tall, before reaching its apex and coming back down, onto the hood of a yellow Arrival.

Archie laughed. A perfect match.

But he didn't want to get just one car, so he spun from his hips, spraying piss like a gardener watering his flowers.

One of the car's water-sensitive wipers engaged as Archie's urine splashed a windshield. That prompted yet another laugh.

That was when he heard something.

A motor . . . an engine . . . a *loud* engine. Definitely *not* an Arrival. These battery-powered wusses couldn't make an aggressive noise like that.

It didn't sound like an honest-to-God car. No,

it was more like a motorcycle. And it sounded like it was racing along one of the mall's perimeter roads.

A couple of the Arrivals inched back, as if ready to go on the hunt.

The motorcycle sounded closer, but it was also powering down, as though turning into the mall lot. The loading bay area was recessed into the mall structure, so Archie had a limited view beyond it. Archie thought this was the first gas-powered engine he'd heard on the island since the beginning of the Arrival experiment, except for maybe the odd lawn mower.

The bike's roar intensified. It was getting closer.

Archie glanced down, saw his open zipper, and pulled it up.

And then—

VROOMMM

The bike raced past. Archie knew a little bit about motorcycles, and he was pretty sure what he'd seen was, indeed, a Harley-Davidson, which happened to be the same kind of bike that Rory's dad owned. A Sportster model, in blue, 1200 cc.

But there was something more curious than the bike itself. It was who was sitting on it.

"Mom?" Archie whispered.

It had only taken the bike a second to cross his field of vision, but he was pretty sure he'd seen his mother. It was a woman, no doubt about that. Skirt hiked up high so she could straddle the bike. She wasn't wearing a helmet or goggles, so he could see her long brown hair trailing behind her in the wind.

The Arrivals had heard the motorcycle, too.

Fresh meat.

The cars farthest away from Archie were pulling out of formation to follow the noise of the bike, like animals picking up a scent.

Could it really be Mom?

There was that old picture in her bedroom, of her with Dad, in their biker leathers. He'd never paid that much attention to it, thought maybe it was a photo from a Halloween party or something. Pretended to be a couple of badass Hell's Angels. Sure, he knew his dad loved bikes and could fix them and had owned some in the past.

But seriously?

He wanted to run from the shelter of the loading bay, out into the parking lot, flag down this biker. Because if it *was* his mom, odds were the person she was looking for—

He could hear the bike coming back.

Even though he couldn't yet see it, he started jumping up and down and waving his hands like a castaway on a desert island trying to catch a pilot's attention.

"*Mom!*" he screamed. "*Mom!*"

In a millisecond, the motorcycle sped past. And half a second later, so did six Arrivals, all in pursuit.

The woman on the bike had not glanced Archie's way. But seconds later, it made another pass. Maybe she'd spotted something in her peripheral vision on her previous pass: the boy's frantic waving. The bike was heading straight for the loading bay area.

Archie waved.

His mother waved.

The Arrivals, unable to turn as sharply or as

quickly as the bike, were struggling to keep up. But if they could corner Sandra in the loading bay . . .

Sandra aimed the bike for the concrete steps. Archie thought: *No fucking way.*

It was stunning enough to discover your mom could drive a motorcycle. It was something else to consider that she might undertake climbing a set of steps with it.

But that was exactly what she did.

The Harley screamed into the loading bay. Sandra braked it so she wouldn't hit that bottom step too fast and throw herself over the handle-bars. But once she had that front tire onto the first step, she gunned it, lifting her butt off the seat at the same time, and landed it, with a roar, on the dock.

Archie didn't have to be told to get on. He ran to the bike, threw a leg over the rear half of the seat, wrapped his arms around his mother, locking one hand over the wrist of the other.

Sandra turned her head long enough to say four words.

"Hang the fuck on."

Archie hung the fuck on. And started to cry.

Forty-Four

Derek had decided to venture out from the safety of the yacht club building to see whether the situation was improving any.

So Derek got up from his table, paid his bar tab—even in the midst of chaos, one must not take advantage—and stepped outside. The first thing he heard, coming from the center of town, were a few more gunshots. People were still doing battle with the Arrivals, trying to bring them down as though they were wild animals. There'd been so many shots over the last couple of hours that no one even turned their head anymore.

Despite the maelstrom, Derek felt strangely at peace. He'd liberated himself from Brandon Kyle. Should have done it a long time ago, but he'd been lured into staying by the money. Kyle had always paid him well, treated him decently. But Kyle, Derek had finally realized, was an evil man. He'd been wronged, it was true, by Lisa Carver, but her misdeeds did not justify the killing of innocent people. What Derek had seen happen here today was unimaginable.

He wondered whether Kyle had found a way off the island, if maybe he'd gotten to the ferry and escaped, although there'd been talk in the club that something pretty bad had happened up there, at the terminal.

Standing outside, looking over a harbor nearly

bereft of watercraft, he inhaled the sea air. He'd never been to Garrett Island before. He liked it here. He wondered, if he sold his house and found a small, one-bedroom apartment here, if he'd have enough to live on the rest of his life. Maybe. It was only him. He'd never married, had no children, and tucked money away over the years. Although he was betting the winters here could be hard. Those storms coming in off the Atlantic, they could pack a punch.

Something to think about.

He walked down the planked walkway and around the back of the club. If he was going to head to the center of town to see what was happening, he'd have to be careful. Take narrow pathways between buildings. If he had to cross a road, do it as quickly as possible. Those fucking Arrivals, quiet as they were, could sneak up on you real fast.

"Derek."

He knew the voice.

Derek stopped and turned slowly. Brandon Kyle, minus his enhanced stomach, his clothes streaked with mud, was half-hidden behind half a dozen tall blue garbage cans at the back of the yacht club.

"Mr. Kyle," he said. "You look a little worse for wear."

"I'm not having a very good day," Kyle said.

"You didn't make it off the island."

"No," Kyle said. "But not for lack of trying."

Derek nodded, feigning sympathy. He offered up a weak smile. "I kind of like it here. Or think I would, when the crazy car thing is over."

"Like to spend the rest of your life here?"

Derek gave the question some thought. "Perhaps."

"I can help you with that," Kyle said, raising his arm suddenly.

"Jesus, Mr. Kyle," Derek said, seeing the gun in the man's hand. "There's no call for that."

"I've been so good to you," Kyle said.

"Mr. Kyle, please—"

Kyle fired, putting a bullet squarely in Derek's chest.

The man's mouth opened wide—as much in shock as in pain—but no sound came out. He put a hand to his chest, held it there, then dropped silently to his knees. Five seconds after that, he fell to the ground completely.

If anyone had heard the shot—and Kyle had no doubt that people had—they weren't coming to investigate. It was the Wild West in Garrett today.

Kyle tucked the weapon into the back of his belt, flipped his jacket over it so it wouldn't be seen, then got out his phone to double-check how to get to the address he'd looked up earlier. He was going to have to do it on foot, of course. Maybe a ten-, fifteen-minute walk, more if he had to take a longer route to avoid Arrivals.

Derek attempted to speak, but his throat was filling with blood. But in his last few seconds, he managed to raise one hand a few inches off the pavement and extend his middle finger.

But Kyle didn't see it. He was already on the move.

Forty-Five

They still had to get home.

Sandra was comforted by Archie's arms locked around her as they sped through the streets of Garrett, but she was constantly watching for more Arrivals. She hadn't forgotten how, while on that bicycle, she'd dropped her guard a moment and nearly ended up as an Arrival hood ornament.

But as they'd sped out of the Garrett Mall parking lot on Rory's father's Harley, Sandra had noticed an interesting development. All but one of the Arrivals that had been pursuing her had given up the chase.

One by one, they had either slowed down, or stopped altogether right where they stood. The lone car still after them—a green one—wasn't keeping up. Granted, the Harley had superior pickup and handling skills, but this Arrival didn't seem to have its heart in it.

And then, checking her mirror, she saw the green Arrival turn into a driveway, pull up close to the house, and stop.

What the hell?

Ahead, a yellow Arrival turned onto the street, coming their way.

"Hang on!" she said, veering off the road and seeking shelter in the narrow gap between two houses. She stopped the bike and killed the engine. The car might have seen them, but now that they were off the road, there was no sense in letting it hear them, too.

They both turned around and watched to see whether the Arrival would turn off the street in pursuit, even if the space between the houses was too small to allow it to reach them.

But the car did not turn. The Arrival rolled right on by.

"Maybe it didn't see us," Archie said.

"It saw us," his mother said. "It *had* to have seen us."

Using her feet, she pushed the bike back out into the open so they could see where the car had gone. About ten houses down, it had turned into a driveway and nosed itself right up to the house, just like the car that had trailed them as they left the mall.

Sandra got out her phone, brought up Joe on her texting program, and sent a message.

U DID IT!

She waited to see if Joe got the text, and whether he would be able to reply. Soon, she saw the three dancing dots.

Then: DID WHAT?

She wrote back: THEY'RE STOPPING. LIKE THEY'RE OUT OF GAS.

Joe replied: COULDN'T DISABLE VIRUS. NO IDEA WHAT'S DOING IT.

Archie, who'd been looking over his mother's shoulder as she exchanged messages with the police chief, said, "Not gas."

"What?" said Sandra, looking away from the phone.

"Battery power," he said. "They must be running out. Like a phone down to one bar. While they still have power, they're heading home to get plugged back in."

Sandra started to smile.

"Yeah," she said slowly. And then her smile turned into a laugh. "All this time, we were trying to think how to stop them, and all we had to do was wait for them to run out of juice!" She let out a triumphant shriek. "What are they gonna do now? Plug themselves back in? I don't think so!" She couldn't stop smiling. "As smart as the little shits are, they need *us* to plug them back in."

Archie wiped away some tears that hadn't been blown away during their ride. "Guess they need arms."

It was the first time it had been quiet enough for them to have a conversation since she had rescued him from the loading dock. Archie was almost afraid to ask, but he did:

"What about Katie?"

"Katie's at home," Sandra said. "Kinda shook up, though. Like you, she's had quite a day."

"I'm sorry," Archie said. "I tricked her. I went to the mall."

"Yeah, I know," Sandra said. "With Nick and Rory. I got this bike at Rory's. No sign of Nick yet."

Archie's face saddened. He told her.

"Oh my God," Sandra said, and put her arms around him and squeezed.

"I saw it happen," he said, his voice breaking.

Sandra gave him another squeeze. "We're gonna be okay. It's over. You're okay, Katie's okay. The cars are running out of juice. The only one I'm worried about now is Bruce."

"Bruce?"

Sandra filled him in, briefly, about what had happened with Katie. It had to be brief, because she really didn't know that much herself about what had happened.

"So he's *not* a serial killer?" Archie asked.

"We need to get home, figure out what to do next."

She got back into the driving position and revved the engine as Archie resumed his grip around her waist, a little opossum clinging to his mother's back.

Sandra gave a wide berth to any further Arrivals they encountered but none showed much interest in running them down. All of them, it appeared, were heading home for supper.

She'd felt a tremendous sense of relief when she'd been reunited with Katie, and again when she'd scooped up Archie, but what she was feeling now was something more. A kind of weight being lifted from her. This nightmare was finally coming to an end.

Sandra turned down their street.

If, as it appeared, the worst was over, the islanders could start the process of putting their lives together. The first step would be to get rid of all these goddamn little cars. Load them up on the ferry and, as far as Sandra was concerned, dump them into the ocean before they reached the mainland. They couldn't get their regular cars back fast enough.

There would be a lot of grieving, and a lot of healing. Plenty of lawsuits, too, Sandra figured. She had no idea how many lives had been lost today, but this was a strong community and it would pull through. Not overnight. It would take months, if not longer, but Garrett Island would move forward.

And what would she do? Would she stick with public relations? Would having represented Arrival become a stain on her record? Would the locals hold it against her that she had played a role in organizing the Arrival event?

She'd have to find a way to forgive herself first.

Up ahead, she saw her house. And there, in the driveway, was an Arrival. A bright red one.

Gracie.

If she hadn't already seen other Arrivals heading back to their home bases, looking to be recharged, she'd have been alarmed by the car's presence. But if Gracie had come home, it had to be because she was wrung out. Like Adam used to say, *Ridden hard and put away wet.*

The little bitch, Sandra thought. *If she thinks I'm going to plug her back in, she's out of her little electronic mind.*

But then Sandra saw something that prompted her to suddenly hit the brakes. Archie's head slammed into her upper back.

"What?" he said.

He peered around his mother and saw what had made her stop.

Pinned at the knees, between the house and the front bumper of the Arrival, was Katie. She faced the wall, her arms outstretched, her face turned to one side.

Sandra turned off the bike. Archie hopped off first, then she swung her leg over and put both feet on the ground.

As she started running toward the Arrival, its lights began to flash, a warning for Sandra to stop.

Gracie spoke.

"Plug me in."

Forty-Six

Joe was leaving the community center when he got Sandra's text congratulating him on disabling the cars. He had no idea what she was talking about, but when he got outside, he started putting it together.

Many of the Arrivals that were still operable after they'd attacked the fire engine and ambulance were leaving. An Arrival that had been given to the community center to replace its staff car came back up the drive and stopped at the charging station that had been set up for it. On a post was a small box holding a cable that, once unspooled, could be hooked up to the car and have it ready to go again in short order.

"Son of a bitch," Joe said under his breath. "Of course."

Then he saw something equally startling.

A Garrett Island police force cruiser was speeding up the road, the cherry on top flashing, the siren engaged. Whoever was behind the wheel—and it was a *real person* behind the wheel—maneuvered around the overturned ambulance and the burned-out shell of the fire truck and drove up to the community center entrance.

And then Joe remembered. There was one car they didn't trade in for an Arrival because it was in the police garage being repaired.

The car screeched to a halt. As the window

powered down, Joe saw that it was Ronny, the well-intentioned but somewhat dimwitted officer he'd spoken to earlier, although it felt like days ago.

"Ronny?" Joe said, stepping toward the car.

"Hey, Chief," he said, smiling. "Need wheels?"

"That would be nice, yes."

"I got someone else to take over the phones and decided to have a look at it myself since today was Ernie's day off, and he's on the mainland, the lucky bastard."

Ernie being the department's full-time mechanic.

"So I looked at the work order on it, and Ernie hadn't figured out what was wrong. But it was mentioned that the car had a full tank of gas, and I remembered one of the guys saying he was driving a car that never seemed to run out of gas and—"

"Ronny, give me the car."

"Yeah, right, okay, but I just wanted to tell you that I started to wonder if the gas tank was actually empty, but the fuel gauge was busted? Showing a full tank all the time. So I put some gas in, and sure enough, it was empty and—"

Joe made a thumbing motion.

Ronny got out of the car and let Joe slip behind the wheel. "I'll drop you off back at the station," he said.

As Ronny was coming around the other side of the car, he said, "All the cars are going back to their houses. It's totally weird!"

As Ronny was getting in, Joe's phone rang. He grabbed it without looking at the screen.

"Yeah?"

"Joe."

It was Sandra.

"Hey," he said. "Got your text. It wasn't anything I did. I think the cars want to be recharged and—"

Her voice very low, Sandra said, "Joe, shut up."

He stopped talking, and listened.

"It's got Katie," she whispered.

"What?"

"One of them. It's got Katie trapped."

"Where are you?"

"Home."

"Coming," he said.

Joe turned and said to Ronny, "Get out."

Forty-Seven

Sandra, taking small tentative steps toward Gracie, asked Katie in as calm a voice as possible, "How you doing, sweetheart?"

Katie, pinned at the knees to the front wall of the house by the car's front bumper, tears running down her cheeks, said quietly, "It hurts."

"You think anything is broken?"

"No," she said. "It's just pressing really hard. Every time I try to move a little it gets closer."

"Okay."

Archie had run past his mother, stopping a couple feet from the car, and looked teary-eyed. Then he looked at the car and shouted, "Let her go, you asshole!"

Sandra caught up to him, and pressed her palm gently on his back. "Go in the house, Archie."

"But, Mom, it—"

"Go in the house," she said firmly. "Gracie and I are going to have a little chat, sort this out. Okay?"

Archie looked as though he wanted to object, but finally did as he was told, heading for the front door but not taking his eyes off Katie the whole time. He went inside, but almost instantly appeared at the living room window.

The charging stand stood up close to the house, inches away from the Arrival's front bumper. Inside was the cable that would, once plugged into the outlet right under the car's headlight, recharge the Arrival in as little as an hour. Clearly, Gracie had made it home before entirely running out of battery life.

"*Whom did you call?*" Gracie asked.

"The chief of police," she said. There didn't seem much sense lying to Gracie. She probably had some Bluetooth feature that allowed her to know what was happening on the phones around her.

"*Plug me in.*"

"So you can recharge and go around killing people again?" Sandra asked. "I don't think so. You're pretty smart, Gracie, but you're dumb as a shoe if you think everyone on the island is going want to let you guys have another go at this."

The car moved ahead a millimeter. Katie winced and said, "*Mom.*"

"Okay, okay," Sandra said. "Don't do that, Gracie."

"*Plug me in.*"

"Let go of Katie first," Sandra said, thinking: *I am negotiating with a fucking car for my daughter's life.*

Gracie said nothing, which Sandra hoped meant the car was considering Sandra's request. After several seconds, the car spoke.

"*No. After you have plugged me in, I will back up far enough for her to get out.*"

Sandra considered her options. Before long, Gracie's battery would die, her leverage lost. Then, if Sandra could get the car open and somehow shift it into neutral, she and Archie could move it back far enough to free Katie. But could Sandra stall until Gracie ran out of juice? Gracie would know how much power she had left. She might choose to use the last bit of it to break Katie's legs, cripple her for life, or kill her outright.

Maybe plugging Gracie in wasn't such a bad idea. Insert the cable, Katie frees herself, and then just as quickly yank the cable out.

And run for it.

But Gracie was no dumbass, and might anticipate such a plan. Sandra was betting the car would not free Katie until it was fully charged.

"Okay," she said. "But, Gracie, you have to promise me, soon as I plug you in, you'll let Katie go."

The car said nothing.

"Gracie, come on. I keep my end of the bargain, you keep yours." Sandra tried to smile. "Hey, we've got a history. In the few weeks we've been together, we've had some good times, right? We've gotten to know each other. Before all the shit that happened today, we were friends. And I know that the way you've behaved today, that's not your fault. Someone did that to you. Someone messed with your programming. I get that. So come on. I plug you in, then you back up far enough to let Katie go."

Sandra, as a show of good faith, opened the box that held the cable, and started to draw it out. "See?"

The car remained silent for several seconds. Then: *"Plug me in and I will back up."*

"You'll back up right away?" Sandra asked.

Another pause.

"Yes."

"Okay then," Sandra said, pulling out more cable.

"No."

She looked around. That wasn't Gracie talking. It was a real live human voice, and it was male.

He was standing several feet away, in the middle of the yard. Sandra didn't recognize him at first, given that he was streaked with dirt and looking a lot slimmer than the last time she'd seen him.

And of course, the gun he was pointing at her was somewhat distracting, too.

But then she realized he was the man who'd passed himself off as Ben Stapleton, of *Wheel Base Trends*. Except there was no *Wheel Base Trends*, and there was no Ben Stapleton. This man, she believed, was Brandon Kyle.

Sandra stood there, frozen, cable in hand.

"I have to," she said. "The car will crush her if I don't."

"I know," Kyle said, and smiled. "Your daughter, right?"

Sandra nodded.

"She nearly blinded me. Put shit in my eyes." He shook his head disapprovingly. "You didn't raise her right."

"I know who you are," Sandra said. "And I know what you did."

"Really."

"You're the guy with the other car company. You wanted to get even. You did all this, made it happen. I don't know how, exactly, but you did it. And I know all about Ruskin."

A puzzled expression passed across Brandon Kyle's face. "What about Ruskin?"

"*Plug me in*," Gracie said.

Sandra said, "He was your inside man. He hated Lisa Carver. He helped you get even with her."

Kyle said, very slowly, "I don't think so." He chuckled. "I mean, where the hell did you come up with that?"

"He confessed," Sandra said. "Just before he died."

"Ruskin's dead? One of the cars got him?"

"No," Sandra said. "Something else. But that's what he said. Guess he wanted to clear his conscience."

Kyle's look of puzzlement deepened. "That's not possible."

"It is." Sandra looked at the cable in her hand, then at Katie. "You have to let me plug this in. Please. My daughter . . ."

Kyle waved the gun. "If you do it, I'll just shoot her, anyway. Or maybe you."

"Please, just—"

"Were you there? Did you hear this?"

"What?"

"Ruskin's confession. You heard him say this?"

Sandra paused. "Not personally. But I was told."

Kyle shook his head, still not understanding. "*Who* told you? *Who* heard him?"

"The chief of police," she said. "Joe—"

Kyle raised his free palm, stopping her. And he laughed. "Oh well, now it starts to make some sense. Bridgeman told you this."

"How do you know his—"

"He told you this, and he says Ruskin confessed to him before he died?"

Sandra, almost a whisper: "Yes."

"Convenient," Kyle said.

"But . . . Ruskin gave him the password, for Lisa's computer. He . . . he knew things."

Kyle nodded smugly. "The password, was it Zenia, but backward? With a numeric date attached?"

Sandra started to reply, but nothing came out. She was trying to figure out what was going on. None of what Kyle was saying made sense to her. And yet . . .

"Plug me in."

Katie whimpered, "Mom . . ."

She raised the cable in her hand. "Please. I *have* to do this."

"I can tell you where Joe got that password," Kyle said obligingly. "He got it from me. I had to go through hoops to get it. Ruskin wouldn't have known it. Lisa would never have trusted him with it." He thought a moment. "So Ruskin's confession comes to you secondhand, from the chief?"

She nodded.

"Gotta hand it to him. That was smart. Saying Ruskin confessed before he died." He was pondering something. "Just how did he die, if it wasn't one of the cars?"

"He . . . he hit his head."

"Were you with him when he died?"

Sandra shook her head.

"But let me guess. Good ol' Joe was."

"Plug me in."

Sandra looked back to the car, and Katie. She said to Kyle, her back to him, "You do what you have to do, but I'm plugging in this cable."

He shook his head angrily. "I don't think so. You—"

But then he and Sandra and Katie were distracted by a noise. It was the sound of an engine, a powerful one, coming down the street.

A car.

They all turned and looked, even Katie, who scraped her nose on the board and batten siding as she moved her head.

Joe, Sandra thought. Somehow, he got a car. Let him save us. Let him be the hero, for now. The questions could come later.

But it was not a police car.

It was a big, black, badly damaged Cadillac.

Forty-Eight

The Cadillac came screaming down the street, its V8 engine roaring like a gravelly jet engine, slowing as it rolled past the Montrose house on its whitewall tires. As it went by, Sandra and Kyle and Katie—and Archie, watching through the window—could see that the driver's side of the car was totally smashed in, starting at the back of the front wheel well, and about a foot beyond the door.

From behind the wheel, a bloody and bruised Bruce surveyed the scene in the Montrose driveway. Bruce only needed a couple of seconds to assess what was happening.

Kyle said, "*Him.*"

Bruce gunned the engine, speeding up as he headed toward the end of the street. But before he got there, he cranked the wheel hard, as though intending to make a U-turn. The car, however, was too big, and the street too narrow, to execute such a maneuver.

It was, everyone soon realized, not Bruce's intention to stay on the road.

By the time he had the car facing in the other direction, he was on the front yard of a house five down from the Montrose residence. And then Bruce floored it. The car's back tires kicked up sod and dirt as the beast lunged forward.

"Oh, shit," Sandra said, realizing what it was

Bruce intended to do. She screamed at Katie, "Get ready!" Then Sandra ran toward the street, careful not to be standing between the Arrival and the approaching car.

Kyle fired off a wild shot as the Cadillac blasted through picket fences and hedgerows set up to mark property lines. Bits of wood and foliage scattered across the massive hood before blowing off. The car continued to growl forward as Kyle took another shot, this one spiderwebbing the windshield on the passenger side.

Bruce didn't even flinch.

The huge chrome grille was full of silver teeth, chowing down on splinters of wood and shrubbery.

Before Kyle could get off a third shot, the corner of the front bumper barely clipped him, sending him, and his gun, flying.

Gracie, sensing an imminent threat, slipped herself into reverse and started to roll back, releasing her pinioning of Katie. Sandra's daughter nearly collapsed, but, realizing she had less than a second to seek cover, hobbled frantically around the corner of the house, not five feet away, to safety.

Bruce, in the last millisecond before impact, gave the wheel a slight turn to the left so he'd be lined up with the side of the Arrival as it tried to get away.

And then he hit it.

It was like a thunderclap. An ear-splitting sound of metal hitting metal, metal *ripping* metal. And under that, the wild cackling of Bruce behind the wheel, shouting, "Not so funny when it happens to *you*, is it?"

The Arrival was knocked first onto its side, then rolled onto its roof, down onto its other side, then—briefly—it landed back on its wheels before starting its second roll, coming to a stop halfway through it, all four wheels in the air, still spinning, like an upside-down turtle wiggling its legs, trying to figure a way out of its predicament.

It all happened so fast that Sandra had lost track of Katie, and when she glanced about and did not see her, panic overwhelmed her.

"Katie!" she screamed.

As if on cue, Katie stepped out from behind the corner of the house and waved weakly. "Over here," she said.

Assured Katie was safe, Sandra turned her attention to Kyle, sprawled out on the grass, clutching his thigh, writhing in pain from that glancing blow with the Cadillac. As Sandra hopped over debris—shrubs, fencing, a tricycle—that the Caddy had brought along on its journey, Kyle let go of his leg and started looking for the gun.

He and Sandra spotted it the same time. It lay in the grass, about ten feet from him. Kyle scrambled for it on two hands and one working leg, while Sandra ran. She dived, covering the gun with her body like a noble soldier throwing himself on a grenade.

Kyle reached out and grabbed one of her ankles as she started rolling to one side so she could get a hand on the gun. She yanked her leg up quickly, breaking his grip, but then just as quickly drove it back down, forcing her heel into his face.

Specifically, his nose.

Blood spurted from it. Kyle forgot about Sandra and the gun and his wounded leg, and put both hands over his nose, blood quickly seeping out between his fingers. He wailed in pain as Sandra scooped up the weapon and got to her feet.

Archie charged out the front door, stopping before reaching his mother to survey the Cadillac's path of destruction, a disabled Brandon Kyle, and a freed Katie, who was running to check on Bruce.

"Crazy," Archie said. He looked down at Kyle and asked his mother, "Who's this dude?"

"A bad guy," she said breathlessly. "A really, really bad guy."

Archie blinked, took a step closer to the man, and all at once the tension that had been building up in him all day—trapped in the mall, losing a friend, wondering whether he'd make it out alive—came out in a kick right to the back of the man's head.

"Archie!" his mother screamed as Kyle's eyes closed and he drifted into unconsciousness.

"He was going to shoot you guys," Archie said. "Nobody does that to my mom or my sister."

Sandra might have taken a moment to kiss him, but a wailing siren stopped her. A Garrett Island police car was heading their way, lights flashing along with the siren. It screeched to a halt out front of the Montrose home.

The door flew open and Joe Bridgeman leapt out. He said, "What the . . ."

He quickly took in the scene—the Caddy, the

overturned Arrival, the ripped-up yards—before turning his attention to the unconscious man on the ground.

That was when Sandra knew.

As soon as Joe saw Kyle, there was something in his eyes. A nervous recognition. A quiver in his cheek.

A hint, Sandra thought, of fear.

But Joe recovered quickly and ran to Sandra, wrapping his arms around her. "You're okay, oh God, you're okay."

"Yeah, we're okay," she said evenly.

When she wrested her way free of him, he saw the gun in her hand. "You want me to take that now?"

She looked him right in the eye. "No, I'll hang on to it." She started walking toward the Cadillac, saying, "I need to see how Katie's friend is."

Katie was leaning in through the window of the broken door, her hand on the back of Bruce's neck. "I thought you were going to die," she said, tears running down her face. "I was going to come back, honestly I was."

Bruce, his face caked with dried blood, smiled weakly, and said, "Wanted to save you the trouble."

"Are you hurt bad?" Katie asked.

"Well, I'm hurt," he said. "Don't know how bad, yet."

"We're going to get you fixed up, we are," Katie said. She gave his bloody cheek a kiss. "You're too cranky to die."

Sandra came up to the window, smiled wryly, and said, "I understand you've been giving my daughter driving lessons behind my back."

Bruce smiled, then winced. "I think she's ready for her test."

Sandra also put a hand out, touching Bruce's shoulder. "Help has to be coming. The cars aren't a threat anymore. It's over."

But then she glanced over at Joe.

"Almost," she said.

Forty-Nine

Joe was standing at the back end of the Cadillac, straddling some fence boards from three properties down, when Sandra approached him.

"So," she said.

Joe pointed to the unconscious Kyle. "Who's that guy?"

Sandra smiled. "Don't."

"What?"

"Just don't," Sandra said, slowly shaking her head.

"I don't . . . Sandra, is something wrong?" Joe asked, trying his best to look sincerely baffled.

The gun at the end of Sandra's arm trembled. Her free hand was shaking. She made a fist to stop it.

"I know that *you* know who that is," she said.

"Sandra, look, whatever you may be thinking, whatever he may have told you, you have to believe that I would never want—"

"Stop," Sandra said. "Don't lie to me. I don't want to hear any lies."

Joe's right hand was moving toward his holstered weapon. Quickly, Sandra raised the gun and pointed it at him.

"What are you doing?" Joe asked.

"What are *you* doing?" she shot back at him. "You were going for your gun. Why would you be doing that? You think I'm going to want to shoot you for some reason?"

Joe raised his palms, as if in surrender. "I just want to keep an eye on him," he said, gesturing toward Kyle.

"Why? You think he's some kind of threat? A second ago you asked who he was. Right now, he's out cold. Why would you want to pull a gun on him?"

"I don't know what—"

"Does he need to die, too? So there's no one who can contradict your story? No one who can implicate you?"

"Sandra, what—what are you talking about? Look, these last few hours, they've been horrible for all of us. We're all on edge, our minds going places they shouldn't." He extended a hand. "Why don't you just give me that gun and—"

Sandra took a step back, careful not to step on a length of broken picket fence, and put her other hand on the gun. She wrapped both hands around it, keeping it steady.

"Put your gun on the ground," she said. "Really, really slowly."

"Don't be ridiculous. I'm not—"

"Do it!" she screamed, keeping the gun trained on him.

With deliberate slowness, Joe lifted his weapon from his holster, bent at the knee, and dropped it carefully onto the ground.

"There. Happy?"

"You killed him," she said, her voice nearly breaking as she said the words.

Joe quickly glanced at Kyle and back again. "He's a liar. Whatever he told you, it's a lie."

"God, Joe, how . . . how could you . . ."

Joe rubbed a palm across his mouth, as though buying time, trying to figure out what to say.

Sandra repeated the accusation. "You killed him."

"That's not . . . that's not really true, Sandra. I swear. He wasn't going to make it. There wouldn't have been anything the paramedics could have done, even if they'd been right there. I did call them. I *did*. But maybe . . . maybe I could have called sooner."

Sandra blinked. Katie had moved away from Bruce, and Archie was standing a few feet away, both of them listening now.

"The thing is," Joe continued, "I was crazy about you the first time I saw you. I felt . . . I felt there was something there. And yes, of course, you were married. I wasn't going to try to break up a marriage. But when I came onto the accident, I guess . . . look, I love you. I do. I love you, and I love your kids, and I think we've really had a good thing. I know . . . I know not calling right away, I know that was wrong, but he was never right for you. I mean, he was a good man and all, I'm not saying he wasn't. But I always knew I could offer you more."

The color had drained from Sandra's face.

"Oh my God," she said. Then, in a whisper, as a tear ran down her cheek, she said, *"Adam?"*

"Like I said, I'm sorry, I truly am. I didn't make him fall asleep at the wheel. I didn't make him drive into that tree. That's not on me. It's not like I ran him off the road. I just . . . I just didn't make the call."

Sandra could barely get out the words. "You . . . watched him . . . die . . ."

Joe was starting to get the sense that Sandra was shocked by what he'd told her. He said, "I don't know how Kyle figured it out. He was . . . resourceful."

Sandra said, "He didn't tell me you killed Adam. I was talking about Ruskin."

Now it was Joe's turn to be stunned. "But . . . how . . ."

"Kyle knew it wasn't Ruskin that helped him. So there'd be no reason for Ruskin to confess."

Katie and Archie were frozen to the ground where they stood, stunned by hearing what had really happened to their father.

Joe was slowly shaking his head. "I was . . . I was doing the right thing. If they'd tried to save him, he'd . . . he could have been in a coma for years. It was better . . . better to let him . . ."

Sandra brought the gun up higher and pointed it directly at his head.

"Christ, Sandra, you're not going to shoot me."

"I don't know," she said. "I might."

"You can't. You wouldn't." He chortled. "I'm a police officer! You can't shoot a police officer! They'll send you to jail."

"I doubt that," she said. "Not when they find out what you helped Kyle do."

"I did that for us! For *us*, Sandra! He—he made it possible for me to put my mother in . . . in a center, so we could move in—"

"Oh, Jesus, just stop!" she screamed at him. "Just shut the fuck up!"

"Sandra, put the gun down. I won't go for mine. I'll just . . . I'll just walk away."

She didn't move. The gun stayed pointed at his head. She said, "I think I *will* shoot you."

Joe, wide-eyed, said, "Look, listen, just . . ."

"But I'm going to give you a head start," she said. "I'll count to five. See how far you can get."

"This is crazy, you can't—"

"*One.*"

"Sandra! Stop and think about what you're—"

"*Two.*"

Joe glanced nervously to one side, then beyond Sandra, as though planning which was the best escape route.

"*Three.*"

He spun around a full one hundred and eighty degrees and bolted, but he didn't get far. On his very first step, the toe of his right foot got caught under one of the pieces of broken fencing that the Cadillac had dragged through the yard.

Joe tripped.

His body pitched forward into the air. He threw both hands out in front to brace himself for his fall, but it turned out he wasn't heading for the ground.

Joe was falling toward the left back corner of the Cadillac.

And its enormous, towering, chrome, dagger-like tailfin.

Joe tried to turn his body in midair to avoid it, but he was too slow. The side of his neck connected with the tailfin, and he struck it with enough force that the point went all the way through and came out the other side.

That was where he hung, impaled, and very dead, until teams of emergency responders swarmed the island later that night.

Fifty

It was nearly a month later when the body shop brought back Bruce's Cadillac. He'd had it sent to a place on the mainland that specialized in restoring old cars, and luckily, this was not an operation that was particularly attentive to legitimate ownership. When they'd taken the car away on a flatbed truck, Bruce made no mention of the fact that it was not, technically speaking, his, or that the plates on it were not, in the strictest sense of the word, legit.

Mere trivialities.

Even before his release from the hospital he was scouting up good repair places. If it had only been the side of the vehicle, where the Arrival had plowed into him, it might not have been that big a job. But then he had to go and drive through half a dozen front yards and broadside that Arrival, then that son of a bitch Brandon Kyle put a bullet through the front windshield.

The repairs were going to take nearly half of Bruce's savings. Oh well, you can't take it with you.

He hoped Kyle spent the rest of his life in jail. And even though Massachusetts had outlawed capital punishment, there was still a chance the guy could be sentenced to death because the US government was pursuing various federal charges against him. It *did* have the death penalty, and

430 | Linwood Barclay

if Uncle Sam wanted to fry his ass, they'd move him to another state to do it.

Garrett Island was, more or less, back to normal. The funerals, which were held over the course of three weeks, had finally come to an end. Forty-eight people had lost their lives. There was talk of erecting some kind of memorial in the town square. Some islanders were for it, others wanted to forget it had ever happened. The debate was expected to continue for some time.

Everyone on the island got their cars back. The Arrivals were put on a barge and taken to a landfill site in New Jersey. The Arrival corporation, which was facing more than a hundred lawsuits, declared bankruptcy. Shares in all companies that produced self-driving cars plummeted.

Gas prices went up.

The somewhat dimwitted Ronny was made interim chief. The island's governing council was still shopping around for a sharper knife in the drawer. Deeper background checks had been promised for when the next chief was chosen.

It was early November and the tourist season was over, but there had been a few gawkers coming over from the mainland, wanting to check out the sites of the most serious mayhem. The mall had seen an uptick in visitors.

Lillian Bridgeman sold her house and moved to an assisted living facility outside of Boston.

Sandra Montrose decided to get out of the public relations business. There was an opening for a manager at one of the island's most prestigious resorts, the kind of place where they held a

G7 one year, and she got the job. She didn't need a man in her life anymore.

Sandra had Adam. She talked to him all the time.

"Don't you worry about Katie and Archie," she would tell him, usually once she had slipped under the covers at night. "I'm looking out for them, one hundred percent, but the good thing is, they know how to look out for themselves. We done good, you and me."

Katie was looking out the window when the flatbed truck pulled up in front of Bruce's house. It was a Saturday, and not only was she home, but her mom and Archie were, too.

The three of them came out and slowly crossed the street as the green tarp shrouding the car was pulled away. Once the bed was slowly angled down to the road, the delivery guy crawled up the ramp, got into the Cadillac, and slowly backed it down to the street.

Bruce signed some paperwork and handed over a check, and once the truck was gone, all four of them walked around the car, admiring the work.

"You'd never know," Archie said. "It looks fantastic."

Bruce's chest swelled. "Yeah, I'm pretty happy with it."

Sandra managed to admire the vehicle without ever once looking directly at that one tailfin. "It's a piece of art this car, honestly."

Bruce continued to smile. He was spinning the key chain around on his index finger.

"Aren't you going to drive it?" Archie said.

The retired teacher shook his head. "Can't."

"Why not?" Archie asked.

"No license."

They were all quiet for a moment. It was Sandra who broke the silence. "Katie's got hers now."

Katie nodded. "Passed the test last week."

"Well then," Bruce said, tossing her the keys.

Katie snatched them out of the air, opened the driver's door, and settled in behind the huge steering wheel. Sandra went to slip into the back, Bruce said, "No no."

He walked her around to the passenger side, flipped the seat forward so he and Archie could jump into the back, and left the front seat for Sandra. She got into the car and closed the door.

Katie keyed the engine, bringing the car to life with a rumble. She looked across the expansive bench seat at her mother sitting there.

Sandra smiled. "Let's go for a spin," she said.